three coins

KIMBERLY SULLIVAN

Copyright © 2021 by Kimberly Sullivan

First paperback edition October 2021

Book design by Maxtudio

ISBN: 978-1-7377293-1-0 (paperback)
ISBN: 978-1-7377293-3-4 / Digital Edition (Kindle)
ISBN: 978-1-7377293-2-7 / Digital Edition (ePub)

www.kimberlysullivanauthor.com

To Francesco, Alessandro and Nicolò.
My very own Three Coins.

CHAPTER 1

Emma

Knuckles already white, Emma clutched the steering wheel even tighter. She cursed as a driver cut in, missing her fender by a hair. She never yelled such obscenities in her own language, but her Italian vocabulary could rival a sailor's as crazy Roman drivers swarmed around her. Remaining docile in the right lane never helped. The drivers still cut in erratically, while others remained stubbornly glued to her rear bumper.

The scooters swarmed around her like locusts, not always traveling in the correct direction. It was impossible to gauge their intentions when they often didn't appear to know themselves. Emma had long been convinced the blinkers never gave out in Italian cars, since no one ever bothered to use them.

Of course, the traffic was more annoying today following the meeting at Chiara's school. Her teenage daughter was in trouble. Again. Her grades were slipping, and she was talking back to teachers. She'd even skipped an afternoon of class and forged Emma's signature on the note.

Headmistress Green had been kind but firm during their meeting. "I've known Chiara since the first grade." Despite her decades in Italy, Mrs. Green's harsh American 'r's and open vowels never faded when she pronounced Italian names. "She's always been such a sweet girl, and so bright. I've seen how good she is with her brothers, too. But she's changed this past year. We've been understanding because we know ..." She turned to the window, distracted by a tree branch scratching the glass in the gentle October breeze. "We know this year hasn't been easy on her."

When she turned back, the intensity of her grey eyes made Emma squirm. She felt like a teenager called into the principal's office.

"This can't continue, Mrs. Rinaldi. She's disruptive, and we have many students to prepare for the International Baccalaureate program. We would be sorry to see Chiara go, of course ..."

Emma's heart hammered in her chest. Her palms were sweaty. She wiped them on her Armani pantsuit. *Don't cry, don't cry.* She couldn't break down before Mrs. Green. She just couldn't.

"But if she doesn't *truly* wish to be here, it may be the best thing for her as well."

Oh, damn. She went ahead and said it. Chiara's being kicked out.

Those grey eyes continued to examine her. "Generally, I prefer having these conversations with both parents present, but we haven't seen Doctor Rinaldi at school for some time, and I hope you appreciate how urgent it was to speak in person. Your husband's ... pardon ... ex-husband's schedule, I garner from his secretary, did not offer much availability."

Emma willed her face to remain placid. For the first time in her life, she regretted not having succumbed to nerve-deadening Botox treatments.

"Yes, Mrs. Green. You were right to schedule a meeting with me. I would have preferred Chiara's father to have been present, of course, but bearing in mind his busy schedule." *Screwing a procession of girls only a couple of years older than Chiara.* "It's best we spoke right away. Rest assured that my ex-husband and I speak with one voice when it comes to raising Chiara, and we *will* find a solution. I promise you."

The corners of Mrs. Green's lips tilted upwards, but her stern grey eyes remained unconvinced. "I'm pleased to hear that. Too often, divorce can lead to decreased involvement by one of the parents. But in these cases, it's our experience that two parents working in partnership can turn a situation like this around."

She stood, signaling the end of the meeting. Emma scrambled to her feet.

"I hope to hand Chiara her diploma on graduation day. Don't hesitate to call me if you or Doctor Rinaldi have any concerns you wish to discuss."

Just shake hands with the woman and make it to the door without crying.

She followed Mrs. Green to the door, her Prada heels clicking with each uncertain step. She blinked rapidly, a desperate attempt to stave off the tears. She offered a weak smile to Mrs. Green at the door, and another to the receptionist, before exiting the office and walking out of the building.

The fresh air calmed her. It was a glorious autumn day, unseasonably sunny and warm for mid-October. The tourists were still wandering around the city's historical center in shorts and tank-tops, wondering at the tropical temperatures compared to Stockholm, or London, or Hamburg. Usually, Emma was pleased to visit this campus, with its lush green yard and rolling hills, always finding it hard to believe this peaceful countryside was still, technically, a part of Rome. But today being on campus afforded her no pleasure.

She hurried down the hill to the entrance gate as fast as her fashionable but impractical heels would carry her. *Please don't let me bump into Chiara or the twins.* She kept her head low, as if that could mask her identity should her children cross her path on campus, on their way to lunch or gym class.

"Emma! Why, it's been ages!" A voice rang out when she'd nearly reached the school gate.

Emma turned on her heel to see a woman she knew had been one of Dario's patients on more than one occasion. Her nose had been redone, her lips plumped, and cheek implants strained against artificially tight flesh.

"Margherita! What a pleasant surprise." Emma stepped forward and kissed the woman on each silicone cheek. "It's been ages. My fault. I need to contact you to see when I can help out with PTO activities. Isn't the international luncheon coming up?"

Margherita waved her hand, attempting a smile on skin that was no longer elastic. "Oh, that. We all do what we can. I know how hard it's been for you, what with ..." she lowered her voice. "The divorce."

The horrified expression accompanying her words would have been equally suitable for "your drug conviction" or "the mafia killings you ordered."

Divorce was surprisingly rare at the Fairmont School, as Emma was quickly learning. "Oh, it's fine. I forget about it half the time." Dragon Lady didn't need to know the truth.

Margherita sighed. "But still, so tragic. I always thought you were such a perfect couple. Although, I must admit," she chuckled. "I never would have pegged *you* for a plastic surgeon's wife. Although that was always part of Dario's charm. He's known for creating perfection on his patients, but never demanding it from his own wife."

A steady throbbing began behind Emma's right temple. "I'm over it, really. Thank you for your concern."

"I'm sure you are, my dear. Especially if Dario could ... sweeten the pot, shall we say, with his departure. It's important we hold them to their financial obligations, eh?" She winked. "But still, it's a shame for Chiara. Lucrezia tells me how upset she is, how she always complains the divorce ruined her life." She shook her head. "You know how dramatic teenagers can be." Margherita stood, expectantly, her head tilted.

Emma silently counted to five. "Thanks for your concern. It was tough for Chiara at first, but I think she's starting to accept it."

Margherita's lips formed a dainty little 'o'. "That's not what I heard. But I'm always behind on these things. How nice that everything is going swimmingly, and I've been misinformed." There was a hard glint in her eyes. "Let's be in touch for the international luncheon. Bye, Emma dear." With quick kisses on the cheek, she turned on her heels and made her way up the slope to the school.

Emma watched the receding figure, her head still spinning. A double whammy of Mrs. Green and Margherita. Surely, things couldn't get any worse. She greeted the guard at the exit and made her way to the parking lot. She scrolled down her mobile to Dario's number. It had to be done. She pressed the call button and tapped her foot as she waited for him to respond.

"Emma, what is it?" His voice was breathless, as if he'd just woken.

Emma glanced at her watch. Noon. Surely her early rising ex wasn't still sleeping? But then she picked up on that familiar smooth, smoky quality to his voice. She heard a high-pitched giggle beside him. Was that a rustling of sheets?

Oh, God. Catching Dario in a postcoital moment. She grimaced. Abundant sex with bimbos or not, he was still a father, and she was sick of him getting a free pass on his parenting responsibilities.

"I'm at Chiara's school." Her voice took on the harsh edge it often had when speaking with her ex. "Headmistress Green discussed the possibility of Chiara's dismissal."

"What?" Dario's voice bellowed, the hazy spell following vigorous sex apparently short-lived. "After all we've paid that school? Three kids there, for Christ's sake! And how many times have I volunteered free consultation sessions for the annual raffle? Those mothers are plastic surgery addicts—I've given away countless billable hours in support of Fairmont."

And raked in countless more after the initial consultations. Emma's mind flashed back to the pinched look of Margherita's face, the same look that graced countless other Fairmont mothers' faces.

"This isn't about you. It's about Chiara. She's struggling. She's acting out. And frankly, you haven't been helping out much since the divorce."

"Oh, that's just great, Emma." His voice rose. "Blame it all on me. Aren't you the one staying home with the kids? You wanted custody, you got it. And now you're whining it's too much for you."

A female voice whispered beside the phone. Emma bit her lip. She'd forgotten Dario wasn't away on business, but on a little getaway in the Sardinian villa that had gone with him in the divorce. She imagined the silicone breasts lounging beside him in their old bed. How she'd loved that villa. And now it was a spacious love nest for his latest conquests.

She took a deep breath. "I'm not saying it's too difficult, but it's getting harder, and one parent isn't enough. I need you to take an active role. We need to work together with Chiara, otherwise she's just playing us off of one another and getting away with bad behavior. She's gone from an A to a C student in less than a year. Surely that's a clear sign something's wrong?"

"Damnit, it's not a sign that I'm a bad father. Let's not forget who's financing this family. If Chiara can't cut it, she can go to public school. Like I did. Maybe it'll prepare her for real life. Anyway, I thought divorce would mean an escape from your constant nagging. In the future, call me only for emergencies. I have better things to do. This can all be discussed when I'm back."

Dario ended the call. The silence on the other end taunted her. "*Bastardo di merda!*" she screeched into her cellphone.

Behind her, there was a sharp intake of air. She turned to see a mother all decked out in Prada holding a nursery school-aged child by the hand. The woman dramatically held her hands over her child's ears, looking appalled. *Oh, please lady. Your daughter's delicate ears, my derrière. I've heard your husband the Parliamentarian use far more colorful language on your run-of-the-mill political programs on TV.* But Emma smiled sheepishly and shrugged. "Those annoying telemarketers. What can you do?"

She ducked into her car. No doubt her outburst would keep tongues wagging at the next PTO meeting. Those endless meetings where coddled, bored housewives debated how the tone of the school was being lowered by certain other parents, who would go unnamed.

She couldn't think about that now. She placed the key in the ignition and maneuvered out of the parking lot and onto the chaos of Rome's beltway. The cars and scooters raced by at death-defying speeds as she worked through her mental checklist.

The twins had separate activities this afternoon—fencing for Marco, soccer for Valerio, and Chiara had invited her friend Stefania over with her parents for dinner. Emma still had to shop. At least she'd prepared the tiramisu that morning. Her mother would probably call this evening with some new complaint about her luxurious retirement community back in Annapolis. Her complaint calls always seemed to coincide with dinner parties.

Emma breathed in deeply through her nose, trying to channel relaxing thoughts as her doctor had advised her when handling stressful situations. It never worked, but Emma kept trying. She stepped on the accelerator after glancing at the dashboard clock and panicking once again.

If only she could be like her ex, spending the day—hell, why not the whole week?—in bed with some barely legal boy, forgetting all her family obligations and telling Dario to shove off if he called her, concerned after receiving news their daughter might be kicked out of school. A car cut her off, causing her to slam on her brakes and releasing a slew of choice Italian profanities.

She breathed a sigh of relief when she pulled off the beltway and made her way through the Roman streets back to Aventino. With any luck, she'd still be in time to shop at the vegetable market and stop off at the butcher's.

She turned onto Viale delle Terme di Caracalla and swept aside her anger for a moment to admire the sharp blue sky forming a backdrop behind the fluffy, umbrella forms of the towering Mediterranean pines. The jagged, red ruins of the ancient baths of Caracalla loomed up from the ground on her left. *This* is what she needed to do more. Live in the moment. Look at the bright side of things.

So what if her ex-husband was always shirking his responsibilities, leaving Emma to pick up the pieces when he disappointed their children once again?

Only a few months ago, he'd promised to take all three kids to a musical they wanted to see. He cancelled at the last minute, claiming an important operation had to be rescheduled. To make it up to them, Emma took them to a movie that evening. How could she imagine she'd spot Dario in the lobby, groping his newest conquest? So much for urgent work keeping him from the children. She turned the twins away fast enough, but Chiara caught a glimpse of her father and a woman close to her own age. The hurt and betrayal marring her daughter's face was still etched in Emma's mind.

Emma hadn't brought it up with Chiara, and Chiara never mentioned it. She suspected Chiara kept her anger bottled inside. But after that night, a period of rebellion began. Increasingly, Chiara took those frustrations out on her mother.

Today was simply the umpteenth example of Dario withdrawing from his responsibilities, leaving the grunt work to Emma. But how could she handle everything alone?

Her eyes filled with the tears she'd been longing to shed ever since leaving Headmistress Green's office. She breathed in deeply to stem their flow, but her efforts were useless. Her vision blurred as she saw a scooter, driving the wrong way up the street, headed towards her car.

It all happened so fast, the rider coming at her with a long cascade of dark hair, a flippy skirt all the high school girls were wearing that year. A girl like Chiara.

She screamed and swerved to the left to avoid the scooter, but her relief was short-lived. She smashed straight into the passenger door of a grey Fiat. The sickening thud of metal on metal clanged in her skull.

How could this be happening? Why is it happening to me? And the kids? The dinner? How will I get to the market on time?

She flinched at pounding on her window.

"What the hell were you thinking? Are you blind? You slammed right into me! You could've killed my mother!"

The large man loomed over her window. Her eyes flickered to the car's passenger seat, at the elderly woman looking as dazed as Emma felt. Emma's hands shook on the steering wheel. She wanted to curl up into a ball, close her eyes tight, and make everything go away.

"Hey, lady!" The man rapped on Emma's partially open window.

She stared ahead with glassy eyes.

"Oh, great. Another lunatic out on the roads. Lady, I'm calling the police."

Caught behind two disabled vehicles on the busy Viale delle Terme di Caracalla, the drivers began honking their horns. It sounded like one, horrendous wail echoing in her brain, threatening to shatter her skull.

Make it go away. Please make it go away.

Rocking back and forth, Emma began to sob. The distant wail of a police siren grew closer, but she kept swaying, ignoring the confusion, the pounding in her head, the pain in her shoulders. She jumped at a second rap on her passenger window.

"*Signora*, I'm going to have to ask you to hand me your driver's license and papers."

Emma looked blankly at the policeman. Dark brown eyes stared back at her.

"Didn't I tell you she's a nutcase?" said the driver of the grey car as he approached the officer.

"Shhh, sir. Please step aside and gather your documents." He turned once more to Emma's window. "Ma'am, if you are unable to get out of the car, please open the window all the way and hand me the documents."

The tears flowed down Emma's cheeks. Her rocking grew faster, she clutched her head tightly in her hands. "No!"

"Ma'am," said the officer, his voice firm. "Please roll down your window."

Emma looked up into the officer's face. She reached for the window switch.

"There now," said the officer. "That's better."

She fumbled in her purse for her driving license, tears cascading down her cheeks. Her sobs grew louder. "I didn't need this. First the school, and now this." Her words dissolved into sobs. She looked up into those dark eyes. "He doesn't care, you know? Off with someone else, he couldn't care less about obligations." She reached out for the officer's sleeve and clutched hard. "But they need him. My husband needs to stay involved."

The officer shook his head, confused. "*Signora*, you've been in an accident. Let's call someone to help you."

Her eyes grew heavy. She struggled for air.

"Give me your cellphone, ma'am."

Emma looked up, but those dark eyes were swirling. She blinked twice. No better. She handed the officer the phone and clutched her head again. The throbbing was like a jackhammer in her skull.

"Your husband's name, ma'am?"

Focusing her gaze was an effort. His face was fuzzy around the edges. Her eyelids grew heavy. She laughed, the vicious cackle of a witch. "My husband of twenty years? 'Til death do us part and all that crap. *That* guy?"

He sighed. "Yes."

"The illustrious Doctor Dario Rinaldi. If I'm scarred and hideous, he can even fix me up. Special family discount." Her eyes grew heavier. Maybe sleep would dull the pounding.

"Dario. Got it." He pushed call as she tried to focus on him. "Yes, Doctor Rinaldi, this is Officer Bonardi of the *Vigili urbani*, Rome. Your wife's been in an accident. She's not hurt, but she's acting strangely ..."

Emma stared at his mouth moving, trying to summon forth the words to stop him, but none came. Who was he speaking to? Certainly not Dario? Had she called Dario her husband? She couldn't hear his words any longer. Could he wrap it up so she could buy the food for the dinner? Would she be back in time to get the kids from the school bus stop? She needed to go. The throbbing was unbearable. Maybe if she closed her eyes only for a moment, it would stop.

Her eyelids fluttered down. A moment later, the officer's voice and the din of honking horns faded.

CHAPTER 2

Tiffany

There was a time when people took Tiffany seriously.

But that was before her waist slimmed, and her hips and bust swelled, and long, shapely legs replaced the bruised, bandaged versions of her tomboy youth. Following those miraculous transformations, Tiffany grew accustomed to being on the receiving end of male attention.

Plenty of it, in fact.

Of course, as any pretty girl could tell you, attention had its advantages. It got doors opened for you and men offering to lift your heavy luggage. It facilitated your entry into clubs and ensured you never had to wait for a drink. It made up for how you were ignored at home. It made you forget your father's drinking, and the speed with which he cycled in and out of low-paying jobs. The attention distracted you from life with your divorced mother. How she constantly took up with a string of younger men, whose presence in their house left you uneasy, and always mindful to lock your door at night.

Male attention managed to take her mind off her home life. But once she became a teenager, no one ever took Tiffany seriously again.

Standing before her mirror, Tiffany coated her lashes with mascara, making her blue eyes appear even larger. Her trump card in Rome. She touseled her long, auburn hair and tilted her face before the bright lights of the mirror, ensuring the bronzer gave her a natural, sun-kissed effect.

It was still warm for October, and sailing on Massimo's boat in Capri two weeks earlier procured her a golden glow. Auditions were coming up, and the Italians did love the bronzed look on their television stars.

She slipped the emerald onto her finger and turned it to watch it glimmer under the light. She sighed appreciatively and stroked the stone, as she'd done thousands of times. But when her gaze dropped down to her chest, she groaned. If only she had the money for breast implants. She knew her dancing and her looks were in her favor, but her bustline—fine back home—was too small for local standards.

Her cellphone rang, and she turned from the mirror. "*Pronto.*"

"Hey, Tiff. It's Lisa."

The South Carolina drawl always brought a smile to her face. More colorful than her flat, Midwestern tone.

"Oh, hi. Just getting ready for Giancarlo's party. What time're you stopping by?"

"Sorry. That's why I'm callin'. I can't make it. I gotta migraine and I'm just gonna wait it out in the dark, here in bed."

Tiffany rubbed one temple. "Please, Lisa. Can't you come? Just a little while? Luana Lella will be there." She paced back and forth, forcing herself to speak slowly. "And you know I just *have* to meet Alessio. He's supposed to be there, too. He'll be personally choosing the *veline* for the new show."

"Yeah, I know. But I'm not up to it. Maybe I can stop by tomorrow and hear how it went."

The finality in her friend's tone was crystal clear. She'd known Lisa throughout the three years she'd been in Italy, and Lisa's migraines put an end to many of their plans. This wasn't the first time she'd been abandoned. She tapped her fingers impatiently. What was the point? Lisa would never budge. "Okay, if you're sure you can't make it. Hope you're feeling better soon. We'll talk tomorrow." She hung up in a huff.

Really, being out would probably help much more than shutting herself up in a darkened room. Lisa was a real drag. Hard to believe she worked in television at all.

Although, technically, she was only a glorified English teacher, who spent her days coaching Italian actors in English. Out with friends, Lisa always slipped back to her Southern drawl, but Lisa could mimic any accent: California, Texas, Long Island, Boston Brahmin. You name it, she performed it, making her the go-to woman for Italian actors aspiring to a career in Hollywood. The irony was, practically all her students emerged with only a slightly tweaked Italian accent, even after all her hours of professional coaching.

Tiffany couldn't understand why Lisa never aspired to a television career herself, but Lisa claimed actors bored her. Still, she was an invaluable connection to parties and events— the very places Tiffany needed to circulate to be discovered. Tonight's invitation was no exception.

She walked into her bedroom and opened the wardrobe, extracting a pair of towering heels. She stroked the delicate straps. They'd cost her a fortune, even during the sales, but they made her legs look longer, and she needed that boost if she was to meet Alessio tonight at the party.

She slipped into a Max Mara dress, fingering its daring neckline. She'd bought it just for the occasion, even if she couldn't afford it. Giancarlo already promised the introduction, winking and saying she had to take it from there. After three years in Rome, trying to break into television, Tiffany knew what that meant. She'd smiled demurely at Giancarlo's comments.

Of course, she knew you didn't get on shows without some exchange of favors, but did it have to be so transparent? Her friends with real jobs always asked her why she tried so hard, why she wanted it so much. Why did she? Because it was so far away from where she was raised? Because her high school yearbook voted her most likely to be famous? Because half those classmates were already married with mortgages and kids, while she felt she was living out an adventure? So what if she lived in a shoebox, and half the time she had no idea how to make ends meet from sporadic teaching assignments? This is what she wanted to do, what she knew she had in her.

The doorbell rang. Gently, she placed the shoes down and made her way to the door. After peering through the peephole, she smiled and flung open the door.

"*Ciao bello. Come stai oggi?*"

Simone's eyes examined her from head to toe. Grasping her by the shoulder, he spun her gently around. "Wow, much better after seeing you. Good thing I never have students like you in my classes. Too distracting."

She tapped him on the chest. "You're such a tease. You didn't even see me in my heels. I'll knock before I go out."

There was a spark in his hazel eyes. "Where are you going, dressed to kill? Out to break more hearts?"

She sighed. "I wish. I'm going to a party. The producer of a show I'm auditioning for will be there. I have to make a good impression."

Simone raised an eyebrow. "Dressed like that, how could you not?" He reached for her hand. "It sounds to me like you need a good, home-cooked meal to strengthen you before the attack."

Tiffany groaned. "Not again. I had to hold my breath to squeeze into this dress. Your cooking will bust the seams."

"There's nothing to you, Tiffany. I may not watch those shows, but I am an Italian male. I don't think skeletal frames are any man's ideal. Just a little. I promise not to force-feed you." He smiled, setting off the crinkles around his eyes.

Tiffany could never resist Simone. He was like a big puppy dog. And since they'd been neighbors, he was more like a brother to her than her own brother had ever been. "Okay, you win. Lead the way."

She allowed herself to be nudged next door. She'd been so many times to this apartment, a mirror image of her own, but so much more grown up. Good quality furniture, overflowing floor-to-ceiling bookshelves, a fully equipped kitchen that Simone actually used on a daily basis. When Simone returned from the high school biology classes he taught, he went for a jog, then got to work in the kitchen. Heavenly aromas wafted from under his door every evening when she returned, while Tiffany wondered if she had enough lettuce left over in the fridge for a salad.

"I still haven't gotten used to cooking for one." He pulled a hot bakery tray from the oven.

Tiffany waited until he'd turned. "How's Ramona? Have you spoken to her?" She knew Simone didn't want to talk about it, while still wanting desperately to talk about it.

He turned his back to her again, placing bread slowly onto a plate. "She likes Chicago. She prefers e-mailing to calling or Skyping, says the sound of my voice makes her nostalgic. Makes her weaken her resolve about our deal." His shoulders slouched.

Tiffany held back rather than slipping comforting arms around him.

"I hate how she calls it 'our' deal, when she's the one who wanted to go to Chicago, free from all ties. I was willing to wait for her."

Tiffany heard a sigh, but when Simone turned around he was smiling. She suspected his acting skills were far more developed than her own.

He placed the serving plate on the table with a flourish. "Crusty, homemade French bread, with melted gorgonzola and hazelnuts."

"You're freaking kidding me. You even bake your own bread?"

"Ah, ah, ah." He slapped her hand playfully. "No profanity at this dinner table, *Signorina* Walker."

"Oh, please." Tiffany held up a steaming piece of baguette, smelling the melted gorgonzola. "Your English is so damned perfect and *precise*. You need to shake it up a bit, make it a bit more colorful." She grinned. "That's where I come in."

"So you see? I lucked out with my choice of neighbor."

"Ha!" Tiffany swallowed a bite. "Luck's got nothing to do with it. Where else could we afford to live on two teacher's salaries? A penthouse on Piazza di Spagna?"

Simone's face clouded over. "Ramona's company pays for some luxurious condo."

He made a face and the word, on his lips, sounded vulgar.

"It overlooks Lake Michigan and the skyline. It has a gym and a twenty-four hour doorman." He allowed his voice to grow soft. "She's not coming back."

Tiffany sighed and placed her hand over Simone's. His hazel eyes looked so vulnerable. A lock of his thick, dark hair fell over his eyes, and she longed to brush it away. "No, she isn't, Simone."

"Yeah, I know."

His voice sounded heartbreakingly sad. For the second time, Tiffany fought the urge to embrace him. "You need to get over her. There must be some gorgeous colleague at work. Cook her dinner and she'll swoon." She stroked his arm. "I can't think of a better boyfriend than you."

His gaze met hers. "Ramona didn't think so. She couldn't sprint away fast enough."

"Ramona doesn't know what she's missing."

One side of his mouth twitched up. "Then why aren't you jumping me when you have the chance? I'm lonely and vulnerable."

"I would, but I'm vain and shallow. I need a man in show business, with a fancy car and a yacht. Someone who'll have the contacts to get me on TV." She shrugged. "A high school biology teacher—no matter how sexy and adept in the kitchen he is—just won't cut it."

Simone laughed. "Fair enough. You're more honest than my girlfriend. I mean, my ex." He poured wine into her glass. The oven timer went off. "The lasagna is ready."

"Lasagna? You're killing me. I'll be rolling into the party tonight."

Simone got up, kissed the top of her head, and returned with a baking dish, bubbling gently. The smell was heavenly. Tiffany calculated how many calories might be contained in one deadly slice. But in three years of living next to Simone, she'd internalized one golden rule. Never turn down his lasagna.

"I'll regret this, but give me a slice."

Simone stroked her cheek and smiled. "I thought you'd never ask."

Two hours later, Tiffany made her way around a grand room filled with half-clad women wearing stiletto heels very similar to her own. Only much more expensive.

Every woman in that room was trying to catch Alessio's eye.

Two-thirds of the women, with their perfect bodies, silky hair, and designer dresses, probably had auditions scheduled for Alessio's new program, *Olé olé*. The comedians Alex and Max had already been signed on as the show's hosts, and Alessio was selecting two women who would dress in scanty outfits and dance between skits. They didn't even have to dance well, the emphasis was on sexy. The Italians ate up that well-worn formula, and a showgirl, or *velina,* was a fixture of Italian life, poised to make a fortune from advertisements and appearances.

Ever since arriving in Italy and seeing those programs, she'd dreamed about being one herself.

And there, in the middle of the room, drawing the envious stares of all the women and the more lascivious gazes of the men, was the star of all showgirls: Luana Lella, in the flesh. And what impressive flesh it was. The gossip mags wrote about Luana's rumored operations with the illustrious Doctor Rinaldi, plastic surgeon to the stars.

Luana's lips were plumped, her cheeks raised and sculpted, her rear perky and firm. And her breasts. Well, her breasts were a revelation. Tiffany couldn't take her eyes off them. Every time she glanced down at her own, she realized how inadequate they were.

How could she ever hope to reach the lofty levels of *Luana Lella*, for Christ's sake? Why would Alessio even look twice at her with a goddess like Luana—a legend, really—hogging the spotlight? Tiffany downed her *prosecco* and fought off the urge to cry.

Why had she turned Simone down when he told her he was going to stay in and watch an old classic, *La grande guerra*? Her Italian was still rudimentary, even after three years in Rome, but she'd seen that movie half a dozen times and loved it. Simone would patiently explain the lines she missed. He always served as her personal interpreter when they watched old Italian films together. She could be in her warm pyjamas and fuzzy slippers now, eating popcorn on Simone's couch, with someone who wouldn't comment on how inadequate her breasts were.

For Simone, nothing about her was inadequate at all. Unlike most men, he even seemed to take her seriously.

"Tiffany." A familiar voice shook her from her reveries.

She turned to see Giancarlo, next to ... *him*. Oh, God. He was even hotter in real life than in the magazine photos.

How many times had she read gossip magazines about his latest success, or his latest fling, or his latest sports car? And here he was in person. Wearing jeans and a cool black shirt, buttoned one button too low to show off his waxed, tanned, muscled chest. Gorgeous. His black hair curled just the right length over his collar, advertising his playboy status. A little grin on his face showed the room how perfect he knew he was, and how he knew that everyone recognized it, too.

Her hands grew clammy. Her heart raced. Alessio Armellini, so close she could touch him.

"Tiffany," said Giancarlo. "There's someone I'd like you to meet."

Oh. My. God. They're here for ME.

"This is my friend, Tiffany Walker. She's an American, from some godawful place out in the prairies. Right, Tiff?"

She nodded her head numbly.

"And this is Ales-"

"Alessio Armellini. One meter ninety centimeters. Born in Treviso on 20 October 1978. Loves sailing, golf, fine wines, and driving his race cars. Favorite book: *War and Peace*. Cheers for AC Milan. Produced three hit variety shows for Mediaset in the last five years."

Oh, God. Did she just blurt that all out? Her cheeks flushed. Both men were grinning at her.

Giancarlo's eyes shone in amusement. "A man who needs no introduction, I see. Okay, Tiff, I'll leave you to it, then." With a wink, he was gone.

Her cheeks were on fire. After all the effort required to blurt out the spontaneous biography, her mouth felt strangely dry. She grinned dumbly at the man she'd so longed to meet.

He smiled that coy, winning smile she'd seen dozens of times in the magazine. "Impressive. Can I send you in my place for journalists' interviews?"

She lifted the champagne flute to her lips and drained its contents. God, she must look like such a hick. Deep breath, engaging smile. "I believe in thorough research. I have an audition for your new show on Thursday."

He cocked one eyebrow. "You don't say? I don't get that an awful lot at parties."

Feeling bolder after the liquid fortification, she placed a hand squarely on his chest. "I bet you don't."

"Why don't you wait here. I'll fetch champagne, and then I'm sure I can ask Giancarlo for a room to see a special sneak preview of what's in store for me on Thursday." He winked.

"I'll be waiting." She watched his square shoulders recede into the crowd.

Now what? She'd wanted this, after all. It's not that she was stupid. She'd heard from the other girls that you were expected to, well, exchange favors for a slot on the show. And it was worth it. Wasn't it? Dancing night after night, before a live audience and television viewers across the country on *Olé olé*? Alessio was so smooth, so handsome, it was hardly a sacrifice at all.

How many men had she slept with since coming to Italy with nothing to gain? Hell, what about her sleazy boss at the insurance agency back in Des Moines, with his cloying smell of Dunkin' Donuts and Old Spice? He'd kept promising to leave his wife. That fiasco led her to Rome in the first place. *You need to relax, Tiff. There's nothing wrong with two people attracted to one another acting on that. And, if it leads him to choose you over hundreds of other women vying for the same job, so what?*

She jumped when the sickeningly sweet smell of "Angel" wafted in front of her. Platinum blond hair swung near her face and a pair of Dolly Parton-sized melons grazed her own modest chest. Luana Lella in all her glorious flesh.

"So, honey," said Luana, in nasally Italian that verged on a whine. "You're the flavor of the night."

"Pardon? Are you talking to me?"

She rolled her eyes. "Ah, Alessio always did have a weakness for foreign women. And an American, no less." She drawled out American with a faux Texas drawl.

This was not going as Tiffany had hoped. She'd always dreamed of meeting Luana Lella. And now, here the woman was before her, fangs exposed.

"I think you've misunderstood. Alessio and I have a mutual friend. We've just been catching up. I'm Tiffany, and I'm *so* thrilled to meet you, Luana. You're a legend. I've watched *all* your shows. How on earth do you do it all?" Her rudimentary Italian made her sound like a slow child, but Luana seemed to soften under the barrage of compliments.

"*Grazie, cara.* People think our job is easy, but what's more difficult than having to be sexy twenty-four hours a day? We can never shuffle around in a housedress and flip-flops. We have to be desirable whenever the paparazzi show up." She sighed and her breasts heaved up and down. "It's a burden, but one I bear proudly."

She stared bravely out in the distance, chin quivering slightly, in a manner that made Tiffany suspect she'd practiced the line many times before. Probably in front of a mirror.

Alessio was returning across the room with two flutes and a bottle of champagne. His face fell when he saw Luana, who turned and flashed him her dazzling smile. Tiffany noticed that her face, with its skin unnaturally tight, didn't move at all.

"Alessio, *tesoorooo* ..." she drawled, shaping her silicone-enhanced lips into a seductive pout. "How long has it been?" Her eyes sparkled and she looked him up and down. "Your boat in Capri, maybe? I don't know if I've ever experienced more rocking, from the waves and from ..." She cast a sly glance at Tiffany. A lazy smile spread across her face. "What you'll learn about Alessio is that he's famous for his endurance."

Tiffany looked down, eager to slip away.

"Alessio, *caro*. I'm looking for something new. Any places for me on *Olé olé*? Wouldn't it be brilliant to work together again?"

For a split second, Alessio looked stricken, before he recovered and flashed a toothy smile. "I wish we could, Luana. But we don't have the budget for a star like you. We're aiming at new talent. They'll be willing to accept less." He winked at Tiffany. "But, if I'm not mistaken, that's Fabio over there. I hear he's got a new program in the works, with a budget rumored to be obscene. You should speak with him."

Luana stood on her toes, scanning the crowd. "Over there? *Grazie, tesoro.*" She gave him a hurried kiss on the cheek. "And let's get together soon. Relive old times." She raced off as fast as her stilettos would allow.

There was a long silence. "So, you and Luana were ... an item?"

"An *item* is a gross exaggeration. I had sex with her. Like ninety percent of the straight men working in television. Signora Lella's fame travels far and wide." He rolled his eyes. "But why are we talking about the old lady? I believe we had a private appointment to discuss your audition." He reached for her elbow and led her down the hallway. They entered a room, empty except for a king-sized bed, a table, and an armoire. He placed the champagne bottle and flutes on the table and moved to the door, slowly clicking the lock. "Privacy is key for these interviews. We need quality time to understand if we could work well together."

When he smiled at her, despite his tan, his expensive Italian clothes and shoes, and his artfully tousled hair, something about him reminded Tiffany of Walt, the sleazy boss in Iowa. She shook her head to dispel the image.

He turned to pour champagne and handed her a flute. "First we drink, then I'll watch you dance. A private audition, eh?"

Tiffany took a nervous sip, then another.

"So what's a prairie girl like you doing in Rome, trying to break into television?"

"I've been dancing since I was three. My mother had a dance school. I've been in pageants from the age of six. Little Miss Corn Festival Queen, Miss Midwestern Teen Knock-Out Queen."

He laughed and filled her flute again. "You're kidding, right?"

She sighed. "No. My parents thought it was the height of sophistication." She drained her glass.

Alessio was rifling through the armoire. He turned, holding a skimpy cheerleader's uniform on a hanger. "Were you a prairie cheerleader, too? Why don't you try this on and show me your enthusiasm for the team." He smiled. "We'll need that on *Olé olé.*" He poured another glass. "Drink this, it'll loosen you up."

Tiffany's hand trembled. She drank from her flute, realizing that Alessio hadn't even had a sip. She turned away from him, slipping out of her elegant dress, clad only in a lacy black bra and panties. Quickly, she slid into the cheap, silky uniform. She turned, standing before him in the tight top, revealing her navel and most of her breasts. The skirt left nothing to the imagination. In her hands, she held matching pompoms. "Giancarlo had this just lying around in his closet?" She heard her words slurring.

His lip curled up. "Sometimes we have to do spontaneous auditions. Be prepared. Boy Scout motto, right?"

The room was spinning. She walked to the window. "I need some air. Isn't it hot in here?"

"Oh, that it is, babe. What do you say about steaming it up even more? Dance for me."

Tiffany felt so strange. She hadn't had so much to drink, and after Simone's dinner, she wasn't drinking on an empty stomach. She began to move, swaying her hips, holding her arms out wide, listening to the music inside her. Life in Iowa had been dull, life in her home even worse. Dancing had always been her escape. She could banish her fears when she turned herself over to the music.

But now her head spun and her eyelids felt heavy.

"Strip, Tiffany. I have to see how you look. You have to be a knockout in a bikini."

Alessio's voice reached her through a deep fog. Feeling hot, she reached down and shed her flimsy top, opened the clasp on the skimpy skirt, allowing it to spill around her legs in a shimmering puddle. Through the haze, she saw Alessio devouring her with his eyes.

"*Complimenti*, Tiffany. You have a great body. Let's see if you have other talents." He closed the distance between them and grasped her by the shoulder, shoving her to her knees. He unbuckled his belt.

A clanging sound exploded in Tiffany's skull. The room began to spin. "Alessio, I don't feel well. I'm dizzy."

He lowered his boxers and clutched her hair firmly with his hands, stepping closer. "You're fine, prairie girl. Just excited.

Who could blame you?"

She struggled to stand, but the room tilted. "It's not excitement. It's nausea."

"C'mon, Tiff. If you prefer the bed, we'll start there."

He yanked her up roughly by the shoulder. She lost her balance and tried to catch her fall on the bed, but the objects shifted under her gaze. Her head hit the metal frame with a sickening thud and she slumped to the ground.

"Oh, shit."

She heard a belt buckling, footsteps receding. She closed her eyes, fighting off the dizziness. Soon two voices spoke above her.

"Damnit, Alessio. Not again. What the hell do you give them? Industrial doses?"

"No, the little bitch probably doesn't know how to hold her liquor."

"Don't give me that shit. She's bleeding." He pressed fabric to her forehead. "It's not the first time. You need to drug them to get them into bed? Tiffany's American. What if the Embassy gets involved? I'm not covering for you."

"Don't worry. I know a doctor who can take care of this."

He leaned down and felt her pulse. "No way. Her pulse is slow. I don't need this crap. I'm dropping her off in the emergency room and breaking up the party. The best I can do for you is to let you get the hell out of here before anyone starts asking questions. That's as generous as I can be."

Tiffany tried to open her mouth. She wanted to tell them she was okay, but she couldn't control her muscles. The voices grew more rhythmic, and she didn't try to fight the blackness enveloping her.

CHAPTER 3

Annarita

"Because you so ball-breaking? I tell you, I no have time to study this week." Tommaso barely looked at Annarita as his manicured fingers tapped away on his iPhone, his perfect, touseled hair gleaming in the afternoon light.

Annarita clutched her textbook tighter, anxious to keep her hands occupied. Tommaso often angered her, and she was accustomed to fighting the urge to slap her spoiled student across his petulant face.

Tommaso had been her student for over a year, but, aside from perfecting a few choice pick-up lines, his English hadn't improved at all.

Still, Tommaso had more money than brains, and he paid well for lessons. Unfortunately, Annarita couldn't afford to lose those types of students.

Usually, she laughed off his rude comments, encouraging him to speak, but that afternoon Annarita's own anger welled up inside her. Her patience was frayed. Her scooter had been stolen, something she couldn't afford. She'd crossed all of Rome to get out to Parioli, only to have her lunchtime student stand her up for her troubles. Then she'd raced back across town, only to put up with Tommaso's temper tantrums. And to make things worse, sitting across from him on his sun-drenched terrace in San Teodoro, Annarita could feel the telltale backache and cramps that signaled her period was on its way.

She watched Tommaso text away and swiped at a rogue curl breaking free from her hair clip. Damn, she needed this, too. Her hideous, southern Italian curls passed down from both parents at least calmed down in the fall, usually. But Rome's hot, humid weather was pushing into October, and her hair frizzed away happily—no respite in sight.

Tommaso's lips curled up in a way that made her suspect he was sexting during lessons. It would hardly be the first time. Maybe their lessons would go better if she adapted their lesson plans to Tommaso's narrow range of interest—procuring sex.

Speaking of which, it had been ages since she'd had any. She'd probably forgotten how it was done. Vincenzo was always away, on tour with the band. He'd told her he was beat tonight, but she knew he could never resist her. Or at least her cooking. It would be a stretch, but she'd get to the market after class and buy the last ingredients. Then she'd prepare Vincenzo a home-cooked dinner.

She'd often cursed her Italian-American family's obsession with food, and how their constant feeding kept her from possessing the model figure that, in a perfect world, she was destined to have. But her food culture did have its advantages, especially with the Italian boyfriends she'd had over the eight years she'd been in Rome.

"You have head between clouds again?"

She snapped her head up. "Pardon?"

"Pardon?" He mimicked her, probably in the best imitation of English he'd ever accomplished.

"Listen, you no pay attention anyway. And I got a hot babe flying in from Moscow tonight. She know how have good time, you know what I say?"

Annarita worked hard to mask her disgust. She hated *figli di* like Tommaso. 'Sons of' was the perfect term for the trust fund crowd in Italy. Hair curling at just the right length over expensive shirt collars, casual clothes that left no doubt as to their obscene price tags, designer sunglasses, Swiss watches—all the trappings to display to the world that they fully knew their place in it. Damned terraces over San Teodoro with 360° views over the Roman Forum and the Palatine Hill—once home to the emperors of the greatest civilization on earth.

She looked out over the ruins of the Palatine, secure in the knowledge that Tommaso knew nothing about the Ancient Roman monuments he was privileged enough to view daily from his home as he sipped whiskey or sexted his stable of bimbos.

Annarita knew that Tommaso was a disappointment to his father, more interested in his cars, his sailboat, and his revolving door of leggy women than in taking over the family firm. After all his father's string-pulling to get him in, Tommaso left Bocconi after barely a semester. She knew that his father, dreaming of a political future for his son that rarely required a college degree, managed to get him campaign work during the last elections. Tommaso excelled at partying and meeting young women, but little else. Soon he was back to his schedule of sleeping 'til noon, stopping off for a coffee at his family firm, then keeping up with his hectic social life.

Working on his English was the only thing his father still insisted on, and that's where Annarita came in. Tommaso, allergic to any form of work, never made much progress, but he was forced to make their lessons. And she appreciated the regular cash infusions that made sitting across from the spoiled golden boy twice a week almost bearable.

"You go—okay? You no tell my *papà*."

Annarita blinked twice, momentarily confused. Dismissed fifteen minutes into their hour and a half lesson? But she stifled a sigh of relief as she saw him removing a wad of cash from his pocket. He'd pay in full for the curtailed lesson.

"Ah, sure Tommaso. You have a good time now with your ... err ... special friend." She jumped to her feet, afraid he might change his mind.

"We talk on Tuesday. I tell you all about." He winked at her. "I teach you new words you no know."

"Ahh, yes. Something to look forward to for next Tuesday then. Thank you." She pocketed the money, and made her way to the private elevator. "*Ci vediamo.* See you."

A moment later, the elevator spewed her out in the lobby and she buzzed herself out to San Teodoro's cobblestoned streets. She dodged the tour groups muttering away in French and German and turned out onto Via di San Teodoro, pausing only briefly to see the displays of sweets in the *pasticceria*. But no, she'd fallen in this trap before. The money needed to be put away. Rent had to be paid, and she had new expenses with the stolen *motorino*.

She'd have enough to buy the remaining ingredients and a good bottle of wine for Vincenzo's surprise dinner. And now she even had extra time. She turned onto Via dei Cerchi, skirting the edge of Circo Massimo on the way to the metro, wondering at her good luck.

Lasagna and *Saltimbocca alla romana*. Vincenzo's favorite. She clutched her thermal bag closer, and checked her watch. The market near Vincenzo's house would still be open. If she hurried. She began to speed up, but a glint of gold caught the corner of her eye. She turned and saw a small plaque on the wall beside the sidewalk. She neared it and read its engraved words. '*Mi sono perso.*' I was lost. Beneath it was a date: XVII. IX.MMX.

17 September 2010.

She squinted, but that was it. No other explanation. Rome was filled with plaques—Gogol lived here, Bernini sculpted in this studio, Verdi lodged here. But this was different. Why would a twenty-first century declaration that someone had been lost be placed alongside the Circus Maximus?

She glanced at her watch. No time to think about it now, or she'd never be on time.

She hurried to the end of the street and waited for a light to cross the Viale delle Terme di Caracalla to the metro. She turned to the left to see an ambulance arriving. A policeman was opening the passenger side of an expensive car that had smashed up a grey Fiat. She watched the medical team gently lift an unconscious woman out, placing her onto a stretcher. The woman's golden hair glittered in the afternoon sun. Her clothes looked expensive. A man was yelling at the policeman, something about the woman being a menace to society, how she could have killed his poor mother.

This is what Rome was—one senseless accident after another. Everyone in a rush to get somewhere. Everyone allergic to traffic rules. How many times had she risked death on her scooter, always lucky not to be the one hauled off in that ambulance? If the cars even bothered allowing the ambulance through.

She turned to the pedestrian light and saw it had already turned green. She crossed quickly, making her way to the metro station.

An hour later, she stood before Vincenzo's building, shopping bag in hand. She dug into her purse for her keys. Her keys. Maybe she used that term too loosely. Vincenzo was headed out on a tour, and the housekeeper's key had broken in the lock. He was packing up and sent Annarita out to the locksmith to make an extra copy for the housekeeper before he left.

Okay, so strictly speaking, he'd never asked her to make an extra set for herself. But surely, that's what he meant. He was just so distracted with gathering his stuff. Heading out on tours, playing drums for his band meant he was often, well, a bit scatterbrained about those types of things. Especially before a tour.

If it weren't for all the travel, surely he would have asked her to move in with him already. His life was just so unpredictable. Here a few days, then gone for long stretches, in little towns with clubs scattered throughout the Italian peninsula. It kept things developing haphazardly in their relationship. If he were an accountant or an office worker, they'd probably be married by now. But when he was home, he loved her home-cooked meals and pampering. She knew Vincenzo appreciated a good thing when he found it.

She was still fumbling for the keys, trying to hold the shopping bag upright, when a man approached the door from the lobby. He held it open for her, and she thanked him and smiled.

This would be a great place to live. Not like her place, with the losers and aspiring hoodlums who hung out in her building's lobby all night long, smoking and listening to music. As if any of them would ever open a door. This was another world.

She stepped into the elevator and pressed six. Ha! An elevator that worked. Hers was broken half the time. And a fourth floor walk-up with grocery bags or luggage was killing her. Living here would change her life. It would be an overnight change to her financial situation, once she stopped paying rent for her dive out in the boondocks, which she couldn't even believe was still considered part of Rome.

She paused before his door, her hovering hand about to knock. Instead, she pulled out her key, but yelled, "Vincenzo," at the door. No response.

She'd let herself in. It would give her time to get the dinner ready. She'd already precooked much of it this morning, but she still needed to prepare. Better to surprise him on his one evening back home. It would be a good excuse to tell him about the key. No doubt his favorite meal awaiting him would soften the blow.

Okay, strictly speaking, he *had* said not to come. That he was only back for one night in Rome and off again tomorrow for two weeks in Sicily. But men never knew what was best for them. He was probably trying to spare her the hassle. He could be so thoughtful that way. But really, it had been ages. Three weeks ago? Four? Of course she was dying to see him. She didn't care if it would be brief—yet again.

She looked around. The place was spotless. The housekeeper had probably been by today. The stovetop gleamed. She started unpacking groceries and the contents of her thermal bag.

Half an hour later, she'd placed the lasagna in the oven and had the *saltimbocca* ready to cook while they ate their first course. She opened the wine and poured herself a glass. *This* was good. The price tag had told her as much. But one had to be willing to invest in oneself.

Maybe tonight he'd ask her to move in.

She surveyed the open kitchen and living room. God, she'd love living here. It could use ... well, a woman's touch. But she didn't want to scare Vincenzo right away.

She could live with his furniture for a while. Her mother would freak out to have Annarita living with a man without an official engagement, but she'd have to get used to the idea. Hell, they weren't back in Benevento in the 1950s, and Annarita *was* thirty-four. Her mother would get used to the idea. Eventually.

She placed down the wineglass. She needed the bathroom, and everything was set in the kitchen. She walked to the bedroom door, the room that was soundproofed. Vincenzo had done it when he moved in, so he could practice his drums at home. Of course, he'd joked with her the first time she'd stayed over that the drums weren't the only reason.

Maybe Vincenzo had been asleep the whole time she'd been cooking. She knocked on the door. She didn't want to startle him.

No answer.

She turned the handle and slipped into the dark room. The sheets were all over the place, so he'd been here after the housekeeper. She saw a box of condoms on the dresser. Aha, so he *was* expecting her.

She turned to the small entryway before the bathroom, and saw the light on. She could hear the shower. He'd probably woken recently, and hadn't heard her out in the kitchen.

She reached out to the door, then changed her mind. She looked at her watch—how much time left for the lasagna? She unzipped her dress and let it slide to the floor. It would be cutting it close, but it *had* been ages. The shower was as good a place as any. And she'd paid a small fortune for this lingerie, wanting to surprise him tonight.

She looked down at her body. God, she was supposed to have gotten back to the gym and dropped some pounds during this last tour. She'd been optimistic buying this set, imagining her new body. Now it pinched uncomfortably in all the wrong places. But hell, how long would it be on, anyway? When she lived here, her commute would be shorter, her life easier, and she'd have oodles of time to get to the gym, constructing the perfect body. For tonight, her own would have to do.

Annarita threw back her shoulders, sucked in her soft belly, pushed out her breasts and called out "*Amore*, want some company?"

She threw open the door and immediately saw his large brown eyes staring at her through the steam, his mouth open in surprise.

"Who the hell let you in?"

His voice was harsher than she'd ever heard it. Oh no, the keys. Awkward to explain it now. She registered his flushed face, saw the steam rising around him, heard the water pounding down. Despite his anger, he was so handsome. She let her eyes travel down, and gasped.

His hands were tangled in the long, platinum blonde hair of a figure kneeling before him. Annarita was frozen in place as the figure turned around. Sharp blue eyes observed her with distaste. The woman wasn't a day over twenty. And she looked like a Playboy bunny. Her large breasts, tight tummy and sculpted thighs shimmered in the shower's spray.

Annarita caught a glimpse of her own pudgy silhouette in the wall-length mirror. How pathetic. She wished she could dissolve with the shower's steam. Instead she felt the tears spilling over as her voice warbled "I had a key made. I wanted to surprise you by cooking dinner."

"Honey," said the blonde, looking her up and down dismissively. "A word of advice. You might want to spend less time in the kitchen."

Tears pricked her eyes. She caught Vincenzo's gaze, hoping he'd defend her, but there was only hardness.

"I told you not to come tonight. Get lost."

She gasped and stumbled back, grabbing the door handle. The tears flowed faster, blinding her. She grabbed her shoes and dress. Hiccupping, she plucked her purse from the table and raced to the door, hurtling out to the hallway without thinking. The door closed behind her and she looked down in horror at her body, clad only in lacy, black lingerie.

"Oh, God," she wailed.

She held out her dress with trembling hands as the elevator opened and two teenagers with backpacks stepped out, mouths agape, their hungry, teenaged eyes travelling over her body. She jumped into her dress hurriedly and raced to the elevator, shoes and purse in one shaking hand. With the other, she pressed the ground floor button. She heard one pimply teenager snicker to the other as the doors closed.

"Oh, man. He's turning women away. I saw the hot blonde he brought back this afternoon. I wanna be a drummer when I grow up."

Peals of laughter followed her down the elevator shaft. She dressed quickly and sprinted through the lobby, the tears flowing stronger with each step.

CHAPTER 4

Emma

The antiseptic smell filled Emma's nostrils. Her eyes snapped open as she took in the room: white walls, rough white sheets. No high thread-count on these. She'd be lucky if she didn't have bedbug bites. Medical machines surrounded the bed. She moved her fingers, wiggled her toes. All apparently in working order. Why was she in the hospital?

Images flashed through her mind. The sound of steel hitting steel. The police officer. Oh, God. Had he called Dario? Had *she* told the officer Dario was her husband? What had she been thinking? Her ex wouldn't have raced all the way back from his Sardinian love nest. That meant he must have called ...

"Ah, cara. Finalmente ti sei svegliata."

A seventy-year-old face, tucked and stretched in a useless attempt to appear twenty, hovered over her. Thick, silicone-plumped lips opened and closed. Emma shrank from the bright, red Chanel. Ready to devour her. The exact shade of her Chanel jacket. Marianna was always so put together. And here she was, looking down her nose at Emma, who must look a mess. Could this be a bad dream?

If only.

It was Marianna in the flesh. The *suocera*. The dreaded Italian mother-in-law.

Like a typical Italian male, Dario called his mother to come to the rescue. His mother had always hated Emma and never considered her worthy of her darling son's notice. The woman hosted a dinner party at La pergola for her friends when Dario announced their divorce.

"Dario called me from Sardinia, even if he was in the middle of an important medical conference."

So that's what he told you ...

"You're lucky to have an ex-husband ..."

The joy was evident in her mother-in-law's voice as she carefully formed the 'ex' with her plumped, red lips.

"... who still looks out for you. Of course, he doesn't want to ignore the desperate—and, let's face it, dramatic—pleas from the mother of his children."

Emma caught a hopeful glimmer in the woman's eyes. Maybe she'd hoped for a more serious crash-up when Dario first called.

Marianna looked out the window. "My son is as sweet and thoughtful as he was as a little boy. He could never turn away when those close to him were in need. I always thought wearing his heart on his sleeve would lead him into trouble."

Emma felt her heart beat faster. This woman always had the ability to make her blood pressure rise. She closed her eyes and breathed in deeply.

"Marianna, I'm tired now. Where are the children?"

"Waiting in the hallway. Worried out of their minds that their mother caused a crash, and accosted a policeman."

Emma breathed in through her teeth. "I did *not* accost a policeman. I was upset, and I may have yelled, because of the ringing in my ears." She closed her eyes and smoothed her sheet, willing the tears down. "Can I see them now?"

Marianna shot Emma a disapproving glance, but she moved to the door and opened it. Marco and Valerio charged in, still dressed in their sports uniforms. They threw themselves on Emma's bed. She rested her face on their touseled heads and breathed in their little boy smells, feeling an overwhelming sense of relief.

"*Mamma*! You're okay. We were so worried. The doctor thinks you may come home tomorrow."

The tears she'd felt welling up earlier spilled over. She wiped them away. "It's so good to see you. You have no idea. And Chiara?" She looked up and saw her teenage daughter, leaning sullenly against the door.

Chiara, with her long golden locks and bright blue eyes, looked so heartbreakingly beautiful. Although, at this age, her daughter didn't realize it. She seemed to spend hours locked in her room agonizing she wasn't pretty enough, skinny enough, good enough. Her daughter chewed on her lip, the same nervous habit she'd had as a girl. It made Emma want to scoop her into her arms and protect her.

"Chiara, honey. Come here." She motioned with an arm that felt heavy.

Chiara took hesitant steps toward the bed, still chewing her lip. "It was my fault, wasn't it? The accident?" Her voice was breathy and unsure. "You were upset after your talk with Mrs. Green. It's why you had the accident, isn't it?"

Emma shook her head, feeling a strain in her neck. "No, Chiara. A moped pulled in front of me, and I swerved to avoid it. It could have happened to anyone."

Her daughter nodded, almost imperceptibly. A thin veil of tears coated her sky blue eyes, softening the defiant look Emma had seen in them almost daily since the separation from Dario.

Chiara leaned in, her soft cheek resting against Emma's. Emma stifled a sigh of satisfaction. When she opened her eyes, her gaze fell on Marianna's face, with its deadened nerves straining to form an impossible grimace.

The older women clapped her hands. "*Ragazzi*, your mother needs her rest. Wish her a *buona notte*, and wait in the hallway. I wish to have a word with her."

Emma squeezed her children tight into her like a talisman, willing the sense of love to ward off the bracing chill awaiting her. Their bouncing forms made their way to the door, turning with faces that shared traces of their toddler selves. She smiled as they waved before Marianna stepped in front of them to gently close the door.

She switched back into Italian for her mother-in-law. "*Grazie*, Marianna, for bringing them to me. I'm so grateful. And thank you for taking care of them tonight."

The red jacket grew closer, the click of heels reverberated off old marble floors. Not a lock of her perfectly coiffed hair dared escape from its upswept look.

"Yes, I will stay with them tonight, since they require the presence of family. And yes, I had to cancel my trip to Tuscany with my wine study group —a trip we planned *one year ago*, I might add."

Her dark brown eyes flashed with a dangerous look Emma remembered seeing far too often during her twenty-year marriage to Dario.

"My English may not be good." Her voice dropped a register. "But I can still sniff out a lie in a language that is not my own. What you told Chiara is not the truth. I'm certain of it. This accident was not casual. You have been a wreck ever since the divorce. Frankly, I'm surprised it took this long." She raised her aquiline nose in the air. "I am only grateful that the children were not in the car."

Emma smoothed the sheets, oddly grateful for the rough texture that rubbed against her skin and calmed her. "You are welcome to your suppositions. You always freely voiced your distaste. But I'm afraid, in this case, you are wrong. It was exactly as I told Chiara. A moped swerved. I avoided hitting the driver."

"And yet, the policeman was adamant that you insisted he call your husband. You told him Dario *was* your husband." Hard eyes stared down. "Not an ex."

Emma forced a smile. "Blame it on the head injury."

Marianna sighed. "Americans are always so superficial. Your tendency to make light of everything was always one of the traits I liked least about you."

Were there ever any traits of mine you admired, Marianna?

"I know this has been hard on you. I won't pretend I condoned your marriage." She sniffed. "I knew you and Dario were too dissimilar for the marriage to last after the initial spark died out. Marriage is hard work, and I never believed you were in it for the long haul."

Emma fought to keep her temper in check. With her former mother-in-law, it was always a losing battle. "I know your son can do no wrong in your eyes, but the end of our marriage was not due to my inability to stay committed over the long haul. That recognition should go to Dario, who seemed to find a vow to just one woman too dull for his voracious appetites."

Marianna waved her hand dismissively. "I know my son is no saint. Men crave variety. Surely you know that. One indiscretion here and there could certainly have been overlooked. Was it worth destroying your marriage over? Breaking up your family? Look what it's putting poor Chiara through."

Emma balled up the sheets in her fists. "Unfortunately, I seem to be lacking that Latin gene that allows a wife to smile cheerfully while her husband sleeps with anything moving within a hundred-kilometer radius. Leaving my marriage allowed me to preserve my dignity."

"Well I do hope your dignity keeps you warm at night, dear. And it seems to be having a splendid effect on your children. Dario informs me Chiara may be kicked out of Fairmont." Her eyes narrowed in her smooth, plastic face. "But I'm sure you know what you're doing, *cara*." She turned and glided to the door. "I'll call the doctor tomorrow, but if you're coming home, I'm certain you can arrange for a taxi. *Buona notte*, Emma."

Emma closed her eyes, concentrating on the sharp glow of the ceiling light. As she focused on conjuring up the breaking waves washing over her, she felt the tears slipping from beneath her closed lids. Her breaths were ragged.

As much as she hated her mother-in-law, as much as the crone had made her married life miserable—charging in and constantly reminding Emma of what she wasn't, weighing in on every decision as if she were an equal player in Emma and Dario's marriage—despite all that, Marianna was often right.

She was right now. Emma *was* falling apart. This hadn't been her first panic attack, just her most dangerous. Her life was unraveling before her own eyes.

She had twins who often cried at night in their sleep, who longed for their father's attention. She had a daughter who, only a year earlier, had been daddy's little girl and a straight-A student, and was now acting out and in danger of expulsion. Her husband seemed to consider the divorce an excuse to pull away from his children. Some new conquest would always take precedence over his own children.

And what if he decided to settle down again and father a new litter? Would he forget Chiara, Valerio and Marco altogether? He'd hardly be the first man to forget his original family. Emma couldn't help but be racked with doubt. Maybe her freedom had come at too high a price.

And freedom for what? She'd abandoned her fledgling career when she married Dario. Now she was a woman who lunched. Thanks to her husband's alimony checks. How much of a cliché was that? The accident was anything but. It was a miracle she and others escaped unharmed. And that the children hadn't been in the car. Marianna was right about that, too.

She closed her eyes and breathed in deeply. The cellphone beside her bed rang.

"*Pronto*," she said in a raspy voice.

"*Ciao, Emma. Sono Sabrina.* How are you feeling?"

Her friend's voice soothed her. "Ah, not great ... I was in a car accident."

"I know, sweetie. I was at the hospital earlier. Dario called Franco, and we found out you were taken to San Giovanni. Franco knew the doctor on call, and I came over to see you. You were still unconscious, but Doctor Neri didn't think you were in any danger. Lina had her dance recital this evening, otherwise I'd be back there now. Do you still want me to come? Franco could call in a favor to sneak me in."

"It's okay, Sabrina. I'm exhausted. I'll probably go to sleep. I feel so much better hearing your voice." She swiped a tear trickling down one cheek.

There was a pause on the other end. "Uh-oh. I'll wager a guess the battleax has been by to see you."

Emma tried to laugh, and felt a dull ache in her ribs. "How'd you know?" How many times had Sabrina been her confidante after painful run-ins with her mother-in-law?

"I offered to take the kids, but Dario said he'd called his mother."

"Ah. Well, it's probably for the best. The kids are a little shaken up. Maybe it's better to be with *nonna* tonight."

Sabrina sighed. "Emma, I hate to be the bearer of bad news, but it seems your mother's on her way, too."

"She's coming ..." her voice came out strangled. "... here?"

"Afraid so. Dario called her, too."

"Oh, God. First Marianna, then Marilyn. The accident's starting to look like the high point of my day."

"Oh, sweetie." Her voice was gentle. "You'll be okay. I'll come by to visit lots while she's with you."

"Promise me?" Emma attempted a tense smile, relieved Sabrina couldn't see her. "Thanks for stopping by today. I'm sorry to have scared you."

"Just rest up and get better. I'll be by tomorrow morning, hoping I can take you home. *Buona notte.*"

"Thanks for calling. Your voice cheered me up. Good night, Sabrina."

She clicked off the phone and placed it on the nightstand. She turned towards a sound at the door, seeing the nurse standing there.

"I see you've woken, and I know you've had your visits. Let me take your blood pressure before the doctor stops by on his evening rounds."

Emma smiled at the pretty, white-clad figure approaching her. She took a deep breath and held out her arm, willing her troubles away.

CHAPTER 5

Tiffany

"We're almost there ... just a few more steps. Makes you wish the condominium board spent less energy fighting and more time concentrating on how to get an elevator installed."

"Simone, put me down," Tiffany said. "I'm not feeling well, but I'm not helpless. I'm sure I could make my way up slowly."

His breaths came quickly, but he continued. "Are you calling into question my manliness? Anyway, you're light as a feather. What on earth do you eat anyway? You're all skin and bones. Still, it's clear the jogging isn't enough. I definitely have to start weight-training if a ballerina can wear me out so easily."

They reached the landing. Simone reached into his pockets for Tiffany's keys, opening the door without putting her down.

"Okay, let's get you to bed."

"No, I'm fine."

"Tiffany, doctor's orders. I don't want to hear any protests. I tried your friend Lisa, but she has the flu. I called in to say I won't go to school tomorrow. I'll stay tonight to make sure you're okay, then take care of you tomorrow."

"You've already done enough. I'm sorry about making you come to the hospital."

He lowered her onto the bed, tucking her under the sheets. He grinned. "I don't know, seeing how you were dressed in that skimpy little cheerleader's uniform, it was a good thing I came when I did. You were the talk of all the doctors on their midnight rounds."

He winked and she felt her face grow warm. Memories of the slutty costume made her cringe. Simone had brought her regular clothes to the hospital. "How mortifying. What they must think of me. What *you* must think of me."

Simone sat on the edge of the bed and stroked back her hair. "Shhh. I was teasing you. I spoke to the doctors. You were drugged. Badly. It's lucky the bastards had the decency to dump you off at the emergency room entrance, even if they slipped away without leaving a name. Thank God you had my name in your cellphone as your emergency contact. I promised them I'd keep an eye on you, and race you back if there were any sudden changes." He smiled. "So you're stuck with me."

Tiffany took his hand in hers and squeezed. "You're such a good friend, Simone. I don't deserve you. I can't believe I was such an ass."

"As I said, they got you to the hospital in time." He shook his head. "But, Tiff. It was a close call. I can't believe you're so desperate to work with people like that. Is this really what you want? Prostituting yourself for those animals?"

"Oh, please. If you had any idea how embarrassed I was to wake up at the hospital." She felt the tears well up. "Don't start in on me, too. I can't take it."

Simone rubbed his hands over his eyes. "I'm sorry. That came out wrong. I didn't mean to make you feel worse. But I teach teenage girls. It's a sickness. Half of them want to dance on those stupid shows, and I can just picture those sleazy producers drugging them like they did with you, and getting their grubby hands all over them before the girls even know what hit them."

"And at least they'd have the excuse of being impressionable teenagers." She swiped at her tears. "Oh, damn. My dress and shoes. I left them at the party. I can't afford to lose them. I'll have to call Giancarlo."

Simone's hazel eyes flashed in anger. "No way in hell are you contacting him. You'll give me his number and I'll call the bastard. And give him a piece of my mind."

"No. It's my mess. You've done enough."

"Shhh ... don't worry yourself now. *Basta*. The incident will never to be spoken of again. Close your eyes. I'm going to cook you your favorite—*pasta e fagioli*."

"*Grazie*, Simone."

She heard pots and pans being taken from kitchen cabinets. She turned to look out the window. The full Roman moon lit up the sky. She loved to take walks around the city on nights like these, smiling at the streetlights shining off the Roman cobblestones, feeling a part of the crowds, and the chatter, and life in Rome. And last night she'd come close to leaving all of this behind. For what? Another one of her dreams?

Maybe Walt had been right. In the end, she was just a small-town girl, one who might leverage her looks as long as she was young, and stayed a big fish in the small pond of Iowa.

What on earth was she hoping for? There wasn't one special bone in her body. Even her own parents had told her as much. Why should all that change coming to Rome? She looked up at the moon—struck for a moment by its loveliness—before dissolving into muffled sobs.

CHAPTER 6

Annarita

Annarita stared out the train window. Sermoneta was visible in the distance, high up on the hills. The medieval castle dominated the entire town, its turrets stretching up to scratch the Robin's egg blue sky. She and Vincenzo had been there for a *sagra*—a local festival—only a few months ago. His band played, and she'd come along to see him.

He hadn't been thrilled by her surprise, she now recalled. Scores of young girls gathered around him after the concert, and he'd been in a bad mood that evening. She'd obviously been in his way.

Come to think of it, she'd probably been in the way of all of them ever since she'd fled Yonkers. Annarita's mother was right. She chased men away with unnerving talent. It was always the same. Vincenzo, Marco, Gianluca, Franco, Antonio … she'd cycled through them in record speed during her eight years in Rome.

She smiled when she thought about Rome in those heady first months. She'd felt like a kid in a candy store. Life in cosmopolitan Rome. Not her parents' Campania. No aunts and uncles and cousins watching her every move. The men were handsome, and thoughtful, and sexy. But they escaped as quickly as they appeared.

Her southern Italian roots always emerged in the initial phase of a relationship. She laughed at all their jokes, found their every utterance endlessly fascinating. She coddled them, cooked for them, ran their errands. They appreciated it for a while, but they always sprinted away from her, with gold-medal-winning speed, in the final stretch.

Even though she'd chosen to ignore them these last months, the signs were there. Vincenzo always made it clear he wanted his space. He rarely called her, almost never invited her to dinner. She was always the one insisting she had to try out a new recipe, begging to sew on his buttons, clean his oven. She was always so damned needy, so delusional, thinking every man was ready to tell her he could never go on living without her. The fact that no man ever said those words should have clued her in.

Unless you counted Rocco. Back then, *she'd* been the heartbreaker. Maybe this was payback for her sins.

The train pulled into Fondi. She gathered her bag from the overhead rack, walked to the parking lot, and boarded the local bus. She'd only been on this bus in the summertime, crowded with Romans smelling of suntan lotion, and full of enthusiasm for the day ahead filled with bronzing and flirting. Now the bus was almost empty, a few elderly locals returning from the weekly market or visits into Rome.

When they approached Sperlonga, Annarita pressed against the window. The old town loomed above, its white buildings poking haphazardly above the ancient walls. The turquoise water glistened in the distance.

She sighed. No one would be in the beach town now, but when she'd seen the offer for a week in November at the

Albergo Paradiso, she'd jumped at the chance. She couldn't afford a week of missed lessons, but she also couldn't continue on this way: working all day and crying all night. A week in Sperlonga—even offseason—would help.

At the final stop, she hoisted the bag on her shoulders. She walked past the cinema, boarded up for the season, and the bare houses that boasted colorful flowers in the summer, their shutters now firmly closed for their winter slumber. She passed the modern church before reaching the path to the walkway over the sea.

The afternoon sun bathed the water in a golden glow. The remains of Ancient Roman Emperor Tiberius' villa lay on the far edge of the beach. The beach, devoid of its colorful rows of summer umbrellas, formed a long, uninterrupted crescent of golden sand. Gentle waves rolled in as the seagulls squawked overhead. She breathed in deeply, feeling the salty sea air penetrate her lungs.

Sperlonga in November. The town deserted. Not a soul in sight.

Still, the solitude and the clean sea air would do her good. She'd be stronger when she returned. She took a last look before turning to the hotel.

The Albergo Paradiso, the only hotel in the center of Sperlonga, faced the Tyrrhenean Sea. Annarita had always wanted to stay here but could never afford the rates. But in November, when no sane person took a beach holiday, she could manage. Barely. She smiled and crossed the way. Entering the reception, she rang a bell.

A man with thick curly hair and wire-rimmed glasses emerged from an office behind the desk. "*Buongiorno, Signora.*"

"*Buongiorno. Sono Annarita Masiello. Ho una prenotazione.*"

He looked down at the register, tapping below a name. "Ah, yes. I see. You're here with us for a week. Welcome. I'm

Maurizio. May I show you to your room?" He picked up her bag and walked up the steps.

Unlocking the door, he crossed the room to open the shutters. Sunlight spilled onto the bright blue ceramic floor. One double bed, a desk, an armoire, a large mirror. He placed her bag down. Beyond the window, a small balcony beckoned, a slice of sea view visible from one corner. Yes, this would do nicely for the week. "It's perfect."

"Call reception if you need anything. Breakfast is served from seven thirty to ten. Dinner is in the restaurant from eight to ten."

"*Grazie.*"

When he left, she began unpacking, placing her few items in the armoire. Afterwards, she dug her cigarettes from her purse and stepped out on the balcony, sinking into the chair. The wind muffled the sound of the crashing of the waves in the tranquil bay, but the rhythmic pattern of the waves rolling into shore calmed her. She breathed in deeply. The Sperlonga holiday she'd dreamed of.

In November, when she could afford it.

Still, it beat moping around in her apartment, with images of Vincenzo and his blonde plaything flashing through her mind.

Canceling all her lessons had been a risk. Rent was due in a week and a half, and the utility bills were always a killer in winter. Thirty-four years old and scraping by from month to month, the same as when she was twenty-one.

There had to be another way.

She took a deep drag from her cigarette. So much for quitting. After racing out of Vincenzo's apartment, she found the nearest *tabbacheria*, blowing all her cash on the habit she'd managed to break.

She tapped her cigarette onto the ashtray, watching the tiny hill of ashes form. Her teaching friends were already putting their heads together, thinking about available men they could set her up with. They took turns calling to ask if she wanted to go out for drinks or to the movies.

Annarita knew she should feel grateful, but their tiptoeing around only made her feel pathetic. Debbie was planning her wedding for the summer, but as soon as she heard about Vincenzo, she'd clammed up. Annarita tried to get her friend to discuss reception plans and guest lists, only to have Debbie turn the conversation back to Annarita's heartbreak.

Around her friends, she felt like the delicate china figurines her mother collected back home, those horrible, gaudy creations brought back from holidays in Italy that her mother dusted and polished with such tender care, the same figurines that made the rest of the family nervous and jittery whenever they stood too close.

She stubbed out the last of her cigarette, returned to the room, and slipped on her coat. Below, she emerged into the late afternoon sunlight. The sea breeze whipped her wild curls.

She walked to the piazza, remembering how crowded and lively it was during the summer. Now a few deliverymen pushed squeaky carts across the square, and one lonely couple occupied a table at the outdoor seating of a café. The woman was young and fashionably trim, a perfect size zero. Annarita looked down at her own pants, marveling at the Herculean button, straining to remain closed. At the very least, depressed over Vincenzo, she'd temporarily lost her appetite. Experience showed it wouldn't last long.

The woman's long, auburn hair was pulled up in a tight ponytail. It swayed prettily in the breeze. She wore a clingy, French sailor-striped sweater far too thin for the season. Even from a distance, Annarita saw how the woman shivered.

The man across from her stood, took off his coat, and placed it gently around the woman's shoulders. He sat down and the sunlight caught copper highlights in his tousled, brown hair. He smiled and his whole face lit up. He laughed at something the auburn-haired woman said. Women like that always brought a smile to a handsome man's face. The couple looked so happy, so beautiful, so in love.

Annarita had wanted a coffee, but she felt like an intruder into the couple's intimacy. The last thing she needed was a head-on reminder that happy couples still existed out there.

Instead, she pushed the lovers from her mind and turned in the direction of the ramp leading down to the beach. She'd only ever walked down it in flip-flops. The path felt different in sturdy winter shoes, without grains of sand clinging to suntanned skin. A stray cat darted up on the wall, before pouncing down behind an Indian fig plant.

The town loomed above, its whitewashed homes arched against the bright blue sky. When she'd first moved to Rome, a daytrip to Sperlonga had helped ease her guilt about Rocco. Sitting on the sand, looking up at the medieval hilltop town above, and all the bronzed bodies around her chased away any lingering guilt she harbored in the deepest recesses of her mind. Her parents would come around. Eventually. Rome was where she was meant to be. Summers would be spent frolicking in the waves of Sperlonga. Life in Italy would consist of endless days straight out of some 1950s Technicolor film.

Too bad she missed the boat by a few decades.

At the edge of the path, she untied her shoes and slipped her socks inside. She shivered at the cold sand beneath her feet before walking toward the water. It was odd to have the beach all to herself. Maybe she was the only tourist in town.

She sank down to the cool sand, watching the waves roll in to shore. She squinted her eyes, trying to envision a warming, golden sun; the shrieks of Roman children on holidays with their families; bikini-clad high school girls chatting bravely with handsome boys; Annarita and her friends, lying on expensive lounge chairs, on the lookout for men without rings on their fingers. The ring of cellphones, the animated chatter of beachgoers. The sounds of summer.

In November.

She shook her head. There was a reason she was here all alone. Why she was always alone. She studied the sameness of the waves breaking on shore, wondering how she'd manage all the solitude.

Annarita suspected the upside of time alone at the beach in November would be the thrill of returning back to Rome in a week's time.

CHAPTER 7

Emma

"How did you manage to make such a mess of your life, Emma? Is this what your father and I worked so hard for?"

Marilyn Patterson presided over the kitchen, a cup of freshly brewed coffee before her. Long, tapered fingers picked through a box of Venchi chocolates, trying to determine which piece was worthy enough to break her iron-clad diet. Sunlight spilled through the window, setting off the expensive highlights in Mrs. Patterson's hair.

Emma's head began to throb. She could never decide who was worse—her mother-in-law or her mother. In the end, at least it was socially acceptable to loathe your mother-in-law.

Her mother picked up one delicate piece of chocolate, rolling it between her manicured fingers as she studied it, much as a diamond cutter examines a precious stone. "In the end, perhaps it's better he's not here to see this. You were always his little golden girl." She placed the chocolate down in its snug nest and picked up another. "What was the point? International Relations at Princeton, then Georgetown. All that trouble and expense, only to be a pampered housewife."

She looked out the window, examining a distant point beyond the green grass and garden palm trees. "And a divorced one at that." She tossed the second chocolate into the box. "It would have broken his heart."

Emma turned away, busying herself with the contents of the refrigerator. Her mother was pulling out the big guns to revert to the well-worn daddy's disappointment argument. And talk about the pot calling the kettle black. Marilyn Patterson managed to spend her husband's ample salary almost as quickly as he earned it. After her husband's death, free from any controls, she'd run through their life savings at an alarming rate. For the past years, Dario had been generous in bankrolling her mother's luxurious retirement home. Now all the extras were coming out of Emma's settlement. And she had to put up with her mother, too. The throbbing behind her eyes grew stronger.

"Of course," clipped tones wafted from the kitchen table, "I should have imagined things would finish this way by how quickly you lost interest in the piano."

From her safe position behind the refrigerator door, Emma balled her hands into fists. The piano. Again.

She stood and firmly closed the refrigerator door, meeting her mother's icy blue stare. She knew that spark in Marilyn's eye. Gearing up for battle. All she needed was a gin and tonic in her hand for the real fun to begin. Emma glanced at her watch. Not yet noon. Surely her mother wouldn't hold out much longer for her first drink of the day.

Her mother had only been in her home twenty-four hours, and already it seemed a lifetime.

Emma walked toward the table, stopping to pour herself a cup of coffee. She sat before her mother, resplendent in a striking cashmere dress, showcasing a figure she'd rigorously maintained ever since her debutante days. Emma knew she had to let it go. But her mother's visits always set her on edge.

Emma sipped her coffee and looked out at the parakeet that landed on a branch of the palm tree. Each year found more of them filling the Roman skies with their tropical chorus. She turned to Marilyn. "Mother, I wish you would stop bringing up the piano. You know I never enjoyed it. I felt like a trained monkey, called to play whenever your bridge club or your Annapolis Historical Society members came over." She looked down at her coffee. "I was merely the in-house entertainment."

Marilyn examined her ruby ring, the one she took pleasure in flaunting all over Rome. Emma had tired of warning her that one should avoid drawing attention to oneself with ostentatious jewelry in a city where robbery was commonplace.

"Alison Tate never had half of your talent," said Marilyn in her perfectly enunciated syllables, polished over years of presiding over charity boards and arts councils alongside those her mother liked to term 'people who count.' "But *there* was a young lady who knew the value of hard work. She's a concert pianist today. I've seen her play at the Kennedy Center." She lowered her voice to a dramatic whisper. "She brought tears to my eyes. I kept thinking it could have been you ..." She trailed off and dabbed at her eyes.

Emma struggled to keep the frustration from her voice. "And the knowledge that I had no passion for it means nothing to you?"

Marilyn shook her head. "And now you fill your days in a much more meaningful way. Face it, Emma, moving to Rome is the only thing that keeps your life from being one big cliché. Had you grown up in a housing project, this would obviously be a step up. But you were raised and educated for much more than this. It was hardly worth the expense and effort, when this is all you have to show for it."

A wave of nausea washed over her. "I know that raising children was never a priority for *you*, even if you had plenty of time in which to do it." Emma heard the dangerous touch of hurt creeping into her voice. With her mother, it was never wise to take the bait.

Marilyn clucked her tongue. "No, my dear. Raising you was not worth throwing away my Smith education, it's true. But I was a victim of my era." She fixed her sharp blue eyes on her daughter. "We had fewer choices than women of your generation. The difference between us is that *you* threw away your chances willingly."

Emma lowered her gaze, balling her hands into tight fists. Her relationship with her mother worked so much better with four-thousand miles of distance between them. She glanced at her watch. Surely it was time for the school bus to arrive. She stifled a groan when she saw it was far earlier than she'd imagined.

"To an outsider, it may appear the sacrifice was in vain. I saw Chiara's latest report card. Certainly nothing to brag about."

Emma snapped her head up, looking into that disapproving face she knew all too well. The one she tried to keep her children as far away from as possible. Distance had certainly been one of the major attractions of raising her children in Italy.

"The twins are sweet boys, of course. They're certainly full of energy, but they've never been much ... in the brains department. Now, for instance, the Barton boys." Marilyn rested a hand under her chin. The light from the window struck the ring, setting the gem aglow in a violent explosion of red. "I often see them visiting their grandmother. About the same age as Marco and Valerio."

Her flat American 'r's hung in the air, despite Emma's countless attempts to teach her mother how to pronounce her grandchildren's names correctly.

"Bright as buttons, those handsome devils. Why, only the other day, young Caleb was explaining to me ..."

Emma fought to control her voice. "It's lovely, Mother, that you take such delight in Matt Barton's boys, when your own grandsons do not appear to be up to your lofty standards."

Marilyn sighed and looked out into the garden. "I can't help thinking that I could have been grandmother to the Barton boys, had you only given Matt a chance. He was crazy about you, but *you* always thought you could do better."

Emma heard the bitterness in her mother's voice. "Matt was perfectly nice, Mother, but I was as fond of him as I was of the piano. You can't plan on spending the rest of your life with someone if you're not in love with him."

Marilyn brushed imaginary lint from her sleeve. "Yes, my dear. I see. Marrying for love appears to have worked out quite well for you."

Deep breath.

"Matt was top of his class at Annapolis. Decorated. He just won his second term as congressman, and there's talk of the Senate. Every time I see him with his lovely wife on the evening news, I think that might have been you." She gazed around the sunny kitchen. "Instead of seeing you here in some far-off place, divorced, and alone. With problem kids."

Emma shuddered involuntarily. Her mother's barbs always felt like well-aimed knives.

"Somewhere in the back of your mind you must share my doubts, or you wouldn't be ramming into cars in broad daylight in Rome."

The faint smile on her mother's lips was at odds with the challenge in her eyes. Emma's heart thundered in her chest. She hoped her mother couldn't hear it.

"Oh, my." Emma consulted her watch. "Look at the time! I always lose track of the hour during our lovely catch-up chats. I forgot about my appointment with Doctor Verde. I'll be back in time to get the kids. You can relax here, or go out shopping if you prefer." She rummaged through her purse for her wallet, pulling out six crisp fifty euro bills. "You wouldn't have had the time to exchange dollars yet. Perhaps this can tide you over."

A language her mother understood.

"I'll see you in a few hours, Mother."

As she cast a rapid glance to the kitchen while slipping on her coat, she saw her mother tucking the bills into her Louis Vuitton purse.

"I can't take it anymore." Emma dropped her head into her palms. "Only twenty-four hours in my house, and I'm ready to strangle her. She's no help at all. She only creates extra work. And misery. I need to get away."

Sabrina sat beside her on the couch, her thick black hair pulled back into a tight dancer's bun. Her long fingers sewed her daughter's ballet costume. Before having her daughters, Sabrina was an up-and-coming costume designer for the theatre. She always talked vaguely about going back to it one day, but she seemed to derive much more pleasure in designing costumes for her daughters' dance performances than she ever had working for high-strung actors and directors.

Sabrina lay down her needle, smoothing the frothy pink chiffon on her lap. She placed one hand on top of Emma's. "I know how hard this year's been on you. Franco and Dario aren't as close as they once were, but Franco still hears an earful about Dario's escapades. You're trying so hard to keep everything as normal as you can for the kids." She squeezed tighter. "And I know how trying that's been on you."

Emma felt the tension beginning to ease. Sabrina had been one of her first friends in Rome, way back when her Italian was still rudimentary. Over the years, they'd shared plenty of laughs and cries, but speaking to Sabrina always calmed her.

"Your mother was just the icing on the cake. I couldn't believe Dario called her."

Emma chuckled. "Yeah, he's more sadistic than even I would have imagined." She fingered the delicate folds of the ballet dress, marveling at the embroidery and the tiny rhinestones that sparkled on the fabric like fresh dewdrops. "What would I do without you, Sabrina? What can I do to maintain my sanity?"

"Does your mother still have that old school friend in Paris?"

"Ah, Marie. Yes, she was going on and on about her last night. How much she'd prefer to be in Paris than Rome. "

"Sounds typical. I'll call my cousin at her travel agency, and see about booking an inexpensive flight. And, while she's gone, I've got the perfect getaway for you."

"Getaway?" Emma shook her head. "For me? Why? And the kids?"

"Talk to Dario—see if he can manage a week. If he can't, they can stay here. Leonora would love to have Chiara, and Lina will have fun with the boys."

"I don't think it's a good time to get away. I need to be near the kids."

"And you will be. It's not far. Franco and I won a week in Sperlonga at the church charity auction. We actually wanted to go, but he's got a full surgery schedule these next weeks. Yeah, it's November, when Sperlonga will be pretty dead, but the sea air and walks will do you good. You're always behind on our reading club books—take them along."

"Sperlonga? Alone? Now?"

"I'll drive you down. If you need to get back, it's only a short train ride away." She smiled. "But you won't need to."

"But all that time alone, when I should be taking care of the kids, dealing with my mother."

Sabrina shook her head. "Your mother will be off being unpleasant in Paris—she'll blend right in. Your kids will be fine for a week with Dario, or with us." She set aside the taffeta and turned to Emma. "You need time for yourself, too. It's only a week. In nearby Sperlonga. I've seen the pressure getting to you." Her voice dropped to a gentle whisper. "Let's face it, with everything building up at once, the accident was bound to happen. And it could have been much worse. You need to get away. You need a rest. Only eight short days ..."

CHAPTER 8

Tiffany

Simone pointed to the white town in the distance. "There it is. Sperlonga."

"I can't believe I've never been here," said Tiffany. "It's so close to Rome."

"I guess you've been too eager to go off on sailboats in Sardinia, or to luxurious villas in Capri. You've snubbed beautiful places closer to home. Although, I should warn you, no jetsetters here in November. I think it'll be a week of quiet reflection. Just what the doctor ordered."

Tiffany chewed her lip. "I still feel guilty about this. You shouldn't be paying for a week's holiday for me. You should put it aside and go somewhere special yourself."

Simone smiled behind the wheel, setting off the familiar crinkles around his eyes. "And you're saying the upcoming week-long holiday with my students isn't enough for me? The London Science Museum? Seminars at the Oxford Museum of Natural History? You're just lucky we weren't closer to the date, or I would have suggested you tag along with the class, too."

Tiffany giggled. "Your dunce student. Better not to embarrass myself. I was always a disaster in science. If Mr. Miller hadn't had a soft spot for his pretty students, I would've failed high school biology."

"Mr. Miller was a man of taste."

"Stop changing the subject. I mean it. You didn't need to do this."

"But I wanted to. Anyway, it was a special offer. A week at the Albergo Paradiso, breakfast and dinner included. It didn't break the bank. And you need some quiet time to regroup." He sighed. "I know what it is to jump back into everything too early, before you're strong enough."

"Oh, Simone. Have you heard from Ramona?"

"Yeah, she's not coming back for Christmas, and doesn't think it makes sense for me to come out to Chicago. Thinks it would be too complicated." He spat out the final word.

Tiffany rubbed his shoulder. "I'm so sorry. I've been wrapped up in my own problems, and didn't even ask about you. I know you were hoping she'd change her mind. I know it isn't the same, but if you don't have Christmas plans, we can spend it together. I may not be much of a cook, but my mama did teach me to make a killer eggnog."

"A Christmas dinner of eggnog, eh? A guy'd be a real fool to turn that down."

"Alright, I know when I'm being made fun of." She looked out the window, at the blue expanse of the Tyrrhenian Sea. Even after her years in Italy, she still felt her stomach flip-flop each time she caught sight of the blue depths of the Mediterranean. Beat the Iowa cornfields any day.

Simone pulled into a parking garage. "Here we are. Madame, please step out. Allow me to take your baggage."

Simone slung her bag over his shoulder. It was far lighter than she usually travelled, but he'd sat on her bed to chat as she packed. Every time she'd tried to fold up elegant clothes, he'd stopped her. "No need, Tiff. Just pack comfortable jeans and layers. There's no one to impress at this time of year. This is about you taking time for yourself, getting away from life in Rome." He'd presented her with books, one of them a chick-lit book she'd mentioned she wanted, and two more novels in Italian. "It'll be quiet, you can work on it when you're there."

Everyone Tiffany knew in Rome agreed with her that her Italian was hopeless. Only Simone refused to give up on her, always clipping out articles from Italian magazines, or giving her Italian plays and novels that sat unread on her sparse bookshelf. She tried not to look at them; they always made her feel guilty.

Most everyone in her circle was willing to accept Tiffany at face value, but Simone always seemed to imply she was capable of more. Even her parents never expected much of her. Simone's attentions made her feel like an imposter, like someone trying to get above herself. She wondered if he'd ever realize there were no hidden depths, no diamond in the rough that only required a bit more polishing. With Tiffany, what you saw was what you got. *Punto e basta.*

She took him by the arm and they walked downhill together, past the closed-up movie theatre, past the shuttered summer houses.

"I'm sorry you can't stay at least one night. Sure you can't play hooky?"

"Afraid not. The students have an important exam tomorrow, and I need to be there. But I'll be back to get you in a week."

"Oh, that's silly. There's no need. You've done enough already. I'll take the train back. You can meet me at the station, if you'd like. Sounds kinda romantic and old-fashioned, doesn't it?"

"Yeah, it does," he agreed. "*Ecco il mare.*"

They emerged out onto a little promenade, with clear views down to the wide beach below.

Tiffany squeezed his arm tighter. "Oh, this must be beautiful in the summertime."

Simone nodded. "It is. Ramona and I ..." He shifted her bag on his shoulder, freeing her arm from his in the process. "I used to like coming here in the summer. The town is adorable, and the sea's much cleaner than near Rome. It'd be great to have a little place here, but the prices are as astronomical as in Rome." He turned her gently around. "And here, *Signorina*, is your hotel."

"Ah!" she exclaimed, clapping her hands together. "Right here, with a view over the sea. Perfect! Oh, you're such a doll." She jumped up and planted a kiss on his cheek. She observed him as she pulled back. "My, my. Is that a blush I see?"

"Not at all. You caught me by surprise. Shall we check you in? I'll still have time for a walk and a coffee with you before I need to drive back."

Tiffany felt the golden afternoon sunlight warming her shoulders. Her long hair was pulled into a tight ponytail. Its ends grazed against her too-thin nautical-striped sweater. Simone had laughed when she packed it. 'A tad optimistic? It's cooling down after our hot October. I don't think temperatures will be so balmy during your stay.' Not surprisingly, he'd been right. She shivered in the gentle but biting sea breeze.

"You're cold, aren't you?" Simone stood, taking off his coat and reaching across the table to drape it over her shoulders. "There, no point coming down with a cold on the first day of your vacation."

He sat down again and she smiled across at him. "Thank you, Simone. Always right, and always a gentleman."

He laughed. "I may have tried to talk you out of that sweater, but it does look awfully fetching on you."

"Really?" She heard the hopeful tone in her voice. "It's just, well. I think it makes my chest look awfully small." She met his eyes and felt heat spread across her cheeks. "Whoops, sorry about that. You're such a good friend, that sometimes I forget I'm not speaking to Lisa."

"Girl talk. I know something about that. I have two sisters. And a gaggle of high school girls in class. Mind you, intellectually they're light years away from the boys. But for all their intelligence, when they get together and think no one can hear them, they're worrying about non-existent cellulite, or too-small breasts on perfect bodies, or that they're not pretty enough, or tall enough, or sexy enough."

Tiffany sipped her caffè latte. "I guess I can relate."

"Maybe I should pretend to be Lisa, imagine all those things you'd tell me then … probably talking nonstop about your gorgeous, sexy neighbor." He winked. "But going back to your concern. It's ridiculous. You're perfect the way you are. It's all those stupid programs you all watch. Those women aren't real—I'm always telling my students. They're tucked and nipped and plumped in all the right places, but I still don't think that's what most men want."

Tiffany watched a woman walking down the path to the sea, her tangle of black curls waving wildly in the wind. "I'm not sure I agree with you. I know I should be fed up with those programs after what happened to me, should give up my dream of dancing on one of those shows." She looked up and met those hazel eyes. "But I'm not sure I can."

Simone groaned. "Really, Tiff? I thought it was a period of insanity you'd gotten over. You're too smart for crap like that."

"I'm really not." Her voice was just over a whisper. "I'm a simple girl. I grew up with nothing. But I always wanted to make it big. I was stupid—so ridiculously stupid. But not every producer is like Alessio."

Simone shook his head. "Actually, I think they all pretty much are. Sleazeballs to the last man. You could do so much more."

"You've always overestimated me, Simone. But when I was at that party, talking to Luana Lella, I couldn't help wanting what she had. Millions of fans, the spotlights on her when she comes onstage, audiences cheering. I can't pick up a magazine without reading about her latest hairstyle, or current flame, or her shopping expeditions, or what she thinks of the economic crisis."

He furrowed his brows. "They seriously ask Luana Lella her views on the economic crisis? You're definitely reading the wrong newspapers. No wonder your Italian isn't getting any better."

"Don't tease. I'm trying to tell you, I'm not sure I'm ready to give up on my dream yet. I hope that doesn't disappoint you."

"Will you at least think about it some more while you're here?"

She lay a hand over his. "I will. I really do think the quiet time will do me good. I'm so grateful."

He picked up her hand and kissed it. "Don't be grateful. Just be happy. And call me if you need anything, or if you just want to talk. I can even do girl talk. Promise."

Tiffany smiled. "You, too. If you're feeling down about Ramona, you know you can always call me. And that eggnog Christmas offer still stands."

"If you don't have some new boyfriend sweeping you off to tropical locales by then, you can join me for Christmas with my family in Perugia. My sisters will be there. I think you three would get along well. And Christmas in Umbria is always beautiful."

"*Grazie*, Simone."

"Shall we take a walk around town before I drive back?"

They stood and walked over to the wall, looking down at the deserted beach below. Almost deserted. One lone woman sat on the cold sand, her shoes beside her. She stared out into the ceaseless blue waves as the wind whipped her black curls around her head.

Simone slipped an arm around her waist. "The benefits of low season in Sperlonga. You and the woman down there might be the only two out sunbathing tomorrow. Maybe you'll become best friends, and your Italian will improve this week."

"Or maybe I'll get her to read the Italian books for me and give me a summary, so you'll think I've read them." She slipped from his grip and held on to his arm. "So, *Professore*. You were telling me how Emperor Tiberius used to come here to escape the Roman heat. You only have two thousand years of history to catch me up on as I walk you to your car."

They turned from the sea view and wandered into a narrow alley, the sounds of their footsteps ringing loudly in the silence of the whitewashed town.

CHAPTER 9

Annarita

The bathwater grew cold. The bubbles had long ago disappeared, but Annarita remained motionless in the tub. Her tiny Roman apartment didn't have a bathtub, and whenever she went someplace where she could slip into comforting warm water, she always made the most of it. If only she had candles and soothing music, her day would be complete.

Grudgingly, she pushed herself out of the bathtub, wrapping herself in plush cotton and wondered if the maid would notice if a towel disappeared into her luggage at the end of her stay. She towel-dried her thick curls. She'd long given up on straightening. Hairdresser appointments were becoming too frequent, and she'd taken a hard look at her monthly budget— what she could afford, and what she'd have to do without. As much as it pained her, curls it was.

She dropped her towel and gave a long, appraising look at herself in the mirror. When had her waist completely disappeared? Okay, she'd have to crunch the numbers another time. Perhaps she'd been too hasty dropping her gym membership. Images of that glistening, golden body in the shower with Vincenzo flashed through her mind again. *She'd certainly never give up gym membership if times were tough.*

But when would times ever be tough for women who looked like that?

Annarita dressed hastily, wondering if she shouldn't forgo dinner calories as a first step to losing weight. But then again, it was paid for. After her weeklong splurge, who knew if she'd even be able to afford groceries in the coming weeks?

Still an hour before dinner. She calculated the time back in Yonkers. Noon. Ma would be home.

She dialed the number on her cellphone.

"Hello, Ma," she said when her mother picked up.

"Annarita, I wasn't expecting to hear from you today."

"No, I'm away from Rome. I needed a break, so I'm down in Sperlonga this week. It's a little town on the coast."

"And your teaching?"

"It's just a week, Ma. I rescheduled. No big deal." Technically, those words weren't true, but Ma didn't have to know that.

"You never liked the idea of a steady job, steady pay, steady benefits."

Annarita heard the familiar thunks, and knew her mother was making a sign of the cross and praying to Saint Jude. Tonight she'd most likely be the beneficiary of additional prayers to the patron saint of lost causes as her mother muttered over the well-worn rosary beads.

"But I still don't think you should be running off on holidays in the middle of your work."

"Ma, not today, okay? I'm devastated. Vincenzo and I split up a few days ago."

Silence on the other end of the line. "Ah, sorry, honey. You sure haven't had much luck with men since Rocco."

Annarita stepped out onto the balcony. The sky was dark; only a few pinpoints of light brightened the sky. The black of the sea stretched out in the distance. "What do you mean by that?"

"Nothing."

Her mother sighed. Annarita heard the clinging of a stirring spoon against a pot. She was probably preparing a traditional Sunday lunch for the extended family. It wasn't the best time to talk, but she often felt the desire to call home at this time. Her family drove her crazy. As far as she was concerned, they should have been locked up in the lunatic asylum long ago, and the key thrown away. But she still found herself missing those Sunday lunches.

"Okay. You know I don't like to get involved when it's none of my business."

Annarita rolled her eyes, glad her mother didn't have Skype.

"You practically left Rocco at the altar, ya know? His parents were furious with us. We lost all that money on the reception. But you always knew better. Little Miss Honor Roll. You were always headstrong. Rome was the only thing you wanted. But now that you're there, it's one boyfriend after the next. Barely enough time for us to keep up with them before they're gone. Everyone here was taking bets on how long Vincenzo would last. Uncle Frank'll win the pot tonight."

"You're all over there taking bets on my love life? Talking about how I deserve it because I didn't go through with a marriage arranged when we were still in diapers?"

"You didn't have to end it the way you did. *Do unto others ...*"

"Yeah, Ma. I get it. Thanks for the sympathy." She took a deep breath. "Who's coming over?"

"Oh, it's only a small dinner. Auntie Teresa and Uncle Frank. Cousin Vincenza. Father Antonio. Cousin Nicola and Auntie Anita and her three boys. Oh, and Assunta, Tony and the kids."

"How are they doing?"

"I wish you could see them. Can't you come back for Christmas? They're always asking after their Auntie."

"Tell them I miss them, too. I got their school pictures. They've grown so much. Sorry, Ma, but I don't think Christmas will work this year. How's Assunta?"

"Well, I imagine she would've wanted to tell you herself. But they're going for the fifth. She's not feeling too well now—the first trimester always gets her. But you know what a doll Tony is. Always looking after her. I bring over some casseroles, but he's helping out so much."

She rubbed a hand over her eyes. "Wow, that's quite the surprise. Congratulate her from me. I'll email her when I'm back in Rome."

"I know I shouldn't complain."

Annarita caught her mother's long-suffering voice, the one she knew all too well.

"Come spring, God willing," The phone bounced along with the sound of the crossing. Thump-thump, thump-thump. "I'll have five healthy grandchildren. God bless your father, who never had the chance to meet them. But I wish you could have a family of your own one day, too."

Sucker-punched. Again.

Deep breaths. "Yeah, well. Not in the cards right now, Ma. Give everyone my love. A big kiss to Assunta and Tony. Gotta run to see some friends, but we'll talk again soon. Bye, Ma!"

The cellphone slipped to the balcony floor. In the nightly silence, Annarita strained to hear the crashing of the waves far below. A world away from Yonkers.

She attempted to pin up a loose strand of hair. Despite her best intentions to sweep her hair up in a presentable, elegant style, her unruly curls did their best to break free. A lost battle.

But did she really have to spend her holiday stressing about not being fashionable enough? After all, there had to be *some* advantages to frequenting seaside resorts during the dead season.

At the far end of the dining room, an elegant woman sat at a window side table dressed in casual clothes like those Annarita's well-heeled students wore. They didn't need labels. The cut and fabric screamed out wealth and privilege in a way that only fine Italian clothes could. Her golden hair was smoothed into an upswept style worthy of Grace Kelly. She sat reading a novel—an Italian novel.

Aside from the clothes, Annarita wouldn't have pegged the woman for Italian. But why on earth would an English or Swedish tourist be in Sperlonga in November?

She showed her room key to the hostess and was shown to a table at the opposite corner from the lone diner. She took her seat, sorry not to have brought reading material. The dining room was cozy, with vaulted ceilings, large windows that must boast spectacular sea views during the daylight hours, and walls decorated with artistic black and white photos of Sperlonga's old town. She recognized many of the stairs and alleys from her solitary wanderings that afternoon.

She studied the menu. The fried seafood looked tempting, but she'd have to stick with her diet this week. Mussels to start, and broiled sea bass. Ooh, but the dessert menu looked amazing. Maybe only a little ...

Her waitress arrived. Feeling proud of herself, Annarita stuck to her healthy order. She had a habit of sabotaging her virtuous intentions at the moment of ordering. But tonight, the image of the shapely blonde bimbo lodged in her brain kept her resolute.

As she ordered, lightning lit up the sky. A thunderbolt caused the waitress to jump back. Rain pounded down, lashing against the windows. The waitress shook her head. "*Sperlonga a novembre.*"

Annarita nodded sympathetically.

Oh, damn. What if it rained all week? Could her solitary walk on the beach this afternoon be the only one she managed during her time here? The waitress left and Annarita attempted sympathetic eye contact with the blonde woman at the far end of the room, but she was absorbed in her novel. Ice Princess remained unmoved by the storm.

Annarita watched the lightning set the sky on fire. After dinner, she could crawl into bed and watch the storm from her balcony door. When she was little, she and Assunta would cuddle together during storms, hugging each other as the thunder grew louder. Annarita always pretended to be brave, playing the courageous older sister—when she was anything but.

Hard to believe that her little sister was comforting her own children now: four of them. Soon five. If she'd have gone through with her marriage to Rocco, maybe she'd be a mother now, too. Her children playing with their cousins, all sitting together around Ma's big dining room table eating Sunday lunch. Rich Italian food, covered in way too much tomato sauce. Everyone talking over everyone else. Everyone driving one another nuts. Everyone delving into one another's business. Everyone knowing they belonged, and that they'd never be lonely.

Her mussels arrived and she looked at the waitress, momentarily confused, before smiling and thanking her. She hadn't noticed another diner taking a seat between her and the blonde woman. She recognized the slim figure, the sailor's sweater, the swingy auburn ponytail. The woman from today, probably waiting to be joined by her tall, handsome husband. One of those couples you hated because they were so damned perfect.

Then again, the woman wasn't wearing a ring. Ha! No wonder they looked so in love this afternoon. Annarita watched her order, then pull an Italian celebrity gossip magazine out of her purse, placing it on the table and studying it carefully.

Who read those rags? Articles chronicling every mundane thought and movement of celebrities like Luana Lella, or the rich-boy sailing and race car habits of TV producers like Alessio Armellini, who, in every interview, claimed that *War and Peace* was his favorite novel. He even made a point of insisting he dreamed of settling down with a simple Italian girl who loves keeping a perfect home and cooking traditional Sunday dinners. *So, Alessio, why aren't you knocking on my door?*

Well, perhaps it wasn't quite honest to pretend she *never* read those magazines. But only at the hairdresser, and now that her visits were so infrequent, she wasn't even up on all the latest gossip anymore.

The clock ticked noisily on the wall between the bursts of thunder and the pummeling of the rain against the glass. Her fellow diners read without interruption, barely looking up as they ate their food.

Annarita ate her mussels in silence, thinking about the noise and chaos around the table of the family home, and wishing she was at her regular seat, listening to the same, boring family stories for the umpteenth time.

Maurizio, whom she hadn't seen since he checked her in, was standing at attention at the receptionist desk. When she'd needed information earlier today, he'd been impossible to find. Now, at nine o'clock at night, when the town was dead, he sat diligently at the desk, busy scribbling on a pad of paper.

"*Buona notte, Maurizio*," she said as she passed on her way up to her room.

He looked up and smiled. "Ah, *Signora* Annarita. But surely you're not going to bed so soon?"

They both stood in silence as rain lashed violently against a window. "Well, it didn't seem the perfect weather for a solitary walk along the beach, so I thought I'd call it a night and get an early start tomorrow."

"Oh. No, no, *Signora*." His face fell. "You simply can't retire to your room now. When it rains, I set up the screen."

He indicated the lobby, where the couches had been moved into a semi-circle around a free-standing screen that reminded Annarita of the interminable family movie nights of her youth.

"*Mamma* makes the popcorn, and we watch films from the Golden era of cinema. Nothing like that dribble they churn out of your Hollywood today. I have selected very carefully. You live in Rome, no? This is the story of three American women who live in Rome in the 1950s. They are—shall we say—rather unlucky in love. I know that must not be a problem for you." He winked at her. "But you can still enjoy. I choose it specially because we have three female guests this week—all from Rome. What do you say? Won't it be fun?"

"A 1950s film about women suffering miserable love lives in Rome? You don't say. And all in Italian, no less. It sounds awfully tempting, Maurizio, but I'm exhausted. I'd have a hard time concentrating on the Italian tonight."

He clapped his hands together. "No need, *Signora* Annarita. It is in English, with Italian subtitles. So I'll take it as a yes. Sit, please. I tell mamma to heat up the stove for the popcorn."

Annarita shuffled into the lobby's lounge area, darkened for the coming attraction, and flopped onto the middle couch. Movie night with Maurizio and his mamma—and a fifties movie at that. Could you get more depressing? Then again, a walk around town in this rain was unthinkable. How dull would it be alone in her room, listening to the rain thundering down? The real cinema was shuttered up for the winter. Beggars couldn't be choosers. At least the film would get her closer to bedtime.

Maurizio returned and began fiddling with the movie reel. Not a DVD, but the old-fashioned kind. He spooled the film through the second reel.

"Maurizio, I didn't even know those still existed. You have a vintage projector."

He smiled proudly. "My uncle ran the old cinema in town. Nothing but the best. Now it's only playing during the summer season. I used to watch all the old films with him." He was struggling with the wheels. "But the old machine isn't what she used to be. I warn you now ... no bathroom breaks. We won't be able to start again."

"And the others?"

"Ah, they went up to their rooms. I said I set up and be ready when they return."

Yeah, right. They're not coming back. Just me, Maurizio, Mamma and lots of greased-back hair and poodle skirts ...

"*Eccolo!*" Maurizio exclaimed as the screen filled with light.

Dramatic music swelled throughout the room. Technicolor images of Lazio and Rome filled the screen. The fountains of the Villa d'Este in Tivoli, The Piazza Barberini fountain, Rome's turtle fountain, and Bernini's Fountain of the Four Rivers on Piazza Navona.

"What year was this filmed?"

"1954."

"Oh, wow. Must have been quite the calling card for Rome." She looked toward the staircase. "Can't you stop it and wait for the others?"

"Afraid not. It might not start again. *Signore ... sbrigatevi!*"

Three coins in the fountain, Each one seeking happiness ... Annarita began humming along to the dramatic music, before she caught herself. "Is this Sinatra?"

"*Ovviamente.* Don't you recognize the voice? You people didn't deserve him." He turned from the screen and smiled.

"I've never heard of *Three Coins in The Fountain*. Was it a famous film?"

Maurizio nodded, still staring at the screen. His silver hair glistened in the light. "At the time, yes. Rome was very glamorous in the 1950s and 1960s. I think you'll like it." He turned. "So you didn't move to Rome because of this film?"

Annarita smiled. "Afraid not."

She heard sounds on the staircase, and saw the two Italian women she'd seen at the restaurant approach the room. The blonde woman had changed into jeans, a taupe-colored cashmere sweater and fabulous Tods shoes Annarita had gazed at longingly through the shop windows only last week. The young woman remained in her nautical stripes and ponytail. They both smiled and said, "*Buona sera.*"

"*Buona sera*," said Annarita.

"Please, ladies. Take a seat. It begins."

The excitement in Maurizio's voice was almost touching. Annarita wanted to ask him how many times he'd seen the film, but she didn't want to seem like the intrusive American tourist to these Roman women. She simply smiled politely as they sat on the couches beside hers.

The song crescendoed on endlessly, accompanied by images of Rome bathed in golden light, and ending on a widescreen shot of the Termini train station, minus the swarms of passengers, tourists, and pickpockets present at the modern version. All three women burst out laughing as a convertible drove up and parked mere meters from the entryway.

"Oh, right," said the young woman with the auburn ponytail. "Parking right next to Termini, just like today." She shook her head. "Where's the chaos? Where are the car thieves? Was this filmed in Switzerland instead of Rome?"

Annarita shook her head. American.

"Rome in the '50s and '60s was supposed to have been a city virtually without cars," said the blonde from her perch on the sofa. "Wouldn't that be fabulous today?"

Surprised, Annarita slid to the edge of her seat. "You're both American?"

"Annapolis."

"Middle of nowhere, Iowa."

Annarita giggled, eliciting a loud *shh*-ing by Maurizio. She slid back into her position on the couch, watching the two women at the Trevi Fountain. Only one threw in a coin, the other begging off, saying she didn't want to jinx her plans for returning home to America to marry.

Annarita watched the city she'd lived in these past eight years with mounting amazement. The two women on the screen—Anita and Maria—maneuvered their car through an oddly empty Rome. Where were all the cars? Where were the crazy scooter drivers? Oh, to live in this 1950s Rome. It would never take hours to cross from one side of the city to the other for her English lessons.

Now Anita was bringing Maria to her new home on the Janiculum Hill. A villa they would share with one other American woman. Annarita slid to the edge of her chair as they entered into the grand salons, with their chandeliers and frescoes and garden views over the city of Rome spread out beneath them.

"*Secretaries do very well in Rome. You'll get spoiled here,*" said Anita on the screen.

"Oh. My. God," said the young woman from Iowa. "You're shitting me." Her eyes darted around the room. "I mean, you're kidding me. That's how secretaries lived in Rome back in the 1950s? Why wasn't I born back then?" She clutched a pillow and sank into the couch, her pretty face tugged into a comic pout.

"Shhh," said Maurizio, never turning from the screen. "They will explain why."

"You're paid at the agency in dollars, and the rate of exchange is in your favor," Anita explained to Maria.

All three women burst into laughter.

"Oh my goodness," said the blonde. "Can you imagine? What do you think a villa on the Janiculum Hill fetches these days? And with the dollar as worthless as Indian wampum." She shook her head.

"My apartment doesn't look *anything* like that," sighed Annarita. "It probably doesn't look even a thousandth as nice as the broom closet in that *palazzo*."

"Join the club," said the auburn-haired woman.

The blonde stayed quiet.

Probably dripping in euro, living in a place similar to the villa in this film. So what's she doing in the Albergo Paradiso in November?

Annarita observed her from the corner of her eye. She really did look like Grace Kelly. Those ice-cold blondes Annarita always despised. She was what the Italians called *bentenuta*. What was she? Late forties? Maybe even fifty? Annarita would never look that good at that age—living from hand to mouth had a tendency to make aging gracefully difficult. But, if she were honest, she didn't look that good now. And the young one, with her emaciated model's figure and Ivory complexion, was even worse. She was the type the Italian guys were wild over—the all-American girls. Annarita was always just a placeholder. The woman to be dumped when someone better, someone like these women, came along.

An old woman shuffled out from a swinging door. She wore a black dress and an apron. Her shoulders were rounded, but she carried a tray laden with bowls and glasses. Her white hair was piled on top of her head, but Annarita stifled a smile when she saw frizzy wisps falling down. This was a woman who knew the frustration of battling humidity uselessly, only to watch her hair corkscrew up out of control.

Maurizio jumped from his seat, "*Mamma*, why didn't you call for me to come? You will hurt yourself." He turned back to the women. "She thinks she is still a young girl of eighteen."

They all smiled as he rushed to his mother's rescue. The dutiful Italian son. He placed the tray on the table before them, scattering the bowls of steaming popcorn so they all could reach them easily. "But we will not drink your American champagne—that hateful Coca-Cola. It is better to toast to Rome and new friendships with *spumante*." He expertly popped the cork and poured the sparkling bubbles into each flute. He passed the glasses around. "*Salute.*"

"*Salute*," they all replied.

Annarita reached for the popcorn. The familiar salt and butter melted in her mouth, reminding her of movie nights long past with her big, crazy Italian family. She looked around her at the glow of faces gathered around the screen. She didn't even know the names of the women, but somehow it still felt like a family. Four thousand miles away, her real family was still gathered around the table, stomachs full with her mother's rich cooking, heads spinning after glasses of Uncle Vincenzo's homemade *grappa*. They were probably arguing. They always did. The same old arguments, embellished after countless years of repetitions. The same gripes she'd heard over three decades.

And still, she missed them all.

She sighed and popped another handful of popcorn in her mouth. So much for behaving at dinner. Here she was, ruining it all.

On the screen, Anita and Maria stood on a balcony feeding the pigeons below. Anita told the newcomer, "*If you're romantic,*

Rome's not the city for you. The wealthy Italians aren't interested in secretaries, and the Italians at the agency are too poor."

Annarita rolled her eyes. So living in Rome was a romantic pitfall even back in the fifties. A moment later, she straightened up as a man appeared on screen. The familiar French accent striving to be Italian. "But that's Gascon!" she yelled. "From *Gigi."*

The blonde smiled at her. "I loved that film. It all seemed so glamorous. I wanted to find my own Gascon in Paris." She smiled at Annarita. "I strayed a bit too far south."

"Shh," said Maurizio. "That's Prince Dino. Maria will use her feminine charms to snare him into marriage."

"So we haven't progressed that much in the past six decades," the blonde said, winking at Annarita. She raised her *spumante* glass in a toast.

Annarita lifted her own, then sank back into the comfortable couch. The film was silly and predictable—the three couples not realizing what every viewer did, that they would wind up in one another's arms by film's end. Maria and Prince Dino, Anita and the young, penniless Italian law student, Frances and her employer. Yes, it was silly and predictable, but Annarita couldn't tear her eyes from the screen. She watched the three women falling in love in a Rome bathed in golden light.

The blonde was right. Six decades made no difference at all. She was exactly the same when she fell in love with a new man—pinning all her hopes on him, dreaming about the perfect wedding. Give her the fifties' clothes and she could be a character in the film. Living in that villa, to boot.

Annarita took another sip of her *spumante*, allowing the bubbles to float to her head, as she watched the misadventures of three young women taking on Rome, with an enthusiasm she herself possessed not so long ago.

CHAPTER 10

The three couples clung longingly to one another, as the cloying music swelled. Frank Sinatra was amazing, but really, this song was sheer schlock.

And yet. As ridiculous as the film was, it still moved her. Those couples all clinging to one another before an uncharacteristically deserted Trevi Fountain. She and Dario had strolled there often when they were first dating. She'd thrown her fair share of coins into those shallow waters, hoping to stay in Rome.

And it had worked. The husband was gone, but she was still in Rome. Most of the time, she was even happy.

She looked across at the young girl, with her auburn ponytail. Pretty. Wholesome. She was wiping away the tears, and Emma stifled a giggle. The girl really was straight from the cornfields of Iowa if *Three Coins in the Fountain* could move her so deeply.

Maurizio jumped up and hit the lights. His eyes were damp, too. She was trapped in some parallel universe—the ones they always showed on *The Twilight Zone*. The brunette with the corkscrew curls was dry-eyed, although she looked at the screen with longing. Doubtless, still dreaming of the perfect man.

When Dario walked out their door, Emma knew it was time to give up the fairytale. Fool that she was, she'd never even seen it coming. The expensive red sports car didn't tip her off. Nor did the tennis club membership, or the fictitious conference in the Seychelles. So wrapped up in the hectic rhythms of family life, she'd deluded herself that they were happy. Possessors of a contented coin in the fountain. She'd never fall for that crap again.

Maurizio turned to them. "Ladies, did you enjoy it?"

"Wonderful."

"Beautiful."

"So romantic. Thanks for setting it up."

Maurizio smiled. "It was my pleasure. And on a night like tonight." He turned to the window. "Let us hope that tomorrow is more agreeable weather. I wish you a good night, ladies."

"*Buona notte.*" The women filed up the stairs.

They all stopped at the landing, pulling out their keys, and approached their separate entries. Emma longed for her soft bed. She plastered a smile on her face and turned to the brunette and the redhead to wish them a good night, but something stopped her.

"Would you care for a nightcap?" *Really, a nightcap? Who used that term nowadays?* "I have wine chilling in the fridge. If you're not too tired, you're welcome to join me."

Two sets of eyes examined her. The women subtly retracted their keys.

"Are you sure?"

"It wouldn't be too much bother?"

"Maybe just for a minute ..."

Emma opened her door and flicked on the lights, wondering what had gotten into her. This week was supposed to be about solitude and regrouping, getting stronger for the return. Ensuring her family didn't see her fall apart again. Why did she need to invite hotel guests to her room? One must be close to her daughter's age. How needy was that?

The other women hung back at the entrance, examining the room.

The woman with the corkscrew hair pulled her cardigan tight around her ample curves, and whistled. "Wow. The Albergo Paradiso has a presidential suite?"

Emma shrugged. "Ah, I didn't realize. Aren't all the rooms like this?"

The redhead shook her tresses, the ponytail swishing back and forth. "As if. Mine's nothing like this." She indicated the glass doors. "And that terrace looks like it's bigger than my apartment in Rome."

"*Mamma mia!*" exclaimed the brunette. "The view must be gorgeous from there—I just catch a tiny glimpse of the sea, if I hang off the balcony at the right angle."

"We can sit out there, if it's not too cold for you. There's a heater, and the seats with cushions are protected under a roof. They should be dry." She walked to the mini-bar fridge, opening the door. "Let me get a bottle, and you can help carry out the glasses."

"Jesus!" exclaimed the brunette. "Someone is well-stocked. Are you expecting the sailors to dock sometime soon?"

Emma looked confused, then saw all the bottles Sabrina had neatly piled inside the fridge when she'd dropped her off at the Albergo Paradiso earlier that day. She laughed. "Ah, the friend who brought me here is a bit of a wine snob. She was terrified the hotel wine list wouldn't be up to her exacting standards." She extracted a bottle. "It's not like I was going to follow her suggestion and BYOB to the restaurant. I was afraid I'd have to haul it all back. If you ladies like good wine, you'd be helping me out."

The brunette examined the label. "French. Chablis. Expensive. I usually can't afford the good stuff. So yeah, I'll do my part." She smiled. "Can I carry it out for you?"

"Thanks. That would be great. I'm sorry, I don't even know your name. I'm Emma."

"Annarita."

"Tiffany."

"So nice to meet you. Please, go out and make yourself comfortable."

Emma picked up three glasses and the bottle opener, and followed the women out to the terrace.

Tiffany studied the heat lamp, looking up when Emma came out. "Did you say this thing works? It's chilly out here."

Emma placed the glasses down on the table and located the switch. "Maurizio showed me how it worked earlier. I'm sure it'll warm up in a minute. It cooled down a lot after the rain." She sank down into one of the lounge chairs and opened the bottle with an expert hand. She poured three glasses, handing them to the women. "What shall we toast to?"

"To Sperlonga, and new friends," said Annarita.

"To three coins in the fountain," said Tiffany, raising her glass.

"To three coins in the fountain," chimed Emma and Annarita, clinking glasses.

"Ah-ha," said Annarita. "I was right. This *is* the good stuff."

Emma smiled. "Nothing but the best for my friend Sabrina."

"Looks like you're doing okay yourself." Tiffany turned back to the suite. "I still can't get over this suite."

"Afraid that's my friend Sabrina's doing, too. She and her husband won the week in a charity raffle, but they couldn't get away. She didn't want it to go to waste." She sipped her wine, willed her voice steady. "And she thought I might need a little time away."

Tiffany observed her closely. "What would we do without our friends? My neighbor, Simone, thought I'd been having a rough time recently, and needed a getaway, too. He booked me here as a present through some off-season sale." She sipped her wine. "He wouldn't even let me pay him back."

"Oh, so that gorgeous guy I saw you with earlier isn't your boyfriend?" asked Annarita, sliding to the edge of her seat.

Tiffany shook her head. "No, just a neighbor, and a good friend."

"Is he single? If I were you, I'd snap him up before someone else does," Annarita winked. "You two chose your friends well. I discovered my lying, cheating boyfriend *in flagrante* with another woman. I needed a getaway and I came here on that low-season sale, too. But I emptied my savings account to do it." She held up her glass. "I suppose at least I can go broke in style."

"Ouch," Emma grimaced. "I'm sorry, Annarita. So we're all here in November, hopelessly out of season, hoping for a reprieve from our daily lives. I can toast to that."

Tiffany fingered the edge of a wicker basket, lifting it up when she discovered a latch. "Ah, blankets. Anyone want one?"

"Here."

"Over here, too."

Tiffany wrapped one around her shoulders. "This reminds me of attempts at campfires at our house. Always a disaster. The wine and the sound of crashing waves are much better." Her voice grew quiet. "Everything's better here in Italy. Hey, do you think Maria's plans to catch a prince would work in modern-day Rome, too? Hell, I'd learn to play the piccolo, too, if it would nab me some handsome, wealthy prince like that."

"I loved that actor—Louis Jourdan," said Emma, with an exaggerated sigh. "I was *so* in love with him as a girl."

"But shouldn't everything have changed since the fifties?" asked Annarita. "Shouldn't *we* have changed? Watching that film, it cut too close to the bone. I feel I'm still chasing men around, just like Maria does with Prince Dino. Although I would've taken the good-looking, penniless law student in a heartbeat. Giorgio, right?" She stretched her feet out on the lounge chair, covering them with the blanket. "Hey, did you see Via Petroselli without traffic? Imagine driving a truck without brakes there today."

Emma laughed. "That's close to my house. I definitely can't imagine a scene like that today."

"Yeah," said Annarita. "But the whole city looked like that back then. I spend my life shuttling from apartment to apartment in Rome, and it takes forever to get from point A to point B. It drives me crazy half the time, all the time I waste just reaching my lessons. Not paid for my troubles, obviously. Apparently, I should've been here six decades ago, when Rome was a little village, and I'd be living in a luxurious villa on an English teacher's salary."

Tiffany sighed. "Guess we all missed the boat on that one."

Well, ladies. Today you could marry a cheating, lying scoundrel, and in the divorce settlement you could get the beautiful villa. How's that for a modern-day fairytale?

Emma smiled at the women and poured more wine into their glasses.

"Maria, Anita, and Frances probably could have pooled their salaries and bought some ramshackle seaside villa here in Sperlonga," said Tiffany, looking out into the distance.

"At least we have the Albergo Paradiso," said Annarita. "Even if I'm not as lucky in love as my 1950s sisters."

"Who needs men anyway?" asked Emma, looking out into the blackness of the sea. "My husband and I parted ways almost two years ago." She looked down into her wineglass.

"Mutual decision. It was right for us both. At least we're not stuck in the '50s, where we'd be trapped in some unhappy marriage." Emma didn't dare meet the women's eyes.

Annarita shifted in her seat. "Well, yeah. I guess that's what we're supposed to think." She placed her glass down on the table. "But here's the thing. *Are* we better off? I feel like we struggle so much, just to keep up, to prove ourselves, to carve out our little niche in the world. And then I feel trampled by all the men I meet. At least my mother had some certainty in life. She's all nervous for me. Am I going to get married? Am I going to have children? I don't know what to tell her. I know we're supposed to laugh at those '50s women." She looked down at her hands. "But sometimes it seems simpler."

Silence hung in the cool night air.

"I don't know. I've kissed my share of frogs, Lord knows there are plenty of them. But it's not just the guys." Tiffany turned to Annarita. "You saw me with my friend, Simone, earlier. He's a great guy. Funny, good-looking, a high school biology teacher. Really laid back. His girlfriend is a management consultant, totally driven. But they were so happy together, you know? I was always at their place for dinners, or holidays. They were finishing one another's sentences, talking about who their future kids would take after." She wrapped herself tighter in the blanket. "Then, one day, she gets an offer from the Chicago office, and she's packing her bags that same afternoon. No explanation. Simone goes around shell-shocked half the time. No idea what the hell hit him, and when everything went wrong. There weren't any signs."

Annarita shook her head, her corkscrew curls bouncing with the effort. "That gorgeous guy? *He* was dumped? Maybe I have been too hard on men in general. Why don't guys like your Simone ever find their way to me?"

"Poor man," said Emma. "And Annarita, you'll find someone else. It takes time."

"It's easy for you to say," said Annarita. "You're among the 0.01% who is happy and secure that separating from her husband was all for the best. I don't know anyone else like you. My divorced friends are all basket cases. Hell, *I'm* a basket case every time I get dumped. Maybe one day I'll develop your wisdom."

Emma slipped her hands under her blanket, hiding the tremors. "I don't consider myself particularly wise. Just wizened, perhaps." She attempted a smile, and saw the women glancing at their watches.

"Way after midnight," said Tiffany. "I may turn into a pumpkin. I'm afraid it's been a long day."

"Me, too," said Annarita. "The trip down, the sea air, and now this amazing wine have knocked me out. I'd better get to bed before I conk out on your terrace."

The women picked up the wineglasses and brought them inside.

"Emma," said Annarita. "Thanks for the invitation. And please thank your friend. The wine was fabulous."

Emma gestured to the fridge. "You've seen my supplies. Be sure to come back and help me finish it."

"Oh, sure," said Tiffany. "I love your place. I'd love to come back and drool at the view in daylight." She leaned in to kiss Emma's cheeks. "Thanks for the invite. I'm so glad we'll be here together this week. See you at breakfast?"

"Of course."

"Yes, let's go for a walk on the beach, if the weather holds."

"*Buona notte!*"

Emma bolted the door behind the women, then retraced her steps to the terrace. She slumped down into the lounge chair, covering herself with a thick blanket.

After the storms, the night had cleared. She looked up at the bright pinpoints of light in the night sky, speaking to the stars. "Mutual decision to separate. See how wise I am?" She breathed in deeply. "Maybe one day I can even fool myself into believing it."

Closing her eyes, she concentrated on the sound of the waves rolling in far below her terrace. She tried not to think about Dario and his young lover, probably back in the Sardinian villa, their naked limbs wrapped around one another, as they listened to the crash of the waves of the same sea.

CHAPTER 11

Tiffany

Tiffany glanced at the clock as she made her way downstairs for breakfast. Twenty to ten. She hoped the Albergo Paradiso wasn't too strict about breakfast rules, because she was in desperate need of a coffee.

She hadn't meant to sleep so late, but the wine last night, and sleeping with the distant sound of the waves, lulled her into a pleasant, uninterrupted slumber. She'd been surprised to see the clock hands when she woke. Emma and Annarita had probably gotten an early start, already out combing the beach. At least the sun shone warmly today, the sky unmarred by a single cloud.

"*Buongiorno*, Maurizio!" she greeted when she saw him sweeping the front stoop.

He turned and smiled. "*Buongiorno, Signora Tiffany. È una bella giornata oggi.*"

Yes, it most certainly was a beautiful day. She'd have some breakfast, and afterwards head out to the newsstand and buy the new *Chi* that was out today. The starlet Jessica Jesoli recently married a soccer player from Juventus, and *Chi* had the exclusive photos. Tiffany couldn't wait to see the dresses, the shoes, and the hairstyles. Luana Lella was one of the witnesses! What had she worn to the ceremony? Oh, but what if Alessio had been there? She'd hate to see a photo of him. Still, she'd have to get used to it. It was hard to avoid photos of Alessio in Italian magazines. It would probably hurt less as time passed. She hadn't even told Lisa what happened that night. Simone was the only one to know, and she knew he could be trusted not to say anything.

Turning into the restaurant with images of a radiant Jessica Jesoli in her bridal gown playing through her mind, she startled to see Emma and Annarita sitting before one of the large windows, looking out over the sea. So she wasn't as late as she'd imagined.

"Good morning, ladies. I thought I was the naughty one sleeping in this morning. I see great minds think alike."

Emma laughed. "I can't even remember the last time I slept past eight. Heaven ..." She indicated a chair. "Pull that up and come join us." She signaled the waitress.

It was such a small gesture, but Tiffany noticed how the waitress ran over. Women like Emma had that effect on people. Tiffany was often around people like that, women who possessed that sense of wealth and privilege that made them so confident. Even if she was light years away from the simple girl she'd been back in Buffalo Plains and Des Moines, she still felt awkward. An imposter next to women like Emma.

Tiffany smiled as she carried over the chair, looking shyly at the waitress. "*Un cappuccino, per favore.*" She always hated asking waiters for anything. It was absurd, especially since she'd spent her high school and college years waitressing, and knew exactly what the job entailed. She'd never felt degraded serving meals to customers, yet she was always loathe to ask serving staff for anything.

Annarita pointed to a table across the room. "You get your food over there. The Nutella croissants are fabulous. Maurizio's mother makes them herself. This cake, too. Wow, I'm blowing my diet this morning."

Yes, you certainly are. Tiffany cast a judgmental glance at Annarita's plate, laden with cookies and cakes. How many gazillion calories were perched on that one delicate piece of porcelain? She fought the urge to wrinkle her nose. "I'll go take a look." She avoided the sweets, placing toast, jam, and fruit on her plate.

"That's all you're having?" Annarita asked, incredulous, when Tiffany placed her plate on the table. "You know that Maurizio's mother is a fantastic cook. You really want to miss out?"

"I've been dancing since I was three. I guess I've always been careful with my diet. Anyway, I've never had much of a sweet tooth."

"Lucky you," said Annarita, plunging her fork into the cake. "That explains why there's nothing to you. You're all skin and bones."

Tiffany carefully smoothed her napkin before placing it on her lap. She breathed in deeply and willed the anger from her voice. "I'm certainly not all skin and bones." *Unlike you, I'm able to practice a little self-discipline.*

Annarita tilted her head to observe Tiffany. "It wasn't meant as an insult. Most of the guys who've dumped me prefer anorexic girls like you." She pushed her plate away.

Tiffany's cappuccino arrived. She accepted it gratefully, sipping the frothy foam and looking out the window at the waves below. Willing them to calm her. How could she avoid these people in such close proximity all week? She'd bolt as soon as she finished breakfast and buy her gossip magazine. *Some time alone to enjoy photos and reports from Jessica's wedding sounds better than facing bitter jabs because I'm not devouring every calorie-bomb within easy reach as a balm to my romantic disappointments.*

Silence hung heavily over the table as all three women sipped their coffee and looked out at the beach below.

Annarita dug through her purse and extracted a pack of Marlboro Lights. She tapped it on the table. "Aw, damn. Sorry 'bout that, Tiff. I'm flying off the handle too easily these days after the spectacular breakup with my boyfriend last week. I walked in on him and some gorgeous young thing with a perfect body."

She clutched the pack tighter. Tiffany thought she might crush it.

"So now I'm an emotional wreck. I came here to escape and get my messed-up head in order." She looked up and met Tiffany's gaze. "Sorry, guess this week might be tougher than I thought. I'm not really over him yet." She turned back to the window, her eyes glistening.

Tiffany placed her hands on her lap. "It must be tough for you. Don't worry about me." An image sprang to mind: opening the door to see her best friend spread naked on the desk in her Des Moines office, with *him* thrusting above her. "I understand. It's fine."

"Well, it's not. And I'm sorry." She clasped the cigarettes in her fist and stood, indicating the door. "Think I'll head out for a second and calm down with one of these coffin nails." She grinned. "Catch you ladies later, out on the beach?" She was gone before they could respond.

Tiffany looked through the plate glass. "Guess it takes a while to get over it when you discover your man's been cheating on you."

Emma looked distractedly at her cellphone. "I suppose it does." Her voice was cool.

What's the point? Someone like Emma would never understand. Pulled together and polished. Separated from a man after a mutual, grown-up decision that the relationship's expire-by date had passed. Tiffany took a deep breath. "Weather's taken a turn for the better, hasn't it?"

Emma nodded. "Yes, lovely today. I hope you won't consider me rude, but I have a call to make." She placed her napkin on the table. "Maybe I'll see you later, out on the beach?"

"Yeah, of course. See you later," said Tiffany, her voice full of false cheer.

Down below, the waves rolled onto the golden sand as Tiffany sipped her coffee and contemplated her lonely plans for the day.

Tiffany sat on her newly purchased towel, with its rainbow-colored threads announcing *Sperlonga* to the seagulls flying overhead. No one else was on the beach to see it. Tiffany had imagined the solitude would bore her. Instead, she found it freeing.

When she'd first walked down the ramp, she took off her shoes and executed a dozen cartwheels across the golden sand of the empty beach. Yes, someone may have observed her up in the town, but even there, there were only a few elderly residents. How nice not to have to care about what others thought, and how one should behave. As much as she despised her Iowa upbringing, the sense of freedom had been an advantage.

Back when she and Billy were kids, back when they still got along, they'd spend hours running around in the cornfields. Cowboys and Indians, policeman and robbers, earthlings and aliens. The sky was the limit. They ran endlessly, the earth stretching out to the faraway horizon, hazy sunlight beaming down on them. Out there, amongst the golden husks of corn, they were light years away from daddy's violent, drunken stupors and mama's constant tirades.

Exhausted from their sprinting, they'd slump down, stretching out and looking up at the expanse of bright blue sky.

"One day, I'm gonna go far away from here," said Billy. "I'm gonna be an explorer."

Tiffany observed her big brother with awe. "You're gonna leave Mama and Daddy and all our friends?" People did that in movies, of course, but how did people gather the courage to do so in real life? If anyone had the guts to go far away, it was Billy.

"Aw, you're just little, Tiff. But you'll discover this ain't much of a life. Mama and Dad fightin' all the time, just scraping by. I wanna be rich. See the world. Have a big, shiny car, and all the girls in love with me."

Tiffany's eyes grew wide; her big brother's words sounded so courageous. "And when you do, will you send for me?"

"Sure will, Tiff. I'll send you a plane ticket to come live with me in Italy. Jack was there in the Navy. He says it's always beautiful, never rains. I'll hang out all day in the sunshine, eating spaghetti and meeting pretty girls."

"Where's Italy, Billy?"

"Far away from here. You gotta cross all the cornfields and get all the way to New York. Afterwards, you fly over the ocean to reach Italy. Italy's surrounded by water—nothing like here."

"Oh," Tiffany frowned. "It sounds awfully far away. I don't wanna leave Mama. Or Heather. Who'll be her best friend if I leave?"

"C'mon, Tiff. You're such a baby. A place like this sucks the life out of you. Ever see the old photos of Dad, for Christ's sake? Star of the goddamn high school football team, strongest boy in town. Look at him now."

Tiffany lay still, watching a fluffy white cloud pass overhead. Billy was right. Daddy kept his old high school football photo framed in the living room. At night, he slouched next to it, drinking a six-pack of Schlitz, a can permanently perched on his gut. He didn't even look like the same person. The few times he'd gone out with Tiffany, she saw older people shake their heads as he passed, whisper to one another when they thought she couldn't hear. "What a shame about Jimmy Walker. Who'd a thought he'd let himself go so early? Just goes to show you ..."

Maybe you did have to leave. Make something of yourself. Maybe this Italy place would ensure she didn't grow as bitter as Mama, didn't try to squeeze into her old high school jeans every Sunday after stepping on the scale, then spend the rest of the afternoon locked in her room, crying for hours about what a mess she'd made of her life.

Maybe it was Iowa that made people unhappy. Maybe Heather could join Tiffany in Italy. She turned to look at her brother. He was twelve, and he knew everything. Seven-year-old Tiffany believed his every word. He'd never lied to her yet.

When Daddy took the belt to her, it was Billy who comforted her, told her stories to forget the pain. When Mama took too many sleeping pills and forgot to go to her Christmas concert, it was Billy who'd cheer from the front row, and tell Ms. Cox their mama had come down with the flu and couldn't make it.

Billy was her bedrock. Until he wasn't. But she still loved to remember those endless summer days out in the cornfields with Billy.

Those days were as close to an idyllic childhood as Tiffany could get.

It was late in the day. The newspaper seller hadn't had the magazines she'd wanted. He told her to stop by later, so Tiffany wandered around the town, and later returned to the hotel for a nap.

She'd been sleeping poorly ever since returning from the hospital. She'd awaken to the feeling of Alessio's hands sliding over her body. When her eyes snapped open, she'd be alone in her bed, her heart galloping as fast as a thoroughbred.

The hospital had provided her with sleeping pills, but Simone cast his scientist's eye on the active ingredients and immediately removed them from her medicine cabinet. "These are way too strong. We don't want to replace one problem with an entirely new one."

But at night, as she lay sleepless in her bed, watching the lights of passing cars illuminate her ceiling, she longed for those little white pills that would usher her into sweet oblivion. That's probably how her mother felt with her own pills, or how her father felt when he reached for his Jack Daniel's.

Now she sat listening to the sound of the seagulls shrieking above. The sunlight filtered lazily between the curtains, not as bright as earlier. When she turned to the alarm clock, she startled to see it was already three. She'd slept three hours, in the middle of the afternoon. Springing from her bed, she finger-combed her tousled hair.

She wrapped herself in her warm sweater and plucked the Buzzati from Simone off the bedside table. Racing down the stairs before anyone could spot her, she slipped out of the hotel and made her way to the trail leading down to the beach.

The sea breeze ruffled the magazine pages. Tiffany battled the gusts to keep the pages flat on the sand. Jessica Jesoli was a goddess in her wedding dress. Although, well, even if Tiffany *hated* to admit it, maybe there was a bit too much *décolleté* for a wedding gown.

Then again, Jessica was rumored to have recently gone under the knife with Doctor Rinaldi especially for the occasion. Jessica denied it vehemently, of course, but one couldn't help but notice how much her silhouette had altered.

A slit in her tight skirt climbed up to the upper reaches of her slim, toned thighs. Oh! And those shoes! Strappy and delicate, but with heels to die for. Jessica towered over her Juventus striker, whose greasy, stringy hair was pulled back in a ponytail for the occasion. Jessica's golden curls cascaded down her back. If Tiffany were being unkind, the lips may have been plumped a tad too much. But still, she looked like a princess.

And there was Luana Lella behind her at the ceremony, wearing a racy Dolce & Gabbana number, her bronzed cleavage competing with the bride's own. There were photos of her clinging to a muscular, young midfielder for Roma. He looked barely out of his teens.

She leaned closer to study Luana's expression as the midfielder whispered something in her ear. To the left of the stocky athlete, she caught sight of a familiar profile at the edge of the photo. Alessio. Alessio Armellini, deep in conversation with a statuesque woman with caffè latte skin and a cloud of shimmering corkscrew curls. She recognized her as the new Colombian dancer on the Saturday evening program *Caliente!* The skirt of the dancer's minidress left nothing to the imagination, and her platform shoes caused her to tower over Alessio.

What were they talking about? A possible new role on *Olé olé*? She bit her lip when she noticed the ghost of a smile on Alessio's lips. The same smile he'd shared with her as they spoke at the party, before everything went so horribly wrong.

"Hi Tiffany, what are you doing there?"

She turned in surprise to the voice behind her. Like a young boy caught red-handed with a *Playboy*, she snapped the issue of *Chi* closed. She covered it with the Buzzati novel.

Emma approached. The edges of her lips curled upwards. "Ah, reading Dino Buzzati, I see. How are you enjoying *Il deserto dei tartari*?"

Tiffany's cheeks burned. She'd always been a hopeless liar. "Well ... uh ... my Italian isn't quite up to it. My neighbor's expectations are far too high. He may need to buy me a grade-school book next time." She smiled. "Or maybe even a comic book."

Emma eased down beside Tiffany and tapped the magazine shoved under the novel. "Or maybe the writing in *Chi* is simplistic enough to handle, even for a beginner student?"

Tiffany's cheeks flushed once again.

Emma smiled. "Oh, relax. I'm teasing you. I have a teenage daughter at home. I always find these things lying around. And then I know she's been catching up on gossip rather than finishing homework assignments on Dante or Boccaccio." She winked. "So what's the news that will captivate my daughter this week?"

Tiffany picked up the magazine and clutched it to her chest. "Oh, definitely Jessica Jesoli's wedding!"

Emma shook her head, a blank expression on her face.

"Jessica Jesoli! You *must* know her. The up-and-coming star of *Caramba la Bamba*." She searched Emma's face for recognition, but saw only confusion. "Ah, here. Page ten. Let me show you." She pointed to the wedding spread. "Here she is. Isn't she a gorgeous bride? The groom plays attack for Juventus. And here's Luana Lella." She fought to control the gushing tone creeping into her voice. "She's a bridesmaid. Look how elegant she is." She handed the magazine to Emma.

Emma scanned the photos. "Afraid I don't know her." She looked up. "But I'm sure my daughter would."

"Oh, but you must know Luana!" Tiffany gushed. "I just met her *in person* for the first time a couple of weeks ago. Even prettier in real life than in her photos, if you can believe it."

Emma shifted in the sand.

"And here's the man who helped nudge her into perfection," Tiffany continued, pointing to a photo of a tanned man in an elegant suit. "Doctor Dario Rinaldi, plastic surgeon to the stars. He's a genius. He's responsible for Luana and Jessica." She giggled. "He's kind of a modern-day Michelangelo—working with flesh instead of marble."

Emma examined the paper and made a face. "I never thought of it like that, although I imagine *he* would appreciate the comparison." Her voice had a harsh edge to it.

Tiffany observed her. "Do you *know* him? Know him personally?" She examined Emma's face carefully, wondering if she'd had work done. "What's he like?"

Emma looked out to the waves. "I imagine he's like most plastic surgeons to showgirls and starlets. Rather full of himself." She ran her fingers through her golden waves. "Before he built up his current client list, he used to do a lot of *pro bono* work in developing countries—working with Operation Smile and other organizations to provide surgery to children in African villages." She released a sigh. "I met him back then."

"Oh!" exclaimed Tiffany. "I had no idea. How impressive. I imagine he doesn't have time for any of that now. He's rumored to have a kilometer-long client list. They say the waiting list can be years." She laughed. "But I'm told by reliable television sources that when he has a ..." she made air quotes, "... 'favorite', she can be bumped to the top of the list." She pointed to a pretty black woman in a sequined gown with a neckline that plunged to her navel and emphasized ample, glistening breasts. "Like this Cuban dancer who's new on the scene. Can't remember her name. I spoke to her at a party a couple of months ago, and she told me she was desperate for an appointment. I can guarantee she didn't have a figure *anything* like that before. But word on the street is, she's his new favorite now."

Emma held the magazine closer and examined the photo. Her jaw was rigid, and she shook her head slightly. She met

Tiffany's gaze with her ice blue eyes. "What impressive handiwork." She shoved the magazine at Tiffany, and stood, the wind whipping through her hair. "Apologies, but I hadn't realized the time. I promised to call my children this afternoon, and I don't want to keep them waiting. Hope to see you later."

"I'd like that, Emma." She looked up and shaded her eyes. "Bye."

Emma's elegant figure cut across the sand and began the ascent up the ramp to town. She'd probably bored the woman to death talking about showgirls' weddings and plastic surgeons to the stars. Simone was allergic to her gushing about articles in *Chi*, too, but he put up with it because he said his students discussed the same topics, so at least Tiffany kept him in the know. But Emma didn't seem like someone to waste her time with such frivolous news. Her blonde head reached the top of the long walkway up, and she turned purposely towards the hotel, without looking back to wave down at Tiffany.

No, she definitely didn't seem like a person to enjoy chatting about celebrity gossip and celebrity operations. Better for Tiffany to indulge in her small pleasures alone.

With a glance at the rapidly fading sunlight, she once again opened the magazine to the wedding exclusive, eager to soak in the glamour of the event before encroaching darkness forced her to make her way back up the ramp to the Albergo Paradiso.

CHAPTER 12

Annarita

"Do you think you could seat me at a table for three?" asked Annarita. "The other two American guests should be joining me."

The waitress shook her head. "Not tonight, I'm afraid. *Signora* Emma called down, saying she wasn't feeling well. We sent up broth. *Signorina* Tiffany was down about ten minutes ago, asking after *Signora* Emma. When I told her, she said she had a sandwich in her room and wouldn't be joining us this evening." She picked up a menu, and pointed to a lone table by the windows. "It seems you'll have the place all to yourself this evening."

"Oh, what a treat." Annarita forced a cheery smile. "All alone tonight." She followed the waitress to the table and took the menu offered to her. When the waitress retreated, she muttered under her breath. "Yet again."

"Would you care for dessert?"

"Most definitely." She accepted the dessert menu with a smile. All dietary restraint flew out the window with the homemade lasagna and the *bistecca alla fiorentina*. Glass upon glass of Chianti probably hadn't helped much either. She scanned the items and looked up at the waitress. "*Tiramisu, per favore.*"

Why the hell not? Who cared if she were as big as a house by the end of the week? Not only did she scare men off at an alarming rate, she sent potential female friends running for cover, too. And they'd all seemed to get along so well the other evening, up in Emma's room, laughing and chatting over the wine. She'd really believed they'd made a connection.

But it felt forced this morning at breakfast with Emma, and then she'd offended Tiffany when she'd joined them. Why had she made that crack about Tiffany's weight? Probably envy. She'd take Tiffany's figure over her own any day. Yes, the girl *was* all skin and bones, but how much did she sound like her mother, trying to suggest the poor young woman should fatten herself up? As she grew older, the transformation was alarming. All she needed was the apron, a strand of rosary beads, and a horrendous china figurine collection, and she would officially become her mother.

She peered out the window into the blackness below, where the sea produced its endless swell of waves—back and forth, back and forth, with the alarming sameness of her dull, predictable life.

Her mother was constantly trying to convince her to return home. It was a testament to the dismal state of Annarita's life in Rome that she'd seriously considered it on several occasions. But what would she do back in Yonkers, returning like a dog with its tail tucked between its legs? Each week at family dinners, her failures would be dissected by her extended family. Or worse, they wouldn't be dissected at all. The pitying glances cast her way over the lunch table would express all the words unsaid.

The tiramisu arrived at her table, topped by a huge wallop of whipped cream. Annarita thanked the waitress. Picking up the fork, she took bite after bite. It was delicious, yet she ate mechanically. She startled at the presence of Maurizio's mother beside her table.

The woman wore a black dress, covered over by a white, lace apron. A delicate white kerchief held her wild, white curls in place and, oddly, managed to look quite fashionable. Annarita touched her own frizzy locks self-consciously. Perhaps they would benefit from a similar look.

The old woman stared into Annarita's eyes without blinking.

Annarita shook her head, confused, before gesturing to the chair across from her own. "*Signora* Renata, would you care to join me?"

The old woman snapped her fingers, and a moment later the waitress materialized with a tray containing a bottle of *limoncello* and two iced glasses. She placed it on the table. Renata looked at her. "È *tardi, Paola, puoi tornare a casa.*"

The waitress smiled at the unexpected reprieve, and turned to the kitchen.

Renata spoke as she poured the bright yellow liquid into the frosted glasses. "I observed you from the kitchen, here alone, eating my food. You do not seem happy. You did not enjoy all the work that went into making the food for you."

Annarita shifted in her seat. The woman's dialect was difficult to understand, but her reproach was unmistakable. She took a deep breath before responding. "The food was all wonderful. I certainly did not mean to give the impression ..."

"I am not fishing for compliments." The old woman waved a vein-webbed hand in front of her face in the universal sign of dismissal. "I have been cooking for the better part of seven decades, and I've had enough compliments on my cooking to feel confident in my skills. I suspect you share my passion for cooking." She pinned Annarita in place with her sharp, brown gaze, taking in her curves and the buttons straining on her blouse, optimistically bought one size too small. "But you did not derive any enjoyment from the food. That is clear. You sat here and you chewed and swallowed. You accompanied your meal with fine Tuscan wine, yet you felt no pleasure. This I do not understand. A young woman, here on holiday, with all the time to relax and enjoy herself. But you are not happy. You look like a prisoner in her cell." She handed Annarita a glass and held her own in the air. "*Salute!*"

"*Salute!*" responded Annarita, following the woman's lead and sipping down the sweet, strong drink.

"I make this, too. For the first time, I detect a smile."

"It's delicious—the entire dinner was. As you guessed, I enjoy cooking myself, so I know all the work that went into the food. I'm only a bit blue."

"And why should a beautiful, young woman like you be blue?"

Her lips twisted into a grimace and she turned to the darkness beyond the windows. "I'm afraid I'm neither beautiful nor young." She traced a warm finger across the frosted glass, melting the thin layer of ice. "I repel people—both men, and even potential friends, like the two women staying here."

The old woman gave another dismissive wave of her hand and lifted the bottle to refill their glasses. "That is nonsense. You may become friendly with the two women, and you may not. You certainly have nothing in common with them. It's clear the blonde travels in different social circles. I am certain even our luxurious suite is below her normal standards. And the redhead is so young and insecure. She is finding her way in the world, and I'm guessing the only way she knows is to trade in on her looks. Something you and I did not have as an option ..."

Annarita startled at the comment. Renata was right, of course. Neither of them knew what it was to have all the men turn to watch them enter a room, to desire them above any other woman. But it was still odd to hear that certainty voiced aloud.

Without regret.

The woman set down the bottle and picked up her refilled glass, pointing it in Annarita's direction. "But you—you are woman at the height of her power, with life experience and practical talents a man appreciates in a woman. Your family is Italian, no?"

Annarita stifled a smile. "Yes, my parents came over as children. Their families were from Benevento."

Renata patted her hand. "So you grew up in an Italian family. You cook, you know the value of family. You are a catch for any man."

Renata was like Annarita's older aunts and uncles, thinking marriageable men still reasoned like they did a century ago—eschewing slim, delicate beauties for robust women with cooking skills and childbearing hips.

"I'm afraid the single men don't see it that way today. I have a talent for scaring them off." She sipped her *limoncello*. Why she was complaining about her love life—or lack of it—to this octogenarian was a mystery, but she didn't have the desire to excuse herself and go to her room.

"I have had my fair share of experience in my eighty-five years. I am willing to wager that your problems are all due to the fact that you choose the wrong men."

Annarita laughed. "That's probably true, but I never seem to realize it until they've eaten their fill of my home cooking, allowed me to clean their apartments, and then they go and run off with someone else."

"And I will also wager that those someone elses look like our friend, the young redhead of the skeletal frame."

Annarita fingered the edge of the tablecloth.

"If I may be so bold, I think you must be less superficial in looking for a man." She pointed a finger across the table. "I speak from experience. I was a young woman much like you, living in Sperlonga of the 1950s. Everything changed after the war. Rome was so glamorous, and people began arriving here for summer escapes. I always fell for the wrong men—handsome, full of themselves. I cooked for them, I mothered them, and they were content to be beside a local girl for a few days here. But they always forgot about me when a glamorous, beautiful woman came along. If I hadn't realized my errors, I never would have returned Salvatore's attentions." Renata stroked her wedding ring.

"Who was Salvatore?"

"The butcher's son. He was quiet and plain, but a steady worker. He was always slipping me extra meat in those lean years, but I never noticed. My head was always in the clouds, dreaming about the handsome young Roman men in their shiny cars."

"And Salvatore became your husband?"

Renata smiled, setting alight her chocolate brown eyes, and momentarily melting away the decades. "He did. And we were married for fifty years, until the Good Lord saw fit to call him home ten years ago." She crossed herself.

"I'm sorry."

"*Grazie.*" She placed a hand over Annarita's. "I know you will find someone as wonderful as Salvatore, someone who appreciates you for all you have to offer. Don't always try to mold yourself into a woman that you're not, only to appeal to men who aren't worthy of you."

Renata removed her hand from Annarita's and efficiently placed the bottle and empty glasses on the tray. With strength and speed belying her eighty-five years, she shuffled with determination to the kitchen, without so much as a backwards glance.

Annarita sat in stunned silence in the darkened dining room, staring out the window at the infinite blackness that lay beyond.

CHAPTER 13

Emma threw open the doors and stepped onto the terrace. Her bare feet were cool on the tile. The sea breeze whipped through her hair. The autumn air was brisk, but the weak morning sun would strengthen throughout the day.

She'd spoken to Sabrina and the children last night. All was going well. The children were behaving—Sabrina even claimed Chiara was diligent about her homework, and that her daughter looked forward to Emma's return on Saturday. Her mother was safely dispatched to Paris, and Emma was convinced she could survive the three days they'd have together in Rome before accompanying her mother back to the airport for the flight back to Washington. The dull rhythms of the days here allowed her to lose track of obligations and rigid schedules. Yes, she would return to them, but she'd go back stronger.

She hadn't even thought about Dario in the past days. Well, unless you counted when that airhead Tiffany spoke in such reverential tones about her ex-husband's handiwork with silicone. Like Michelangelo—what a load of crap. She could picture a naïve girl like Tiffany gushing such nonsense to her ex and performing special talents to gain a more favorable position on his patient list.

She paced back and forth on the terrace. No, it wasn't fair to take her anger out on Tiffany. She was young and empty-headed. It was Dario's fault for allowing them to behave like that in the first place.

The Dario she used to know would never have been such an ass.

He used to be her hero. She'd thought those six months they'd worked together for NGOs in Bosnia after the war, living outside of Mostar, would change them forever. Dario operated eighteen hours a day in a simple hospital. She'd overseen efforts to open local schools. They'd met up nightly in their one-room flat, with its poorly repaired, shell-marked walls. She'd cook dinner from the meager ingredients to be found in the markets. Those dinners were the time to recount their days, to give voice to the emotions they needed to keep in check during their working hours.

Dario spoke about the children he operated on—with their shrapnel damage and their limbs lost to mines. Emma recounted the children who returned to school with racing hearts, always jumping at the slightest sound, ready to dive under their desks when snipers attacked. The teachers could never convince the children with constant terror shining in their eyes that the snipers would never return.

After dinner, despite their exhaustion, Emma and Dario would tumble into one another's arms, grappling with buttons and zippers. Later, on the misshapen mattress on the floor, their heartbeats slowing, Dario would wrap her in his arms and breathe in the scent of her skin. He'd tell her she was the only thing that mattered, that their work put everything into perspective.

He swore the gratitude on the faces of parents who'd travelled kilometers to reach their simple hospital was worth countless fat checks from spoiled Italian starlets eager for a smaller nose or larger breasts. "Let's never forget what we've seen here, Emma ..." he'd whisper as he drifted off to sleep, his naked limbs entwined with hers.

For a while, they hadn't. He'd returned to his fledgling practice, steadily adding clients, while still departing for missions *pro bono* to Asian fishing communities or African villages. When Chiara was born, the missions were never as long, and Emma no longer accompanied him to volunteer in the local schools or orphanages. By the time the twins came along, his practice was booming, and clients no longer looked favorably on his charitable work. A nose job or breast implants should be scheduled around the patients' needs—not those of distant Burundian villagers.

Emma, exhausted by the demands of their growing family, decided not to press. She'd always assumed—when the kids were older—they'd return to their earlier arrangements. Seeing glimpses of Dario in his new world of silicone and designer gowns, talking about purchasing sailboats and expensive cars, made her doubt whether those hazy memories of their idealistic youth had been mere dreams.

She shivered at a gust of cold breeze and turned back to her room, locking the terrace door behind her. She plucked up the clothes laid out on her bed and dressed efficiently, willing memories from her mind.

Clutching *The Economist* to her chest, she made her way to the breakfast room. The weather forecast promised it would be beautiful today, and she'd take her book to the beach and prepare herself for the next book club meeting. Sabrina was right. She needed to make more of an effort. This past year she'd let too many things slip.

When she turned into the breakfast room, she saw Tiffany and Annarita deep in conversation before the tall plate-glass window. She paused when she saw the clear blue sky beyond them. It really was shaping up to be the perfect day. As she continued walking to a quiet table at the far end, Annarita looked up and smiled. Waving her over.

Too late.

Emma paused for a moment before walking toward the table. Tiffany smiled up shyly, with an expression that reminded her of Chiara. She shouldn't have snapped at her yesterday.

Annarita was indicating a free place, already set for a third. "We were hoping you'd join us. Cappuccino, right?" She signaled the waitress, without waiting for a response. "Tiffany and I were busy planning. What are you up to today?"

"What am I up to today?" Emma stalled for time. Some time alone would do her good, but what pressing appointments could she conjure up in Sperlonga? "Maybe I'll take advantage of the sunshine to do some reading out on the beach. I'm hosting my book club next week. I can't be behind on the reading."

"Aw, no, Emma. *Signora* Renata told us there's a local festival going on in Gaeta. We're headed down on the bus—it leaves at ten o'clock. Join us. We'll see the festival, walk around, and have lunch. We'll be back in plenty of time for you to do your reading."

"It's awfully nice of you to invite me along." She hesitated. Tiffany's eyes were downcast, maybe she wasn't keen on Emma tagging along. "But maybe you two girls should go ahead. I'll only slow you down. I'll stick to my reading today."

"No way." Annarita clutched Emma's wrist, removing her hand when the waitress placed Emma's frothy cappuccino on the table. "Bring your book along and read on the bus, if you need to. It won't be any fun without you, will it, Tiffany?"

Tiffany nodded politely. Still, Emma could tell she wanted Emma along as much as she herself desired to be there. But Annarita was a force of nature.

Emma sipped her coffee. "Okay, you win. Gaeta it is." She forced a smile.

"Here, Emma. You have to try this cake Renata made. I saved it for you. It's delicious. I'm going to ask her for the recipe."

"Thank you." From the corner of her eye, she caught a glimpse of shimmering green. The sunlight caught a gem on Tiffany's finger, setting it off in a burst of sparkling emerald light. She turned to it. "Oooh, what a ring. It's exquisite."

Tiffany straightened her fingers, examining it herself as if for the first time. "Thank you."

"I didn't notice it the other day."

"No, I wasn't wearing it. I don't know why I brought it at all, but I don't feel comfortable keeping it in my apartment when I'm gone. It's the only valuable thing I own." She looked up at the women.

"I wouldn't mind if the only valuable thing I owned was a rock like that," said Annarita.

"It was left to me by my grandmother. It was an engagement ring—her fiancé was an adventurer and gem trader. He got this in Colombia." She smiled. "My grandmother was all set to take off with him on his adventures. But he died of malaria."

"Oh, how sad," said Annarita.

"Yes, it was." Tiffany turned her finger, observing the sparkle of light. "Even more tragic than it had to be, because she wound up marrying my grandfather—a corn farmer and a hopeless drunk, with a weakness for cards. He wound up losing the farm and working on someone else's. My grandmother never owned one thing of value. Except this ring." She stroked it. "She didn't tell Grandpa about it. He would've sold it off right away. I asked her why she didn't use it to buy back the farm, and she told me he'd just lose it again. And then she would've sacrificed the only proof that her life might have turned out differently."

"That's so sad," said Emma.

"Yeah." Tiffany nodded. "It is. But when I was little, it was our secret. It made me feel so special. Even my father didn't know. She let me wear this ring at her house while she told me stories about her fiancé, and the adventures they would have had. My poor Grandma never travelled far beyond our little town. She told me I was the only one in our family she could imagine carrying out her dreams of adventure. She always promised me she'd leave me the ring in her will." She looked out the window. "I never expected it, but she really did. I was working in Des Moines when she died. And she did leave it to me in her will. A month later, I had boyfriend problems and wanted to make a change. I moved to Italy."

"Oh, wow," said Annarita. "That's a great story. And you are, aren't you? I mean, living out your Grandma's adventures?"

Tiffany kept her eyes fixed at a far point on the horizon. "I guess in some ways, I am. Though I'm afraid Grandma had awfully big dreams for me."

Emma examined the beautiful ring, marveling at the hopes and dreams it symbolized for one woman. Could all those aspirations be encapsulated in one lovely gem, and passed down through the generations? "It's stunning, Tiffany. I imagine it means a lot to you. You should be proud your grandma left it to you with such love in her heart."

Tiffany's gaze caught hers for the first time that morning. She broke out in a wide grin. Her face transformed into a look of such youth and beauty, that it almost hurt to observe it.

"*Spigola*! Just caught this morning. Three for the price of two."

"*Gamberetti*! Fresh shrimp! Bring it home for your pasta tonight."

"This is incredible, isn't it?" Tiffany looked around her at the fish vendors. "Can you believe I'd never even eaten seafood until I moved to Italy? We're so far from the sea in Iowa. And look at this fish market, all these fish that were swimming in the sea this morning."

Annarita stepped over to a stand, looking at the piles of shiny, scaly creatures. "What do you think if we bring some back for Maurizio? Think they'd cook it up for us?"

"You really want to do battle with Renata?" laughed Emma. "Show her you don't trust she buys the best-quality fish in Sperlonga?"

"You have a point there. She's been so good to me, I don't want to insult her." Annarita stepped away from the stand, straight into a sailor in a crisp, white uniform. "Oh," she exclaimed, as he slammed into her.

He stepped back. "Sorry, ma'am. Have I hurt you? Oh, sorry ... I mean, *Scusi, Signora*."

Annarita brushed herself off. She looked up and smiled. "English is fine. No harm done."

"Thank you, ma'am. My first port abroad, and I'm already late back to the ship. I'm happy I didn't hurt you."

"I'm fine. Please go back. Don't want you getting in trouble on my account."

The relief in his face was evident as he flashed a smile. "Thank you, ma'am." They watched him race off to the ship docked at the port.

"Texans in Gaeta. Who woulda thunk it?" Annarita said.

Emma shook her head. "I suppose Gaeta being a NATO base, with that big American ship docked right there," Emma pointed to a hulking, grey ship flying the Stars and Stripes, "should have clued us in."

"Good point," said Annarita. "But it's odd seeing all these U.S. sailors around these little streets in Gaeta."

"The locals must be used to them by now," said Tiffany. She extracted a pair of sunglasses from her purse and put them on.

The sun glistened off the Bay of Gaeta. Emma had been to Naples before, but never Gaeta, which looked like a miniature Naples. The mountains stretched behind the city; the blue water of the port sparkled in the morning sun. The fishmongers loudly hawked their catch to the passing crowds. Discerning housewives haggled down the prices, filling their baskets with the daily catch. Scooters weaved in and out along the seaside road. In the distance, a palace stood on a high point in the city's old town. Bell towers punctuated the cityscape. Maurizio and Renata had been right to suggest a visit.

Annarita interrupted her reveries. "Renata gave pretty precise instructions for the procession today. She told me the route to follow from the fish market. Should we head there, and then explore the old town afterwards?"

"Sounds good."

"Why not? Lead the way."

Annarita followed Renata's handscrawled notes. Emma and Tiffany followed her lead, moving from the wide, sunswept spaces where the fish stands had been set up, to the darker, winding streets farther back from the port.

The crowds were already gathering along the sidewalk. Annarita squeezed through a noisy group of kindergarten children, wearing their multi-colored smocks, and gestured for the others to follow her to the edge of the sidewalk. "Guess we've found it."

"Wow, quite a turnout," said Tiffany.

"Yeah, I can't remember which saint's day it is. I'm Italian American, you'd think I'd know these things." Annarita made a face. "But Renata and Maurizio said it's a big celebration. They'll have a procession with the saint's statue, and carrying some of the church's holy relics."

Police were lining the streets, exchanging greetings with those crowding in to see the procession. The school children chattered noisily, oblivious to the teachers' attempts to quiet them. Parents hoisted toddlers up on their shoulders. Old ladies gossiped together, as middle-aged men argued about the latest soccer matches.

Emma smiled inwardly at all the excitement surrounding these Italian rituals. Even after years of living in Italy, these moments still made her feel a bit like an outsider trying to be part of the community. She'd grown up in a cool, Waspy Annapolis household. She'd once taken her mother to a Good Friday procession in a little town outside of Rome. Emma loved the pageantry, the participation of young and old, the statues being led down the streets and the songs, the old women crossing themselves. Marilyn looked on with distaste at the enthusiasm of her grandchildren as they observed the procession, muttering about the Latins and their slavish devotion to ritual and superstitions.

Emma always envied her children their sense of belonging as they watched this ritual of Italian life, so different from the uptight chill she'd lived with in her own home. Years ago, Emma hadn't stood a chance when she'd come to Italy, embracing its warmth and chaos, its ritual and traditions.

A little boy pushed up beside her, and she stepped aside so he could pass and reach his mother and baby sister on the other side of the street. He was about the same age as Marco and Valerio. How they would have enjoyed being here.

Annarita turned to her. "This whole town's a microcosm of my family—uncles discussing sports, aunts exchanging recipes, all waiting for the church processions to begin. I was always packed off in the train with my family, getting dragged to Little Italy as a kid for every saint's day or festival. Heck, I've probably clocked enough hours at church functions to qualify as a nun. As much as I've grumbled about all our church activities, there's something about seeing them here that makes me appreciate how Italian Americans have managed to keep the traditions alive." She laughed. "It's one of those things you hate when you're growing up. Please don't tell my ma how sentimental I'm becoming in my old age."

They all turned when the strains of a brass band broke out across the crowd, silencing the gathering of twittering observers. A ragtag mix of octogenarians marched unsteadily beside young musicians barely out of high school. The trumpets, flutes, French horns and drums mingled through the streets of Gaeta. A throng of altar boys followed, a float held on their shoulders. A saint, his arms outstretched to the masses, floated above their diligent heads. The crowds crossed themselves as the float passed. A priest, holding the Bible, passed behind the saint, making friendly eye contact with his parishioners.

The same ritual, generation after generation, passed on from father to son, father to son, and down the line. Even if he wasn't being much of a father now, Emma recognized how much her ex-husband shaped the characters of their children. She'd considered returning to Annapolis when she and Dario had separated, but what was the point? Her children didn't belong to that world. If she was honest with herself, after all these years, neither did she.

To her left and right, she observed the rapt faces of Annarita and Tiffany. Like their fictional 1950s sisters in *Three Coins in the Fountain*, they'd all uprooted their lives to settle in the Italian peninsula. Was Italy a temporary stopping point? Or were they all here to stay?

The line beside her began to move, the spectators taking their places behind the procession. Tiffany and Annarita took her by each hand. Wordlessly, they followed the crowd, the band, and the priest leading the procession through Gaeta's winding streets. In that moment, they joined the centuries-long line of Gaeta residents paying homage to their saints and their traditions.

CHAPTER 14

Tiffany

"Ooh, this fish is fabulous." Annarita cut through the layer of salt to extract another piece of *orata*. "Renata will be so offended when I don't have any room for dinner." She tilted her head up to the sun, partially obscured by a twelfth century bell tower. Stretching out her legs beneath their table on the sunny *piazza,* she sighed. "It's gorgeous here. Who wants to go home to work, and bills, and hectic schedules?"

Tiffany raised her glass of white wine. "Hear, hear. But you know, in the end, this is how my friends back home assume I spend every day. Sitting in the sun, sipping a cappuccino or a glass of wine, depending on the time of day. All the films about Italy don't help at all—the ones showing people hanging out all day, doing nothing, always with some fabulous apartment right off Piazza Navona, never having any real source of income." She shook her head. "I keep telling them it's nothing like that ... unfortunately."

Emma swept a lock of hair from her forehead. "The Hollywood Effect. At least our 1950s film shows us it has a long tradition."

"Yeah, but they never see how we scrimp and save just to get by in Rome, how much apartments cost—and nowhere near the center. I've thought about going home about a million times. The latest time being when I walked in on my boyfriend and his new toy." Annarita reached for the wine bottle and filled her glass. "But I never manage to make the break. I know if I go back, it's for good. And I'm not sure I want to give it all up."

"That's how I feel most of the time." Tiffany examined her ring in the sparkling sunlight. "I was so convinced I was going to make it here. I'm afraid everyone will recognize what a failure I am if I go back."

"But you're both so young," said Emma. "It's okay to be finding yourself, and going back home if that's what you want. It sounds like you're being hard on yourselves."

Annarita shook her head. "It's different for you. Even if you and your husband decided to split, you have children here. Roots here. I can see why you'd stay."

"I did consider going back at first. But it's not easy after two decades. I don't know if I ever will. Then again, I'm blessed with an impossible mother. If I go back, she'd drive me insane within a month. Oh, sorry. That probably sounds awful. She's not a monster or anything. I don't want to sound ungrateful."

Tiffany laughed. "Don't worry. I'm not offended. I didn't have any luck in the mother or father department. I don't know why they bothered having kids at all. My mom only remembers my birthday one year out of three. I held out some hope for my brother, but I don't even know where he is right now. He contacts me every couple of years, when he needs a favor. Or money."

"Oh, yikes," said Annarita. "Guess I have no right to complain. My ma's actually great. She loves my sister and me. But she's traditional. Wants to see me married off."

"Mothers and daughters. Now that I'm a mom with my own daughter, I see how complicated everything is. I think most days my daughter hates me, too." Emma rolled her eyes. "The teenage years."

"Yeah, but we were all impossible as teenagers." Annarita pushed back her chair. "Assunta and I tortured our mother at that age. God, I don't know how I'd put up with a teenage daughter."

Tiffany's cellphone beeped. She clicked into the messages.

'Not responding to my texts. Met some hot Sperlonga fisherman? Forgot your neighbor? XOXO. *Bacio*. S.'

She smiled, picturing her neighbor as he texted the words.

"Hey," said Annarita. "Earth to Tiffany."

Tiffany looked up from her cellphone. "Ooh, sorry. Just had a message from my friend Simone. Poor guy. He's always coming over to my house to complain about his teenage girl students. I think about half are in love with him, and that's why they give him such a hard time. I mean, I never had a teacher who looked like Simone in high school."

"How's Mr. Perfect doing?"

"You want me to tell him I'll be setting him up with an Italian American?"

"In a heartbeat, but I think you'll come to your senses and fall for him yourself." Annarita winked. "You saw him first, after all."

"Don't think so. I've developed expensive tastes living here. Nothing less than a filthy-rich boyfriend will do. Anyway, I met Simone when he was living with his girlfriend. I was friends with both of them, and I just can't think of him that way. I doubt he thinks of me like that, either."

Annarita shook her head. "Tiffany, you're gorgeous. You're tall, thin. You look like a model. What guy's going to say no to you? I saw him at the café with you. I was so convinced you two were a couple. Friends don't give off that same vibe."

"That's all it is. And I like it that way."

"Don't listen to her." Emma reached across the table and put her hand on Tiffany's. "It's not always easy having a male friend, and I think it's wonderful that you have this close friendship. He even organized this trip for you because he thought you needed a rest. Friendships like that don't come around too often. He sounds special."

"He is. I'm lucky to have him."

"So don't listen to the teasing. Annarita's only nursing a broken heart, and now she's trying to set everyone up. I'll be next."

"Maybe that's not such a bad idea," said Annarita. "You said you've been separated two years. What're you waiting for?"

"Hmmm, let me think." She rolled her eyes. "Raising three kids doesn't exactly give me lots of time to throw myself back in the dating scene. And honestly, I have zero desire to be back out there."

"But how'll you ever meet anyone?"

Emma groaned. "Didn't you say your mother was such a pain in the neck, always putting pressure on you about relationships? Don't you ever wonder if you've taken after her?"

"God forbid. I've become my mother. Entirely possible. It was just a matter of time." She pushed her plate away. She signaled the waiter. "What do you girls say to some *limoncello*?"

"Oh, no," said Tiffany. "No more alcohol."

"It's not like we're driving. We just have to hop on the bus. C'mon." She signaled three glasses to the waiter. "You're such a lightweight. Next week at this time you'll be back at work, wishing you were out in the sun with fabulous women drinking ice-cold *limoncello*."

"At the rate we're going, I'll be ten pounds heavier and still hungover a week from now."

"Tiff, you could put on ten pounds and there'd still be nothing to you. Do you really have to be so skinny to dance on those programs?"

"You have no idea. There's so much competition. And yes, the camera really does put on ten pounds. Even more." She slipped her sunglasses down over her eyes. "But it's not just TV. I teach a dance class in Rome, at the Central Studio. Don't get me started on my fellow instructors, or the students. I swear, at least half those girls are anorexic."

"Oh." Emma leaned in closer. "You teach at Central Studio? My daughter wants to take dance classes there with some friends from school. She's already so obsessed she's fat, when she's perfect the way she is. Do you think being in that environment might make it worse?"

"Nah, I probably exaggerated. Most of the girls are fine. But it makes an impression, ya know? These young girls obsessing about something that's not a problem. Never appreciating how they are."

"Yeah, well," said Annarita. "That won't get better with age. We women never learn. After I caught Vincenzo with that blonde bimbo ... you know, in the shower ... the image that keeps flashing through my mind is how damned perfect the other woman's body was. That's what he wanted all along."

The waiter arrived with three glasses of bright yellow liqueur.

"Well, if that's not perfect timing. Gets me out of exploring forbidden corners of my disturbed mind. Raise your glasses, ladies. This is a toast to us. Perfect women who should spend more time appreciating how special we are, and who should spend far more time enjoying our lives in Rome. Our chaotic, expensive, messed-up lives in Rome."

Tiffany and Emma held up their glasses.

"I don't know. We all came over because we wanted to, right?" Tiffany ignored the catcalls directed at her by the American sailors passing by her table. She shrugged dismissively. "Probably all from Iowa. But seriously, why can't we be like those three women in *Three Coins*? What's wrong with being optimistic, and believing it's all ours for the taking?"

Emma shook her head. "I hate to extinguish youthful optimism, but I have a few years on you both. I'm not sure that 1950s Hollywood can really serve as my mantra on how to live a fulfilled life."

"I don't know, Emma," said Annarita. "Maybe Tiff's onto something here. Those women weren't stupid. They came to Rome back when it couldn't have been easy for a young, single woman to leave home all alone and move half a world away. They worked, they lived in a new culture, and they were determined they'd meet Mr. Right. What's so wrong with that? Call me sappy, but I agree. I've been letting Rome and my romantic disasters drag me down. I could handle some *Three Coins* optimism."

"I'm now a single mom with three kids. I'm used to being outnumbered. If it'll make us happy, why not?" Emma raised her glass. "To *Three Coins*."

"*Three Coins*."

"To *Three Coins*."

They clinked glasses before downing the sweet, lemony liquid. The medieval clock tower struck the hour. Tiffany looked up as a seagull perched on the bell tower's roof took flight. It escaped the tolling bell to soar across the bay and toward Orlando Mountain. Tiffany followed its journey, remembering all the times she'd sat out in the cornfields, watching the birds flying above, wishing she could do the same.

And hadn't she?

It doesn't have to end badly. It's my life, and I can turn things around. Italy, it is. Three Coins? *Why the hell not. If they can do it, so can I.*

CHAPTER 15

Annarita

The rain pelted against the panes of glass. A sudden crack of lightning illuminated the starless black sky. Annarita shuddered. Storms still scared her.

"Wow," said Tiffany. "It's like the first night we were here."

Emma broke off a piece of bread and dipped it into the mussels sauce. "Do you think Maurizio is setting up the screen for movie night?"

"Doesn't that seem ages ago? Movie night with *Three Coins*?" Annarita shook her head. "And it was only last week. Can't believe tomorrow I'll be back in Rome, and back to lessons with my spoiled students. Are you sure it's not a problem to drive us back?"

"Not at all," said Emma. "I rented the car anyway. It's you two doing me a favor. I haven't driven since the accident. It'll make me less nervous having you both with me." Her cellphone rang and she lifted her purse to her lap, digging out her phone. She frowned at the screen, before looking up. "I don't know who's calling. If you'll excuse me a moment. *Pronto* ... Yes, this is Emma Patterson ... Oh, you're kidding me. Mark

Daniels!" She smiled. "It's been a lifetime since I heard that name. How've you been?"

Annarita nudged Tiffany in the ribs and made an exaggerated face at Emma.

Emma shook her head. "I'm so pleased you got my number. I'm not in Rome now, but I'll be back tomorrow. How long are you staying?"

Annarita leaned forward in her seat. Beside her, Tiffany was doing the same.

"Okay, if you're free Thursday evening, you can come over for dinner ... Eight sounds perfect. It's in Aventino, I'll text you the address ... Great, Mark. I'm at dinner with friends. I need to go ... See you soon ... 'Night." She tucked her phone away.

Annarita whistled. "I don't know about you, Tiff, but it sounds as if Emma has a date lined up, doesn't it?"

"It does indeed."

"How long have you known this *Signor* Mark?"

"It's *not* a date. We were at Georgetown together, eons ago, doing our master's program."

"Rekindled college romance," said Annarita. "Even better."

"What an active imagination you have. There's nothing to rekindle. We were only friends." She handed her empty plate to the waitress. "Sounds like he may be getting involved in a business in Umbria, and he needs advice."

"Classic ruse."

"Annarita, you're impossible. He's married. Don't try to turn everything into a romance."

"Ah, but someone has to. Especially someone with a love life as disastrous as mine. You never know, is all I'm saying."

Tiffany shook her head. "Annarita, you do have a one-track mind about fixing people up. Let Emma have dinner with an old friend. We'll bug her for details after. Anyone else having dessert?"

"You?" Annarita clutched her chest in mock horror. "Maybe we should call a press conference."

"Oh, please. Back in Rome, I won't have Signora Renata's delicious *babà* tempting me. Have to enjoy it while I can."

Annarita ordered dessert, too. She'd completely abandoned her diet during the week. She'd pay for it later, but this week, in off-season Sperlonga, chatting each day with her new friends left her feeling better than she had in a long time.

She observed Emma carefully. Her face announced the conversation about the mysterious caller was over, but Annarita had enough experience with her sister, female cousins and girlfriends to suspect this Mark had been more than a friend. There'd been a glow in Emma's eyes when she'd spoken to him. He hadn't merely been the geeky lab partner. That was for sure. Fine—she didn't want to talk about it—but Annarita was convinced her hunch was right. She had a weird sixth sense for these things. Sadly, however, her special talent never worked when applied to herself.

The rain thundered down against the glass as their dessert arrived. Maurizio arrived at the table, rubbing his hands together in anticipation. "Ladies, it looks like we have another storm ruining any plans for midnight strolls. I wanted to let you know I've set up the screen for movie night. I'll give you three clues: Burt Lancaster, Claudia Cardinale, Alain Delon."

"*Il gattopardo*," said Emma.

"Right you are."

"But isn't that a rather long film?"

"Perhaps, but you all leave tomorrow. What better way to spend your last evening here?"

Annarita would miss Maurizio's earnestness.

"What do you say, ladies? A classic film to wrap up our week at the Albergo Paradiso?"

"Why not?"

"Don't have other plans."

"So, it's settled." Maurizio smiled. "Bring your coffees in, and I'll set up the projector."

The storm was too strong even to sit under the terrace roof. With the sliding doors open, they listened to the pounding rain and watched the sky light up with frequent crackles of lightning, all from the safety and comfort of Emma's spacious suite.

Emma uncorked the wine bottle and returned to her seat. "First *The Leopard*, followed by Mother Nature's performance. Now that's what I call a double feature. At least while we're all warm and dry." She poured wine into the three glasses. "Enjoying the last of Sabrina's excellent wine."

"I can drink to that." Annarita had been doing far too much drinking this past week, but tomorrow would start a new era. She'd only be able to afford water. The kind that was free from Rome's fountains. "God, did you see how young and gorgeous Claudia Cardinale was in that film? Alain Delon wasn't so bad, either."

"Do you know," said Tiffany, "I'd never seen the movie before. But thank God for the subtitles, or I wouldn't have understood anything."

"I hadn't seen it in ages." Emma slipped an expensive-looking cardigan around her shoulders. "I should watch it with my daughter sometime. If she doesn't protest about spending an evening home with her mom."

"Oh, she won't," said Annarita. "My sister and I fought tons with our ma, but we'd always call a truce over the old Italian classics. Our special time together."

Tiffany groaned. "Ha, I'm trying to picture classic Italian movie nights in my family. If cars weren't getting smashed up, my family couldn't be bothered. Although, my mom..." She took a sip of her wine and turned to the storm raging outside.

"... Way back when I was a kid, really young, sometimes she'd watch the old musicals with me. She used to be a good dancer, even used to stage some of the numbers for the students in her dance studio. But that was long ago. By the time I was a teenager, all that enthusiasm was long gone. Every year, it was the same sad numbers, the same dusty sets. She didn't care anymore."

"Is that where you learned to dance?" asked Emma. "In your mom's studio?"

"Yeah. I was always there. I probably learned to dance around the same time I learned to walk, then I followed up with lessons when I turned three. Then I was a source of free labor for many years. It wasn't just my dad who hit the bottle. Mom always had a hangover, and I was the one to fill in last-minute for lessons when she was 'under the weather.'"

"But you're not in your mother's shadow here. You said you teach the occasional class at The Central Studio. Ever considered teaching more regularly there? I don't know that much about it, but my friend Sabrina designs ballet costumes, and she's always telling me how talented the students there are."

"They are. But I'm not classically trained. They have more ballet classes, although I've filled in for modern dance and choreography work. The pay's not bad, definitely better than English lessons. But yeah, I guess I do worry about becoming my mom."

Tiffany twisted her ring, angling it to catch bursts of light on the stones. Annarita would be scared to wear anything so valuable around. How hard would it be to knock down someone as waif-like as Tiffany to steal the ring from her? But over these past days, she'd often seen Tiffany admire her ring, or stroke it absently, as if she needed to assure herself it was there, still a part of her. Her grandmother must have meant a lot to her. Annarita got that. She'd certainly seen her own family obsess over family heirlooms, though nothing nearly as valuable and exquisite as Tiffany's ring. People were funny like that.

"I dunno, I guess I have my heart so set on television. I'm afraid to commit too much to the dance lessons. I don't want them becoming a full-time job."

"You're able to make ends meet cobbling together part-time jobs?" Annarita looked up to see two sets of eyes staring at her. She sunk deeper into the plush cushions of the couch. "Sorry, my ma always tells me I should be minding my own business. Look, I'm hardly flush myself. Living in Rome is damned expensive. I'm always living from month to month. Without the complicated teaching schedule, I'd never manage. Plus, I babysit sometimes for neighbors, or fill in bartending at the pub downstairs when they need extra staff. But if I had an unforeseen expense, I'd be flat-out broke."

She caught Emma's gaze fast enough to see a look of pity reflected in their arctic blue depths.

There was a woman who didn't understand hand-to-mouth. She would probably have been at ease in the ballroom of the film, waltzing along with the aristocracy. Had she ever worked? Fancy-pants degrees from brand-name schools, followed by a life wandering around one of those luxurious Aventino villas, scheduling lunches and tennis matches. Nice work if you could get it. Not that she'd ever be getting it.

Tiffany was twisting her ring back and forth. Annarita held her breath, wondering if she might screw her finger right off with the effort.

"Yeah, well ... it definitely hasn't been easy. I do bits and pieces. English tutoring, dance classes, a bit of modeling, hostessing at conventions. I've danced as a backup on a few stage shows, but the pay's awful. Juggling and chasing after jobs saps the energy out of me most days. But I got my associate's degree in accounting. I worked as a bookkeeper for an insurance agency back in Des Moines. Even struggling here is better than what I had before."

The glow was gone from Tiffany's skin. Her crumpled face transformed her. She was still beautiful, Annarita would give her that, but her radiance was gone. Annarita's unnerving talent for sticking her foot in her mouth had struck again.

"Sorry, Tiff. I really didn't mean to pry. Misery loves company, and all that. I'm only worried about my own financial woes when I get back to Rome." She raised her glass. "To the last evening of carefree holidays. Here's to holding real life at bay."

She looked up to see Tiffany smile. Her radiance had returned. Here was a woman who must have men racing to open doors for her, begging to lug her suitcase up flights of stairs. The kind of woman she'd always envied. Maybe she still did, but she liked Tiffany, too. That was new.

Tiffany leaned closer, reaching her glass out to clink against Annarita's. "To holidays. This week has cheered me up more than you'll ever know. I'm ready to go back now." She tapped glasses with Emma. "I'll be sorry to lose you ladies. I hope we can do it again. I mean, when we're back in Rome."

"I'd love that." Annarita's voice was too eager to her own ears. She must sound desperate to the others. She smiled woodenly. Only Emma remained silent. Tiffany and Annarita may have been acceptable company on a lonely week off-season at the beach. But somehow she didn't imagine them becoming regular fixtures in Emma's more sophisticated social circles. Emma's smile was tight as she poured the last of the wine into their glasses.

"That would be lovely."

Her voice was hardly convincing. Annarita reached for her purse. "Then it's settled. Let's exchange contacts, and we can arrange a post-Sperlonga evening sometime in Rome." She handed a pen and a small notebook to Emma first—better to strike while the iron was hot. Emma paused a moment, but wrote on the page before passing it on to Tiffany.

"Oh, this is so exciting," Tiffany said as she wrote. "I'd love to see you both in Rome. I've had such a great time this week. Maybe we can even do a movie night when we're back. What about *Three Coins in the Fountain*?" She looked up, an eager smile transforming her face into that of the television star she so longed to be.

Annarita sensed Emma stiffening beside her. She turned to Emma and smiled. "That would be fun, wouldn't it? I can't wait for a movie night back in Rome. All three of us together again."

Emma arranged the white roses in the vase, placing it on the side table and fussing once again with the blooms.

"Yes, she got back in one piece. I spoke to her today. Already whining because I'm not sending her the money for another luxurious Caribbean cruise. *Mamma mia*, she just went a few months ago. Is it written anywhere you have to spring twice a year for your mother's expensive holidays?"

"In your mother's book, I think it's rule number one." Sabrina popped a tiny mozzarella into her mouth. "These are fabulous. Volpetti?"

Emma changed her mind, shifting the vase to the mantelpiece. "Yes, I got them this morning."

Sabrina picked up another. "You're going to a lot of trouble for an old schoolmate who needs to pick your brains for some Italian investment. What's the deal?"

Emma shifted her full attention to her friend. "Nothing. What are you suggesting? I told you he's married. There's nothing there. It's just that Mark ..." She trailed off.

Sabrina shifted forward in her chair.

"Mark knew me when I was young and ambitious. He hasn't seen me since graduate school. Now I'm ... old, and not at all ambitious. I'm a pampered housewife. Even worse, a housewife without a husband. I don't want to come off as pathetic." She sighed. "What will he think of me?"

Sabrina shook her head. "Emma, he'll think what everyone does when they meet you. That you're a beautiful, intelligent woman. One who's fun to talk to, and living well, even if you didn't go for a career in international relations in the end. After all, he didn't either."

"No, but he's some hotshot consultant up in Amsterdam, advising international corporations and governments and I don't know what. He'll only be bored when he sees me."

"Stop knocking yourself. He'll be thrilled when he sees you. You'll catch up on old times. It'll be good for you to see some old friends. Some pre-Dario friends."

Emma sat down across from Sabrina and popped a mozzarella into her mouth. "Mmmm, these *are* good. I love Volpetti. Yes, he's definitely a pre-Dario friend. We kind of lost touch when I moved over here to be with Dario."

"Because he was madly in love with you, and you trampled his heart by falling in love with some Italian heartthrob."

"Hardly." Emma trailed off. "It's true we'd gone on a few dates before I did the semester working at the Embassy in Rome. When I met Dario. But he probably won't even remember."

"Trust me, no man forgets being thrown over. Even if it was a long time ago." She pulled out her car keys. "Okay, I have to pick up Lina and take her to ballet. But I am *definitely* going to want to hear about this tomorrow. Coffee at San Teodoro tomorrow morning, after school drop-off?"

"There'll be nothing to tell, but I'd love a coffee tomorrow. Ten okay?" Emma walked her friend to the door.

"Perfect. *A domani*." Sabrina kissed her friend on each cheek. "Have fun tonight!"

Emma returned to the kitchen, took the parmesan out of the fridge and began grating. Maybe Sabrina was right. She shouldn't be so silly about seeing Mark again. He was an old school friend who needed some Italian advice. It's not like he'd sit across from her all evening judging her life.

Maybe it was a good thing to see a pre-Dario friend. After all, even if some days it was hard to believe, she had created a life for herself before Italy.

"I don't get why you didn't manage to meet my mom when you came to Rome. Why didn't you just text her?"

"You know, Valerio," Mark smiled at the boy, his blue eyes lighting up. "Back when your mom and I were in school, we didn't have cellphones, or even email. It was harder to agree on meeting up, especially when you were travelling abroad."

"You didn't have *cellphones*?" Marco's face was a study in confusion. "How could you, like, even have friends without cellphones?"

Mark met Emma's eyes. He laughed the booming laugh she remembered from so many years ago.

Actually, he was remarkably like she remembered him so many years ago. Maybe a little *too* much the same. Life was treating him well. Men always got away with aging gently. The salt-and-pepper look around the temples and a few character-enhancing lines around the eyes were the only major changes. His shoulders were still broad, his hair still thick, and his build still trim and athletic.

She'd been nervous earlier in the evening when he showed up at their doorstep, looking handsome as ever, sporting a bottle of wine and a bouquet of flowers that quickly replaced the carefully positioned roses.

The odd fluttering in her stomach subsided as they sat down together, and he joked with the twins and even coaxed smiles out of Chiara. He told her about his own daughters, one a year younger than Chiara, and the bicycle trips they liked to go on in Holland, and all the things they did around their home in Amsterdam. It broke Emma's heart to see how her daughter warmed to her old friend immediately when she saw what an active father he was with his girls. The way her own father had been with her not so long ago.

Between courses, he traipsed up to Marco and Valerio's room to see soccer and fencing medals, and he was conversant about Rome's football season. He even promised to take them to see an Ajax game if they were up in Amsterdam. That was more than enough to win the boys over. Their father had taken them to one Roma game, right after their carefully rehearsed announcement about their split to the kids. After that, it had been a string of broken promises. "Believe it or not, Marco, we still managed to have friends. Even without cellphones."

"But, like, how did you contact your friends if you had to change plans?" Valerio asked.

"Your mom and I didn't live in the Stone Age. We had home phones, but you couldn't get in touch once you went out of the house. I'd say people were better about being on time back in our day."

"But that would *never* work in Italy," Marco said. "No one would ever do *anything* if they had to be on time."

Mark laughed. "I wasn't blaming Italy for not seeing your mom when I was travelling through. I think your mom had just met your dad, and they were off someplace romantic. The Amalfi Coast or Capri, or somewhere. She forgot all about her promise to meet up with me when I passed through Rome on holiday."

Emma snapped her neck around so quickly she felt a twinge in a neck muscle. "Surely I didn't take off on a weekend

I'd promised to meet you." She searched her memory in vain. "You must have been so angry."

"At your ages, you don't understand." Mark looked at the children. "Time is the great healer. I've had over twenty years to get over being mad at your mom for abandoning me in Rome." He smiled the lopsided grin she remembered from school. "A place, I should add, that was completely off the map of the trip in northern Europe I was on with friends. I only came to Rome to see your mom, so I was shocked as anything when I was finally able to get in touch with an Embassy colleague of hers who told me I'd been abandoned for some handsome, young Italian." He winked at Chiara. "I think you know him? So you see, you can never trust good friends in the end, especially when they're blinded by love."

Valerio turned to Emma. "How could you do that?"

Had she really stood him up? It was so long ago, that semester interning at the Embassy in Rome.

Yes, she'd been swept off her feet by the handsome, young Italian medical student. Yes, he had taken her to Capri for a holiday weekend. She hadn't remembered that Mark planned to pass through Rome on those days. Of course, back then, her couch served as a place to crash for dozens of cash-strapped grad students passing through Rome during her time there. She was constantly fielding calls from classmates and acquaintances hoping to stay for free. But to have forgotten all about an agreement like that ...

"Now, kids," said Mark. "I certainly didn't want to start a third degree on your mom. That's how things were back then. We'd make plans and then find it hard to see them through. I stayed in some dive hostel in Rome, threw a few coins in the Trevi Fountain, and drank way too much wine. No harm done. I even got back in time to meet my friends in Copenhagen." He pushed his chair back. "And the best thing is, more than twenty years later, I can tease your mom about it."

Emma smothered a smile. She rose and began clearing dishes.

Mark jumped up. "Let me help."

"Absolutely not. You're our guest." She placed the silverware on the top plate. "And it seems I owe you one after behaving so shamefully all those years ago. Stay where you are. Marco, come help me get dessert."

For once, he jumped up without being asked twice. A sure sign he liked Mark.

When she and Marco returned with dessert plates and the cake she'd baked, Chiara and Valerio were laughing so hard tears were streaming from their eyes. Chiara broke into fresh peals of laughter when she met her mother's eyes.

"Did you really mud wrestle naked with your roommates when you were at Georgetown?"

Her hands began to shake and she lowered the cake to the table before it could slip from her grasp. She fought to keep a hint of panic from her voice. "What exactly has Mark been telling you?"

Mark chuckled. "Your daughter is as dangerous as mine are. I never said the word 'naked' alongside 'mud wrestling.' In fact, your mother was quite fetching in a yellow bikini. Well, come to think of it, it wasn't yellow for long once she started rolling around in the mud."

"Is it true, Mommy?" asked Valerio. "Did you really mud wrestle back in school?"

She looked sharply at Mark. "Why did this come up?"

"Aha!" said Chiara. "So you're not denying it."

"Now, kids. What did I tell you? This wasn't a regular habit of your mom's. She did it to raise money for a charity. But she did happen to have a remarkable talent for it. She was the uncontested Georgetown female mud wrestling champion." He winked. "She could have turned it into a career."

"At least she would have had a career," Chiara muttered under her breath.

Emma prayed Mark missed the comment.

"Wow, Mom. I can't believe you used to be so cool!" Marco's gaze was admiring.

"Cool doesn't even begin to describe your mom. She was bright, funny, beautiful, and so ambitious." He took the slice of cake Emma offered him. "And a champion mud wrestler to boot."

She caught his eye and broke into a smile. That girl had long ago been dead and buried. Maybe it was time to revive her, or at least the memories of her. But that still didn't mean the kids needed a play-by-play account of days long past.

"Yes, centuries ago, maybe I was cool, and maybe I did miss out on professional mud wrestling. But tonight Mark needs my help with a property he's looking at, and you three have school tomorrow. So let's finish up dessert and get ready for bed."

"See?" said Valerio, turning to Mark. "She's not cool anymore." He shrugged. "She's just our mom."

Mark met her gaze over the table and winked.

The house was awash in a pleasing silence. The time of evening she always savored. There were no soccer balls bouncing in Marco and Valerio's room, Chiara wasn't in loud, animated, and endless blow-by-blow conversation with a friend about who said what to whom and when. No one was screaming for Emma to take sides in the latest sibling fight.

Upstairs, the children slumbered peacefully. Downstairs, she motioned Mark to pick up his wineglass and the wine bottle and to follow her into the living room. Despite the brisk evening, she opened the French doors leading out to the backyard, allowing the bracing breeze to enter the room.

"Does it bother you? I like to get some fresh evening air into the room, but I'll close it in a minute."

"No, it's fine." He settled into the leather sofa. "I can't believe how warm it is here in November. It's already miserable weather in Amsterdam. I'm envious of your Roman life."

Envy her? The man with the successful career and an intact marriage had nothing to envy in this house.

"Don't be. It sounds like you have everything you could ever want. How are Lieke and the girls?"

He shifted in his seat, resting his wineglass on his leg. "They're great. Thanks. Lieke's really pleased you'll be able to give me your views on this property I've inherited. It's kind of messy. She's supporting me if I decide to come down here and make a go of it." He smiled sheepishly. "I hope I'm not getting in over my head."

"And your consulting in Amsterdam?"

"Ah," he coughed. "Well, it's my father-in-law's consulting firm. So I have some flexibility if I want to take time off, to pursue this investment opportunity."

"It sounds like you have it all figured out."

"All figured out? Hmm …" He looked out into the darkness beyond the open doors. A waft of breeze tousled his hair. "Remember back when we were in grad school? Didn't you imagine our lives would be perfect at our age? I certainly thought I'd have everything figured out. Turns out I was wiser in my mid-twenties than in my late forties."

"Oh, come on, Mark. You're being tough on yourself. It sounds like everything's going well for you."

He smiled. "Well, maybe I bounced back somewhat after you deserted me in Rome, shattering my heart."

Emma flushed. "Oh, my. Your dinner story. You know, I didn't remember it. We went out for a few dinners before my semester abroad, but I'd forgotten we had plans for your visit to Rome. You never mentioned it later."

"You were so in love with your exotic Italian when you came back to Washington. I didn't have the heart to bring it up. It seemed you were only counting the days to graduate and to move to Rome."

"Back then, I guess I was."

The flashbulbs from the graduation ceremony had hardly dimmed before she was hopping on a plane direct to Rome, mindlessly turning down job offers from the World Bank and prestigious Washington think tanks in exchange for unemployment in Italy. Two decades ago, the idea of being without Dario was too much to bear. Her love-addled brain could easily have forgotten Mark's visit to Rome.

"What's the statute of limitations on apologies?"

Mark's eyes crinkled as he met her gaze. "I think about twenty years, give or take. So we're fine. Plus, you agreed to come with me to see this Todi property. I don't know what I'd do without you."

"So this was some distant aunt?"

"Yes, I never even met her, but she and my mom had been close as children. She was artistic. Kind of the black sheep of the family. Spent all her money on some rambling farmhouse outside of Todi. Apparently, she had a studio there and took in other artists when they passed through. I understand she never had commercial success, but she got by okay. I was shocked when I learned she'd left me the farmhouse in her will. Mom's health is failing. She couldn't come over to see it, but I promised to tell her all about it, and to let her know if I could do something with it."

"Such as?"

"I've only seen the photos. It looks like a fixer-upper, but not a disaster. If I'm right, I'd love to turn it into an *agriturismo*." He laughed. "Apologies for my awful accent on that. A farm holiday—where people can come to stay in the country and relax, maybe take Italian classes and cooking classes. It's easy walking distance from Todi. Guests can also use it as a base to travel around Umbria and Tuscany."

"It sounds great, but you'll have to see what shape it's in. Then there are Italian permits and regulations. I don't think things will be as easy as they are in Holland."

"That's why I was hoping I might lure you away—for a while. I could pay you to be my consultant. Help out overseeing the work, the permits. Everything."

"Me? I don't know anything about setting up an agriturismo business. Plus, I have the kids, responsibilities in Rome."

Mark leaned closer. "I know that, of course. I wouldn't want it to get in the way of your family obligations. It wouldn't be full time. But I could use help from an old friend, someone I can trust. I need someone to hold my hand through this."

"I don't know, Mark."

"Please say yes. You walked on water back at Georgetown. You could have done anything. There's no one else I'd want fighting in my corner."

She sighed. "I think my fighting days are long gone. When do you plan on going up to see the place?"

"On Saturday."

Emma sighed. "I'll go with you. If it's a disaster, I'm out. If it's workable, then we can talk about it. But no promises."

Mark reached out and grasped her hand. Her heart raced in a way she preferred to ignore.

"Thank you. I can't tell you how happy it would make me to work with you on this project. Let's toast." He lifted his wineglass, and slid over to toast. "To rekindled friendships."

"To rekindled friendships."

She clinked her glass against his, trying to ignore how her heart flip-flopped in her chest as his body moved closer to hers.

CHAPTER 17

Tiffany

Tiffany threw her bag down in front of the door and fumbled for her keys. Her fingers flailed uselessly around the depths of her purse, never finding the cool metal shafts.

Her temples throbbed. Two weeks wasted perfecting her choreography and shelling out for singing lessons to ensure her Italian pronunciation was perfect. She'd been so convinced this musical was perfect for her, and she'd been damned good in her callbacks.

Who'd have expected one of the producers to grope her in the hallway after her audition? When she slapped him away, he'd made a face and mumbled how there were plenty of other girls, more cooperative girls, who could fill the part.

Rent was due next week, and she still hadn't returned Central Studio's call about filling in for a modern dance class starting next month. Back when she was evading the calls, she hoped to be able to say she'd be too busy rehearsing for her tour with the musical. Now, it was time to beg forgiveness with the studio and grab the class before someone else did.

She breathed in deeply. Her muscles ached, and she needed a hot shower and an early bedtime. Maybe things wouldn't look so disastrous in the morning. Ah, the keys!

She extracted them and opened her door, anticipating the feel of the pounding spray of a hot shower on sore muscles. She flicked on the light switch and took in the chaos of her living room. Muddy men's work boots sat in the middle of the floor, a barn jacket was flung over the sofa. Empty beer bottles cluttered the table, and an empty bag of potato chips glimmered on the couch. She instinctively took a step back to the hallway. Someone broke into her apartment and settled in for the long haul?

The loud flush of her faulty toilet reverberated through the apartment, and she felt her heart thump. She dropped her bag to the hall floor, ready to sprint to the emergency exit. A door slammed and footsteps approached the living room. Who the hell was the brazen thief? Would Simone already be home? Could he come to her rescue?

A man rounded the corner. He was skinny, with close-cropped, dark hair, a familiar scar marred his right cheek. His skin wasn't as taut as she remembered it, his stubble now looked more degenerate than rugged, but she'd know that walk anywhere.

"Hey, Tiff. What kind of welcome is that?"

She stood perfectly still in the hallway. Her muscles still retained the survivor's instinct to flee. But surely this was unnatural. One didn't flee from family.

"How ... how did you get in?"

He laughed, the hollow laugh of one unaccustomed to using those muscles. "You're so predictable. Keys over the notch above the door. Just like back in Des Moines. Not a brilliant move for a pretty girl like you. Anyone could wander in and catch you off guard when you're asleep. Not everyone plays nice, Tiff."

"So I've learned."

"Aw, c'mon. Is that the way to treat me? It's been ages. Come and give your big brother a hug."

Tiffany remained immobile, frozen outside her front door. "What brings you here, Billy? I haven't heard from you since Des Moines. To what do I owe the pleasure of this visit? How the hell did you even know I was here?"

"Ma had your address. A Christmas card she had hanging around. You always were the family member with the holiday spirit." He gazed around the room. "Seems you sugar-coated your life in your letters to Ma. I was expecting, well, a bit more."

Billy reached out to touch the back of a chair. His eyes were more bloodshot than the last time she'd seen him. His youthful good looks were long cashed in.

"Gee, Billy. So sorry it's not up to your usual standards. I can book you in at the Hotel Hassler, if you prefer."

He smiled, revealing tobacco-stained teeth. "Now there, lil sis. Don't go gettin' all huffy. This'll do just fine. About time we caught up. Haven't seen you in ages. I been missing you."

"You'll be needing something."

"Can't a big brother stop by to see his sister if he's stopping through her city? What's all this suspicion?" He held out his arms like he used to, back when they were kids. But her little-sister worship had faded long ago.

"Why are you stopping through Rome now? Do you need money?"

"Always doubting me. I'm flush now, little sis. Surely Ma told you."

"Ma told me about the meth lab, and your jail time, but she never mentioned your new Trump-like status."

Billy shook his head and tucked one quivering hand under his elbow. "Water under the bridge, Tiff. A man can't be defined by his mistakes. I ran with a bad crowd for a while. I'm clean now. Paid my time. Running a legitimate operation out of Amsterdam now. Down here to meet with prospective investors."

She raised one eyebrow. "What kind of legitimate business?"

He evaded her gaze, smoothing down a crease in his jeans. "Ah, you know. Coffeehouses, appealing to the tourists. Nothing hard, all soft stuff, *perfectly legal* in Holland."

Tiffany shook her head, stepping into her apartment and gingerly closing her front door behind her. "You haven't changed one bit, Billy. Listen, I don't want to sound ungrateful. It's fantastic seeing you. I'm happy to invite you to dinner tomorrow, but let's find you some B&B where you can stay."

"But here's the thing. I don't want some anonymous B&B. I wanna stay with you. I was only giving you a hard time. Your place is great. I'll be fine here. I wanna be able to report back to Ma and Dad."

Her heart raced again. "Did they ask about me?"

"All the time." He smiled his yellow grin. "Dad's not lucid, most of the time. But he sends his love. Ma's reeling after Vincent left, but she's trying to keep the studio afloat. Asked me if I could convince you to come back and work there."

Tiffany snorted. "As if."

"Yeah, you always were too good for us, but that doesn't keep Ma from hoping you might come back one day."

"To Iowa? To Buffalo Plains? Ma only needs someone to fill in when she has a hangover. She never writes or calls. I have to call her on my own birthday, fishing for a greeting. She forgets half the time. What kind of mother is that?"

"Don't be hard on her. It wasn't easy on her."

"Not on me, either."

"Boxing gloves off. I don't speak for Ma. But I do want to see my sis and catch up on her fancy Eye-talian life. Come here, let me open you a beer."

"I see you raided my fridge."

He chuckled. "I remember you and your dancer's figure. I was doin' you a favor, lil sis. Not that you need any help. You're as slim as you were when you were sixteen."

Tiffany sighed. "I'm afraid I'll regret this, but you can stay. Have a beer and wait for me. I've been in rehearsals all day today, and I need a shower. Stay here. I'll be back in a few minutes, and I'll cook you some dinner."

"Sounds good, sis." He picked up the remote control and sank into the couch. "I'll wait here."

Freshly showered, Tiffany felt better able to face her brother. She slipped into a pair of well-worn jeans and a soft fleece sweater. She'd longed for silence and the chance to regroup. She would have to call Central Studio, and hoped no one had scooped up the dance class. She'd need the money.

The Giulianis, the neighbors upstairs, had been asking if she'd tutor little Eduardo in English. His mother claimed he was so gifted with languages, but was making no progress with the horrible teacher he'd been saddled with. Tiffany had tutored the boy a few afternoons when he was desperate before exams, and was convinced Shakespeare himself could return from the dead to teach Eduardo, and the boy would still make no progress. Still, beggars couldn't be choosers, and the boy was just upstairs. Lessons a few times a week would add to the cash flow needed to help meet rent. If she managed to pick up a few more modeling jobs, maybe hostessing at a few conferences, she might be back on track again.

She sat before her dresser mirror, combing her freshly washed hair into a high ponytail. She looked at her reflection, rubbing cream across her cheeks and under her eyes. Why did everything have to be so hard? Why couldn't she enjoy a stroke of luck? What a difference one little spot on some new show would make. If only things hadn't gone so wrong with Alessio back at that party, maybe she'd be dancing on *Olé olé* right now, sitting pretty as her bank account ticked up, not worrying about every single purchase.

She rubbed her eyes. Not tonight. She needed all her concentration with Billy here. How long did he intend to stay? What was he up to? She didn't buy the change of heart/newly flush story at all.

She averted her eyes from the mirror, and her gaze fell on the jewelry box. Her heart beat faster as she opened it, then calmed when she saw the emerald sparkle against the dark mahogany wood. Grandma's ring. Safe. Her gaze darted around the room for a safer hiding spot. Maybe she was overreacting, but her family had disappointed her so many times. She couldn't risk being gullible once again.

Lifting a delicate chain from the depths of the jewelry box, she threaded it through the ring, placed it around her neck, and tucked it safely under her fleece sweater. Out of sight, out of mind.

She heard laughter above the sound of the television. Sliding sore feet into her slippers, she stood and moved to the door. Two heads turned when she opened the door. Beside Billy's ravaged face, Simone's skin looked taut and golden. His hazel eyes sparkled with warmth. He gave her a wink.

"So this is the famous Billy."

Tiffany struggled not to show her confusion. In all the time she'd known Simone and Ramona, she'd worked hard to deflect their questions about her family. Their tight-knit families always left her feeling insecure. She brushed off their friendly attempts to draw her out, speaking in vague terms about her parents and Billy, making only passing references to Billy's troubled past.

And now, despite her best efforts, here sat Simone next to her lying, cheating, drug addict brother. She closed her eyes for a moment, then opened them and plastered on what she hoped was a believable smile. "Simone, I wasn't expecting you. Weren't you supposed to be in London with your class?"

He rolled his eyes. "Yes, I was." He gave an exaggerated sigh. "Alitalia strike." He stood up. "I didn't mean to interrupt, but I knocked, and Billy told me you were exhausted after rehearsals today." He searched her face. His eyes looked hopeful.

He knew about the final selection for the musical. She grimaced and shook her head slowly.

Turning away from Billy, Simone mouthed "I'm sorry." He slapped his palms on his jeans, turning to face them both. "I've been cooking, and it's way too much for one person. Why don't you come over for dinner? Billy, it would be a great opportunity to speak some more with you, hear what you're up to. And to get all the embarrassing stories about Tiffany growing up." He smiled. "It'll cheer me up about London being cancelled."

Tiffany paused. On the one hand, she preferred keeping Simone far from her messy family life. But on the other hand, she needed support. Who better than Simone? She knew he wouldn't judge her.

They followed Simone into his apartment, where the aroma of fish stewed in pacchino tomatoes, cooking over a bed of thinly sliced potatoes, filled the air. Her stomach growled. She'd only eaten a few rice cakes all day.

She sank gratefully into the chair when Simone signaled it to her, and poured her a glass of chilled Vermentino. As she sat beside Billy, sipping the wine as Simone puttered around the kitchen, it took her a moment to realize she was sitting in Ramona's former place. Ever since his ex-girlfriend left for Chicago, as if by some unspoken arrangement, the two of them had left the place free.

She absently answered some of Billy's questions, while stroking the stem of her wineglass. The whole atmosphere was charged, when all she longed for was to curl up in bed after a long day of disappointment.

Simone soon emerged with a seafood salad, and she forced a smile. Simone asked Billy questions about life in Amsterdam, and his business, but her brother was evasive with his answers. She felt a sinking feeling in her stomach as she watched Billy's gaze size up Simone's room. For the first time, she appraised it herself, ensuring nothing of value was too prominently displayed. The tense knots forming in her stomach caused even Simone's cooking to seem unpalatable.

The mood eased somewhat when the fish platter arrived on the table. Perhaps she'd just needed time to get used to having her brother in Rome—or else Simone was particularly attentive in filling her wineglass. Whatever the reason, tension began to dissolve from her body.

Billy was in full storyteller mode, regaling Simone with stories of their Iowa upbringing. Laughing along, even Tiffany was hard-pressed to determine how much was true. Listening to his tall tales of their hillbilly childhood unfold, she remembered how awed she was in his presence when they were children, how she'd loved to hear his stories. How she almost started believing them herself, even though everyone knew only about a quarter of what Billy said was true. At times, his facial expressions, a simple gesture of his hands, made her feel that same sense of pride, that same love she'd once felt for him.

The chatter continued through dinner, dessert and the *digestivo*. Billy put back glass after glass until she hardly knew how he could stand straight. When he excused himself to smoke a cigarette out on Simone's balcony, Simone scraped his chair closer to Tiffany's, and placed one warm hand over hers.

"I'm so sorry to hear about the musical." He whispered close to her ear. "I know how hard you worked on it, and I was so convinced this would be the one."

She laughed, a mirthless sound filling the room. "You and me both. I hadn't counted on one of the geriatric producers groping me backstage. My reaction dropped me out of the running."

He reeled back and shook his head. "Not again. Who *are* these people?"

He didn't move his hand away; he rubbed her hand in his. She felt a warm glow inside, one she hadn't felt in ages. He brought his face closer to hers, and she was aware of her quickened breaths as she smelled his familiar cologne, felt his shirt brush against her sweater.

"Am I interrupting something?" Billy stood at the doorway, swaying unsteadily, his eyes more bloodshot than they'd been earlier in the evening.

Simone snapped back, scraping his chair noisily away. "No, Billy. I was only comforting Tiff about a disappointment at work."

Billy leaned heavily on the doorframe. "Yeah, I bet you were comforting my sis all right. You'd hardly be the first. Tiff's had lots of *comforting* in her life, haven't you, little sis?"

Simone rose from his chair, hands balled into fists. She stroked his arm, and in a low voice whispered, "It's okay, Simone. It's been a long evening. I think Billy needs to sleep it off."

He looked at her, confused for a moment before he shook his head and relaxed his hands. He nodded. "You're right. Of course, I overreacted." He walked over to Billy, who seemed to have fallen asleep standing, and took him by the arm, leading him to the couch. "Billy, why don't you stay here tonight? Give your sister a rest this evening. I have an extra room."

Billy's head lolled onto the back cushion, and he began to snore.

"No point dragging him to your place and making up the couch. Help me move him into the guest bedroom."

Tiffany shook her head. "No, you've done more than enough. He's my brother, in the end. He must need something if he's come all this way."

"And you can handle all that tomorrow. You've had a bad day, and you need to rest tonight. He shouldn't have just showed up on your doorstep like that."

"What's family for?" She stood and walked over to her brother, looking down at him. His lifestyle aged him. He was only thirty, but he already looked decades older. "At least my family thinks that's what I'm for. An ATM when they're in need."

Simone stood and slid an arm around her shoulders, pulling her into his solid chest. Her stomach clenched, and she stepped from his embrace.

"You're sure?"

He nodded.

"How can I ever thank you?"

"You don't need to. I'm sorry your family has let you down in the past, but I'm your friend. I want you to trust me."

She leaned back into his embrace, her voice muffled in his chest. "I have no idea what I'd do without you." She stifled a sigh, before stepping back. "Okay, let me help you get him to bed, and he can sleep it off. He's a mean drunk—just like our dad."

Simone pulled Billy up, half dragging, half carrying him to the spare room. Tiffany rushed ahead, pulling down the soft, flannel sheets. Simone rested him on the bed, and she unlaced his sneakers, ignoring the holes in his socks and slipping his feet under the covers. She glanced around her, at the bookshelves lined with biology textbooks, and Italian and English classics. The moonlight spilled through the large French door. A balcony beckoned beyond, the same balcony Tiffany shared from her own apartment. She wondered if Billy would realize where he was when he woke. How was his life in Amsterdam? She felt certain he didn't pass his time in comfortable rooms like this. She pushed back the sleeve to his ragged sweater, rubbing her fingers across the fresh track marks. The tears welled up in her eyes.

Simone ushered a small cough from the doorway. She pulled the sleeve back down, and pulled the sheet and comforter high up on her brother's neck. She placed a gentle kiss on his forehead. Turning to Simone, she willed her expression to be untroubled.

"He's lucky to have a sister like you."

"I don't know about that. We haven't even been in touch these past years."

"It doesn't matter. I see how much you love him." He grasped her shoulders and maneuvered her to the front door. "Now, go home and sleep. You must be exhausted after the auditions."

"*Grazie*, Simone." She kissed him on the cheeks. Opening her front door, she hoped she could make it to her bed before collapsing.

The pounding grew louder, the voice calling her name more insistent. She shifted in her bed, anxious to slip back into a deep sleep.

But the pounding continued, and she opened one eye. Sunlight tumbled through the open window. She shivered at the rush of cold air, sitting up in confusion as she realized the pounding on her door was not a dream. Her heart raced.

"Tiffany! Tiff, open up!"

She pulled the covers to her chest. "Simone? What are you doing here?"

"Tiff, just open the door."

She swung her legs over the edge of the bed, shivering as a blast of cool air blew in from the open window. She rubbed her eyes and snapped back the lock. Simone filled the doorframe, a wild look in his eyes. Involuntarily, she stepped back.

"Thank God you're okay, and that you locked your bedroom door. Nothing's been touched in the rest of the apartment."

A wave of dizziness washed over her and she stumbled back to the bedroom and slumped down, resting against the headboard. She looked down, surprised to see she was still wearing her jeans and sweater. She'd fallen straight into her bed. "You're not making any sense. Why wouldn't I be okay?"

He sat down on her bed, taking her hands in his. "It's ... uh ... Billy. He's gone."

"What do you mean gone?" Her voice was loud to her own ears. She took a breath. "Maybe he got up early and went to get a cup of coffee."

Simone took a deep breath. When he spoke, his voice was strangled. "Your brother is long gone. Trust me." He squeezed her hand harder. "He trashed my apartment."

"What? How?" Panic coursed through her body.

"There was a handkerchief next to my bed. Chloroform. Outwitted a science teacher with chloroform. The oldest trick in the book for train thieves in Italy. I wasn't as smart as you. I didn't think to lock my door."

She breathed deeply. "What did he take?"

His gaze fell down to her comforter. "About 500 euro I had in my dresser. A Montblanc pen my father gave me for graduation." He swallowed hard. "And a watch my grandfather gave me before he died."

The tears streamed down Tiffany's face. "The bastard. It's all my fault ..."

His eyes met hers. "No, Tiff. It's not. You're not responsible for your brother's behavior."

She spoke through her sobs. "But I know what he is. What he's capable of. I should have stopped you yesterday when you invited him to stay. I wanted to believe he'd changed somewhat, and I was so tired. I just wanted to come home and sleep ..." She dissolved into sobs.

He shifted over on the bed and wrapped her into his arms. "It's okay."

"It's *not* okay! What have I done?"

"Shh."

He pulled her in tightly, stroking her hair. She could feel his heart beating against her chest. Her breath was still erratic, but his touch and his embrace made her feel safe and protected.

"It's not your fault, Tiff. You could have shipped him off to some hotel, but he would have found a way back anyway. I won't lie and say I'm not upset about the watch. I loved my grandpa, and it reminded me of him. But I'll survive." He rocked her gently. "You know I don't care that much about possessions. I'm only glad he didn't get to you in the end." He sat back and stroked her face.

Her tears were steady, but her sobbing stopped. His warm fingers felt comforting on her face. His face moved closer to hers, and his warm breath tickled her cheeks. She narrowed the distance between them, pleading with her eyes. His gaze dropped to the ground. He moved away and reached down to the ground, picking up a handkerchief. He sniffed it and his eyes flashed in anger. "Chloroform."

She startled at the force of his voice. "But—how?" A gust of air rushed in.

He turned back. "Was that window open when I came in?"

She felt the panic well up again. Her mind raced. "Uh ... yes. But I always close the window at night. With our balcony ..." Her voice trailed off and she leapt from the bed and raced to the window. "The balcony," she whispered. The tool marks were clear on the window frame. The window had been forced by someone on the balcony. By Billy on the balcony.

In a panic, she spun around. She clutched a wild hand over her chest. Not feeling anything, she tore her sweater over her head, not caring that Simone stood before her as she bared her chest. She stared down uncomprehendingly at her naked breasts. She hadn't removed her necklace last night before falling into bed. With a cry of anguish, she sank down to the floor.

"My grandmother's ring. He stole it." Her words dissolved into uncontrollable sobs. "The only thing of value I ever had. Will ever have. It was all I had to prove I was special to someone."

Her cries grew louder as the crisp November breeze swept over her bare back.

CHAPTER 18

Annarita

Annarita slammed the front door, ripped her heels off, and threw them across the room. The only thing her crap apartment had going for it was the freshly painted walls. She hardly needed to ruin even that with shoe marks, but it had been that kind of night.

She knew she shouldn't have listened to Debbie when she said she had the perfect man for her. She should have refused the blind date.

When the man, a good twenty years her senior but pretending to be in his late thirties, showed up, she should have found an excuse. As they waited for their table in the bar and he cried on her shoulder about the fiancée who left him, and how he'd done everything to win her back, she'd stared over his head at the clock, lamenting all the time she'd never be able to reclaim.

But when they stood to go to the table and he'd pinched her rear and said he'd love to get lucky later that night to get his mind off his ex, that had been the final straw. She followed the waitress to the table, excused herself to go to the women's room, and never looked back.

And here she was. Alone at home at nine on a Saturday night. Forty euro poorer after the hairdresser's appointment, although the Bangladeshi manning the convenience store under her apartment had winked at her and told her she was looking particularly hot that evening.

So went the story of her life.

In her room, she slipped the Marina Rinaldi dress off. Despite her anger, she was careful to place it gently on its silk hanger. She pulled on worn flannel pajamas, and slipped her aching feet into soft slippers.

She caught her reflection in the mirror, slumping into middle-aged frumpiness. But as she appraised the luster of her curls, the way they sprang softly as she shook her head, she couldn't help but smile. Her hairdresser really could work miracles. Too bad she couldn't afford to visit her often. Too bad she couldn't afford anything, really.

On Monday, she'd call her language school and offer to take on extra classes. The private lessons were going well, but students cancelled all the time, and she needed a steady flow of income.

Flicking off her bedroom light, she returned to the living room. She opened the freezer in her kitchen corner, pulling out the hazelnut ice cream. *Why the hell not?* After the date hell she'd been through—again—she more than deserved it. She slumped onto the couch, eating straight from the container.

Her cellphone rang, and she plucked it from the side table. Debbie displayed on the screen. The dream date had probably called and complained about her running off. He'd have omitted the ex-girlfriend saga and his attempts to get lucky that evening, and Annarita wasn't in the mood. How could her friend have done this to her in the first place? She let it ring and dug into her ice cream again.

Her friends were great. They really were. She knew they were only trying to help. But they were all happily paired up, and wasting their energy trying to find a boyfriend for her. For the first time in her life, Annarita didn't feel the need for a man in her life. She couldn't handle more disastrous blind dates. She thought back to Sperlonga. Emma and Tiffany didn't have men in their lives, and they seemed happy and fulfilled.

Emma and Tiffany.

Since she'd been back in Rome, Annarita had been insistent about getting together. Okay, she'd probably sounded needy, inviting them to concerts and theater performances, suggesting girls' nights out. She sensed their hesitation.

Emma always had something conflicting—activities with the kids, fundraisers. The last time she'd called Tiffany she'd sounded distant, saying she was recuperating from her brother's visit. Okay, on that count Annarita could commiserate. Family visits were always enough to leave her running for cover for at least a week after their departure. But during that phone call, she could sense Tiffany's eagerness to get off the phone.

The deep friendship Annarita had been certain would materialize following their return to Rome never took off. This time, she'd go for casual. Coffee—tomorrow, even. Half an hour, forty minutes at most. A low-grade commitment. San Teodoro was near Emma's house. She knew the perfect little café. How could Emma say no to such a short outing?

Convincing Tiffany first would probably be easier. She'd sensed something in her voice the last time she'd called. A sadness. A beautiful girl like Tiffany was certain to be surrounded by friends, but sometimes a new acquaintance was what the doctor ordered. Hadn't they had fun together, back in Sperlonga? Why couldn't they do the same now that they were back?

She picked up her cellphone, scrolling down to Tiffany's number. *Keep it light*, she coached herself. Just a quick get-together for coffee and a chat tomorrow afternoon. *Don't sound needy and pathetic.* It's only a casual suggestion, not something she was counting on or anything.

"Hi, Tiffany. It's Annarita, from Sperlonga. Hope I'm not disturbing you. I was wondering if you might be free for a coffee tomorrow. Maybe I could call Emma and make it all three of us ..."

It was one of those November days in Rome that seemed more like June. The tourists were thrilled to perform an elaborate strip tease, joyously peeling off layers of clothes to luxuriate in the feel of late autumn sunshine warming their skin as they walked through San Teodoro's cobblestoned streets.

Annarita passed the farmers' market, with hordes of well-heeled Romans and tourists following guidebook instructions, all queued up to buy organic meat and vegetables, cheese fresh from the Sabine Hills, wines bottled in Frascati, and crusty bread baked that morning, dense with olives. The market was tempting, but expensive. She couldn't afford the yuppy prices.

As if on cue, she spotted her student Tommaso at the cheese counter, with a leggy blonde on his arm. It was clear they weren't fresh out of morning mass. The supermodel lookalike was painted into a slinky dress Annarita assumed she'd worn the night before. The walk of shame through the neighborhood organic market. That was a new one.

Annarita hurried by before Tommaso could spot her. Lessons with him tomorrow afternoon was enough contact to endure. She wasn't paid for the odd run-in.

She continued down Via San Teodoro, dodging through the throngs of French and German tourists. She turned left onto Via dei Fienile, veering right when the road forked. The buildings were the yellows and burnt oranges of Rome. The honeysuckle crept up their exterior. The flowers were all dormant now, but in May the tiny white petals would blossom and fill the neighborhood with their fragrant perfume. Annarita always lingered in the streets of San Teodoro after her classes with Tommaso when the honeysuckle was in bloom.

The sign for Café Teodoro announced the meeting place she'd arranged. She took an outside seat, with a view over the Conciliazione church. As she sat in the warm sunshine waiting for the others to arrive, she observed the church's roof, seeing how grasses and weeds grew from its rooftop tiles, sprouting out around the saints. Even after all these years in Rome, these little glimpses into the real Rome convinced her that life for her was tied up with this crazy, chaotic, beautiful city.

Even if her love life remained a disaster.

"Hello, Annarita."

Emma stood before her, resplendent in a light grey cashmere sweater, a pencil skirt and suede Tod's shoes. This woman couldn't possibly own a hoodie and a pair of sweats. They'd look so out of place on her. Her blonde hair fell in glamorous 1940s-era diva waves, framing her face. Large sunglasses, designed to keep the paparazzi guessing, concealed her eyes.

Annarita jumped up, kissing Emma on each suntanned cheek. "I'm so glad you could come! I've been thinking of you so often after Sperlonga."

Was she gushing? Maybe she was, but she couldn't completely hide her enthusiasm.

Emma waited a few moments too long before responding.

"And I've been thinking of you and Tiffany. Such a nice surprise when you called last night." She looked at her watch. "I don't have too much time—theatre tickets tonight—but I'm glad we can catch up."

So Annarita was simply shoehorned in, when meeting Emma and Tiffany was the highlight of her day, maybe even her week. No matter. She smiled broadly. "I just love it here."

Emma sat down, smoothing her skirt. "So do I. I meet my friend Sabrina here quite often for coffee. Can you believe today? Christmas is only a month away."

"I know. What will you be doing? Do you and the kids go back to the States?"

"No, we don't travel much for the holidays. We have to divvy up Christmas Eve and Christmas between my house and their father's family, but it all works out well in the end. Dario, my ex, will take the kids up for some days for skiing in Cortina. I always prefer avoiding that crowd."

Annarita would have imagined Emma fitting right in with that crowd. She smiled. "Skiing sounds heavenly. Not that I've ever been. Usually I go home for the holidays, but airline tickets were sky-high this year, so I'll stay put."

A shadow fell over the table. Both women looked up to see Tiffany dressed in tight jeans, boots, and a soft suede jacket. Her hair was tucked up in a neat French braid hanging down her back. Her smile was broad as she greeted them, but her eyes looked tired.

They all sat together in the November sunshine, talking about Sperlonga, examining the menu, lamenting the fact that it was too early for the cocktails when they had other plans for the evening. Annarita chose not to volunteer that drinks in the afternoon would not be problematic for her, since her only plans for afterwards were a date with her couch and her remote control.

Pots of tea and a plate of *mignons* were brought to the table.

"Tiffany," said Annarita, pointing to her ring finger. "I was hoping to see your grandmother's beautiful ring. But I suppose you don't like to go out walking in Rome with something so valuable on your finger."

Tiffany reeled as if she'd been slapped. Her eyes appeared to fill with tears. Or might it be the effect of the bright sunlight? Tiffany sipped her tea, her hand trembling ever so slightly.

"I'm sorry if I said something wrong."

"No, but it's a little upsetting." Tiffany took a deep breath. "There've been a few break-ins in my apartment building and ... I felt safer putting my jewelry away in a safe deposit box."

Emma shook her head. "Such a shame, all the theft in Rome. That's wise, Tiffany. You'd never forgive yourself if you lost something so valuable."

Tiffany coughed, and her tea splattered onto the table. She looked stricken. "How clumsy of me. It was so hot. I burned my tongue."

Annarita helped her wipe the table with a napkin. Afterwards, she took a sip of her own tea, which had cooled quickly. She gazed up at Tiffany from below her thick eyelashes, but she seemed to focus on a distant point over the roof of the church.

"Emma," ventured Annarita, "last time we spoke to you, you were meeting an old schoolmate of yours. How did it go?"

Emma looked up, surprised. "Oh, you mean Mark. Yes, lovely seeing him after such a long time. He hasn't changed a bit. Why is it men are always so lucky on that count?"

"Didn't you say he was investing in some hotel?"

"Yes. You remembered that? An aunt left him an old place out in Umbria. He's dragging me up to take a look at it. I'm supposed to help him decide if it's hopeless, or if it has potential as an agriturismo."

"Sounds exciting." Annarita felt she was grasping at straws, but the atmosphere was more tense than during the days they'd spent in Sperlonga. She felt a desperate need to keep conversation humming. "You know, since I returned, I've thought a lot about our time at the Albergo Paradiso, about movie night with *Three Coins*."

Tiffany laughed. "Yeah, me too. I'm often wandering around Rome and I think of some scene from the film. I was up on the Gianicolo last week, looking at all those villas and wishing I could scoop one up for a song, too."

"We should watch it again sometime. My place is nothing like where Anita, Maria and Fran live, but you're welcome to come over sometime for dinner and the film. Signora Renata shared some recipes with me. I'm sure they're not as good as when she cooks them, but they're still pretty impressive."

"You shouldn't always put yourself down like that. I'm sure you're a great cook," said Tiffany. "Sounds like fun. I'd enjoy that sometime. Anyway, I was hoping not to be in Rome much over the next few months. I auditioned for a part in a musical going on tour nationally, but it fell through."

"I'm sorry you didn't get it," said Emma.

"How could they have found anyone better than you? I would have gone on the road to see you," said Annarita.

"Thanks. Maybe I'll be luckier next time. But it does mean I can manage a dinner and movie night sometime."

"Well then, I'll check next week to see if there's a day that works for both of you."

"Great," said Emma, pulling her wallet from her purse. "Then we'll have the chance to see one another fairly soon. It makes me feel less guilty that I have to leave. Let me at least take care of the check." She signaled the waitress. "And you two can stay on."

"Oh, but I have to get back, too. I hadn't realized how late it is. Are you headed back past Circo Massimo?"

"I'm headed there, too. Let's all go together. There's something I want to show you along the way," said Annarita.

They split the bill and walked together through San Teodoro, turning onto Via dei Cerchi. At a certain point, Annarita stopped. "Here it is. Here's the plaque I saw a few weeks ago. Any idea what it is?"

Emma bent down and read the engraved words. "*Mi sono perso. 17 September 2010* ... I've never noticed this before. Why would a modern day plaque be put up to announce that someone is lost?"

"I couldn't figure it out either. I was hoping one of you might know."

"All we know for sure is it's a male who wrote this," said Tiffany. "Even I can catch that it's the masculine form with my bad Italian grammar. Anyway, a woman would never announce it to the world on a plaque. Let's hope he found himself."

Annarita smiled to herself. "Maybe he did."

They continued walking to the Circo Massimo metro, the sun warming them as they chatted. Annarita continued to think of the plaque, hoping the mysterious stranger had indeed found his way in Rome.

CHAPTER 19

Emma

The sun poked out behind the clouds, but the breeze was strong. Todi's church bell chimed through the ancient cobblestoned streets. Emma pulled her pashmina more firmly around her shoulders, watching the old men chatting in clusters, the women hurrying by, rolling their bags full of fruits and vegetables from the market.

"You were brilliant in there, Emma." Mark paused when the waitress returned with their cappuccinos. "How on earth would I have managed building permits, and cutting through all the red tape without you? Where would I even have started looking around at building contractors?"

"Don't flatter me too much. You haven't seen them work yet."

"You know what I mean. You're shivering."

"It's nothing." She sipped her cappuccino. "Better already."

He stood and walked to the other side of the table. He took off his jacket and slipped it over her shoulders. Instead of moving away, he leaned in, his light stubble tickling her cheek. He whispered in her ear. "You see, I'd give you the shirt off my back."

She felt an involuntary shiver down her spine, grateful he couldn't see her face. She composed herself as he moved back to his place.

"Technically, the jacket off your back, but thank you. Much warmer. Back to business, Mark. You know I've been happy to help out, but I'm sure you can take it from here."

His blue eyes shone in amusement as he shook his head. "But I can't, Emma. It should be obvious that I'm hopelessly lost without you. I won't let you get away this time. I want to hire you, pay you a salary, have you as my project manager. You name your price."

"But it's absurd. You need someone on-site, and I need to be home for the children. I can't be up here all the time."

"I've thought about that, and we can fit this all around your needs. I won't need you here every day. What do you say about two times a week? I'm sure you can handle things by phone the other days. And you don't need to drive. You can take the train up and I'll pick you up with the car. You'll be back in time for the kids."

"Why?"

He pushed his cup aside and leaned across the table. "I need you. I'm here in a strange land." He smiled. "You can help me get through this smoothly. I need hand-holding. I need to feel I'm not going to get ripped off because I'm a foreigner. I need you to speak to the planning boards like you did back there." He cocked his head and examined her closely. "You're the same as when I knew you back at Georgetown. You may have taken some time off in your career, but you could jump back in in a heartbeat, if you wanted to."

Emma laughed. "What planet are you living on? Twenty years is hardly some time off to reflect. Kind of hard to brush over a gaping hole like that on the job resume."

"Maybe I'll get lucky and it'll turn out you like the hospitality business. I want to make this a guest home that can attract Italian and European clientele. I want it to be elegant, but authentic—all local foods and wines, cooking classes, maybe even Italian and English classes, sports and local activities. I want it to be a place where people come for an escape, a place they're longing to return to each year. I know you can help with that authenticity." He winked. "You can help with the elegance, too."

"Mark, I'm flattered. But I'm sure you could get someone with better experience, someone who knows the hospitality industry."

"But I want to work with you. I've worked with the hospitality industry before. I can handle the figures, the budgets; I have a good idea about the costs and commitment involved. But I need you to make sure I'm staying true to the Italian lifestyle. You know what Italians and foreigners want when they're coming here." He twisted his empty cup in his hands. "And, I admit it, I'm selfish. After over twenty years of not seeing you, I'd like to spend some time together."

Her heart thumped in her chest. Part of her was flattered, but the other part, the sensible one, was horrified. "And Lieke? What does she think of all this? She can't like the fact that you're asking an old friend, and a divorcée at that, to help you out."

He opened his mouth to speak, then seemed to change his mind. He glanced around him for a moment, at life unfolding before them on the streets of Todi. Slowly, he turned to her, meeting her gaze. "I've told her all about you. Told her I'd be lucky if you'd decide to work with me on this. She wants this to work out, wants me to have the best people who can make that happen."

"But she can't be happy having you far away from her and the girls for so much time."

He drummed his long fingers on the table. His wedding band gleamed in the sunlight. Self-consciously, Emma touched the place on her ring finger where hers used to rest. For a long time after she removed it, she continued to feel its weight.

The activity around them continued. Todi was alive with the chattering of its residents, the delivery carts clattering noisily over the cobblestones, the women hollering hellos to friends up at windows above. But the silence at the table was deafening.

"Lieke's okay with it," he said quietly. "But I miss the girls."

"I imagine you do."

He reached across the table, taking her hand in his. She fought the urge to pull it away. His large hand over her own felt too warm, too comforting. Even if she'd never act on them, she hated the feelings his nearness stirred up in her. She knew the consequences. She'd suffered them.

"Please say yes, Emma. I need you."

She inhaled sharply. The rational side of her brain was screaming out for her to refuse. She wouldn't act on anything, but her heart would still feel trampled. Did she need to suffer any more emotional dramas? Hadn't her heart been through enough over the past years? Wasn't it time to settle in and accept how things were?

But Mark was offering her a chance. It wasn't only about working with him. She'd been home so long, she'd forgotten what it was like to be out in the world, taking charge of work and projects. She *could* do this. How many employers would offer her such flexibility, the chance to dip her feet back in without the pressure of long hours and proving herself to a new employer?

Why not?

She met his gaze, those bright blue eyes with their spark of hope. She smiled. "*Sì* it is. Hope we won't both wind up regretting this."

"Never, my darling Emma. This will be perfect." He looked around for their waitress. "This calls for a celebration." He signaled the woman. "Two glasses of *prosecco*." He turned back to Emma. "You won't regret this, I promise."

She hoped he was right.

The waitress returned with their flutes. He waited until she picked hers up, before raising his. "We'll always have Todi, my dear. Here's to the start of a beautiful friendship."

She looked at him quizzically, and he laughed.

"I know, I'm mixing up lines and characters. My girls say I'm hopeless."

"No, it's a good sentiment. Here's to the start of a beautiful friendship. I can toast to that." She clinked her glass against his.

The glint was back in his eye. He reached down and plucked out the map of the agroturismo. "I'm thinking about placing the pool here. There's such a great view over the town from this point. It would be the perfect place to gather guests for drinks at sunset. What do you think?"

She leaned her head in and they studied the map together. The Todi clock tower chimed the hour throughout the medieval streets as a blonde and dark head touched, their faces low and close together as they discussed the transformations they planned to oversee just beyond the edge of the ancient Umbrian town.

CHAPTER 20

Tiffany

Corso Vannucci could have been Broadway for all the time it took to walk its length.

The street was the main drag for the *passeggiata* in little Perugia, decked out with sparkling Christmas lights and a gentle dusting of snow. Every time she, Simone, his sisters and parents walked more than five meters, a cry would ring out, directed at one of the family members. There was always an old classmate of Simone's or his sisters, someone from his mother's school, someone with a question for Simone's physician father, a neighbor requesting help for this or that committee, or some church benefit.

Each time, Tiffany would be introduced proudly as Simone's American neighbor from Rome who was visiting for the holidays. She would be greeted and pampered, asked how she was enjoying Perugia, whether she was eating well. Her Italian would be complimented, even though she knew this was a polite lie the townspeople offered her.

In the brief moment after they left one townsperson and before they were accosted by the next, Simone would link his arm in hers, smile and tell her how well she was holding up under the scrutiny of the town busybodies.

She'd chuckle good-naturedly, but Simone had no reason for worrying. She was born and raised in a small town, bred to this friendliness and the environment in which everyone knew everyone else. Sometimes she missed that in anonymous Rome.

Ever since arriving in Perugia yesterday, she'd been embraced by his family. They chatted with her, fussed over her, insisted on feeding her, and told her to spill all of Simone's secrets now that he'd deserted Perugia. Simone's sisters, Anna and Tiziana, had claimed her immediately, chatting about American movies and music, asking her to go out to holiday parties with them.

Simone pouted and joked about his baby sisters stealing his friends. They shot back that someone like Tiffany deserved a better class of friend, and he retorted with a look of exaggerated hurt. "Stop stifling the poor girl," he'd tell them.

But truth be told, Tiffany had never before felt part of such a close-knit family. She envied them their closeness, their teasing, their laughter and jokes. She loved how they gathered around the table and spoke over one another. She envied their affectionate teasing. This was the family she'd always wanted. The family she'd often conjured up in her mind when her parents got drunk and went on a hollering spree, when she raced to her bed and pretended to be asleep in order to avoid the vicious crossfire.

She sat at the table and smiled on them all. Seeing Simone in his home only made her appreciate him more. Now she fully understood his kindness. He'd grown up surrounded by it, and it was in his nature to offer it to others.

She wondered if Ramona had been a frequent guest at his parents' home. If so, how had she ever gathered the courage to leave them all behind when she moved to Chicago?

They passed a jewelry store window display. She paused to admire the emeralds glittering under the Christmas lights.

"Aw, Tiff. I wish I could afford to replace your ring. You know I'd do it in a heartbeat if I could. You must miss it."

She turned to him, patting his nose that had grown rosy with the cold. "No, I'm fine. I only notice them when I pass shop windows, but it's a bad habit. Mostly I prefer to forget about it."

He led her away and they continued to walk behind her family. "Are you sure you want to go out dancing with my sisters tonight? I thought we could go to a concert, and then out to dinner. Just the two of us."

She turned to him. "But your mother would be so angry with me. She said she's cooking tonight and inviting your neighbors. And Tiziana wants me to meet the new man she's interested in. He's asked her out, but she's been putting him off. She needs another woman's opinion."

His explosive laugh rang out through the streets of Perugia. "Twenty-four hours here, and you're already part of the family. Next you'll be telling me you're baking cakes with my mother for the church benefit."

"I thought you wanted me to like them. You see, it was no trouble at all. You're lucky to have such a wonderful family, to come from such a special place."

He squeezed her arm tighter into his side. "It's even more special having you here. I'm glad you could come. I never thought I'd actually get you here."

"Don't you miss living here? I think if I grew up in a place like this, I'd never leave."

Simone laughed. "Listen to you. One day in Perugia, and your small-town roots come back. I think we're more alike than you realize. I think we must both have a bit of gypsy blood in us. I know how much you love Rome, the crowds, the excitement. I feel the same. Yeah, it's great to be back, but after too long I miss the city."

"Maybe you're right." She looked up and pointed. "Oh, Simone. Look! *La neve*! Snow." The snow was drifting down in slow, weak patterns, but everyone looked up, and children started to squeal. "Thank you for inviting me." She kissed his cheek, and they set off, only to be stopped by an old soccer teammate of Simone's who wanted to catch up on old times.

"Oh, no. Thank you, Signora Bordonaro. I couldn't eat another bite."

"Please call me Livia. How many times have I asked you, Tiffany?"

"I'm sorry, Livia. This has been such a feast. I've never had such a delicious Christmas dinner."

She stood alongside Simone to clear away the dishes. Simone's mother tried to stop them, but Simone insisted. He picked up the serving plate containing the remnants of the *orata*. They'd worked their way through several seafood plates that evening, and Tiffany could feel her pants button straining at her waist. In the kitchen, she patted her waistline self-consciously.

"Oh, please," said Simone, setting down dishes. "Don't tell me my mother's cooking has ruined your figure. You know I think you're perfect. An extra kilo or two would do you some good."

"Now at least I know where you developed your skills in the kitchen. Your mom's a fabulous cook."

"And you haven't even tried dessert yet."

Tiffany groaned.

"If you want, we can go out for a jog tomorrow."

"I'd never be able to keep up with you."

"*Mia cara*. You know I'd wait for you."

Anna entered with a tray of dishes. She shot her brother a sharp look, before breaking out into a smile. "Always the flirt.

Tiffany, you're way too good for our brother, but Tiziana and I like you. And we've *never* liked anyone Simone's brought home. Have pity on us. Date him."

Simone snapped her with a dish towel. "Anna, you little pain in the neck. Get out. She hasn't changed since she was a little twerp playing pranks on her teenage brother."

Anna stuck her tongue out at her brother before returning to the dining room.

He took her hands in his. "Don't listen to her. They know we're only friends."

Her stomach clenched. In disappointment? Wasn't friendship what she wanted? Being on Simone's home turf was playing tricks on her brain, weakening her resolve about the well-heeled boyfriend with television connections she was convinced she needed.

"I hope you won't kill me, but my family would love for you to join us at midnight mass. I told them it didn't make sense, that you weren't even Catholic. They don't want to pressure you, but I promised I would ask."

"Oh, but of course I'll come. They've been so kind, made me feel so welcome. And it's such a small thing to ask. I won't have any clue what to do, but you'll help me, won't you?"

He raised up her hand and kissed her knuckles. "You'll be perfect." He pulled her to the door. "Now come. It's time for *mamma*'s dessert, and *papà*'s homemade grappa. You'll have to tell him you love it, a little lie we all perpetuate. Luckily, he only makes it once a year."

She smiled and allowed herself to be dragged into the family embrace. They ate and drank, opened presents, laughed and joked—did all the things she'd dreamed families did when she lay alone as a child in her narrow bed after another family holiday debacle.

Glancing around the living room, with wrapping paper strewn across the floor, the love and affection was palpable.

And she was grateful to be a part of it, even if for just one evening.

Watching Simone open presents, the handsome lines of his face concentrated as he ripped open the paper, his hazel eyes glowing as he laughed with his family, she realized how lucky she was to have him as a neighbor and friend. How lucky she was he'd invited her into his life.

"Tu scendi dalle stelle, o Re del cielo; E vieni in una grotta al freddo e al gelo ..."

The voices of the parishioners filled the cavernous cathedral. This Italian Christmas song was new to her, although she'd heard it sung on Roman streets by school children in past Christmas seasons.

Simone stood to her left, squeezed tightly against her. He was tall and handsome in his grey cashmere overcoat, a gift from his mother. She felt the warmth of his arm pressed against her. It gave her confidence. Never much of a churchgoer in her family, she felt even more alien with the Catholic rituals—uncertain when to sit or stand, when to pray or sing. But she basked in the sense of community, the following of rituals passed on from generation to generation. She felt a warm glow inside as she observed the flickering lights of the candles, the ornate carving of the nativity scene on the altar, the vaulted ceiling and delicate frescoes. She breathed in deeply, the pungent smell of incense mixing with the heady scent of Simone's cologne.

All these people gathered at midnight to mark the birth of the baby Jesus. The exhaustion she'd felt earlier in the evening dissipated as soon as she walked into the church with the Bordonaro family and began greeting their neighbors and friends. Simone kept his arm fully anchored around her shoulders, ferrying her from one acquaintance to another.

On her right, Tiziana stood beside her, smirking whenever she got a line wrong from the prayer book, rolling her eyes when Tiffany flubbed a hymn. "Let's hope you make a better dancer than a singer," she'd whispered in her ear, and Tiffany felt her cheeks burn, while still feeling proud to be the object of this little-sister-style of teasing.

When the mass ended, Simone tucked her arm through his and followed his family down the aisle. He shook the priest's hand, introducing him to Tiffany.

"Ah, the famous *americana* I've been hearing is visiting Simone. Tell me, is this young man giving you a positive impression of Perugia?"

"Oh, yes, Father. I'm not sure I want to return to Rome. It's so beautiful here."

His booming laugh ricocheted around the church. "That's what all the young people say, before they hightail it to Rome." He jabbed a finger at Simone. "Take my former altar boy here. We were so proud of him when he went off to the university in Rome, but don't you think Perugia would welcome back one of its own to teach biology at our high school?"

"Okay, Father. Now you're embarrassing me."

"Hmm, I know when I'm being shushed." He winked at Tiffany. "Maybe one day a nice woman will convince him to come back and settle in this family-friendly community. Ah, I see you're both blushing now. Very well, I'll wish you a *Buon Natale*. Enjoy your time with us, and come back soon."

"Thank you, Father. And *Buon Natale* to you, too."

They walked out into the bracing night air, chatting with other parishioners on the bustling piazza as the church bells echoed through the ancient streets of Perugia.

Simone's family walked home, their breath visible in the cold night air. As they turned onto their street, a light but steady snow began to flutter down from the sky. A squeal rose from Simone's sisters.

"A white Christmas! Oh, you'll love it, Tiff. The town is so pretty covered with fresh snow."

By the time they reached the house, its comforting warmth was welcome.

"Will you be up a while longer? Should I start the fire?" asked Simone's father.

"Don't worry, *papà*. You must be exhausted. I'd like to watch the snow a bit, but if we stay up late, I can start the fire myself."

"Of course, of course. Good night."

"Good night, *papà*."

"Good night, Mr. Bordonaro."

"Well, lovebirds, I think that Tiziana and I are going to call it a night, too. See you tomorrow morning."

"It is tomorrow morning."

"Always the smart aleck, Simone. Night, Tiff!"

"*Buona notte, ragazze*."

When everyone had gone upstairs, Simone went to the liquor cabinet and poured two glasses. He handed one to Tiffany, placing a finger to his lips. "Shh, not my father's grappa. This is the good stuff." He clinked his glass against hers. "To Christmas in Perugia."

"To Christmas in Perugia. How can I ever thank you for inviting me? I love it here, and I love being with your family."

"I'm just glad I got you here. I know it's been a tough year on you."

She sighed. "Tough doesn't even begin to describe it."

He turned to the staircase. "Get your coat on," he whispered. He opened an armoire, taking a heavy blanket from its depth. "Let's take our drinks outside and watch the snow."

She laughed. "Really? Won't we freeze out there?"

"It's hardly Mount Everest. I'll keep you warm. C'mon. I never have you to myself here. I want to talk before we head off to sleep. Tomorrow will be the big family lunch, then the neighbors and friends will all stop by for drinks and cards, and I'll have to share you with everyone else."

Tiffany slipped on her coat and a warm, wool hat. "Okay, if you insist. But I'm back inside at the first sign of frostbite."

Simone turned on the front light and led her to a bench positioned on the edge of the old stone house. She'd loved the house the moment she'd seen it, with its honey-colored stones and green shutters, the garden outside and a view of the cathedral in the distance. She could picture Simone and his sisters growing up here, walking the short distance to Corso Vannucci, meeting up with friends to play soccer on the piazza, running to the church on Sunday mornings to serve as altar boy.

"Maybe your priest is right. Why did you ever leave here?"

He sat down next to her on the bench and placed the thick blanket over them. He put one arm around her, squeezing her into him for warmth. They both sipped their grappa to feel the warm, burning sensation work its way down their throats.

"I actually did plan on coming back. I wanted to teach biology at my old high school. But I met Ramona at the university, and she never liked Perugia. Always called it provincial. She kept me in Rome." He looked up at the snowflakes gathering speed. "But I must admit, Rome grew on me, too. I feel at home in both. But eventually, when I settle down and have a family, I think I could be tempted to come back."

"So your parish priest is on to something." She smiled at him. "Altar boy, huh? You never told me."

He laughed, his eyes crinkling up in their familiar way. "A good, Catholic boy. How could you not have guessed that about me?"

She felt her stomach flip. Snuggled against him, the heat from his body managed to stave off the cold. The snowflakes hurtled down, forming a thick, white carpet on the grass. Tomorrow morning the town would be magical.

She touched the watch on his wrist. "I hope you really do like it. I obviously couldn't make it up to you. What Billy did. I didn't have the money for a Swiss watch like your grandfather's, but I told the salesman you were preparing for the Roma-Ostia half-marathon. He convinced me you'd love the stopwatch function for your training."

He placed a warm hand on her cheek. "I do love it, Tiff, and I'll love training with this. You didn't have to get me anything. It wasn't your fault, what happened. I wish you'd stop feeling guilty about it."

"But I do." A tear slipped from her eye, working its way down her frosty skin. "How could I not? I let him in. I let you offer to have him stay at your place. I *knew* what he was." Another tear slid down, and he reached up with his thumb to wipe it away. She longed to grab his hand and kiss it, but instead closed her eyes and took a deep breath. "I'm so stupid where Billy's concerned. I keep hoping he's changed. But he'll never change. Your watch, your pen, my ..." She sucked in her breath "... my grandmother's ring. All stolen for a few hits for Billy, and probably whoever he's crashing with these days. How can he keep sucker-punching me like this? What the hell is wrong with me to fall for it?"

"Shhh." His face came closer. His eyes were firm as they gazed into hers. "Absolutely nothing is wrong with you, Tiff. You can't keep beating yourself up about it."

"Yeah, but you've had a tough year, too. And it's not like you're falling apart all the time."

He placed down his glass and shifted to face her, placing his hands on either side of her face. "Maybe my problems haven't been as bad as I imagined them to be. And I can count on good friends like you to help me through it."

She felt his warm breath on her face. The glow from the living room cast light and shadows over his handsome face. She took shallow breaths, hoping he'd move in closer, ready to surrender to whatever he decided.

Instead, he removed his hands and shifted back on the bench. He reached into the inside pocket of his coat with one hand, looking up at her from under thick lashes. "It wasn't really true that I left your present back in Rome. I didn't need my sisters giving me a hard time."

He pulled out a small jewelry box and held it out to her. She caught her breath.

"I know it can't replace what you lost. I don't have that kind of money. But I did hope it would take some of the hurt away."

She met his gaze. "But you didn't. Simone, there was absolutely no reason ..."

"Shhh, open it before you get all excited. I don't want you to get your hopes up thinking it looks anything like your grandmother's."

With trembling fingers, Tiffany opened the velvet box. Inside, a small but delicate emerald glistened against blue velvet. Tiny diamonds chips shimmered around it. Tiffany caught her breath. "Oh, Simone. You shouldn't have. Tell me you can take it back. You can't afford this."

"How's that for killing a guy's ego?" He plucked it out of the box and slipped it onto her finger. He wiped his brow and smiled. "Whew! My guess was right. Fits perfectly."

She smiled up at him, tears welling up once more in her eyes. "It does. It's beautiful." A snowflake fell on the glittering stone, and she brushed it away.

"It killed me when you told me it was the only possession you had that proved you were special to someone." He clasped her hand in his. "How could you think that? Don't you know how special you are to your friends? To me?" He moved closer. "Don't you realize the effect you have on people? Look at these few days—my parents love you, my sisters, everyone in town is asking why you'd be friends with someone like me." He smiled, and his perfect teeth matched the color of the falling snow. "I know it's not the same as what you lost, but I hope this can serve as a daily reminder of how very special you are, and how much your friends love you, and how lucky we feel to have you in our lives." He stroked her cheek with his fingers, and whispered, "How lucky I feel to have you in my life."

Her heart clenched, and she moved closer. His lips brushed hers. A warm tingling spread throughout her body. He crushed his solid chest into her, his heart thumping against her breast. His hands rubbed along her back, sliding up to tangle themselves in her long hair. Surely, her heart would explode. She groaned with pleasure.

"*Che cazzo!* What the hell is going on?"

They broke away at the same time, turning to the voice. There, before them stood a woman bundled up against the elements, a thick goose-down coat covering her figure. Glossy black curls, coated with snowflakes, tumbled down from a black hat. Two suitcases lay beside her where she had dropped them.

Tiffany was slow to connect the face with a name. She reared back on the bench. "Ramona! I wasn't expecting to see you here."

"Well that's bloody obvious by how you were carrying on, Tiffany. What the hell was that little display?"

Tiffany looked to Simone, hoping he would break in, but he sat in stunned silence, staring at Ramona as if she were a ghost. She tried to catch his gaze. "Simone, did you know Ramona was coming?"

He shook his head, almost imperceptibly.

"Well, clearly he didn't know. It was supposed to be a surprise. I obviously didn't expect to find him with his tongue down the neighbor's throat."

Tiffany waited for Simone to intervene, but he continued staring at Ramona without uttering a word. Panic welled up inside her. He was still in love with her. That night, he'd convinced himself he could move on. That he could move on with Tiffany. But now that Ramona was back, she was only his second choice. Only special with the competition a continent away.

She took a deep breath. "You know, Ramona, we both had a bit too much to drink. It really wasn't as bad as it seems. I had some family problems—my brother's been ill. Simone was only comforting me, and, well, one thing led to another. It was a silly mistake."

She paused, waiting for Simone to break in and deny her lies. The silence was deafening to her ears. Standing, she slapped her hands on her jeans. "Well, you two probably have lots to catch up on, and I'm beat. I'll be off to my room. See you tomorrow."

Ramona's hard black eyes glared at her as she moved away. She heard Ramona walk over to the bench as Tiffany retreated to the door. She shot a quick glance back, seeing Ramona slip under the blanket. The same spot where Tiffany had been a moment earlier. She stood frozen as Ramona slipped into Simone's embrace.

Simone glanced up at her, but his gaze was impenetrable. She couldn't handle pity. Not tonight. She slipped into the house without another word.

She lay sleepless in her bed, trying not to think of Simone and Ramona with their naked limbs entwined in the room next door. At least they'd had the decency to be quiet about it, but maybe that was more for Simone's parents' benefit than out of concern for her own feelings. Despite straining her ears the entire night, she heard only silence from the adjacent room.

As the rosy fingers of dawn streaked the dusky morning sky, Tiffany abandoned any hope of sleep. She climbed out of her warm bed and quickly packed up her small bag. She dressed in haste, pulling on her jeans, her warmest sweater, and her boots. At the desk, she rummaged in the drawer to find paper and pen, and scribbled a note to Simone's parents, apologizing for the early departure to Rome to care for an ill friend.

Slinging her bag over her shoulder, she crept down the staircase, unlatched the door, and stepped out into the frosty air. The town was blanketed in fresh, virgin snow. This early on Christmas morning, not another soul stirred in the silence of the town. As she passed the bench, she looked down at her finger, stroking the emerald Simone had slipped on her finger only a few hours earlier.

She wasn't feeling all that special now. Breathing in deeply, she forced herself not to cry. She tramped out into the fresh snow, her footsteps a muted echo in the silence of the white town as she made her lonely way to the train station.

CHAPTER 21

Annarita

"Okay, class. Remember that the discussion will go better if you actually read the chapters each week." Annarita tried to smile encouragingly at the row of bored students. "Remember, you selected *The Great Gatsby*. And it's a fairly easy read. Let's repeat the assignment: Chapters one through three for next week. *Please read* this time." She plastered a smile on once more. "C'mon now. It'll be fun. Can't wait for next week. And Happy New Year everyone!"

The students filed out, chattering over one another now that they were free to speak in Italian. In English, they never had a thing to say. She sank into her chair. Working over the holidays really sucked. The students were even less motivated, but fewer teachers were around and Annarita could easily pick up the extra hours that needed filling.

"Ciao, prof." A young man stood at the door, a cashmere scarf tied carefully around his neck, his hair gelled and touseled to perfection.

"Ciao, Fabrizio." She packed her books into her bag. "You didn't make it to class tonight."

"Yeah, well." He leaned against the doorframe. "Lots going on tonight. My band has a lot of gigs lined up over the next weeks, and we need to practice."

She sighed. She'd seen Fabrizio in the same circles when she'd been with Vincenzo, and she'd been surprised to have bumped into him in one of her English classes. His English was hopeless. But in the tradition of Tommaso, her superlatively hopeless student, Fabrizio really only bothered trying as a way to pick up girls, and to get closer to his dream of moving to Malindi one day.

Annarita really would have preferred to have steered clear of this rocker so full of himself, and so similar to Vincenzo, but he'd let it slip that he owned a café. He'd heard her mentioning wanting to teach a cooking class and told her it was exactly what he was looking for during this holiday season—a cooking class taught in English, before the café's busy dinner hour. How could she resist?

"Okay, Fabrizio. Should we get a move on? I bought all the ingredients, and they're all home in my fridge. Still able to drive me there to pick it up?"

"Your wish is my command." His black eyes sparkled, and he flashed her his perfect smile.

Vincenzo in the shower with the silicone blonde. She gave a tight smile. "Okay, let's get going."

In her apartment, she packed the clams, mussels, calamari, shrimp and the *orata* into a cooler.

"Wow, you really went all out."

"I was at the fish market before seven. You have to be there early to get the best. Well, you must know from the café."

Fabrizio slouched back on the couch. "I don't actually do the shopping myself. I'm happy to delegate to my staff, but they've managed to build up a network of good suppliers."

Annarita stacked the packages carefully. "I'm surprised. I thought you'd want to be more hands-on with the purchasing."

He sipped from the grappa she'd offered him. "This is good." He met her gaze. "Well, you know. I'm a busy man. The café, the band. Can't follow everything personally, but I like to manage good people. Trust my staff."

"It's admirable, I guess. I don't think I could be so hands-off if I were lucky enough to have my own place."

He stood and came over to the kitchen counter. "A good manager needs to hire good people, and trust them to do their jobs well."

Annarita pulled bottles of wine from the refrigerator and placed them on the counter. "I'm sure you're right. That's probably why I don't own my own café, and you do. Hope you can help me with these."

"Wow, you have quite a bit of wine here."

"The students need to try their dishes paired with excellent wines. I'm a bit surprised you couldn't manage from the café."

He shook his head. "Yeah, I'm sorry about that. Ya know. We're a bit in the red right now. Can pay you back, no problem, next month. But for the bookkeepers, we need to keep it off the records until next month."

"Yeah, I understand. I mean, I get the purchases. But even the money the students pay needs to go directly to you? And not even the wine couldn't have been provided by the café?"

Fabrizio smiled and stepped closer. "Again, thanks for your patience. We'll take the fees, then write you a check for your share of the fees, and all your expenses for the materials and wine. Next month, I promise."

Annarita took a deep breath. She couldn't afford it, but here was a chance to teach cooking classes in English, in a trendy café in the center. She was always too cautious. Sometimes, you had to take a chance. Especially if a little risk could lead you where you wanted to go.

Fabrizio stepped closer and examined a bottle. "Nice." He narrowed the distance between them and stroked her hip. "Nothing's sexier than a woman who cooks a three-course seafood meal." He smiled. "We have a bit of time before the course starts." He nodded toward the open bedroom door and smiled. "Why don't you put me out of my misery? A quickie before your class?"

Before Vincenzo, Annarita may have fallen for him. A handsome musician, with a successful café of his own. But now she saw through his shallowness, saw that there was no way they'd ever be together in the long-term. Renata had been right back in Sperlonga. He was all wrong for her. It didn't matter how much she cooked for him, how many times she cleaned his apartment or sewed his clothes. It wasn't meant to be.

She breathed a sigh of relief. "Very tempting, Fabrizio. But I want to be there early to prepare for my students. I'd hate to let you down, or let down the café." She picked up the cooler, and indicated the bag filled with bottles. "Could you get those?" With a smile, she strode to the door with a determination she'd too often lacked.

The following evening, Annarita stood outside the *enoteca*, wrapping her thin cardigan more firmly around her. The wind was picking up, and she'd been waiting for Francesca for a half hour.

At first, she'd reviewed the success of the cooking class last night, how much the students had enjoyed themselves, how well their dinner had turned out, and all the fun they'd had eating their seafood feast over fine wine and lively conversation. She'd spoken to Fabrizio about scheduling future courses, and he'd been positive.

But the course had set her back financially, at least until next month when she would be reimbursed for her expenses and paid her share of the registration fees. Tonight's lesson would at least provide her with some desperately needed cash.

Francesca was one of her regular students. Usually, she went to Francesca's home for their weekly lessons, but Francesca had called her, sounding depressed again. She told Annarita it sounded much more fun and bohemian to meet and speak English over a glass of wine than to go over grammar in her living room. As if Francesca ever worried about reviewing grammar.

Annarita knew the drill. Francesca's husband had recently left her for a younger woman, and Francesca wanted to complain while being out around people having fun. It gave her a semblance of a social life, especially during the holidays. But even if you were going through a separation, did you ask your divorce attorney to meet you in a bar? Did you ask your hairdresser or your cleaning lady? Why was your language teacher considered less professional? When her hour was up, Annarita wanted to go home, but she knew it would be difficult to sneak away from the wine bar.

She saw Francesca rounding the corner, an expensive leather coat brushing the tops of what looked like dominatrix boots. No wonder Francesca was so late. How on earth had she managed to arrive at all over slippery cobblestones with heels like that? Francesca caught sight of her and waved.

"Oh, you wait me here outside? Why you no go in?"

Annarita always meant to introduce Francesca and Tommaso, putting her two most grammatically challenged students together.

Annarita opened the door to the Monti bar. Not her scene at all. Overpriced and packed. Lots of exchange students, the young, foreign women ardently pursued by a pack of Italian men. She usually steered clear of places like this, but

Francesca was in her element, happily eyeing up the young men. Annarita glanced at her watch, hoping Francesca might get lucky early and allow her to slip out.

Inside, Annarita spotted a free table and raced for it. No way was she elbowing her way up to the bar. She waited for Francesca to join her.

But Francesca was having none of it. She would not be rushed when she was set on having her grand, Sophia Loren-style entrance. She shook her jacket down over her shoulders, allowing it to slide down her back. Annarita gaped in horror. Francesca, easily the oldest woman in the bar, was dressed in a skintight minidress that left absolutely nothing to the imagination. Where on earth had she bought such an outfit? And why in God's name hadn't the saleswomen talked her out of it?

Francesca was happily oblivious to the pointing and snickering of the beautiful twenty-somethings around her. She'd shed her jacket and slung it over one shoulder, an ill-advised attempt to look like a runway model on the catwalks of Milan. She walked slowly to Annarita's table, wobbling her hips at each painful step her dominatrix boots took across the terracotta floor. At a certain point, she flipped her hair and winked at a young American boy in a baseball cap. His friends burst into laughter and slapped him on the back.

Annarita grimaced. Surely there must be a more dignified way of allowing a woman scorned to sow her wild oats. She wondered if she could dig out the cellphone number of her disastrous blind date last week, the one who wanted to get lucky. Maybe she could set him up with a sure thing like Francesca.

Instead, she picked up the menu, holding it high before her face and praying she could be anywhere other than in this wine bar with Francesca.

Francesca slipped down into the seat in front of Annarita's, chest projected firmly forward. Annarita lowered her menu, and immediately regretted it. Her student's breasts were barely contained in the tight leather. Wrinkly flesh spilled over the décolleté, flabby arms reached up to tousle her hair à la Brigitte Bardot. Annarita squeezed her eyes shut, hoping she was trapped in an unpleasant dream. When she opened them, Francesca was still there, examining the wine menu with an artfully seductive puckering of her blood-red lips.

"Very very nice here, no? I must to ask. Where do you go to meet the young men, Annarita?"

"Well ... uhhh ... I don't actually spend a lot of time meeting young men. I've been concentrated a lot on work and going out with girlfriends."

"A real waste of time, *mia cara*. You are only young one time. Once it is gone, your husband, he leave you for a younger one. Then you must to restart."

"Start again, yes. I'm a little off men right now, Francesca. No time or interest." She drummed her fingers on the table. "So what have you been doing with yourself these days?"

"I speak every day with my expensive, expensive lawyer. We plan how to get more money from the *bastardo*. I am on list of the famous Doctor Rinaldi. With new money, I get new breasts, new nose, young face. What do you think about it? The young boys will love me then, no?"

"Francesca, don't you think you're taking this a little fast? What about some time away—a little holiday? Separation can be a tough time."

She waved a bejeweled hand in the air. "Not for me— separation no tough. I am better without that horrible, horrible man. Now, where are our drinks?" She rubbed her hands together. "Do you see the tight jeans on our *cameriere*? Oh, *ragazzo*, come here!"

Annarita slouched down in her seat.

The young waiter arrived at the table. "*Buona sera*, ladies. What can I get you?"

"Oh, you are English."

"No, American."

"Like my friend here."

She patted Annarita on the cheek. Annarita made brief, apologetic eye contact with the young man. Surely Francesca could not be the first cougar on the loose in this bar.

"I love Americans. So young, so strong." She reached out and stroked his arm. "Oh, yes. So very, very strong. What is your name, beautiful boy?"

"Uh, Jake."

"Jake, what a nice American name. Now Jake, what time do you finish to work here tonight?"

"Uh, ma'am. I hear my boss calling me from out back. Can I take your order?"

"*Sì, spumante.*"

"And for your daughter?"

Black eyes burned with anger. Annarita examined her fingernails.

"Two glasses of *spumante*, Jake. Now run away." She sighed heavily. "Really, these young people today."

Annarita took a deep breath, wishing she could be anywhere else. "So, Francesca, seen any good movies or exhibitions recently?"

A young woman placed their flutes on the table. Jake was nowhere to be seen. Annarita smiled at her, Francesca glowered.

When the woman left, Francesca's attention was concentrated on a small group of men in Chelsea football shirts. They looked out of place at the wine bar, inexplicably stranded on their way from the stadium to the pub. A man with a ruddy face and sandy hair stumbled over. Then again, perhaps they'd already been to the pub.

"Evening, ladies." He swayed on his feet beside their table. His eyes were unfocused.

"*Buona sera*, handsome English man. I just love the English men. So much more *raffinati* than Americans. What is your name?"

"Rupert."

"Rupert, what a nice English name. I am Francesca." She reached out to shake his hand, freeing more of her breasts in the process. "Rupert, please take the chair."

He looked around stupidly for a free chair, swaying dangerously with each turn.

"No need," said Annarita. "Rupert, I was just leaving. Here, take mine. I haven't touched my drink either. It's all yours. Knock yourself out." She patted him on the shoulder. "Francesca, we'll speak about your next lesson. Nice evening."

With a quick wave, she strode to the door. Rupert's football friends tried to stop her, but she pointed to her watch and said she needed to hurry back to her husband.

Outside, the rain had started. No umbrella. She hurried over slippery cobblestones on her way to the metro. Only when she dug out the money for her metro ticket did it occur to her. Francesca hadn't paid her for that evening's lesson.

CHAPTER 22

Emma

Emma sat in the sunshine at an outdoor table of the Café San Teodoro. After the cold rains of the past two days, the sun had made its appearance once again. A group was already drinking *aperitivi*, probably gathering strength before going on to a wedding mass around the corner at the Chiesa di San Giovanni Decollato.

Emma always got a kick out of that name. What bride would choose to be married at the church of Saint-John-with-his-head-cut-off? Although, with the benefit of hindsight, maybe the church could have been the perfect setting for her marriage to Dario.

She caught sight of Sabrina climbing up the steps, her slicked-back, black hair gleaming in the sunlight. Spending time with ballerinas had an effect on her. Sabrina always appeared to be floating rather than walking.

"Ciao, Emma. Sorry I'm late."

"Don't worry. I've been enjoying the quiet after the holiday chaos."

"I know. I'm so glad Christmas is over. I was going to burst if I had to eat another bite. But I bet you'll be enjoying the silence even more in a while. When does Dario take the kids up to Cortina?"

She signaled the waitress to bring two cappuccinos. "Day after tomorrow. I'm heading back to help them pack."

Sabrina tucked her bag under the table. Pink tulle and sequins poked out from the top. "Is the sex bunny—I mean, snow bunny—still in the picture?"

Emma sighed and looked out over the church, with its grasses and bushes growing wild on the roof poking out between the saints. She loved this view, these private glimpses of ordinary Roman life. These scenes usually kept her grounded, when so many other aspects of her life attempted to rip her up from the roots.

"I'm afraid so. But I've made him promise to spend his time exclusively with the kids and to not introduce them to his harem girls. That makes me the nag." The coffees arrived. Emma stirred sugar into hers. "But things are finally starting to get better with Chiara. We've seen small improvements at school. I don't want to start going backwards."

"God, you'd think he could keep it in his pants for a week." Sabrina rubbed her hands over her eyes. "Sorry, that was crude. It's just ... I just remember him from before. Remember both of you from before. Seeing Dario during his midlife-crisis-on-steroids makes me nervous. Like, if it could happen to him, it could happen to any man."

"It won't happen with Franco. He's so different. I didn't realize it at the time, but there were small signs. I was blindsided because I was too busy to notice them. It's not the same for you. Franco's much ... steadier than Dario. Let's change topics. Lucky duck. Mauritius, huh?"

Sabrina smiled. "I can't believe it. We leave the day after tomorrow. Ten days of heaven. I've been dreaming about this for a month."

"I can imagine. Are the girls excited?"

"Are you kidding? Franco, too. He's been pulling long shifts. He needs the break."

"It'll be good for all of you. Mind if I stow away in your suitcase?"

Sabrina laughed. "What about you? Still planning on Paris?"

Emma shifted in her seat. "A radical change of plans. Who knew I could shift back into being such a diligent worker bee? I've got the construction crew working over the holidays. One of the apartments is all completed, even the heat is working. So I've decided to move in and use this next week to really move things along."

"You're kidding me. What about when the workers go home? You'll stay in that big *casale* all alone?"

Emma played with her spoon. "Well, I won't exactly be alone."

Sabrina raised an eyebrow. "You don't say. Mr. Hot American will be in Umbria during the holidays?"

"Sabrina ..."

"I'm only saying. Look, you two seem to be getting awfully close. I keep thinking about that time I stopped by when he was at your place to go over plans. The way he was looking at you, as if you hung the moon. Talk about smolder alert."

"Sabrina, he's only grateful I'm helping him out."

"As he damned well should be. How much would he be paying for a project manager as good as you've been? I'm Italian, and even *I* don't understand how the hell you managed it all. You've got your construction crew working *ahead* of schedule. It must be the first time that's ever happened in Italy since construction on the Colosseum. And they were slaves and didn't have much choice."

"Don't exaggerate. They're serious workers, and they're simply working well. But this is exciting for me. I haven't worked in years. I didn't think I could still do it."

"*Mia cara*, you've already proven you can. If we'd known about these hidden talents for miracle-making, we could have named you Italy's Economic Minister years ago and we'd never be in the trouble we are now."

Emma smiled and shook her head.

"But as your friend, I have to tell you. I'm worried about you." She leaned into the table, her voice dropping a notch. "It goes beyond old college friends. I know he relies on you, but I think it's more than that. I think he's falling for you."

Emma opened her mouth to protest.

"And, I hate to say it, because I'm your friend, and you know how much I love you. But I think you're falling for him, too." She leaned back in her seat. "I get it, Emma. After all you've been through, this is the first man you've had eyes for. Maybe it's the first time you're ready to get out there again, and Mark just happens to be in the right place at the right time. Or maybe you really did use to have feelings for him, and seeing him again brings them back." She placed a hand on Emma's arm. "But I'm worried. He has a wife and daughters. This can't end well. After all you've been through, I know this isn't what you'd want for another woman."

Emma felt the blood throbbing in her ears. Sabrina knew her better than anyone, and she'd seen through her flimsy excuses. But Emma really did need this job. She needed to prove she could make things work. She needed to regain that confidence in herself and fill up the emptiness that came with years of being simply a wife and mother.

Yes, Sabrina wasn't entirely off the mark. She was attracted to Mark.

Still, she was hardly a lovestruck teenager who couldn't control her emotions. He was married. He wasn't free. He made her feel special, but she knew where the lines were. And nothing would convince her to cross them. She knew from firsthand experience the pain that caused to the unsuspecting wife and family.

She gently extracted her arm from under Sabrina's, and looked her directly in the eyes. Her voice was low and measured. "You're a wonderful friend, and I honestly appreciate your concern. But you have no reason to worry. Yes, Mark is handsome and charming. Yes, we do have a shared past. But this is work. *Only* work. I want to pull this off. The kids are older, and I'm tired of relying on Dario's money. I'm doing this to jumpstart a career for myself. If that means a little flirting with the hotel owner, so be it. It won't go any further than that."

The incredulity was evident in Sabrina's eyes, but it faded as quickly as it appeared.

Emma called to the waitress, signaling for the check. "It's on me this time. Let's walk back together. I need to get the kids sorted, and I imagine you have your own packing to do."

On the walk back along the Circo Massimo, a glimmer of copper caught Emma's eye. '*I am lost*,' she thought, as she passed the engraving that exploded in a burst of sunlight.

She turned back to glance at the hidden message, but she had no desire to share the mysterious plaque with her best friend.

"*Sì, sì*, now move that right in here."

She motioned the men in. They grunted with the effort of lifting the solid oak table. When they placed it down where she'd indicated, she led them into the kitchen to pour them freshly squeezed lemonade before they returned for the benches.

As they drank, she returned to the table, running her hand over it, feeling the smoothly polished wood. It was so perfect when she'd seen it at the Antiques Fair in Arezzo. She'd snapped a photo on her cellphone, haggled the price down with the seller, and insisted Mark let her purchase it on his behalf. It had been in one of the Umbrian castles. It easily seated thirty. Emma had told Mark it would be perfect for the dining room, the only room finished outside of the ground floor apartment.

She admired the heavy wooden structure over the gleaming terracotta floors. With the high-backed chairs that accompanied it, this would create a perfect first impression for future guests. A crackling fireplace, a large rustic table where guests would chat over dinners, meeting one another over hearty courses of locally sourced foods. Mark was going for the full local experience for his guests.

She pulled her cardigan tighter around her. The heating had only been turned on that morning, and old houses like this needed time to warm up. She checked her watch anxiously as the men went back out to the truck for the chairs. She had an interview for a cook in an hour. She'd already met with two this morning, and they'd failed to impress her.

Mark was supposed to have been here, but his flight was delayed. By the time he flew into Florence and drove down here, who knew what time it would be. But he trusted her to do the first round of interviews.

Finding the right cook was crucial. They needed someone committed to promoting local culinary traditions, to overseeing the gardens they would create, and ensuring they were supplied with the best local ingredients. Mark was hoping to find a chef open to offering cooking classes for the guests. Emma wasn't hopeful they'd find someone who could teach in Italian and English—Mark was far too optimistic after all his years living in Amsterdam. But she hadn't anticipated problems in even finding someone willing to teach in Italian. The chefs she'd met earlier that morning had been appalled by the idea.

The men returned with the chairs and placed them around the table. It really was perfect. Now she'd need to find the perfect chandelier to go with it. She'd had her eye on one at the Arezzo antiques market. Maybe she could get there with Mark. The men were eager to be on their way; she thanked them and saw them out.

In the kitchen, she set water on the stove for tea. The rest of the kitchen was a work in progress, but a beautiful old oven and a decrepit refrigerator stood alone in the empty space. She still needed to work with the architect to design the kitchen, but if they had the chef on board, she'd give him a say. The light was beautiful in the room, with big windows overlooking a garden. The garden was horribly overgrown, but it would be in shape for spring.

She sighed. She loved this place. It wasn't only Mark, or even feeling useful once again. She'd known the minute she saw the rundown farmhouse, with its old stone exterior, its open ground-floor spaces and the rooms above, with their airy windows looking out onto the town and the countryside beyond. She loved the little footpath that led up to the spires of Todi. It was an easy, gentle walk in, one that allowed the visitor to admire the view of the town as it loomed ever closer. Much as medieval travelers would have viewed it. She suspected in the summertime, the path would be surrounded by wild strawberries and blackberries.

She envied Mark his inheritance, and she respected him for wanting to turn the property into a hotel, rather than trying to unload it quickly on some rich English or German buyers. She would have loved to visit a place like this for a restorative holiday. She knew the pampered mothers at the Fairmont School would love a place like this. She'd already talked to Mark about converting one of the old dépendances into a spa.

Another would serve as a space for children—to do arts and crafts, bake cookies, learn about working on the farm— caring for the animals and tending the garden. There would be not a video game in sight, but wooden construction sets to build, and maybe a ping-pong table and a swing set out on the lawn. While the mothers were waxed and peeled, massaged and pampered, the kids could be put in the care of some of the local teenagers.

She'd already floated the idea with some of the mothers at Fairmont, and they'd enthusiastically asked her to sign them up—whatever the price tag.

The kettle whistled, and she turned from the window facing the garden. She switched off the gas and poured the steaming water into the teapot. She touched the ceramic, delighting in the burning sensation on her palms.

"Oh, wow. I see my timing's perfect."

She startled at the familiar voice behind her.

"Hi, honey. How was your day?" Mark smiled the slightly crooked smile she was familiar with once more. "Tell me— that amazing table is the one you found in Arezzo? It's even better in person than it was in that grainy photo you sent me. You have *carte blanche* to spend all my money if you make purchases like that."

She felt a blush creeping across her cheeks. Just like some silly teenager.

"The tea will be ready in a moment. Would you like some?"

He nodded and came closer. She instinctively took a step back, before turning to cover her embarrassment. "I was admiring the garden, or what I think you can make of the garden come springtime."

He stepped beside her, looking out the window as he slipped one arm around her shoulder. "What *we* can coax out of the garden come springtime." He looked at her. "I couldn't have done any of this without you, Emma. You're a powerhouse. I managed to snag the best damned organizer in all of Italy."

Her cheeks grew warmer, and she slipped from his grasp to pour the tea. She returned and handed him a mug, careful to allow for distance between them.

"How was your flight? The drive down?"

"Oh, all fine. Not much traffic. That was a nice surprise."

"How was Christmas with Lieke and the girls?"

He sipped his tea. "The girls were great. Thanks to your help—yours and Chiara's—I got them all the right presents. They loved the handbags and the shoes. They already want to go shopping with Chiara when they come down to visit." He laughed. "And you? How was Christmas? How are the kids? Did they get off okay with Dario for skiing?"

It was strange hearing her ex-husband's name roll off his tongue with ease, as if they were old friends.

She nodded. "They were so excited. The snow's fabulous. I know they'll have a great time."

His eyes were concerned. "Am I keeping you from them? Would you have gone if it weren't for me and my neediness with this place?"

"Me? Join Dario and the kids? No, no. You didn't keep me. It's important they have time alone together. But I'm afraid you took my availability to work the wrong way. I didn't mean for you to give up family time with Lieke and the girls to come here."

There was something rigid about the set of his jaw. The eyes that were usually laughing looked hard as they stared out into the overgrown garden. "No, the getaway was Lieke's idea. A friend's cottage up north. My presence wasn't strictly necessary." He turned to her, and his face changed. The smile was warm and genuine. "This tea is perfect. Thanks. Hits the spot after the trip."

"I wish I could tell you that you could rest after the voyage, but the chef interview is set in a few minutes. The two this morning were a disaster. The man this afternoon is Giuseppe Giordano. He comes highly recommended from a woman at my children's school. She's from Todi, and her mother still lives here. Apparently, Giuseppe had a successful restaurant, but he had to sell it when his wife was ill and they needed expensive treatment." She placed her cup down. "She died about a year ago. I've been told he's a genius in the kitchen, but he's not yet ready to start his own restaurant. His house neighbors your property, so this would be convenient for him." She whispered. "If he's up to it. I've been told he's been a wreck this past year."

"I don't know if we can handle someone who's a wreck. I mean, I can imagine this year must have been hard on him. I really feel for him. But a start-up is tough, and it's hard to be charitable if people aren't committed a hundred percent. We'll flop if we don't have a reliable cook."

She picked up the teapot and poured some more tea into her cup. She looked at him and he nodded, and she poured into his as well. "That's why I'm glad you're here for the interview, too."

"You know I trust your instinct on everything. It would have been the same with the chef. But if it makes you happy, I'm glad we can discuss together. Can we take a look at the finished apartments?"

"Sure—these are going to be for you, the manager, and staff working here who may have to stay overnight." She led him back into the grand entrance hall and through to the private quarters. "This is the largest—it will be yours. See, there are two rooms for the girls. I've put in bunk beds, in case they have friends sleep over. There's a shared bathroom and a small kitchen, so you don't have to get in the way of the chef during dining hours." She walked him around. They'd talked about keeping costs down in the private portion of the house—the ones that weren't destined for the guests, but she was still pleased with the finishings.

"It's beautiful, Emma. I hadn't expected anything so luxurious."

She laughed. "Trust me. It's not luxurious. Wait 'til you see the level of design in the guest rooms. Now *those* will be impressive." She opened another door. "No locks yet, but we'll put them on. This will be for the hotel manager. Simple, but spacious enough. An extra room if they have a family. A small living room, dining room, kitchen corner, and a small patio." She opened onto a patio with a view over the rolling hills of the countryside beyond. "Think this'll be enough to tempt a good hotel manager?"

He whistled. He stepped behind her, so close that she could feel his warm breath on her cheek.

"I don't know. Could I tempt you?"

She laughed and turned, taking a self-conscious step backward. "It'll tempt me in these days, but I meant when you need to get a real manager in here."

He tilted his head. "I know. And that's what I was asking you. Would you consider moving to Todi? Taking on the job?"

She shook her head. "I'm not a hotel manager."

"You weren't a project manager either, and look how well that's working out."

"But it's different."

"Of course it's different. But I've no doubt you'd ace that, too. I'll be down here much of the time. I'll be going back and forth to see the girls ... see Lieke and the girls, but I've spoken to my father-in-law about starting to hand over my projects, so that I can concentrate on the hotel." He shoved his hands in his pockets. "I really want to make this work."

She smiled at him. "You will. I know you will. I'll be on call if you need me, but I'm sure you'll find someone competent to run this place."

He shook his head. "I already have. Now I only have to try and convince her. I'll take the smaller apartment, you and the kids could have the owner's flat. I've asked around. The school is supposed to be great up here. Even checked out that there was a soccer club and a fencing group for Marco and Valerio." He grinned. "Tell me you'll at least think about it?"

She rolled her eyes. "You're impossible, Mark. You know my life's in Rome."

"It's close by. You'll get back whenever you want."

The doorbell rang.

"Saved by the bell. I'll get it." Emma walked through the manager's apartment and to the front door. She opened to a towering man, with wild black curls swirling in the wind. He had the broad shoulders of a rugby player, a generous belly, and sparkling black eyes. "*Buongiorno. Lei è Giuseppe Giordano?*"

"*Sì, Signora Emma, vero? Abbiamo parlato al telefono.*"

"What a pleasure. Please come in. This is Mark Daniels, the owner. He doesn't speak Italian. Do you speak English?"

"Not much, I'm afraid."

"That's okay. I'll translate for you. Please come in and sit down."

Mark shook hands, and attempted to welcome him in Italian. Emma smothered a smile at his Dutch-accented Italian. Still, she was pleased to see him hard at work studying the language he would need to run the place.

She translated, and they had a pleasant conversation with Giuseppe. Despite his bulk, or perhaps because of it, the man was a force of nature. He shifted in his chair and bounced his leg the whole time they conversed. He looked ready to spring from his chair at any moment. His hands performed complicated acrobatics to complement his rapid-fire Italian. He was so different from the candidates she had interviewed that morning, so enthusiastic and excited to take on a new project.

"But enough talk," he said at a certain point. "May we go through to see the kitchen?"

"Yes, of course," said Emma. "But you'll see there's not much there. We still have to design it. Come." His rapid-fire speech meant simultaneous interpretation had been abandoned long ago. She gestured with a nod of her chin that Mark should follow them.

"*Sì, sì,*" said Giuseppe as he looked around him. "There is much potential here. And I like the light and the garden, which should contain all our herbs and vegetables. But this will not do."

Emma raised an eyebrow.

He stared at her, his black eyes even darker. "I cannot cook in an empty kitchen. And how can you decide I am right for the job if you do not try my cooking? You must come to my house. I will cook for you there, and you can decide."

Emma turned to Mark and translated for him. He shook his head. "Tell him it won't be necessary."

Giuseppe would hear none of it. "I insist. You come now, and we have an early dinner."

They followed him out the door and along the path leading to town. Less than three hundred meters from the hotel, they passed through a gate in the stone wall. A stone cottage was visible behind olive trees. Emma had noticed this home before, seen the welcoming lights shining from its windows, and had meant to stop by to introduce herself. When she'd been told Giuseppe lived close to the hotel, she hadn't understood he was their direct neighbor.

He opened the door with his key and flicked on the lights, for dusk was settling in quickly on the shortest days of the year. The room filled with a golden glow. Emma took in the dark wooden beams, the stone fireplace, the colorful pottery on shelves, the heavy, wooden *arte povera* furniture, all so cozily arranged. It was a pleasant home. On the mantelpiece, numerous photographs were arranged. Giuseppe on his wedding day, next to a short, stout woman with a mountain of black curls and a beautiful smile. There were numerous photos of this woman next to Giuseppe, at family events, in front of their home, on Saint Mark's Square in Venice, in London. The deceased wife.

There was a cough behind her. Giuseppe strode over the fireplace and plucked a photo of the woman in front of the Eiffel Tower. He handed her the photo in its heavy frame. "This is my wife, Luisa. She died last year. Breast cancer." He crossed himself as he spoke the words. He took the photo back wordlessly and placed it gently on the mantelpiece. He kept his back to her as he spoke. "It's been hard. We both grew up in Todi. We were elementary school sweethearts."

"We are so sorry for your loss, Giuseppe," said Emma.

"Thank you." His voice lowered to a whisper. "It hasn't been a good year." He poked at the fire in the fireplace, coaxing the flames. When he turned around, his black eyes were luminous. He rubbed his hands together. "Now, let me get to work in the kitchen. You stay here and make yourself comfortable. I will be right back with wine." He indicated a large, blue couch before the fire.

Emma and Mark sat beside one another in silence. Giuseppe returned a moment later, handing them two glasses of wine. With a smile, he returned to the kitchen. From beyond the open door, they heard the sound of chopping accompanied by a booming, rich tenor. "*La donna è mobile. Qual' pium' al vento. Muta d'accento, e di pensiero ...*"

She smiled at Mark. "A singing chef, no less. Did you understand when he was speaking?"

He nodded. "Enough, I think. What a difficult year it must have been for him." He held his glass up, clinking against hers. "*Salute.*"

Emma sipped from her glass. "This is excellent. We'll have to ask him if it's local. You'll need to start filling your wine cellar."

"That sounds like a pleasant burden. This is really good." He leaned back on the couch, his leg brushing against Emma's. "Emma, look outside."

She turned to the window. "*La neve.* Snow." She stood and walked to the window. The flakes were coming down slowly. "I hope your heating is up to it."

"I hope my rental car is up to it." He patted the cushion. "Come back here. We can watch together. You're always in motion. Let's relax and enjoy this dinner. I have a feeling Giuseppe will impress us. I can already picture him in our kitchen, and I haven't even tasted his food yet."

"You can?" She smiled and crossed the room, sitting beside him, but not as close before. "I'm glad you feel it, too. It's not everything he's gone through, although that makes a difference. But I can picture him at your hotel. I'm happy you can, also."

"Let's wait until the dinner, but I've been asking around, too. I understand his restaurant was pretty amazing." He looked back out the window. "It's nice, Emma. Being here with you, bringing this hotel to life. This is the most fun I've had in a long time."

She lowered her head to hide a smile. "It's the most fun I've had in a long time, too. It's been a long time since I've worked. I'd forgotten how much I enjoyed it."

He shifted in closer. "You're good at it. You'd be good at anything you do. But I'm glad I was able to convince you to help me." He placed a hand on her leg. "And I hope I'll manage to convince you to make it more permanent."

Her heart thumped in her chest. His touch had the power to do this to her. How could she agree to work long-term in his proximity?

The kitchen door swung open. Giuseppe filled the doorframe, an apron tied around his waist, a wide smile on a face flushed by bubbling stovetops. "*La cena è pronta. Venite al tavolo.*"

Mark squeezed her leg. He stood, holding his arm out for her to grasp. They followed Giuseppe into the kitchen, struck by the comforting aroma of stewed tomatoes, garlic, and roasting meats. Emma felt her stomach grumble as she reached the table.

The three hundred meters separating Giuseppe's cottage from the hotel might as well have been three hundred kilometers.

With their stomachs full with Giuseppe's rich foods and their heads spinning with the strong Umbrian red wine, Emma and Mark slipped through the snow-slicked path to the hotel like a couple of kids. Mark scooped up snow, forming messy snowballs that he aimed at her with remarkable accuracy. Emma ran off, slipping on the snow and falling headfirst. Mark was on top of her, pulling her up and laughing, his lips so maddeningly close to hers. She shook her head and saw the hazy outline of Todi in the distance. It would be beautiful tomorrow. It was beautiful tonight.

He pulled her to her feet, brushing her off. "I'm sorry. I've gotten you all wet. Let's get you home and warm you up." He rubbed her arms, his warm breath caressing her face. He slipped an arm around her waist and they continued their unbalanced walk back to the hotel.

Mark fumbled with the keys, flicked on the lights, and yelled, "Wait here!" at the entryway as he jogged toward the apartment.

He returned with an old pair of his sweatpants and a Georgetown sweatshirt. "Something warm. Go get changed and then come back out. I have cases of wine I bought, but I don't think they're as good as what Giuseppe has. We may have to get a new supplier."

"More wine, Mark? I don't think so. But I'll take you up on the warm clothes."

"Take the owner's suite! I want you to test-drive it so you'll accept the hotel manager offer."

She returned in the dry clothes as he stood before the fire, trying to get it started. He looked up and smiled. "This takes me back. You look just like you did in our dorms."

She felt her cheeks burning. "I don't believe that for a minute, but it's still nice to hear." She rubbed the material. "Do you know how long it's been since I wore sweats? I've been conditioned by an Italian husband. The idea of wearing sweats, or—the horror—of ever going out in public with them is unthinkable. Maybe it's even punishable by death for the wife of an Italian plastic surgeon." She collapsed on the couch.

"Then perhaps, based on entirely selfish motives, it's better that you're not married to him anymore." He gave a last stoke to the fire and stood up. "I like seeing you this way."

He plucked a bottle off the mantel and strode to the table, pouring two glasses. "I know that we've had way more wine than we should have at dinner, but you have to at least try this. I need your professional opinion. Giuseppe's is better, isn't it?"

She took the glass offered to her, twirled the wine in her glass and took a small sip. "Yes. Giuseppe's is definitely better. I'll ask him tomorrow for the vineyard, and ask them about bulk prices. It'll be easy now that Giuseppe will be working for us."

He sank into the couch beside her. "That was the most amazing meal I've ever had. I can't believe you found him for me. And that he lives 300 meters from my hotel and accepted immediately. You walk on water, Emma. He'll make this hotel. With cooking like that, I'll have a line of Dutch families booking every holiday with us for the next decade."

Emma rubbed her abdomen. "I don't know. With cooking like that, we'll need to set up hiking excursions and soccer matches to burn off the calories. I put on five kilos with that dinner alone."

Mark smiled and stroked her hair. "You did not, but even if you did, you'd look fine with an extra five kilos. You're even slimmer than you were back in college."

She gently pulled back from his touch. Her head was spinning, and his nearness wasn't doing anything to calm her thoughts.

"I told him he could design the kitchen."

"Of course. Whatever he wants."

"He's okay with teaching occasional classes, but they'll have to be in Italian."

"Maybe we can get an English-speaking cook to help him every once in a while, depending on the clientele."

"Careful, Mark. Giuseppe will be fantastic, but he has a Pavarotti-sized ego. Let's ease into things slowly. Let him be involved with certain decisions."

"You see? That's why I need you." He slid over on the couch, until he was touching her. "I didn't want to admit to it before, but now that we're friends again, I should confess that you did break my heart back in Rome."

Emma shook her head. "Back in Rome? What're you talking about?"

He reached for the bottle and filled her glass. "Back in grad school. You didn't know how in love with you I was, but I foolishly thought I could impress you on my visit to Rome. I had a Roman classmate tell me all the right restaurants and clubs to take you to, all the best walks. I was shattered when I found out an actual Roman had beaten me to it."

She longed to pull back. She could feel the heat of his body through her sweatshirt. She willed her heart to stop pounding. "That was years ago. Decades ago, actually. You seem to have fallen on your feet. You met Lieke right after graduation, didn't you?"

He shifted in his seat, and stared into the fire. "Yes, the next summer in Amsterdam. Quite the cliché. I fell for the boss' daughter."

Emma edged imperceptibly away. "Okay, but these things happen. They'd hired you on your own merits. It's hardly that you weren't worthy of your position."

"But that's what people think. No matter how well you do, they're always speaking behind your back, saying you only have your position because of your wife."

"But Lieke works there, too. You're not the only one."

"You know, it's different with a man. The way you're judged by others. I married into it. She's the heir apparent."

She examined his face, lit by the orange flames. "Is that why you were so happy to take on this hotel? To have something that was all yours?"

He placed his wineglass on the ground, rubbed his hand over his face. He ran his fingers through his hair, leaving wild tufts. Even with disheveled hair, he looked handsome. Emma found herself wondering what he would look like if she woke up beside him, but she quickly banished that thought.

"Always the star student, Emma." He smiled. "Yeah, I guess it was. It came at a good time." He put a hand on hers. "And you came at a good time, too. I'm happy to have you back in my life. As a friend. I didn't mean to embarrass you earlier with my Rome story. I've kept it inside so long. I only wanted to be honest with you. My head is throbbing. This is exactly why I never overdo it with alcohol. Do you mind if I sit here with you for a minute before we go off to bed?"

"That would be nice. Let's enjoy the last of the fire."

He slipped his arm around her shoulders and pulled her to him. Her head rested on his warm shoulder, and she inhaled the scent of his cologne. She heard his breathing grow more rhythmic, and she didn't fight the heaviness she felt as her own eyelids dropped down. Tight in Mark's embrace, with the crackling of the fire and the steady snow falling outside the thick, stone walls, Emma felt more content than she had in ages.

Sunlight streamed through the window, the bright, cool sunlight of a snowy winter day. Her head ached. All that wine last night. Today would be tough. She'd have carpenters and plumbers coming later in the day, a meeting with the architect's project manager that morning, and lots of work schedules to be organized. She moved to sit up, but something constricted her.

She turned to one side and gasped. Mark lay next to her on the couch, his arms wrapped around her chest. Someone had pulled a blanket over them during the night. Mark? Maybe she had done it, but she had no memory of it. The sunlight fell on his face. He was so handsome in the first rays of the day. His tousled hair looked as she'd imagined it last night. Maybe even better. They'd spent the whole night out here on the couch? In one another's arms? She remembered their talk, remembered the ill-advised extra glass of wine.

Slowly, she lifted his arm from her body, and slid out from under him. If she got up and made breakfast, maybe he wouldn't even recall last night. After all, he'd had too much to drink, too. Then they could avoid any awkwardness.

But as she searched her memory of the previous evening, she could come up with no mistakes. Yes, they'd fallen asleep in one another's embrace. But it was the exhaustion, nothing untoward. There had been no kisses, no caresses, just the solid feel of Mark's arms around her. That was enough.

She closed her eyes for a moment, stretching her arms over her head. Embarrassing, to be sure. But not improper. Or at least not seriously improper. She rubbed her temples and slowly opened her eyes. She gasped.

"Who are you?" she asked the woman seated in a chair in the corner.

"I could ask the same of you." The woman stood. She wore an elegant camel hair coat and wool trousers. Her long, dark hair was sleek and full. "But the Georgetown college gear and finding you asleep with my husband's arms around you gave the game away. You're obviously Emma. The old college flame."

Her heart galloped. "Oh, Lieke. I can imagine how terrible this looks." She stepped closer and offered an outstretched arm, retracting it when no move was made to reciprocate. "We weren't expecting you." Her cheeks began to burn. "I only meant … of course you needed no advance notice. You're always welcome."

"The odd thing is, Emma." She drew out the name in a way that made it seem almost ugly. "That from where I'm standing, it doesn't seem I'm all that welcome." She looked out the window. "I didn't expect to come down to surprise Mark, and find him in the arms of another woman."

The hangover wasn't helping. She needed a hot shower and a big pot of coffee, not a confrontation with an angry wife. "Lieke. You have every right to be angry. But I assure you, *nothing* happened. We ate a huge dinner last night with the new chef, and drank far too much wine. We fell asleep talking on the couch. That's it. I promise you."

"So says the divorcée." She spat out the last word.

Mark shifted on the couch. Thank God. She was his wife, after all. It seemed only fair that he should deal with this. She stepped back, cautious to keep her distance. She touched his leg cautiously. "Mark, wake up. Lieke's here."

He sat up quickly, rubbing his eyes. "Lieke?" He opened his eyes, focusing across the room. "Lieke." His face fell. He ran his fingers through his hair, creating wild peaks. "What are you doing here?"

"Yes, we've been through this before. You obviously weren't expecting me."

"No, we weren't."

Emma cringed.

"I mean, I wasn't. You made it clear you were at Jelle's."

"The girls missed you. " She swiped at a tear. "*I* missed you. I came here to convince you to come back." She paced through the sunlight spilling through the window. "I thought it would be a surprise. I obviously wasn't expecting *this*."

Mark placed a hand over his eyes. His shoulders heaved up and down. His deep breaths thundered in the silent room. "Lieke, we only fell asleep. Nothing happened."

Would Dario have said the same if she'd caught him with one of his flings? How quickly she'd gone from the wronged woman to the homewrecker. Or at least, the perceived homewrecker. Only she could manage all of the guilt, with none of the sinning.

He stepped closer to Emma and placed a hand on her shoulder. She fought the urge to step back. "Emma, I'm sorry. I know I've embarrassed you and made you look bad, when it was all an innocent misunderstanding." His blue eyes searched hers. "I will have to go with Lieke, but I'll call you. You don't have to stay here on your own. We can schedule appointments in a few days, when I'll be back."

"That's rich, Mark. Come running back. I'm sure Emma will keep the bed warm." Lieke strode to the front door, slamming it noisily as she went out.

Mark clutched her in an embrace, kissing her hair. "I'm so sorry for this."

Emma reached up, placing her hands firmly on his chest and pushing back. She fought to keep her voice controlled. "Go, Mark. I've had enough for one day. I know about being the betrayed wife. Go to her, and leave me alone."

She turned to the window, afraid the tears would start to flow. She stood there until she heard the click of the front door.

In the distance, the snow-capped roofs of Todi sparkled in the bright sun, and the church bells began to peal.

Emma slumped to the floor and sobbed, drowning out the clanging of the bells.

CHAPTER 23

Tiffany

The air was brisk, but the sun warm. A nice change from all the rain since she'd returned from Perugia. Each morning she'd opened her shutters to see that the grey, rainy skies perfectly matched her melancholic mood.

She passed by the Circo Massimo, dodging the groups of Chinese tourists snapping quick photos before they hopped back onto the tour bus, only to be unloaded at another monument for another five minutes of photo-taking.

She heard Simone and Ramona return last night, heard their lock click, heard Ramona's high-pitched giggles. She'd checked to see neither was in the hallway before she dared go out this morning. But how long could she avoid them? Sooner or later, she'd have to see her neighbors. And then what?

Frankly, she'd expected more of Simone.

A phone call, at least. An apology for how she'd been made to feel she'd done something wrong. His girlfriend came back, and he jumped into her arms willingly.

Fine.

But why was Tiffany the ogre in this scenario? He'd pretended to want her when she was the only game in town, but didn't he owe her at least an apology? She hadn't thrown herself on him in Perugia. He was the one leading her on. And what a fool she'd been to follow him.

She checked her watch. She'd have to hurry to make the dance class. Christmas and New Year's had been miserable, but at least she had picked up decent-paying dance classes in the new year. She needed the cash.

A flash of copper caught her eye, and she stopped short. *Mi sono perso*. I am lost. The plaque she saw that day with Emma and Annarita. That was before she was lost, when she was still looking forward to an Umbrian Christmas with Simone. What a stupid fool she'd been. She took one last look at the engraving, and hurried on to Central Studio.

An hour later, she was making notes in her roster. Some of the girls were promising, but all had a lot of improvement to make over the coming months.

"Chiara," she yelled at a tall blonde girl. "Your arms are slack. Look at me. This is how they should look. Head straight up, look ahead."

The girl mumbled something, not making eye contact.

Tiffany walked over to her and placed her hand under her chin. "Chiara, in here you will listen to what I say and respond by looking me in the eye. I need commitment from you. Dance is passion, and I don't see the passion in you. You're a pretty girl, but that's not enough for a dancer. I want you to show me what you can do."

God, she could be talking to herself. But the girl bit her lip, looked straight at Tiffany with her shy eyes and repeated the sequence. She really was remarkably pretty, but she was at that awkward age. Probably in constant fear that she wasn't good enough. Then again, did most women ever outgrow that phase?

She smiled. "Much better. That's the level I want to see you performing at from now on." She turned and called to a girl with her long, black hair pulled into a high ponytail. "Manuela, stop right there. What did I tell you about that kick? No, stop. Come here. Copy me ..."

Showered and back in clean clothes, Tiffany felt a new energy on the way home. She'd been worried about taking on too heavy a class schedule, but now that she was regularly at Central Studio, she found she appreciated the certainty. Regular schedules, regular paychecks. She was tired of scrounging for money, hoping she'd have enough by month's end to cover her rent.

If she continued with these work rhythms, she might even manage to set a little aside, fatten up her bank account, and still have something left over for a little holiday. A vacation paid for by herself, not by the latest rich man she relied on to take care of her.

Lugging her heavy bag, she emerged onto her landing with a sense of relief. She heard the high-pitched giggles before she saw the couple nuzzling one another beside her door. Too late to escape. Only a few minutes earlier or later would have rescued her. She sighed. It was bound to happen eventually.

The couple broke apart. Ramona observed her with cool eyes. Simone avoided her gaze entirely. She readied her stage smile, the false one she used for auditions.

"Ciao, Ramona. Ciao, Simone. Got back okay? Happy New Year."

"You, too, Tiff. You were out of Perugia so quickly, we didn't really have the time to chat properly. It's starting out to be a *great* year." Ramona slipped her arm around Simone's waist, pulling in tightly.

Marking her territory in case Tiffany had other ideas. Simone still refused to meet her eyes.

"How 'bout you?"

"Yeah, well. You know. Stuff to do. So you're back now?"

"Apparently I can't leave my Simone alone too long. You never know what he might get up to in my absence." She pinned Tiffany in place with her razor-sharp gaze.

Tiffany struggled to keep her face neutral. Simone hadn't looked at her once. Why had she ever let her guard down? Her first instincts were always right. She never should have thought about getting romantically involved with him. Look where that had gotten her. Her temples throbbed. She was tired and thirsty after her class.

She slipped her key into the lock and turned back to the happy couple. "Great chatting with you. I've got some calls to make, but I hope we can catch up another time."

"Sure, Tiff."

Ramona ran a hand through Simone's hair. If Tiffany waited a few minutes more, would she throw him down on the hallway floor and have her way with him?

"Hey. Great ring! Looks a lot like your grandma's, only smaller. Guess that's safer to wear walking around Rome instead of that huge rock you have."

Tiffany looked down, confused. The ring. Simone's ring. She looked up quickly, catching his full gaze upon her. She recognized the shame.

"Yeah. Less chance of getting mugged with this one. See you two soon." She jumped inside, closing the door firmly behind her.

Sitting down at her dressing room table, she ripped off the ring and threw it into the jewelry box. Her face looked pale in the mirror's reflection. Pale and wan. The golden glow of the Indian summer was only a distant memory.

First her brother, then Simone. Men would always let her down. Why did she always let them? At least when she found rich men, *she* was using *them*—for the dinners, the yachts, the connections, the vacations she'd never be able to afford on her own.

The phone rang. She hesitated a moment before picking it up. "Oh, hi Lisa. It's good to hear your voice ... No, I'm just wiped out after dance classes. Think I'll stay in ... Oh, a party? You're sure they're producers from the new show on RAI? ... Okay, maybe just for a little while. See you at eight."

She hung up the phone and stared at her reflection. Was this what she wanted? She'd avoided parties since ... well, since that night. But why should she have to hide out, when she hadn't done anything wrong? It wasn't a given Alessio would even be there. And even if he were, she'd avoid him and hold her chin high.

An unconvinced woman stared back at her from the mirror. *You won't be young forever, Tiffany. You need to at least try.*

She opened her makeup case. The exhausted, put-upon dance instructor look wasn't going to impress anyone. Sexy was what she needed to achieve. She dabbed foundation onto her fingertips and got to work.

"Why haven't I met you before? Lisa, are you keeping your beautiful friends away from me on purpose?"

Lisa favored her student with her most insincere smile. Tiffany knew from Lisa's frequent stories what an arrogant ass Pierpaolo was, but he cornered her early on, and Tiffany knew he would be having auditions soon.

"And so you're a dance teacher? Have you been auditioning for television?"

"Not as much as I should." Tiffany shook her head with what she hoped looked like nonchalance. She didn't want to look desperate. "I've been concentrated more on musicals, but they're few and far between in Italy."

Pierpaolo shook his head dismissively. "And decidedly B-list. Or maybe even C or D." He looked her up and down. "If you dance as well as I hope you do, I think you'd be perfect. Looks are almost a ten, too." He sipped his drink. "Notice I said *almost*." He reached up and stroked her cheek, before sliding his hand down her neck, and boldly resting it on one breast. He squeezed gently. "These," he raised an eyebrow, "still need to grow. A little appointment could take care of this, and make you perfect."

His hand remained on her breast and Tiffany fought the urge to slap it away. From the corner of her eye, she caught Lisa's look of pity. After all, Lisa taught these people English, but she wasn't one of their possessions. Tiffany had never told her friend the full story about Alessio. She'd been too embarrassed.

Gently, she pushed Pierpaolo's hand away. "I'll think about it."

"Do more than think, baby. I'm not sure that's your strong point. I'd hate to not be able to take you on because you're thinking too much." He stepped closer, his groin rubbing against Tiffany. "So how about we get out of here, have a drink, and discuss what I can expect from your auditions?"

Lisa moved off. Tiffany saw all the glances being cast in her direction. The aspiring showgirl offering her wares to the television producer. A frequently rehashed plotline. If she got a part on Pierpaolo's program, the rumors about her discovery on the casting couch would all mention that party. Why hadn't she stayed home tonight?

She smiled at him in the admiring way she knew all men loved. "That sounds great, but I have a few people to see tonight. Let's talk later, okay?"

He leaned in and whispered in her ear. "I'm gonna find you later and take you up on that." He squeezed her breast again, but this time it wasn't gentle. He walked away without so much as a backward glance.

Tiffany surveyed the crowded room, looking for Lisa. In the corner, she saw a familiar profile. She studied the woman, no, a girl really, more carefully. She knew her. From where? Of course, her student from Central Studio. The one with such promise. Chiara.

With her blonde hair piled on top of her head, the makeup and the low-cut dress, she looked much older. Wasn't she only fifteen or sixteen? Her heart clenched when she saw who was beside her student. She'd recognize that artificially tanned profile anywhere. The crisp shirt buttoned low, the arrogant smile. Alessio. He seemed to be telling the girl to drink, he kept pointing to her glass of champagne. She sipped it and he moved closer, whispering something into her ear. Was she imagining it? Or was Chiara unsteady on her feet?

She moved closer, trying to conceal herself behind a column. Alessio continued talking to the girl. He whispered in her ear, stroked her arm. When Chiara turned in Tiffany's direction, her unfocussed gaze was obvious. Was she drunk? Or was Alessio up to his old tricks?

The poor girl was too young for this. What the hell was she doing here in the first place? Why had her parents ever let her go out? Then again, what would she have done at sixteen if she'd had a chance to impress television producers? At least she'd been far removed from that danger in Iowa.

She watched Alessio, running his eyes up and down Chiara's body. Fresh, virginal. He was indicating a back hallway, probably suggesting they have a private audition. The room would be miraculously equipped with a bed and a cheerleader's outfit. Or maybe, in a nod to variety, it would be a nurse's outfit this time. He sat her down in a chair and signaled her to stay put for a minute.

Tiffany waited until he'd disappeared to approach her student. She bent down before her and immediately saw the unfocused look in the young girl's eyes.

It took a moment, but Chiara blurted out, "Tiffany, what are you doing here?" Her words slurred together.

She took Chiara's glass from her hand, placing it on the ground. "Honey, you're coming with me."

Chiara shook her head. "No, no. Alessio wants to see me dance. Says there might be a place for me on his show."

Tiffany stroked the girl's cheek. "I bet he did. Believe me, Chiara, you'll thank me for this later. Let's get out of here."

She leaned Chiara against her body, placing the girl's arm around her neck. Chiara was already unbalanced, but the high heels weren't helping. Tiffany half dragged her, half carried her to the exit.

"She needs air," she said to the man closest to the exit.

He opened the door and let them through. They made their way to the elevator. Although she should have been fully concentrated on her charge, Tiffany couldn't help but reflect on the fact that the sentence she'd uttered at the door had been her most perfect command of Italian throughout her entire time in Rome.

If she were being immodest, she almost sounded like a native.

The San Giovanni Emergency Room was a depressing place to be on a Saturday night. Ambulance workers passed by with young people on stretchers, seemingly victims of drunken misfortunes. Knife fights, car accidents, the aftermath of drunken brawls. You name it, Tiffany saw it.

Tiffany was fine with allowing the serious cases to pass before her, but she blanched at the Italians and their dramatic talents as the ones with minor injuries groaned and cried when the nurses came by, attempting to hop to the front of the queue.

The well-dressed man beside her was calling on his phone, asking his contacts to perform miracles getting his father to the see a doctor before everyone else. Tiffany kept telling the nurses, "My sister's been drugged at a party. You need to look at her first."

The sister ruse had been a lie to accompany Chiara into the waiting room. Family only. Chiara was slumped on her lap. Tiffany kept feeling for her pulse and monitored her breathing, but this wait was endless. When Chiara finally opened her eyes, Tiffany said, "Chiara, honey, you have to give me your parents' number. I need to have them join us."

Although still groggy, the fear in her eyes was evident. "My parents? Why? You're here. Please don't tell them."

"I can't stay quiet about this. The doctors have to see you. I lied and said I was your sister, but your parents will need to speak with them."

A tear ran down her cheek. "Not my father. He's a well-known surgeon. Dario Rinaldi. He'll kill me."

"Dario Rinaldi's your father? The plastic surgeon?"

Chiara nodded. "But please don't call him. Call my mom. 3338967444."

Tiffany dialed the number. Dario Rinaldi, Chiara's father. The famous Dario Rinaldi. A woman answered. Tiffany paused a moment as she constructed in her mind the Italian sentence she needed to say, with her limited language skills. "*Buona sera. Sono qui al pronto soccorso con sua figlia.*"

"What? Emergency Room? With Chiara? I hear from your accent you're an English speaker." She switched to English. "What's happened? Is Chiara okay?"

"Oh, you speak English? Yes. Please don't worry. I think she was slipped drugs at a party. We're at San Giovanni's emergency room. Her pulse is steady. They still need to examine her."

"A party? What party? She was sleeping over at a classmate's house." The woman gulped for air. "Oh, God. I'll have to drop my sons over at a neighbor's house. I'll be right over."

Tiffany hung up the phone. There was something so familiar about the voice. She looked down and saw the big, blue eyes on her lap gazing up at her.

"Is she furious? Is she going to kill me?"

"She's worried. As any good mother would be. You should feel lucky. My mother wouldn't have roused herself out of bed for me." She stroked Chiara's hair back from her forehead. "You didn't tell me your mom was American. I thought your English was so good from international school."

Chiara closed her eyes. "Not just school. Mom was always insistent."

"I didn't know Doctor Rinaldi was married. He always seems to have so many ... uh ... friends."

She breathed in deeply. "Well, yeah. Those friends were the real problem. They seemed to get in the way of his marriage. My parents are separated."

"I understand. My parents divorced, too. But it was my mom who had all the friends. My dad's only friend was the bottle."

Chiara sighed. "So you know what hell it is."

Tiffany took her hand, and they sat in silence in the chaos of the waiting room.

"Emma?"

"Tiffany?"

"Oh." Tiffany sat frozen, seeing the fear radiating from Emma's eyes. "I didn't make the connection. You're Chiara's American mother? I ... I ... didn't know."

Emma ran over, crouching before Tiffany and looking down into Chiara's face. "How are you, honey?"

"Groggy. Dizzy." She looked up into her mother's eyes, appearing like a little girl. "I just want to see them, so we can go home."

Emma stood and began pacing. "This is ridiculous. Tiffany, how long have you been here?"

"An hour and a half, at least. I've spoken with the nurse, but people keep jumping in front of us, and the nurses aren't doing anything about it."

Emma's face was concentrated. "No. They never do. I hate to do this, but I'll have to get Dario to pull strings, otherwise we'll be here all night."

"No, not *papà.*"

"We can't keep this a secret, darling. He'll have to know one way or another. I'll be right back." She extracted her cellphone from her purse, and went out to the hallway to make her call.

Tiffany stared down at the teenager still sprawled over her lap. Now that she was looking for it, she saw all the similarities with Emma. Why had she never noticed it before? The girl was so beautiful. Who knows what would have happened to her if Tiffany had bowed out of the party. How could Alessio not have guessed her age? Or was that part of the attraction?

Chiara rubbed her temples. "If there's a positive side to emerge from this, at least *papà* will be grateful for your help. For me, you're perfect as you are, but if you wanted any work done, I know he'd do it to thank you. I mean, I know lots of dancers feel the need for little interventions here and there."

Tiffany took a deep breath. "Thanks, Chiara. But we have more important things to think about now. Getting you better. Just rest."

Chiara closed her eyes again. Her breathing grew slower and more rhythmic.

Emma's shouts from the hallway were audible in the waiting room. Screaming choice words in Italian, Tiffany would have assumed it was a local woman fighting in dialect. But each time Emma crossed before the open door, Tiffany confirmed the aggressive language was originating from the mouth of her elegant friend. A quick glance down assured her Chiara was asleep.

Emma entered the waiting room, snapping her phone shut and slipping in the seat beside Tiffany's. "Okay, I spoke to Dario. He's calling the head of the ER right now. It shouldn't be a moment."

"It sounds like you gave him a piece of your mind."

Emma's eyes flashed. "It was nothing less than he deserved. I have two years of pent-up rage putting up with his playboy lifestyle, not allowing him to prioritize his kids. He's been pulling this crap long enough, but at least now he knows I won't put up with it anymore. It felt good to finally let him have it." She took a deep breath. "But that's not what's most important now." She looked at Tiffany, her eyes glazed with tears. "I can't thank you enough. I don't even want to think about what could have happened if you weren't there tonight. You shouldn't have to stay here. Could I offer to call a cab and pay for your return?"

Tiffany shook her head. "It's okay. I'll stay."

Emma took Tiffany's hand in her own. "Thank you. I'll drive you home when we're done here." She dropped her voice to a whisper as she sat down beside Tiffany. "Thank you for rescuing my baby girl."

CHAPTER 24

Annarita

Annarita stormed into her apartment and collapsed on the couch, certain she wouldn't move from her perch until the next morning.

Her language school course schedule was turning out to be a killer, and she'd topped off her evening with an hour-and-a-half lesson with Tommaso.

Tommaso and his sexual prowess, Tommaso and his endless circle of well-heeled friends, Tommaso and his difficulty in deciding whether to spend Easter holidays in the Maldives or in Thailand. One, long me-fest she was forced to endure. He'd snapped at her the few times she'd tried to correct his abominable English. In the end, he'd settled on the half-English, half-Italian formula that seemed to work for him.

Then there was the complete disappearance of Fabrizio. When she stopped by the café to collect her reimbursement and her fee for the course, the waitress revealed that Fabrizio not only wasn't the owner, but he'd long been blacklisted from the locale after fighting with his former friend, the real owner. She had only allowed him back because the owner was away on holidays, and she was sleeping with Fabrizio. She hadn't been expecting Fabrizio to decamp to Malindi, breaking her heart. Of course, he'd also pocketed the money the students paid for Annarita's class. Not to mention leaving her in the lurch for the hundreds of euro Annarita shelled out for supplies.

Screwed once again. But as she took in the waitress' shell-shocked gaze, at least she took pride in the fact that her former student had never managed to seduce her.

But still, she and her café cooking students had laughed so much that evening, had worked so hard preparing their feast. Then they'd sat at a long table together and enjoyed the fruits of their labor, accompanied by fine wine. They'd talked about other courses after the holiday. Courses the café owner hadn't the foggiest notion about.

If being swindled by Fabrizio weren't enough, the holidays had been miserable, too. Most of her friends were away. The few that were in town wanted to go to parties and concerts Annarita really couldn't afford. She was filling in for double and triple shifts at the language school and their "holiday crash lessons." She'd tried to speak with Janice, the owner of the school, to suggest a new holiday cooking seminar—all taught in English.

Janice shot the idea down right away.

She flipped through a cookbook on her table. The only thing Annarita found herself enjoying these days was cooking. She'd always found it rewarding, always been good at it. Now it was the only thing she looked forward to at the end of her monotonous days.

Flipping through the recipes, she stopped at a page with steamed mussels in wine sauce. She'd have time to go to the fish market before work tomorrow. Why not? She picked up her cellphone and scrolled down to Tiffany's number.

"Hi, Tiffany. It's been a while since our coffee. What do you think about dinner and a movie tomorrow night? *Three Coins* if you want to see it again, and I was thinking seafood."

"Tomorrow I have dance classes most of the day. But I should wrap up a little after six."

"Perfect—what about seven at my place? I'll text you the address. I'll call Emma and see if she can come, too. I've missed you both."

"Me, too. The holidays have been tougher than usual. It'd be nice to see you and Emma again. Thanks for the invite."

"I'm looking forward to it. The holidays have been awful for me, too. It'll cheer me up to have a little Sperlonga reunion."

She hung up the phone feeling better than she had in a long time, and flipped through the cookbook choosing recipes for the following evening.

Frank Sinatra's singing swelled on the screen as the three couples embraced at the Trevi Fountain.

"Annarita, you're not even seeing this. Get back here," yelled Tiffany.

"Just have to check the oven. I'm starving. You two must be, too."

"It smells amazing," said Emma.

"Let's hope. Tiffany, can you switch off the television? Come on in here, *ragazze*. Dinner's served." Annarita set the pot of steaming mussels on the table.

Emma and Tiffany walked through the door.

"Oh, that looks good."

"Takes me back to Sperlonga."

Annarita held up a wine bottle. "Thank Emma for this. It's much better than what I had in the fridge for you. Our supplier of expensive wines." She poured into three glasses, and held hers up. "To our Sperlonga reunion. And *Three Coins*. I could certainly use some of that luck in love in the new year."

"Hear, hear."

"Tell me about it."

"Sounds like we all have the same New Year's resolution," Annarita sat down and began scooping mussels into each bowl. "The problem is, I never meet any decent men in my work. And I've had enough blind date disasters to last a lifetime." She lifted up her fork. "*Buon appetito.*"

"Oh, this is delicious," said Emma. "I'm glad she's out of earshot, but I'd be hard-pressed to say whose is better. Yours or Renata's."

"I take that as a real compliment. We're having Renata's cake tonight. I wrestled the recipe out of her."

"Oh, wow, spoiling us tonight," said Tiffany. "It seems like ages since I've eaten so well. Now that my neighbor ..." She trailed off and refolded her napkin. "I mean, a neighbor of mine used to entertain a lot, and he hasn't in a while. So I haven't been eating well."

"This is really amazing," said Emma. "I can't believe you whipped this all up after your teaching."

They ate in content silence, the piles of empty mussel shells piling up high on the plate in the center of the table.

Emma was the first to break the stillness. "You know, since we're all here for this reunion, I have to apologize to both of you. I wasn't exactly honest with you in Sperlonga. I've been having a hard time coping with the end of my marriage, and I made it sound like a mutual decision. It wasn't. He left me, after a long string of lovers I was too blind to notice. I was a wreck and prone to nervous breakdowns. That's why I needed the Sperlonga getaway in the first place." She took a deep breath. "A few nights ago, Tiffany rescued my daughter Chiara from a situation I can't even stand to think about."

Tiffany shook her head. "There's no need to mention it."

"But there is. It's all my fault. It wasn't the split, but my problems in dealing with it that led to the tense atmosphere in my family. It seemed easier to pretend I wasn't a mess. Chiara never would have gotten herself into that position if I'd been more attentive." She rubbed her eyes.

Tiffany put down her silverware. "Emma, don't blame yourself. It's not your fault at all. Okay, you couldn't cope and needed a break. So what? We all do sometimes. Do you have any idea why I was in Sperlonga, back when we first met? I needed to get away because I was drugged at a party. By Alessio, the producer who tried the same thing with Chiara. That's why I freaked out when I saw him with her. I'm an adult, and he tricked me. What chance did a young girl like Chiara have?" She put a hand over Emma's. "What more could you have done? You thought she was at a friend's. You had no idea she'd go to that party."

Emma wiped at a tear. "I encouraged her with dancing, I wanted to see her excited about something again after the rough time she's been having. But maybe I'm placing her in a situation that will create more pressure."

"She's talented, Emma. And she loves it. I'll speak to her, and you'll follow her closely. We don't have to fall victim to predators like Alessio."

"Did he ... I mean, did you?" She shook her head. "I'm sorry. That's none of my business."

"No, it's okay. I haven't told anyone because I've been so embarrassed about it. But I shouldn't be the one to be embarrassed. I was brought to the hospital when I passed out. My friend Simone was the only one who knew. But I've spoken to the owner of Central Studio, and we agreed I'll tell my story to the girls, let them know about the dangers out there."

"That's really brave of you," Annarita said. "It could make a real difference to your girls to hear a warning like that from their teacher."

"I know how much it meant to Chiara, what you did for her. She loves you, and loves your classes. I know from her how much those girls look up to you."

"I've been enjoying my classes. I was afraid to settle into teaching, but it's been a good decision. I like the studio owner, too. We've even talked about having more professional end-of-year shows."

Annarita spooned the last mussels into their bowls. "I think teaching is great if you have a love for it. I can see how this could work out well for you, Tiff, especially because your work is so creative. I'd be the first to go to your shows. But I'm stuck in a rut with my teaching. It bores me to death. I'm starting to hate my students, and I hate teaching English. I tried to suggest a cooking class to the school owner, but she wouldn't even hear me out."

"You'd like to teach cooking?" asked Emma.

"Would I? Is the Pope Catholic?" A timer went off. She stood. "Give me those plates." She gathered them and stepped into the small kitchen, returning with a steaming clay cooking dish.

"You're freaking kidding me," said Tiffany. "You made *orata* baked in salt?"

"You remember? From Gaeta. The potatoes are underneath. Tiffany, can you grab those plates from the table behind you while I cut the portions? Emma, will you pour more wine?"

Tiffany and Emma watched as Annarita expertly cut the fish and slid the portion of salt-layered fish and potatoes onto their plates.

Emma took a first bite. "Annarita, this is delicious."

"It's even better than what we ate in Gaeta."

Emma sipped her wine and observed Annarita. "Do cooking classes have to be in Rome for you to consider them?"

"Well, if you have something lined up in some posh hotel in Bali, I won't say no."

"Not quite what I meant. You know I'm working with Mark to open his agroturismo. We're hoping to have a soft opening by March, and be in full swing for Easter. There are lots of European holidays in May, so we're hoping for steady bookings right into the summer." She met Annarita's gaze. "If you remember, it's up in Todi. The place is coming along nicely. We have an Italian chef, but he doesn't speak English. We'd like to offer cooking classes to the guests, so we've been talking about trying out an English-speaking chef to work beside him."

Annarita stifled a smile. "Are you serious? Springtime up in Umbria? Teaching cooking? I'd love that."

"Wouldn't you miss Rome?" asked Tiffany.

"Well, if Emma agrees, I could give it a try. I could sublet this place easily for a few months, see how it goes. I hate the language school anyway, and the pay is awful. I'm assuming it will be better at the hotel?"

"I don't want to get your hopes up. You and Giuseppe—he's the main chef—would be working a lot at first. But I hope we'd hit our stride by early summer, work out a schedule for both of you. He's incredibly talented. He owned a restaurant in town." She smoothed the tablecloth. "But his wife had cancer and he had medical bills. He had to close, and now that she's died, he's looking for something new."

"Poor man," said Annarita. "But how would it be working for him? Does he seem ... difficult?"

Emma smiled. "He's an Italian man. Surely you know them enough to know, they're all temperamental."

"Yeah. That's true. Do you think we'd get on?"

Emma paused. "Honestly, I never considered it before sitting at this table. But yes, I do. He's demanding. He's a perfectionist. But for someone like you who loves to cook, I think you'd enjoy working with Giuseppe."

"Why don't you talk to him? See what he thinks. Talk to Mark, too, and get an idea what the salary might be. I'd love to play hard to get, but if it covers my expenses and lets me put a little aside, I'd jump on it. I'm at my wits' end here. I need to shake things up."

"Hear, hear," said Tiffany, raising her wineglass in the air.

Annarita shook her head. "Tiffany, you're tall, young, gorgeous, with a body that's a ten plus. You're a dancer, for crying out loud. What's your big complaint?"

"The same one that our 1950s friends had. Unlucky in love in the Eternal City."

"Oh, please."

"It's true. And it's partly your fault, Annarita." She fixed her with a mock severe look. "Remember Simone, my sexy neighbor? Remember how you told me I should give it a try?" She studied her wineglass carefully, avoiding their gazes. "Well, he invited me to his family's house in Perugia. Yeah, I always knew he was gorgeous and sweet and kind. But I was set on ignoring him and finding a rich TV producer who could secure my career. Then he takes me up to his place, and everything is so perfect and romantic. I love his family, and his sisters."

"But that's great, Tiff." Annarita edged forward in her seat.

"Well, yeah. I suppose it could've been. He told me how he's felt about me, he gave me a gorgeous ring. He brought me out in the perfect snowstorm in Perugia, where it was all so magical and romantic. And he kissed me." She placed her glass down. "And then, just like in a film, Ramona showed up."

"Who's Ramona?" asked Emma.

"The girlfriend. The one who left him for the hotshot job in Chicago." She sighed. "She shows up ... in Perugia ... when we're finally ready to move beyond friendship, and she decides she wants him back. All these months in Chicago were just a big mistake. They're living together again, for Christ's sake. I see them every single day and I want to tear her eyes out. And I want to punch him for being so spineless, for reeling me in only to cast me off the minute she comes crawling back."

She leaned back in her chair. The room was silent.

"What did you do?" asked Emma.

"I hightailed it back to Rome. I was so ashamed. Humiliated, really. I snuck out like a thief in the night. I couldn't bear to see them cuddling and touching one another over the breakfast table the next morning."

Annarita put her hand over Tiffany's. "Ouch. That's tough. But you were right to leave. How could he play with your heart like that? He seemed gorgeous back in Sperlonga, but it must have been the flattering light. You know how these romantic Italian landscapes can fill a woman's head."

Tiffany smiled. "Thanks, Annarita. I knew I could count on you. But I'm still a brainless idiot to have let him do that to me."

Emma shook her head. "You're not. And you're not the only one. This is only between us, but I fell for Mark. My partner. My boss. I said I wouldn't, that it was water under the bridge. He's married, for goodness sake. I, of all people, should know what that means. Know how important it is not to put other women in the horrible situation I've been in these past two years. And then I go and start falling for him. Old times, and all that crap." She swipes a hand across her golden locks. "Nothing happened, but we fell asleep in one another's arms after a long day of work. The wife came down to surprise him. I felt like such a tramp."

"But you didn't *do* anything," said Annarita.

"It doesn't matter, though, does it? I wanted to. At least in my mind."

"But you're beating yourself up over nothing. Maybe this is the sign you're ready to get out there. You haven't dated since the breakup with Dario, have you?"

Emma shook her head.

"So maybe it's time. It won't be with Mark. But Mark was able to convince you it's time. Don't punish yourself over this."

Emma smiled. "Maybe you're right."

"I know I am. Remember, I come from a meddling Italian-American family. What good are we if we're not dissecting everyone's lives and passing judgment? This is *nothing*. What would our friends in *Three Coins* do? They'd go toss a few coins and head out on the lookout for some available men. Who's to say they weren't onto something?" She raised her glass. "To Tiffany, who is embarking on a promising career as a dance instructor. And who is so young and gorgeous that she'll soon have a line of men showing Simone what a spineless ass he is. And be sure to flaunt them in his face to drive the message home."

Tiffany blushed and shook her head.

"And to Emma, who's ready to get herself out into the heartless world of dating again, and to her career as a hotel manager extraordinaire. And to *moi*, too. Here's to hoping my dreams as a chef will materialize. And, as we all know, the way to a man's heart is through his stomach. So it's only a matter of time until a prince on a white horse is pounding down my door."

Emma and Tiffany smiled and raised their glasses in the air, clinking theirs with Annarita's.

"To *Three Coins in the Fountain*."

"*Three Coins*."

"To finding love and happiness in Rome."

The three women sipped their wine, feeling much more optimistic than they had earlier that evening.

Annarita smiled inwardly. Her days had been miserable lately. She'd been right to take a chance and invite Emma and Tiffany over. They seemed so perfect and glamorous, like two women who'd have millions of better things to do than to spend an evening having dinner with Annarita. But they were struggling, too.

And what if Emma could help her out with her dream of cooking professionally? Hadn't she been begging the school director to let her teach cooking classes? Her pleas had fallen on deaf ears. Yet tonight, it was Emma herself who suggested it. She didn't want to get her hopes up, but it might just work out for her. It might work out for all three of them.

After all, if Maria, Anita, and Fran could do it, why couldn't they?

CHAPTER 25

Emma

"Giuseppe, no one's suggesting you'd take a back seat. Think of Annarita like a sous-chef. She's eager to learn, and she can take some of the pressure off you."

"Take the pressure off me?" He thumped his barrel chest with great force. His disheveled curls shook with the effort. "Who needs help from an untested ... *little girl*. And an American, no less! She'll probably want to serve hamburgers and hotdogs to our guests."

Emma suppressed a smile and leaned back on the gleaming kitchen counters installed only yesterday. She struggled to keep the angry, pacing Giuseppe at the center of her thoughts, not to be distracted by the sleek countertops and the sparkling new appliances. The workmen had done an amazing job. She pictured the guests in this space, taking cooking classes. There was no way Giuseppe's kindergarten-level English would cut it with the foreign guests. He'd need to accept Annarita. She'd have to make him see it was the only way.

"Oh, please, Giuseppe. *Per carità.* Annarita's family is Italian. She grew up with the same cooking you did. I've eaten her food. Believe me, she's a pro. She doesn't have as much experience as you do." She met his fiery black eyes. "But she's bright, and she's willing to learn. She most certainly will *not* wish to serve hamburgers and hotdogs to our guests."

"But she's a *broccolina*, a fake Italian. I cannot work with someone like that."

Emma took a deep breath. "Giuseppe. We open in two months' time. We already have a waiting list. It's fine for the Italians. But what about the English, the Germans, the Dutch? They're already asking about our cooking classes. Annarita can help you. We'll need her. I know her—she's a friend. She knows you're in charge. She'll be here to help—to follow your orders. I really think the two of you will hit it off."

He grunted. "Hit it off with a *broccolina*."

She reached out to put a hand on his sleeve. "Will you try? I can invite her up later this week, and you can meet and discuss your plans. See what you think." She stepped closer. "But Giuseppe, please promise me you'll give it a try. We'll need both of you to make this work."

He stepped back, out of her reach. He tied an apron around his waist and shook his head. "I will meet her, if you insist. But I can promise nothing. All will depend on her behavior."

"Well, then, I can guarantee it will be fine. Annarita is very diplomatic. You'll love working with her, I can assure you." Emma pulled her cellphone from her purse. "If you'll excuse me, I have a few calls to make."

She walked to the door as Giuseppe pulled vegetables from a basket, placing them on a large chopping board. They were still far from having their first guests check in, but Giuseppe had insisted he stop off today to try out the new kitchen. She patted her firm abdomen self-consciously. Goodness knows how much he'd expect her to eat this evening. Giuseppe would not take no for an answer when it came to accepting seconds or thirds for his cooking.

At least she'd be back in Rome tomorrow. She had to stay overnight for her morning meeting at city council. Things were moving along with the work, and it looked as if they would have the soft opening for Easter, as long as everything ran smoothly with the permits. Hiring Giuseppe was a stroke of genius, not only for his culinary skills, but also for cutting through the red tape. He was related to half the town. He made a call here and there, and eased her way with the local authorities. They were all thrilled to see him back to his old self, excited about his new project, eager to eat at the restaurant and support him.

Mark would be back tomorrow afternoon, so she'd made an excuse to get back to Rome early enough to avoid him. Dario had the children another night, but Mark didn't have to know that. She hadn't seen him since the embarrassment with Lieke. He'd called her as soon as he'd returned to Amsterdam, apologized for the misunderstanding, and told her she had nothing to feel ashamed about. But her cheeks burned every time she thought about it.

Something could have happened that night. She'd been attracted to Mark. She'd felt so at ease in his embrace. And what if something *had* happened? What if they'd betrayed Lieke? Wouldn't it be worse from someone like her? Someone whose world had crashed down around her only two years ago? How could she do that to another wife and mother? To those two beautiful girls?

She didn't trust herself around Mark, and so she worked hard to ensure their paths never crossed. She'd managed these past weeks. But Mark was pressuring her to come into the hotel full-time, offering her a stake in the hotel if that's what it would take to get her to agree.

A part of her was tempted. She wanted to ensure the hotel was a success, and she believed she could help to ensure it was. After such a long time not working, it was rewarding to see she could jump back into the workplace, knowing that she wouldn't have to feel she was relying on Dario's money forever. But how could she pluck the kids from their school and life in Rome? The twins might even be excited—they'd love to live in Todi, where they could walk or bike to friends' houses and soccer practice. But Chiara would never agree to moving to a small town in her last years of high school.

And, on top of those difficulties, she didn't trust herself around Mark all the time. He planned on spending more time in Todi once the hotel opened. How could she live in the hotel with him, worried all the time she might act on her attraction?

For a short time, over at Annarita's apartment, she'd allowed Annarita and Tiffany to convince her the attraction she'd felt for Mark that night in Todi was merely a sign she was ready to start dating again. She'd wanted to believe it.

She even made some offhand comment to Sabrina, who immediately clapped her hands together in excitement and blurted out "Finally!" Two awkward dinners had followed. Emma was often invited to Sabrina's home for dinners, but the last two were obvious pair-ups with single doctors working with Franco. One of the potential suitors had even gushed on about how much he admired Dario's practice and his reputation with actresses and well-heeled Romans. Emma shot a withering look at her friend across the table. Over coffee the next morning, she made it clear that she wasn't quite ready for the dating world.

Maybe she would eventually feel ready again. But not yet.

Mark must have been a first attempt. After all, he was familiar, a friend from the past. That's all it was.

It certainly wasn't the fact that one look from him could make her insides melt like a school girl. It wasn't that she felt her knees grow weak when he smiled. It couldn't be how he made her feel younger and more attractive every time his hand accidentally brushed hers, or the warmth of his touch when he wrapped her coat around her, or placed an arm on her back to lead her into a restaurant or a shop.

No, that was all her imagination.

But even so, working with Mark would be disastrous. It broke her heart to admit it; she'd invested so much in the successful opening of the hotel, but she had to get moving to find someone to replace her. Her work would end following the Easter opening. It had to end.

She couldn't trust herself around Mark.

CHAPTER 26

Tiffany

Tiffany caught sight of the clock in her living room. "Shit, shit, shit!" She threw a leotard into her bag, grabbed her coat from the coat rack, picked up her keys from the shelf, and raced out.

Hastily locking the door, she ran to the stairwell and gasped when she barreled headfirst into Simone, knocking him down. He managed to catch himself on the railing, and she placed a hand over her mouth.

"Oh, God. I'm so sorry! I wasn't looking where I was going. I'm running late for my classes today."

His hazel eyes met hers and he smiled that familiar smile, the one she hadn't seen in ages. He patted his chest. "No lasting damage done, Tiff. I wasn't looking either. You're welcome to barrel into me anytime. Just ... er ... not on the staircase next time." He grinned again and his eyes lit up.

She missed that look. The old Simone. And she was too late to stop and enjoy it. Better that way. It wasn't meant for her. It belonged to his girlfriend.

"I'm glad you're okay. Sorry again. You know what a disaster I am getting myself organized."

He grabbed her wrist. She met his gaze with stunned eyes.

"You're not a disaster at anything. You're perfect the way you are."

Her heartbeat accelerated, and she silently cursed herself. *Off limits!* screamed her brain.

He withdrew his hand, but the warmth lingered. "I'm ... uh ... sorry things have seemed tense between us." He looked down and kicked the railing. "I know it's my fault."

Oh, God. Not this. Not now. For weeks she'd wanted an apology, but not now that she'd moved beyond the humiliation.

She looked pointedly at her watch, then up into his hazel eyes. "Water under the bridge, Simone. But I do have to go—rehearsals are really important now."

She tried to edge around him, but he shifted, blocking her path. "You have a show coming up, don't you? The National Theatre, isn't it?"

She shook her head. "How did you know that?"

His eyes sparkled. "I have a student in your class. Leonora D'Andrea."

"Ah, Leonora's one of your high school students? She's talented."

He looked down. "She said she studied at Central Studio, and I asked if she knew you. She was so impressed you were my neighbor. She gushed on and on about your classes."

Tiffany felt her cheeks burn. "She's exaggerating."

Simone shook his head. "I bet she's not. I'm guessing her glowing reports about what an amazing teacher you are are one hundred percent accurate."

"That's sweet, but if I don't get a move on, we won't be ready for Friday's performance."

"Leonora will kill me in class tomorrow if I keep you from rehearsals. Friday night, huh? I may be in the mood for a dance performance." He tilted his head and observed her.

Great, Simone and Ramona in the audience, hands all over one another as they dissected her onstage.

She gave a tight smile. "No need. I know you have better things to do with your time. Better be off. See you later!"

She shouldered her heavy bag and raced down the stairs, hoping Simone would forget all about the performance. Friday was still a long way off.

CHAPTER 27

Annarita

Annarita looked out at the spires of the distant hill town. It was a perfect winter day—bright blue skies, sparkling sunshine, a bite to the crisp air. She'd never been to Todi. As the town grew closer, her nervousness increased.

It didn't help seeing the town for the first time on such a perfect day. What if she fell in love with it, fell in love with the hotel? And what if Giuseppe refused to work with her?

Emma warned her the hotel cook was somewhat tempestuous. High-strung had been another word she'd used. Annarita had taken the news in stride. Didn't she have a family of high-strung, tempestuous relatives, especially when you got them together in a kitchen? She assured Emma she could handle it, but as they grew closer, she began to doubt her earlier confidence.

Could she handle it?

She wanted this too badly. As she taught English classes at the dreadful language school, she imagined herself in chef whites at the Umbrian hotel, teaching cooking classes to foreign tourists. The traffic in Rome was bothering her more;

the noise and chaos sounded louder to her ears. She caught herself daydreaming about a simpler life in Umbria.

Emma told her she could live at the hotel. That there was a bedroom with a small living room-kitchen corner and a bathroom for her use. It would be part of her pay package. She could sublet her Roman apartment those first months to see if things worked out. Debbie already had a friend clambering for her place. That's how crazy apartment-hunting was in Rome. Who the hell would be dying for her place in any other city in the world? She'd come out ahead financially if she didn't have to scrimp and save for a Roman apartment and utilities, even for a few months.

And all of these considerations made the decision today far too high-stakes. Seeing the fairytale-perfect town looming in the distance only made things worse. What if Giuseppe said no?

Annarita knew Emma counted on this star chef. One complaint from him would deflate all her hopes for a new life.

"Annarita."

The voice broke her train of thoughts. She turned to Emma, in the driver's seat beside her. She'd been silent as they neared the town. She looked down at her hands, embarrassed by how they were clenched into tight fists.

"I can tell you're getting yourself all worked up about nothing."

"No, I'm fine." Her voice sounded as confident of that of a little girl sent to the principal's office.

Emma cast her a sideways glance and grinned. "Stop it. Giuseppe will love you. I'm sure of it."

Annarita felt her heart flutter. She was not at all sure Giuseppe's approval was a certainty. But she forced a wooden smile and looked out the window. "You're right. I always get nervous for any type of work. First-day-of-school syndrome, I guess." She smoothed down her pants. "So tell me again about the pool you'll be putting in. It sounds like heaven. Will you manage groundbreaking before Easter?"

She sat back and listened to Emma rattle on about work on the hotel. Todi loomed closer with each turn of the road, and Annarita fought to control her rising terror.

The kitchen windows were open, despite the brisk day. Annarita's cheeks were flushed from the stove, and from the relentless nervousness she'd felt as soon as she'd stepped into the perfect, gleaming room. She'd loved it the second she walked over its threshold. Sunlight tumbled through its large windows. It was beautiful, and shiny, and new. She could already envision chopping ingredients alongside the guests, sharing wisdom and advice her mother and grandmother shared with her. She stifled a smile.

After her initial glance around the room, her gaze fell upon an imposing figure in chef's whites standing in the far corner. Her gasp was audible. She gulped and stepped toward him, forcing a smile when every muscle in her body longed to flee.

"You must be Giuseppe," she said in a confident voice she didn't recognize. "I'm Annarita, and I'm so thrilled to meet you."

"Yes, the New Yorker who Emma tells me has an idea or two about how to get around in the kitchen." His black eyes appraised her with detachment.

She stepped back and wiped her sweaty palms on her slacks. "Well, uh ... of course I don't claim to be an expert like you. Emma's told me so much about your successful restaurant and the reputation you have here in town. But, uh ... I believe I do know a thing or two, and I'd love to learn more. I'm a quick study."

"Enough chitchat. You will find an apron and hat in the closet. Please put them on, and we will get to work to see what you can do."

Annarita felt a telltale pounding at her temple. "You, ah, want me to cook for you? I thought you might ask me to follow a recipe with you, or work alongside you."

"And I prefer to see what you are capable of. There is no point in us working together if I can't see this promise from the beginning. This will be a high-pressure kitchen. We will have to cook for the guests every day, and what we prepare will determine if they come back, if they tell their friends about us. I need someone who is up to the task, not someone who only dabbles in cooking and happens to speak English. I must meet with a supplier later this afternoon. Let's hurry up. Change and wash your hands, and decide what you will be cooking for me today. I will show you where the supplies are."

Annarita made her way to the closet, her heart sinking with each step.

There was no need to speak on the trip home. A political talk show was on the radio, and they listened to it on the way back. It ended as they approached Rome's National Theatre, and Emma broke the silence.

"I think that went quite well, don't you?"

Annarita took a deep breath. "Well? You think that went well? Giuseppe hates me."

Emma shook her head. "He doesn't hate you. He's a bit ... prickly, I guess. He was devastated after his wife's death. He can be a bit brusque at times. But he means well."

"Prickly? A bit brusque at times? Throwing me out of the kitchen and telling me never to return again because I used garlic and onion together 'like a stupid American' in one of the recipes? I mean, all five dishes before that were perfect. Okay, my ma does mix those ingredients sometimes, and I did it automatically."

"Yes, well." Emma bit her lip. "I'm sure he'll get over it. Giuseppe's temper tends to boil over quickly, but when he stops to think about things he's quite rational. I'm sure he'll understand what an advantage working with you would be."

"I appreciate your optimism, but I think that's the last thing he's thinking. I think he wanted to boot me over the ocean back to America. You know how badly I wanted this position—it would be such an opportunity for me. But even if he did accept me, I have no idea how I'd work with that man. He's so overbearing."

"He's a man. A man with an ego, and one who's hurting now. I don't want you to get too upset about this. I do think it will blow over."

Annarita sighed. "I hope so. Oh, look. Here's a parking spot."

"Good eye. We don't want to be late. Chiara will kill me."

"I can't believe Chiara is dancing at the National Theatre—under the direction of Tiffany. I can't believe I know two of the dancers performing tonight."

Emma maneuvered the car into the tight spot, got out and locked up. "Chiara's so nervous. She couldn't get to sleep last night. I have to admit, I have butterflies in my stomach, too, and I'm only in the audience. She loves having Tiffany as a teacher." She turned off the engine and stepped outside.

Annarita waited as Emma locked the doors. "Aren't you excited? Sixteen years old and already performing at the National Theatre. Pretty impressive."

Emma smiled. "It is, isn't it?" She took Annarita by the hand and pulled her across the busy road. "C'mon. Let's hurry. I want to see my baby when she comes out onstage."

CHAPTER 28

Emma wiped away a tear. She thought she'd managed it discreetly, but Annarita leaned in closer beside her and handed her a tissue. She waved it away.

"Don't be silly," Annarita whispered. "I'm over here tearing up, and I don't have a daughter onstage. I'd think you were heartless if you weren't weepy. Chiara's so talented. And beautiful."

Emma smiled and took the tissue. It was true. Chiara was performing beautifully—she'd really taken to dance classes under Tiffany's instruction. Tiffany told Emma how well Chiara was doing, but this was the first time she'd seen for herself. And here was her daughter, looking so self-assured as she glided across the stage. And so beautiful. Emma couldn't tear her eyes from her. In her costume and stage makeup, with the stage lights on her, she looked so much older than her sixteen years. How had all those years raced by in the blink of an eye?

She dabbed her eyes once again, this time making no attempt to hide her tears.

The applause had ended and the theatre was now empty, but backstage was a beehive of activity. Stagehands were dismantling the backdrops and sweeping the stage. Students were racing to change out of their costumes, and proud parents and friends waited to congratulate the performers they had come to see.

Emma stood next to Annarita, waiting for Chiara to change and for Tiffany to have a break in conversation from all the enthusiastic well-wishers. It had been a triumph. When Central Studio managed to finagle the National Theatre for a charity performance, Emma hadn't been expecting much. She was excited for Tiffany, of course, who was put in charge of the choreography, and she knew it would be a good opportunity for her friend. But she'd never expected a packed audience, and such impressive performances from the students.

And it was the first time she'd seen Tiffany perform onstage. Of course, Tiffany was so beautiful, with the perfect dancer's body. For months now, Chiara had been raving about Tiffany, how talented she was, what a perfectionist she was, and how she demanded the best from her students.

But even knowing all of that hadn't diminished her awe when she watched Tiffany's lithe movements under the blazing lights. She was so poised and professional. She possessed a remarkable stage presence as she glided across the stage and floated through the air. Her partner lifted her in the air as if she weighed nothing at all, and the two of them danced as if they were one person, driven by the music inside them. The audience watched in rapt silence. Emma had been one of the first to jump to her feet for a standing ovation that seemed to go on forever.

She hadn't even known she'd liked modern dance, and had attempted to talk Chiara out of her choice, trying to convince her to study ballet. Chiara was insistent, and after seeing the performance, Emma would never try to change her daughter's mind again. She'd chosen well.

The tall, young man to her left bumped into her. When she turned, his face was crestfallen.

"*Scusi, Signora.*" He turned his hazel eyes to her, apologized once again.

She assured him it was nothing, smiled into his handsome face. He wore an elegant coat and tie. She noted the large bouquet of dewy, red roses he held in one hand. For his daughter? There was always something special about a girl receiving roses from her father. Although the young man looked far too young to have a daughter Chiara's age.

She felt a gentle nudge on her side once again. This time it was Tiffany's dance partner making his way through the crowd. From the corner of her eye, she saw the handsome man beside her stop him and exchange some words. The dancer pointed in the general direction of the dressing rooms before he hurried off.

She watched the dancer weave through the crowds, as elegant walking through the throngs of dancers and family as he was when he was gliding across the stage. He reached Tiffany when there was a miraculous lull in the crowds around her. Emma watched as he kissed her gently on the lips and placed a proprietary, muscular arm around her shoulder. He pulled her lithe body into his powerful embrace. She couldn't tear her eyes away. They looked as lovely as they had onstage, and she wondered if the powerful emotions they conveyed in the performance had anything to do with feelings they had for one another in private life.

There was a sharp intake of air followed by a strangled sound from the young man beside her. A sideways glance revealed the now harsh lines of his face, with its resolute scowl. A temple throbbed angrily. She watched him tap the shoulder of a young dancer before him. He leaned in closely and said something to her. She nodded and he shoved the bouquet roughly into her hands. He turned on his heel and strode away from the crowd with long strides.

Emma shook her head. To her other side, Annarita looked up from her texting and followed the direction of Emma's gaze.

"Isn't that Tiffany's neighbor?" said Annarita.

Emma turned.

"What was his name again? The one I saw in Sperlonga? The one she said she was starting to fall for, but the old girlfriend came back and he broke her heart. Samuele. No, what was it? Yeah, Simone."

Emma thought back to their conversation at Annarita's dinner. He was her neighbor? The one who invited her to Perugia? The one she ran away from on Christmas Day?

Her gaze shifted back to Tiffany and her dance partner, his arm still around her as they laughed and chatted with Tiffany's students. Simone had seen the same thing she had. Maybe he didn't know Tiffany had moved on, too. One thing was clear: he must still harbor feelings for her.

"*Mamma!*"

She was distracted from her thoughts by her daughter, standing before her in jeans and a t-shirt, her hair still slicked back in a tight bun. Her heart filled with love as she gazed on Chiara, and she wrapped her into a tight embrace. "Oh, Chiara, sweetie. I had no idea how wonderful you are onstage. You made me so proud out there in the audience."

She reached out to Annarita and introduced her to her daughter. They all chatted about the performance, and Emma forgot all about her earlier train of thought and the frustrated young man beside her who gave away the bouquet of roses she suspected had been destined for Tiffany.

CHAPTER 29

Tiffany

Tiffany stepped out of the shower and dried herself before slipping into a silky nightgown.

The smooth fabric caressed her skin as it slid down, and she sighed with pleasure. This shimmering, pale pink lingerie had been purchased at an obscene price at *La perla* on a whim over a year ago after an audition she was convinced she'd aced for a show. Unfortunately, she hadn't. A woman with half her talent got the part and the lucrative contract.

Although parting with so much money had been tough, the whisper of luxurious fabric against her bare skin always felt celebratory.

And that's what she needed tonight.

She'd been destroyed after the performance, but speaking to the students and parents backstage energized her. She and the other dance teachers had even gone out for a bite to eat once the theatre cleared out. The evening had been a success, and they spoke about another performance in a few months' time.

Sitting with her colleagues, laughing, and discussing plans for the new semester no longer scared her. Being a dance teacher didn't mean she was a failure. It didn't mean she would become her mother. She was nothing like her mother, and never would be.

She walked out into the living room and stretched out on the couch. Eyes closed, she thought back to the performance, and the heady mixture of excitement and terror the girls expressed as they prepared in the dressing room.

Emma and Annarita had been there. They'd waited until everyone cleared away before congratulating her. For some reason, it was their approval that meant the most to her. The admiration of her new friends.

She opened her eyes and sat up, leaning over to the side table to smell the red roses she'd placed in a vase. Cristina, one of her students, presented them to her, smiling and saying a man had shoved them in her arms, asking her to give them to her teacher. She'd laughed. "Seems you have a secret admirer."

The doorbell rang and she startled. She glanced at the clock on the wall. Almost midnight.

Her heart beat faster as she crept to the door and looked through the peephole. She breathed a sigh of relief. "Oh, Simone. It's you. Is something wrong?"

"No. I'm sorry about the time. I just wanted to stop by for a minute, if I'm not disturbing you."

She sighed. She could turn him away, but it seemed mean. "I'm not dressed."

"That's okay for me."

"Yeah, but it's not for me. Just a sec." She went to that bathroom and plucked down her thickest, most shapeless terrycloth robe and slipped it over her form-fitting nightgown. She returned. "Okay. I'm decent now."

She opened the door. Simone stood before her in jeans and a soft, grey sweater. In one hand he held a bottle of champagne and in the other, two flutes.

He smiled. "I hope you don't mind, but I wanted to offer a toast to you. I won't stay long."

She peered out into the hallway. "Isn't Ramona coming over?"

He looked down. "She's in Chicago on business."

Every instinct told her to shove him into the hallway and double-bolt the door, but her sensible side won out in the end. After all, they were neighbors. And he'd fixed her plumbing more times than she wished to count.

"Okay, Simone. But only a few minutes. I'm really beat." She stepped back and motioned him in. She gestured to the couch and took a place at the farthest point from where he settled.

Simone placed down the bottle and flutes. He turned away from her and looked at the roses on the side table. They both sat still in an uncomfortable silence.

Tiffany forced herself to speak. "It's thoughtful of you, but you really didn't have to. You probably imagined the performance much more impressive than it actually was. It wasn't such a big deal."

He looked at her directly for the first time that evening, and shook his head. "What do you mean it wasn't a big deal? I was there. It was amazing." He took a deep breath. His voice was almost a whisper. "*You* were amazing."

She looked at him, confused. "You were there?"

"Yes, I was. I could lie and say I never miss a modern dance performance. But you'd see right through me." He picked up the champagne, unraveled the foil and expertly popped the cork. He poured into the two flutes and handed one to Tiffany, before picking up his own. "What can I say, except it was a triumph? To my incredibly beautiful and incredibly talented neighbor and friend." He clinked his glass with hers.

She felt the butterflies pounding their wings in unison in her stomach. The same ones she'd felt in Perugia and must absolutely *not* feel now, because Simone could never be anything more to her. A neighbor and friend. A neighbor and friend, with a live-in girlfriend.

She sipped the champagne, feeling the bubbles pass through her body, fraternizing with the raging butterflies. Why had she opened the door to him? Why hadn't she feigned a headache and said she'd stop by in the morning?

She took a deep breath and gave herself the courage to meet his gaze, those warm hazel eyes that always seemed to see right through her to her true feelings. "Wow, I don't know what to say. I know you have better things to do on a Friday evening than watch dance performances. But I know Leonora must have been thrilled to have her teacher there to see her. She performed well. They all did." She rested her left arm on the back of the couch. "I was so proud of all my students."

Simone gazed at her intently; his eyes crinkled in that way she'd always found irresistibly sexy. Simone spoke and broke her inappropriate train of thought.

"I hope you won't take this the wrong way. It's meant as a compliment." He placed his flute on the table. "You're an extremely talented teacher. Leonora's been raving about you these past months, and I was curious to see for myself. It didn't even seem like a student recital. And how they raced around you at the end. That was genuine. Not all teachers have that effect on their students, but it's clear you do." His voice dropped almost to a whisper. "It's obvious you love them."

She took another sip of her champagne.

"Tiff, I know you've been set on a television career. And I want you to do what makes you happiest. You deserve it. But I do hope you'll seriously consider teaching as an option. Talent like yours—both onstage, and in motivating young people—is much rarer than you think." He smiled. "Can you imagine any of those talentless bimbos on those godawful TV programs having anything to teach to young girls?"

She shook her head and looked beyond him, at the roses. "Teaching always seemed like the last option, only if I couldn't make it as a 'real' dancer. But these last few months I've truly enjoyed it. I've stopped seeing it as a failure."

"I know I'm biased. I chose teaching over research, and my parents took it hard at first, but they know I love what I do. Why were you so afraid to teach?"

Tiffany looked down at her flute. "Because my mother taught. She dreamed of making it big, and, in the end, she had a little dance studio in Buffalo Plains, Iowa. She became a pathetic drunk, and I had to take over running the studio to keep it afloat. I had to drop out of college and come back home to community college to slave away for my mother, until I escaped to Des Moines." She looked up at Simone. "My father was a failure, and, well, you've had the misfortune to meet my brother." Her laugh was bitter. "He takes the prize. With a family like that, is it so surprising I dreamed of something more?"

He shifted over on the couch. She felt the warmth of his body through her thick robe. She smelled the heady scent of his cologne, and she fought the urge to shove him back across the couch. Instead, she remained rigid as he slipped an arm around her shoulder.

"Tiff, you never told me much about your family. And I never wanted to pry. I understood you hadn't been happy back home, but I wish you wouldn't let them cloud your judgment now. No one who knows you would consider you a failure. You light up a room when you enter it. You're smart and funny, beautiful and kind."

She felt herself melting under his embrace. This was wrong. Terribly wrong. He was comforting her as a friend, but she was moved by the words of the man she was falling for back in Perugia. Before Ramona returned and Simone made it perfectly clear she was only his fallback choice.

He leaned his head into hers and kissed the top of her hair. "Gosh, when I think back to our short time together in Perugia and how much everyone loved you. You know I'm still getting calls from neighbors and friends asking after you?"

A sharp pain felt like a knife slicing into her heart. Her whole body went rigid. She freed herself and slipped out from under Simone's arm. Pacing the room, she tried to calm her pounding heart. She poured herself more champagne and fought the urge to gulp it down in one sip.

Simone sank his head into his hands, and groaned. "Sorry, Tiff. What an ass I am."

He looked up at her under thick lashes. She wanted so much to hate him, but he looked heart-breakingly handsome gazing up at her, with his tousled hair and contrite expression. How could she hate him simply because he couldn't feel the same about her as she did for him?

"I know we never talked about it. My fault, too. I was such a coward, and I couldn't face you." He took another sip of his champagne.

She couldn't handle revelations now, his telling her he'd let things get out of hand, had allowed himself to get carried away by feelings for her that were never real. She couldn't handle hearing she'd only been a placeholder for Ramona, one to be ceremoniously dumped the second the real love of his life returned. But that she should realize what an incredible person she really was, and that she was bound to find someone special soon.

She couldn't listen to all that crap tonight.

She'd been getting better these months. Growing stronger. Tonight had been a moment of triumph for her. He couldn't ruin that for her, too. Hadn't trampling on her heart been enough for him?

She looked straight at him and moved to the opposite end of the couch, where he'd sat earlier. She willed her voice to be strong and confident, something she didn't feel inside. "I don't want to talk about it, Simone. It was a long time ago. We both got carried away by the romantic setting—the snow, the night air, spending so much time together, and by everyone assuming we were a couple." Her hand shook and she lowered it, hiding it in the pocket of her robe. "It wasn't real. It was just make-believe. Two friends pretending their friendship could turn into something more." She averted her eyes from his. "Ramona came just in the nick of time. She saved us from making fools of ourselves."

The silence was deafening. The noisy wall clock she'd always meant to replace ticked out the endless seconds. She observed Simone from the corner of her eyes. He was slumped in his seat, staring straight ahead. At least he had the decency to hide his relief, pretending to be devastated by her announcement. Saving face for her. Exactly as friends did for one another.

He turned to her, looking beyond her at the roses. "I guess I deserved that. It's what I'd assumed, of course. And would have learned earlier had I had the guts to ask you." He stood up and paced. "You deserve so much better than me."

Oh God, here it was. The stupid line she couldn't bear tonight. The one she'd hoped she could avoid. All the triumph of the evening deflated within her.

His back was to her. "And I see you have. Moved on, I mean." He took a deep breath, and turned around. "I'm happy for you. I hope you'll bring him by one day, and I can meet him properly."

His face looked far from happy, and Tiffany knew hers must look confused. What the hell was he talking about?

He plucked up his glass and took another sip. "Sorry, I'm still not making any sense. You're wondering how I know." He pointed to the table beside her. "Those roses. They were from me." He gave an ironic half smile. "I went backstage like a love-struck admirer to surprise you, and I waited for the crowds to thin out. I saw your new boyfriend kiss you and put his arms around you, and I didn't want to ruin the moment for the two of you. So I left the flowers with one of your students and took off like a scared teenager." He gave a hollow laugh. "Funny that I'm paid to teach and be a role model for teenagers, but I'm no better than they are."

Tiffany shook her head. "You mean Valentino?"

"Ah, that's his name." He shook his head. "Go figure. Yes, and I'm happy for you, Tiff. I watched the two of you onstage, and I was so moved by how sensuous the performance was, how you danced as one, how the two of you seemed so much in love. I suppose I never appreciated that about dance. How it expresses emotions so perfectly." He dropped his gaze. "I'm sure you would have conveyed that with any partner. You're so talented. But I guess it helps when you happen to be so in love with your partner in real life. Makes it ..." he paused, "... more real." He trailed off in an awkward silence, standing rigidly.

Tiffany stared at the flowers, confused.

Simone strode back to the couch, poured himself another glass of champagne and downed it all in one quick gulp. He coughed, before sliding closer to her on the couch.

"Tiffany, I needed liquid strength to be able to confess this to you. I'm begging you, just let me speak and get it all out. It's killing me."

His hazel eyes were intense as they stared into her own, pleading with her to understand. She wouldn't have been able to utter a word anyway, so she sat in silence.

He placed a hand on hers, and she felt a jolt of electricity spread through her body. Then she kicked herself for allowing her emotions to control her.

"I was in love with you from the day I met you, when you moved in here, fresh to Rome. You were so open and friendly, so ridiculously beautiful. You made me laugh, and I loved our long conversations. Loved feeling I could help you out as you were settling into Rome, loved knowing you'd turn to me when you needed things."

What was he saying? She furrowed her brows.

"Yes, I know. I was with Ramona. Had been for some time by that point. But see, I knew you didn't feel the same about me. I saw the guys you went out with. The TV types, the ones who liked to show off their money with their sports cars and their yachts. You were always honest with me that you wanted that kind of man. I knew I never stood a chance with you, so I worshipped you from afar and got it into my head we were only friends."

"But that's not true. You loved Ramona. You were a wreck when she left."

He sighed and sat up straighter. "It's true. I'd pushed you so far to the back of my mind, and I concentrated all my efforts on making things work with Ramona. I thought things were good. We'd been talking about settling down. Getting married and starting a family. It seemed like we both agreed it was time." He turned away. "And then one day I come home and she's packing her bags. I was blindsided. And desperate." He turned back to her and smiled. "As you know."

He slid closer and placed one hand over hers. All her senses were heightened, but this was the point where he was going to say he'd been given a second chance. She looked him straight in the eyes, careful not to betray any emotions.

"And then, when she was gone, I thought I sensed a change in you." He sighed. "Not at first, but after the horrible things you went through after the party, and some time away to think in Sperlonga, and how you used to talk to me about possibly working more at Central Studio." He lifted the hand covering hers and wiped away a stray tendril of hair, tucking it behind her ear in one, precise swoop. "For the first time, I thought you might have changed, might consider being with a teacher." His voice dropped a register. "Being with me. When you were so down after your brother came, I suggested you spend the holidays with my family. I knew they'd love you, of course. How could they not? And I hoped seeing me in my hometown might help you to think about me as more than a friend." He looked at her and laughed. "Pathetic, I know. And transparent. But I loved those days with you. And I thought it was working."

She blinked quickly, determined to keep any tears from forming. "Yes, Simone. It was."

With one hand, he stroked her hair and wrapped a tendril around his finger. He smiled at her. "I've always loved your hair." He released the lock gently onto her shoulder. "Yes, Christmas Eve. I built up so much courage to give you that ring. I knew it didn't replace your grandmother's, but hoped would show you how much I felt for you. And everything was perfect, with the snow, and the silence, and you next to me on the bench out in my yard."

She felt frustration building inside of her. Why was he doing this to her? "I really don't see what the point is in rehashing this."

He placed two fingers gently on her lips, and she cursed herself for the way she longed to kiss them.

"Please." His eyes pleaded with hers. "You promised to hear me out. Then I swear to never raise the matter again." He lowered his hand and rubbed his leg. "Unfortunately, I made one fatal error. I'd spoken to Ramona. She seemed so well settled into her Chicago life. She was so happy. I was tired of always being the pathetic one, telling her how miserable I was, begging her to come back. So I made the mistake of telling her I'd invited you to Perugia, and hoped I might convince you to see me as more than a friend." He sighed and clapped his hands together. "You see how well that worked out."

Damn, one phone call. And if he hadn't said anything? Ramona would still be in Chicago and she and Simone might have been together. She stood. She needed to move around. She wished again she hadn't let him in. What good could talking about this do for anyone?

She avoided his eye. "Look, Simone, I would have appreciated this explanation two months ago. But I'm not sure what good it does now. You're back together with her now. I appreciate your honesty ..." Her breaths were coming too quickly now. "But it would be best to bury this and pretend nothing ever happened." She met his eye. "In the end, nothing did. One interrupted kiss." *One amazing kiss I haven't been able to forget since that night, as much as I've tried.*

Simone looked down at the floor. "I know. I'm done now. I only wanted to let you know that Ramona is back in Chicago. I told her to go. She did go over for business, but she'll be staying, and I'll ship the rest of her things for her." He looked up at her. "It wasn't working. She begged me to give it another try, and we did, but there was nothing to salvage. I don't love her anymore." He stood, but kept the distance between them. "I love you, Tiff."

She shook her head. "What are you saying?"

He grimaced. "Now you see why I asked you to let me get it all out. I wanted to tell you tonight. I've been looking forward to seeing you dance. I knew you must be talented, but I was spellbound watching you onstage. I was even more in love with you and nervous as a schoolboy waiting for you backstage." He took a deep breath. "And then I saw Valentino. Saw how he kissed you, how at ease you were with one another." He took a step closer, took her hands in his.

Her breaths sounded ragged to her own ears.

"And I was heartbroken, I'll admit it. But I also know I deserved it. It was my punishment for being such a coward back in Perugia. I let Ramona manipulate me, and humiliate you. How you must have hated me. You deserve a boyfriend like Valentino. I want you to be happy, Tiff. I wanted you to know how much I loved you, but to also assure you I can handle just being your friend. I want to meet your *innamorato*. I promise I'd never tell him any of what I'm telling you tonight. This will be the last time I mention it. But I think your boyfriend is the luckiest man on earth." He took a deep breath and smiled, but it didn't reached his eyes. "I envy him more than he'll ever know."

Gently, Tiffany extricated her hands from Simone's grip. Her heart beat uncontrollably. She walked to the couch and sat down, still feeling dizzy.

Simone broke the silence. "*Che figura che ho fatto*. Listen, I know it's a lot to take in. I told you I wanted to tell you everything, but I also mean it when I say I won't ever mention this again. Can we change gears tomorrow? Maybe go see a movie?" He stepped over and gave her a quick peck on the cheek. "I'll ... uh ... call you tomorrow and see if you're free. Ah, goodnight, Tiff." He raced to the door, his hand quickly on the doorknob.

Tiffany looked over, imagining Simone's nerves wound tight as a sprinter's on the starting blocks. She took a deep breath. "Simone."

She stood as he turned around, his hand still grasping the doorknob. She stayed silent for a moment and looked at him, at his cheeks flushed with emotion, his thick hair tousled at the end of a long night, his broad shoulders slightly slouched, and those hazel eyes she'd always dreamed of losing herself in.

"There's something you should know."

He dropped his hand from the doorknob, but he didn't move any closer.

"You were very honest with me tonight, but you got one thing wrong."

"Look, if you need a bit of time, I don't want to rush you. I can wait to call you if you want. We'll take a rain check on the movie. I'd understand." His voice sounded strained.

She took a step closer and untied the belt of her robe. It fell away to reveal shimmering pink satin, and she shrugged the robe from her shoulders, allowing it to fall around her feet. Simone took a deep breath. His eyes travelled the length of her body as she approached him. His admiration was evident.

"No, my desire to go to a movie with you is not what you got wrong." She stopped before him and tilted her face up to meet his gaze.

"It's not? So what was it?" His voice was ragged. "What did I get wrong?"

She paused, gazed into his eyes, watched his breaths go in and out. "Valentino's not my boyfriend."

He arched an eyebrow. "He's not? But I saw him …"

"He's very special to me, and I know he loves me, too." She smiled and paused again, enjoying his confusion. "But Valentino's not interested in me romantically. I spend a lot of time with him and his boyfriend, Philippe." She stepped slightly closer. "I think you'd like him."

There was a spark in Simone's hazel eyes. This time, the smile reached his eyes, forming the crinkles Tiffany loved. She reached up with her index finger to trace one. He sighed.

"I'd go a little farther than that." He placed a hand on Tiffany's hip, rubbing his large hand along the shimmering fabric. He placed his other hand on her shoulder as he stepped closer, leaning in his forehead to touch against Tiffany's. "Right now I'm prepared to say I absolutely love Philippe. I can honestly say that no man has ever made me so happy as Philippe has tonight."

"I'm so glad."

She stood on her tiptoes and pressed her lips against his. He responded immediately, his kiss so insistent she would have collapsed had he not encircled her in his strong arms. When she broke away for air, he placed one arm behind her back and the other under her legs. Lifting her up, he carried her to the couch. He laid her gently down.

He sat beside her and caressed up and down her body with gentle fingertips. "All this time I was baring my soul to you, and you were wearing this under that big, shapeless robe."

She smiled. "Didn't I tell you I wasn't decent when you rang my bell?"

"Yeah, well I wasn't imagining this." He leaned down and kissed her neck. "You're so gorgeous, Tiff. I'm going to be staring at you all night."

She propped herself up on her elbows. "I'll kick myself for saying this, but are you sure? You know we're neighbors. Things could be awkward if we rush into anything. What if it doesn't work out?"

He stroked her hair back from her face. "Tiff, my heart was breaking earlier tonight when I saw Valentino kiss you and thought he was your boyfriend. I've already messed things up and lost you once. I'll never let that happen again." He leaned down and kissed her. "Introducing you to the parents will be easy, too. They already love you and wanted to disown me when I got back together with Ramona. Don't even talk about my sisters and how furious they are with me." He kissed her eyelids. "They were right. When I think of you leaving us on

Christmas morning and coming back here alone on the train, I'm so ashamed."

She reached under his sweater and rubbed her hands over his shoulders and then across his broad back. "Let's forget about these things. The important thing is we're together now. And you better not have plans for the entire weekend, because I'm not letting you out of my sight."

"I wouldn't dream of it. I'm all yours, if you'll have me." He stood and gently pulled her arms up. He scooped her into his arms and kissed her before carrying her to the bedroom. "I'm all yours from now on. And you have no idea how happy that makes me."

She threw her arms around Simone's shoulders and pulled herself into his chest. She knew it was ridiculous, but in her head, even as she tried to suppress it, she simply couldn't stop her inner soundtrack, Frank Sinatra crooning, *Three coins in the fountain.*

CHAPTER 30

Annarita

The air was brisk and the clouds threatened rain, but the weather looked like it might hold up for a bit more. Annarita, Emma and Tiffany sat optimistically outside, sipping their tea, eating cookies and catching up on new developments.

"Tiffany," said Annarita. "Will you wipe that smile off your face? You're texting Simone again, aren't you?"

She looked up and blushed.

"Oh no, it's true. You're away from one another for one hour and don't know how to survive."

"Annarita, leave the poor girl alone. She's smitten. We all remember what that feels like." Emma rolled her eyes. "Although for some of us it seems like centuries ago."

Annarita sipped her tea. "I know I'll regret saying this, but how's it going?"

Tiffany's whole face lit up. "Oh, he's so *perfect*. I can't believe it took us so long to get together. Did I tell you what a great cook he is? Did I tell you he's taking me to Venice next weekend?"

Annarita made a face. "If she's this bad, can you imagine how *he* is? He's surrounded by teenagers. Maybe it's rubbed off on him."

"Haha. He wants to meet you both, suggested I ask you over to dinner one night."

"It's very sweet of him, but do you think we could stand a whole evening with the happiest, most-in-love couple on the planet?"

"Annarita, get used to it," said Emma. "We'd love to."

Emma shot her a look Annarita swore she must use with her children.

"Oh," continued Tiffany. "I know you'll both be happy about this. I've promised Simone I'll improve my Italian. His English is perfect, but he says it's time I learned seriously—that he wants to teach me."

"Well, you know what they say." Annarita winked at Emma. "The best way to learn a language is in bed." She smiled at Tiffany. "With all the time you must be spending there, you should be well on your way to fluency."

Tiffany shrugged and took a cookie. "I'm not rising to the bait, Annarita."

"Oh, my. Tiffany's eating cookies. It must means she's burning millions of calories a day with her nighttime exercises."

"You're impossible." Tiffany smiled.

"I am most certainly not. Instead, this is my chance to say '*I told you so*.' Remember when we first met back in Sperlonga, and I told you that you should be with that gorgeous man? What did you say?"

Tiffany rolled her eyes.

"Well, if you won't 'fess up, I'll say it myself. You said, basically, no chance in hell. That he was just a neighbor, and that you weren't interested. Emma, didn't I tell you those two should be together?"

"It's true, she always was insistent. Did I tell you he was standing beside me after the performance? He had a huge bouquet of roses and he was so nervous. I'd never seen Simone before, so I didn't know who he was until he was leaving and Annarita recognized him."

"I'm so glad he confessed everything to me that night. What if he had kept it all inside?"

Annarita and Emma looked at one another and smiled indulgently.

Emma turned to Tiffany. "With two people as ridiculously in love as you are, you would have found your way to one another eventually. So, Perugia's not far from Todi. We'll expect you to stop by sometimes to see the hotel. The pool should be completed by May."

Tiffany's face lit up. "Oh, we'd love that. Simone's taking me up to Perugia soon. And I love his family, so I hope we'll go more often in spring."

"There's another reason to stop by when you can." Emma placed an arm around Annarita's shoulders. "We managed to snag a very talented sous-chef. And our restaurant is bound to be a hit."

Tiffany beamed. "You're kidding! You didn't tell me anything."

"Well, I only found out two days ago," said Annarita. "And who could get a word in edgewise with new lovebirds who have to go on, and on, and on yet some more, about how perfect their new man is?"

"Okay, point taken. I'm insufferable. But you know what a hard year it's been for me. I'm only amazed things are looking so good now. And it looks like it's the same for you." Tiffany stood to hug her friend. "I'm so happy for you. Tell me how it happened."

"Well, our diplomat here arranged for a Camp David-style meeting. Sadat and Begin were a piece of cake compared to what our Emma had to face. She brought me up for another sit-down with *Maestro* Giuseppe, and somehow she softened him up, because … he agreed to work with me!"

"Wow, that's big news from what you told me after your first meeting. You were convinced it would never happen." Tiffany turned to Emma. "How did you manage it?"

Emma shook her head. "Nothing special. I suggested they meet again, after Giuseppe had thought about it. He's a bit gruff on the exterior, but he's a teddy bear underneath."

Annarita leaned in closer. "Says the woman who has never shared a kitchen with him. Do keep in mind that there *are* an awful lot of sharp knives around my new workplace …"

Emma raised an eyebrow.

"But, despite the gruffness, I've decided I'll enjoy working with him. Aside from being ridiculously talented, when I tried to turn down one of his gazillion-calorie desserts, he chewed me out, said women like me were an abomination. That I was too skinny, and always counting calories instead of enjoying food to the fullest. He said he liked a woman with curves, and that I should stop fighting nature and put on a few pounds, like God intended." She beamed, and poured more tea into her cup. "Can you *believe* it? The first time in my life I've ever been called too skinny. How can I *not* like the man?"

Emma and Tiffany exchanged smiles.

"When do you start?"

"At the end of the month. I need to get there by the end of March to prepare for the Easter opening. Giuseppe will be taking me to the fruit and vegetable markets, introducing me to all the local suppliers. We'll even have our own chickens for eggs. If he talks Emma into it, we'll have cows, too."

Emma shook her head. "It's true, Giuseppe doesn't give up. He's planning our vegetable garden, insisting on fruit trees. The man's unstoppable."

"And will you live there?" asked Tiffany.

"Yes, I've sublet my apartment starting in April. It's a four-month trial period. And I have a little apartment in the hotel complex. Thanks to Emma, it's quite luxurious."

Emma smiled modestly. "The apartments did turn out pretty nicely."

"Nicely enough to convince you to live in one?" asked Annarita. "We could be next-door neighbors."

Emma smiled. "I don't know. Mark keeps asking, but I haven't decided yet."

"Giuseppe says your new hobby is avoiding Mark."

Emma's mouth opened in surprise. "That's not true."

"I didn't say it was. I said that was his impression. He thinks the two of you like one another, but neither of you will admit it."

"That's just silly. Mark's a married man. And I am *not* avoiding him. Our schedules are different. That's all."

"Methinks she doth protest too much." Annarita winked at Tiffany. "A little like you when you tried to convince me that Simone-who-now-walks-on-water and warms your bed every night would never be anything but a friend." She leaned back in her chair. "Mark my words. Our second coin is ready to land in the fountain."

Emma tsked and looked at her watch. "Unfortunately, ladies, I have another appointment. But let me pick up the check." She signaled the waitress, who arrived in a heartbeat.

Annarita felt a twinge of envy. She never had that effect on the waitstaff.

CHAPTER 31

"Yes, I know," said Emma. "I can hardly believe it. Less than a month from opening. But we're almost there. The pool will be the toughest. The ground's still frozen, so they can't start until it thaws. Work will have to go on while guests are here. But in spring, it's mostly weekend bookings. I think we should manage." She paced with her cellphone before the large windows, looking up to the grey skies. "How is it up where you are in Milan? Will you be taking the train down? It looks like there might be snow here. I didn't believe the forecasts, but maybe I should head back to Rome soon."

"Oh, Emma. Can't you stay a bit longer?" Mark's voice had a pleading tone to it. "I still have to catch two trains to get there, and a taxi from the train station. I'll never be there in time for the appointment with the Councilman. He'll be there in an hour. Then you can head back to Rome."

Emma looked out the window again. The sky was making her nervous. "An hour? I hope the Councilman is on time. I don't want to be blocked in the storm."

"You did say Dario has the kids the next two days, didn't you?"

Damnit, why had she told him that? "Yeah, well. You know how it is. Still lots to organize on the home front."

"I understand." His voice was quiet. "We're only weeks from opening, and you still haven't given me your answer. I haven't even seen you in person since ... well ... you know, since the holidays when Lieke came down."

Her heart clenched at the memory.

"If I didn't know better, I'd think you were avoiding me."

Emma laughed, but it sounded hollow. "Avoiding you? How silly you sound. Of course I'm not avoiding you. I'm always here."

"Yes, but strangely, never when I am. But I'm sure it's just bad luck. Today will be another missed opportunity. I was hoping to see you."

She placed her forehead against the cool glass and willed her heart to slow down. Of course she was avoiding him. Any fool could see that. But it wouldn't be for much longer. Couldn't be for much longer. She'd stay for the opening, then she'd need to cut herself loose. She hated the idea, but she couldn't continue like this.

Once the hotel opened, there would be no way to avoid him. And her heart could never bear the proximity.

"So it's only my imagination. That you're avoiding me, I mean."

"Of course, Mark. I've been sorry not to see you."

"Really?"

"Really."

"I must admit, that's a relief. And here I thought you've been purposely blowing me off. Running away as fast as you could whenever I was in the vicinity. And now I realize I was just being silly."

She paused. "Yes, silly."

"But I do miss talking to you face to face, you know." There was silence. "For instance, even if I'm kilometers away, I can picture you now, standing at the big plate-glass window facing Todi. Your forehead pressed against the cool glass, staring out onto the distant spires."

She smiled. "Wow, you're good."

He laughed. "So I've been told. Okay, let's see how accurate I can be. You've got your gorgeous blonde hair piled up perfectly in a French twist, with a few tendrils escaping out in the back, curling on your shoulders." His voice grew quiet on the other end of the line. "That's how I like it most."

She reached up and felt the tendrils that had fallen down from the pins.

"Let me see ... You're wearing grey wool pants that make it abundantly clear your figure hasn't changed at all since your grad school days when you used to mud wrestle in a bikini. And that blue sweater may have been put on for warmth, but if it clings to you any better than what I see from this angle, I can tell you I'm quite jealous of that cashmere."

Emma's heart beat faster. She took a deep breath. "Mark. Where the hell are you?"

"Look outside."

He stepped out from the trees and waved. He wore a long, wool jacket, a thick grey scarf tied around his neck, and a broad smile plastered across his face.

"Damn you. So you were never in Milan?"

"*Assolutamente no.*"

"Good trick. You're even more *furbo* than the Italians. And that's really saying something." She sighed. "Come on in before you catch your death."

He placed a hand over his heart. "I thought you'd never ask."

Mark emerged from the kitchen with a tray bearing a teapot and two mugs. He placed it down on the table and motioned Emma to the couch. "Nice, hot tea. Just what the doctor ordered."

Emma kicked off her boots and pulled her feet up under her on the couch. Mark tossed her a blanket. He poured tea into the mugs, and handed one to Emma.

"Thank you. So you made up the whole Milan thing? Not one shred of truth to it?"

He shook his head and smiled like a boy who just brought back his first trophy.

"But why?"

"Why? Because I wanted to see you, of course. And because it's obvious to anyone over the age of three that you're avoiding me like the plague."

"Am not."

"Are to."

She shook her head. "Okay, this has to stop. We can't start sounding like our kids. I'll have tea with you, and then I'm on my way."

"No, my dear Emma. You're not going anywhere."

She sighed. "Are you some psychopath? Have you tampered with my car?"

"No, but two decades living in northern Europe has taught me a thing or two, and gives me an advantage over a girl from Annapolis. See those clouds? Did you walk out in that air? It's going to snow soon, and I'm not sending you out on roads that will soon be blocked, or dangerous."

Emma wrapped her hands around the warm mug. "So that was your idea all the time? To try to get me to stay until it would be too late."

He smiled and tilted his head. She hated when he did that—he looked far too handsome, and it was the last thing she needed.

"I know it sounds devious, but you told me the kids were with Dario, so I knew they wouldn't be inconvenienced." He held up his hands. "I'm a dad, too, and it's the last thing I'd want." He looked over at her. "But you've been avoiding me. For two, almost three months." He sighed. "And yes, I needed to talk to you. I'm sorry I had to get you here under false pretenses."

She raised the tea to her mouth, allowing its steam to tickle her lips and nose, willing her frustration away. Of course she'd been avoiding him. Wasn't that the point? How had she allowed him to trick her? Why hadn't she been suspicious of the whole Milan flight story? It made no sense at the time, but she hadn't even questioned him – only happy that the long drive from Milan would allow her adequate time to escape. She sipped her tea and allowed its warmth to work its way through her body.

"Mark, I don't know what it is you want." She placed her mug down. "I know it's a shame we haven't seen one another since ... since the holidays. But you're a busy man, I'm a busy woman. Our schedules don't always match. It doesn't mean I'm avoiding you. Haven't I gotten all the work done I promised you?"

His blue eyes pierced her with their intensity. "Yes, you have. You always do. But it's *you* I've missed. And you have been avoiding me, that's clear. After that night."

Emma shifted in her seat, untucked her legs and placed them before her, resting her hands firmly on her thighs. It was ridiculous to pretend with Mark. "Okay, you got me. You're right. Yes, it was rather embarrassing having Lieke, *your wife*, walking in on us and drawing her own conclusions."

Mark ran his hand through his hair. "I wanted to talk to you about that." He paused. "But you never gave me the chance."

"The chance for what? She was right. We were wrong."

"But nothing happened."

"It's true. Nothing happened. But it could have." She met his gaze. "I told you my marriage ended badly. I alluded to Dario's cheating. But do you have *any* idea how much I suffered?" She dropped her head into her hands. "What a fool I felt like? That was the worst of it. If he'd at least have been honest with me. But he'd cheated on me multiple times, and I had no clue. I was so busy with my family, my commitments. I sat beside him at our dinners, made him look good in front of surgeons visiting from America and Germany and France. And all that time, he was using me, playing me for the fool." She wiped away a tear, then looked up at him in defiance. "Can you imagine what that feels like? How stupid I felt?"

He met her gaze as she wiped away another tear.

"Yes, I know. Nothing happened. But would I have stopped it if it had? How could I possibly put any other woman through the hell that I've been through? The pain it's caused my children? I can't do that, Mark. I'm sorry if that makes me dishonest, but I lied to you because I can't trust myself. And I won't be the cause of Lieke's pain, your daughters' pain, because of my weakness."

He reached out and clasped her hand. She tried to pull away, but he held her tight.

"So at least I know. And it only makes me respect you more."

She stifled a sob.

"Please don't cry, Emma. I can't bear it."

"I'm not crying." She swiped a tear. "It's just my allergies."

"You're allergic to snow?"

She laughed.

"Look, I know how uncomfortable you were. God, how I've wanted to speak to you since then. I'd be a liar to say I didn't want anything to happen. My feelings for you haven't changed since Georgetown. I've put you out of my mind all these years, but seeing you again brought it all back. Then you came in here and pulled all this together." He gestured around the grand room. "How could I not be impressed? Plus I was furious for you—that your bastard of a husband could cast aside a woman like you." He placed a hand on his heart. "I know only you are allowed to say that about your ex, but it's how I feel." He smiled. "For obvious reasons, I've never liked him."

She shook her head.

"And I thought: here's my chance. Can it be only coincidence? I inherit this house. You agree to help me. Was it wrong to want to try to turn back the hands of time?"

She sighed. "Yes, it *is* wrong. You're married."

He stood up and walked toward the plate-glass window. The snow had begun hurtling down from the skies. Todi was shrouded in white snowflakes; soon, it would no longer be visible in the distance.

He spoke with his back turned to her, still looking out the window. "As you learned all too painfully, marriage vows require the fidelity of both parties." He took a deep breath. "I kept up my end of the bargain. Lieke had more difficulties."

Emma snapped her head up, watched him observing the snow that was gathering strength as it fell to the ground. "Lieke ... was unfaithful?"

He turned, but didn't face her. He looked down at the table. "More than once. But she also managed to fall in love with one of them. Jelle." He spat out the name. "You see, I never thought I'd stay with someone like that, but she always claimed she would change. And my livelihood depended on her daddy. The same man who raised her to be so spoiled, always eager to be the center of attention. She'd always apologize, claiming an affair was a mistake. That she loved the girls and me. Begging for forgiveness. But when she met Jelle, it was different. And I'd grown tired of it."

He walked to the bar and poured himself a glass of whiskey before returning to the couch. "She held the trump card. Daddy employed me. But Jelle. That crossed a line. She invited him home for dinner, introduced him to our daughters. She rubbed my nose in it. When my aunt left me this house, it seemed like an opportunity to make a break. We agreed we'd give the separation a try before breaking the news to the girls. We spent Christmas together. Played happy families." He shook his head. "Then she surprised me by deciding to take the girls up to Jelle's cottage. That wasn't part of the bargain." He sipped from his glass. "Something didn't work out, because soon she was down here, playing wronged wife and making you feel guilty." His eyes pleaded with hers. "When you did absolutely nothing wrong."

She released the breath she'd been holding.

"She played her part brilliantly, didn't she? She always had hidden talents as an actress. But the truth is, nothing did happen that night. Even so, it was the first time in a long time I've felt so happy and complete, having you beside me. Nothing had to happen." He reached out for her hand. "Being with you was enough. Working with you, and laughing with you. You have no idea what it's meant to me, how you rebuilt my world after so much heartache."

He slid closer beside her, and she felt her heart beating double time.

"I understand, Mark. I went through it, too. And I know how much it can devastate you, make you doubt yourself."

"I appreciate your support. I don't want you to feel any pressure. You don't have to feel the same about me. I don't want to force you to feel things you don't. But I love having you next to me. And if it means only as friends, I can accept that. I want to work with you. I love that we rekindled our friendship." He shook his head. "I don't want to lose that."

He placed a tentative hand over hers and her heart galloped away, full speed. Surely this was ridiculous. Acting like a schoolgirl. Feeling like a teenager, the same as Chiara. She hated how Mark could do this to her. And yet, she loved it at the same time.

Hadn't he brought her confidence back, too? Not just that she could love again, but that she was useful, that she could get back into the workplace and pick up where she'd left off over two decades ago. She'd feared there might not be anything left. Working with Mark allowed her to prove her worth to herself. And she'd loved it. Loved every minute of it. Leaving the hotel would break her heart.

Mark looked into her eyes, making her insides melt.

"Couldn't you consider it? Coming here? If you had your own space, and I swore to consider you only as a friend and colleague? At least the first year—help us get off the ground. It would be great for your CV, too. And you know you could count on the best references ever. No strings attached."

She laughed. "Mark, you never give up, do you?"

He tilted his head to the side. "Uh, no."

"Let's say I'd even consider it. I can imagine Marco and Valerio would warm to the idea. You buy them two goals and set them up out back, and find them a place to play soccer and a fencing club. But Chiara will be harder. It'll be her last two years at school."

"I've thought of that."

"You have?"

"I've spoken to tons of locals about the schools here, and they have a great reputation. I've also found a dance studio everyone's raved about. I've even spoken to the director."

"You have not."

"Yes. I have. I've had to be strategic and creative to find ways to lure you here." He stroked her cheek. "And, the icing on the cake. The *tocco finale* that shows I've learned a thing or two from Machiavelli's 'the ends justifies the means'? Well, it seems that Giuseppe has a nephew who's got a reputation as the Umbrian Brad Pitt. I met him and told him I was trying to get you here, but thought your teenage daughter might find it difficult to adjust to Umbria after Rome." He smiled. "He declared it his personal crusade to ensure Chiara makes lots of friends and finds it agreeable here in our sleepy hamlet."

"You did not."

"But I did." He laughed. "Okay, I might have sweetened the pot by letting slip the information that Chiara was blonde, and beautiful, and an accomplished dancer. But can you blame me?"

Emma shook her head. "So Chiara decides our fate? A change might be best for us, for her. And with her father back in Rome, she could still get back for rehearsals, and performances, and school vacations. She wouldn't have to feel she was missing out."

"Do I hear what I think I hear? You're *actually* considering it?" Mark slid closer, and took Emma's hand in his own. "I wouldn't want you to feel you were missing out. And I get the feeling that a change might be best for you, too."

She breathed in deeply. "It might be."

Mark stroked her shoulder. "I couldn't do it without you, Emma. Say you'll come. Say that, if the kids agree to it, you'll come here to Todi and be my hotel manager."

She reached up and placed her hand over his. She took a deep breath and ignored the thundering of her heart. "And what if I want more than a mere business partnership?"

His smile lit up his face. His blue eyes sparkled.

"Only say the word. I'll do whatever you want. I'm not stupid enough to let the opportunity pass me by a second time."

She shook her head. "But we're so hurt after what we've been through. Maybe it doesn't make sense to try again."

He placed two hands on either side of her face, and forced her to look at him. "Emma, who knows how things work out? What if you were meant to be with me all along, but you fell for Dario, and he swept you away? What if my hurt led me to Lieke? What if that's not how things were meant to work out all those years ago, but we mucked things up?" He moved in closer, until his warm breath brushed her cheek. "This is our second chance. I don't want to throw it away."

She ran her fingers through his short hair, tracing the greys at his temples with her fingertips. "Neither do I, Mark. I was too stupid to see it all those years ago. But I've grown wiser with age."

He embraced her and whispered in her ear. "I'll cherish you even more now than I would have two decades ago. I'm smarter now. I promise I'll make you happy, Emma."

She pulled back and looked into the depths of his deep blue eyes. He was so beautiful, and fun, and kind. There was nothing holding them back now. No reason to feel she was breaking up a family that hadn't really existed for some time. No reason to resent Dario anymore for his revolving door of available lovers.

She could have so much more.

"I know you will, Mark. And I want to make you happy, too."

The snow swirled through the air at full speed now. A blizzard alert would probably hit Todi and its surroundings, but Mark and Emma would never notice. They had nowhere else to go.

Mark pulled the blanket to the floor, and ran to his room to return with a goose down comforter. He unbuttoned each tiny button on Emma's sweater, kissing her each time new skin was revealed.

"You have no idea how long I've dreamt of doing this."

He kissed her neck, caressed her breasts. He smiled when she moaned, and slipped out of her wool pants. She yanked his sweater off him and rubbed across his sinewy muscles, unbuckled his belt and edged his pants off with her foot.

He laughed. "Here we've squandered a quarter century, but now there's no time to lose?"

She bit his ear and whispered, "Exactly."

He rolled on top of her and kissed her. He pulled the comforter up around them, enveloping their bodies in a cocoon of soft feathers and warm flannel.

Kissing and exploring the contours of one another's bodies, neither heard the key in the lock. They both looked up in shock to see Giuseppe looming above them with a basket of supplies. Emma pulled the comforter up to her neck.

He chuckled. "It's about time, you two." He placed down the basket filled with candles, flashlights, antifreeze and salt for the driveway. "Guess you're oblivious to the storm raging around you. Better get back, and leave you to it." With a wink, he was gone.

After the door shut and the lock clicked, Emma released her breath.

Mark kissed Emma firmly on the lips and pulled her on top of him. He kissed the top of her head, then began gently plucking the pins from her hair, running his fingers through the strands falling around her face. "You see? We even have the blessing of our chef. Looks like we'll be snowed in for the next few days, and I, for one, have decades to catch up on."

As Mark's lips met hers, Emma felt a warmth radiate throughout her body, and she groaned in pleasure.

Who said the first coin in the fountain was thrown with accuracy? Maybe you needed those practice coins to prepare you for the real thing.

She forced herself to stop thinking, and to concentrate on the pleasure of the moment. When she turned to the wall of windows, Todi was completely shrouded in white clouds of snow. Beneath her, she felt Mark's heartbeat thumping soundly against her chest. She looked into his eyes, moved by his look that was so filled with love, and she kissed him with all the ardor accumulated over more than two decades.

Epilogue

Three months later—June

Emma stood at the intersection of Via San Teodoro and Via dei Cerchi. At this early hour, Rome was still silent. She kicked herself for being on time, when she knew Tiffany and Annarita never would be.

She moved to the far edge of the intersection. An army of seagulls gathered on Circus Maximus for their early morning pow-wow. The few times she'd been here so early, she'd seen them. Hundreds of those hulking birds scattered across the ancient grounds for Roman chariot races never failed to create a sense of unease. Unwelcome snatches of disturbing images from Hitchcock's film flashed through her mind, and she did her best to banish them.

She looked at her watch. 6:35. When would they arrive?

Annarita had been insistent that they needed to see one another before picking up all the guests. "Just a bit of time alone together. Only the three of us. It's important to me."

Emma couldn't refuse her request. And here she was. Alone with the seagulls out on Circus Maximus, banishing irrational fears of having her eyes pecked out as an army of robust, squawking birds descended on her.

A familiar form walked briskly on Via dei Cerchi. The swingy fabric of the woman's yellow sundress swayed theatrically in the morning breeze. Her long, auburn hair shone in the golden morning light. She was the type of woman that men, and particularly Italian men, would always crane their necks to observe as she passed. As if on cue, a *motorino* roared by, the rubber-necked driver taking in the spectacle with obvious appreciation and narrowly missing collision with a parked car.

Emma stifled a smile. She was growing used to the same effect her Chiara had on young men. And Tiffany in love was even more radiant than she was before, if that was possible. Life with Simone was treating her well.

Tiffany reached Emma and placed her small bag on the ground. She smiled and kissed Emma on both cheeks.

Emma indicated the bag. "Is that all you're taking for five days?"

Tiffany shook her head. "The rest is with Simone. He'll bring it up when he comes to Todi on Friday. I said I'd kill him if he doesn't hang my dress up in the car."

Emma laughed. "Simone would never do anything to anger you. If he wrinkles it, he'll probably press it himself."

"Let's not exaggerate. So where's the star of the show? Isn't she taking this everyone-has-to-wait-for-the-bride tradition a little too seriously?"

"Maybe, but she has a lot on her plate these days. All the family came in yesterday, and she tells me they're going to run her ragged. I've had to pull all my strings in town to book group tours to get them out of her hair for a few days."

"Oh, they're gonna love Umbria. And the weather's perfect. Still not too hot. Will you have the pool open?"

"Mark says it's still pretty cold at nights, but he's opened it. His girls are visiting, and they've been swimming every day."

"Yeah, but they live in Amsterdam. They don't mind subzero pool temperatures." She raised one eyebrow. "How do you all get along? Do they like the idea of the new hotel manager moving in with their dad?"

Emma squirmed, remembering the first awkward meeting. "Well, uh, let's just say it was a bit uncomfortable. This summer will be a trial for us all. Once we all move out at the end of the month. The boys are excited, of course ..."

"I've spoken to Chiara. She doesn't seem upset. Well, at least any more upset than any teenager would be about moving. She already promised me she'll be coming back often on Saturdays for classes. Todi's not that far away."

"I know. I'm glad she'll still have the tie with Rome. She'll stay with her father some weekends. Did she tell you the reason for her enthusiasm?"

Tiffany smiled. "Not in so many words, but judging by all the giggles I reprimanded her for with the other girls, I'm guessing there's a boy involved."

"There is. A nephew of Giuseppe's."

"No way!"

"Uh-huh. He's a local Adonis. We introduced the two of them, and Chiara's been all moon-eyed ever since. They even went to a party together when we were up there one weekend earlier this month. That's when she stopped arguing with me about the move." Emma glanced at her watch. "Any idea why we had to come so early if Annarita's a no-show?"

A minivan pulled up, and Annarita hopped out, followed by a white-haired man with a large toolbox.

There was a wild glint in her eye, and she greeted them with a manic smile. "You're here! Good. Sorry, girls, I haven't slept all night—up with my jet-lagged family." She picked up the bags beside Tiffany and Emma, and half-threw them in the van. She turned to the driver. "Antonio, go wait for us at the Piazza della Concilazione. You should find a spot at this hour. We'll have a coffee and meet you there after this, in about forty-five minutes." The van drove off.

"What exactly does 'after this' refer to?" asked Emma, her eyes on the man beside Annarita.

Annarita placed a hand on the man's shoulder and spoke, switching to Italian. "Ladies, this is Mario. He's going to give us a hand before we go get some caffeine in our veins."

He gave a tight smile to both women, before following Annarita's gestures to continue down Via dei Cerchi.

"I just came from that direction," said Tiffany. "Where the heck are we going? What's all the mystery for?"

"Shh, just a second. Don't be so impatient, Tiff. Humor me."

Tiffany walked behind with Emma and rolled her eyes. "Bridezilla. We're in for it these next days. It happens to the best of them."

Emma shook her head.

Annarita stopped short halfway down the street. "Do you remember this?"

"Remember what?" asked Tiffany. "The Circus Maximus. Yeah, it's been here for the past two thousand years. And?"

"No," said Annarita, looking disappointed. "Here." She indicated a plaque on the brick wall beside her.

"Ah, yeah. The 'I am lost' plaque," said Tiffany.

Emma shook her head. "Didn't you show it to us once after we met up for coffee?"

Annarita's face lit up. "So you do remember!" She reached out and took their hands, her voice rising with excitement. "I have no idea what this was put here for—but I understood it when I first saw it. I *was* lost. I don't want to speak for both of you, but I got the impression that we all were." She smiled.

"And now, just a few months later ... look how things have changed!"

Tiffany rolled her eyes again. "Oh, brother. And that's why we're here."

Annarita blushed. "Kind of. I had Mario make a new plaque for us, and we'll place it here under the other one." She pulled a brass plaque from her purse.

Tiffany leaned in to read it. "*Ci siamo trovate*. And underneath it reads what I assume is this today's date in Roman numerals, and then A.E.T. *Three Coins*. What's A.E.T.?"

Annarita beamed. "Us! Annarita, Emma, Tiffany. I was gonna do reverse alphabetical order, but T.E.A. read weird. E.A.T. was even worse."

Tiffany sighed. "Okay, it's true my Italian isn't as up to speed as it should be, but the original sign is masculine singular, and yours is feminine plural."

"Exactly! Because *we* did it. Three women. Three women just like the ones in *Three Coins*."

"You really are a romantic." Emma shook her head. "All that wedding planning must have gone to your head. What do you plan on doing with it?"

Annarita exchanged some words with Mario, and he pulled out his power drills.

"Mario will place it on the wall before people are out on this street. Isn't it wonderful? Under the 'I am lost,' there will be a 'We are found.' And we have a little piece of immortality right here in the center of Rome."

Emma shook her head. "Tell Mario to hurry it up, or we have some jailtime and a fine to chalk up alongside our immortality, right here in the center of Rome."

Mario knelt down and began drilling through the bricks, placing the plaque just below the other. As ridiculous as the idea was, Emma gazed on the plaque and felt a strange sense of pride. With all of the plaques announcing famous people and their deeds around Rome, here was one where she was immortalized, albeit secretly. Every time she walked by, her gaze would fall upon it. And hadn't she found herself this past year?

Her relationship with Mark cancelled all the bitterness she'd felt towards Dario since the separation. They were so well suited, so in love, that it made them both wonder why they'd never connected decades earlier. She loved being back to work and took immense pride in the hotel's success these past months. They were booked solid for months to come. Even the locals found their way to the restaurant. Giuseppe and Annarita made a formidable team in the kitchen, and their enthusiasm for their cooking came through in their classes with the guests. She even believed the move to Todi would be good for the whole family. The boys would love it, and Chiara would have companions this summer while Mark's daughters were visiting, and she'd soon make new friends in town. She was already pining away for the potential boyfriend.

Yes, when she thought back to her desperation only a few short months ago, she supposed it wasn't much of a leap to say she'd found herself. She looked at the shining faces of her new friends. She supposed they all had. Annarita was right.

Mario stood, his work done. The new plaque shimmered like gold in the early morning light.

"*Grazie, Mario. È perfetto*," said Annarita, handing him euro bills.

He left, and Annarita slipped one arm around the shoulders of each friend. "It's starting to get busier, so we shouldn't stay at the crime scene much longer, but I wanted you both to know how much you've meant to me. How much my life has changed ever since our movie night back in Sperlonga."

Emma laughed. "Yeah, I could kind of tell by the fact you've made us set up a movie night at the hotel with *Three Coins in the Fountain* the night before the wedding."

"Simone will be up in time for that. I've made him promise."

"Well, this way you won't forget that I mean it. We may not have known one another that long, but you've become my closest friends. And you've been there as my life changed ... for the better. And I wanted to thank you."

"You've already thanked us by making us witnesses," said Emma, placing her hand over the one Annarita rested on her shoulder. "But thank you for this, too. It's very special."

"I agree," said Tiffany. "Our names on a plaque in Rome. How often does that happen? I thought I wanted my name in lights, and in all the gossip magazines, but this is better." She smiled. "Now, what about that coffee, before we all dissolve into tears, and we're discovered?"

"*Andiamo,*" said Annarita, steering them in the direction of San Teodoro.

They walked down Via di San Teodoro, where traffic had started to pick up as people made their way to work. They turned left into Via dei Fienile and made their way to the café, just opening its doors. The sun was bright and warm, and they took outdoor seats, watching the street come to life. The tabaccheria opened its grated doors, and the little mini-market began accepting supplies from the tiny vans that were the only vehicles able to maneuver the narrow streets.

Emma sat facing the Chiesa della Conciliazione, observing the seagulls that perched on the statues' heads, the grass growing from the roof tiles. The sun warmed her face, and the people began to pass by, setting off on their busy days.

"What time do we pick up your family?" asked Tiffany.

"We'll pick up Ma, my aunt and uncle and two cousins. I have a separate van for my sister, her husband and kids. I can't

believe she managed to come over with a two-month-old."
She smiled. "She insisted. Said she never thought she'd see the
day I got married, and wouldn't miss it for the world. Wait 'til
you meet my nieces and nephews. They're adorable. And they
are going to *love* the hotel, and the pool." She laughed. "And
our neighbors have a pony. They've already said the kids can
ride on her. You have no idea the shrieks the kids gave when I
told them the news last night."

Their cappuccinos arrived.

"I need all the caffeine I can get these next days. Emma,
thanks so much to you and Mark for your wedding present.
I can't believe you're letting us take over the whole hotel for
the next five days and have our reception there. This will be so
special for everyone."

"It's the least we could do for our star chefs. Mark and I were
so worried in the beginning that the two of you might not get
along, and then we'd be stuck with two temperamental chefs
walking out on us. How could we have possibly imagined
you'd not only get along, but fall in love and hold a shotgun
wedding at our hotel?"

Annarita blushed and patted her stomach. "No shotgun
wedding, I promise. But we do want to start trying soon. At our
age, we said, why wait? What's the use of a long engagement
when we know how we feel? And with Giuseppe's house right
next to the kitchen, and his mom and sisters nearby to help
us, we're sure we can work and eventually have a family." She
shook her head. "I can't even believe it's all happened so fast.
But he's so amazing. I should have known he was the one
when he said he hated girls who were always dieting, and
that I was too skinny." She picked up a cookie and bit into
it. "I think it's the first time since I was about sixteen that I
haven't been obsessing about my weight and finally feel happy
accepting how I am."

"Mark and I have loved seeing you and Giuseppe together. You make such a wonderful couple. He's changed so much since he's fallen in love with you. He's been heartbroken for too long. You both deserve this."

"I'm only sorry Signora Renata can't get up there for the wedding. June starts their high season at the Albergo Paradiso—and the weekends are busiest. But she sent up two bottles of her special *limoncello*, and she offered Giuseppe and me a weekend in Sperlonga at the hotel in September." She looked up at Emma. "If that's okay for you, that is. We have our honeymoon in July, and we don't want to create problems during your busy season."

"It's not the same, but Giuseppe's set up a good backup system for your honeymoon in July, with two cousins who used to work in his restaurant. If we can arrange it in the same way for a weekend in September, why not?"

"Thanks, Emma. In the end, it was Signora Renata who got me to realize I was always falling for the wrong men. She told me I wasn't giving the right men a chance, always chasing after the heartbreakers who never loved me. I thought of her words when Giuseppe asked me out the first time."

"So Signora Renata's responsible for getting you two together?" said Tiffany.

"Yes, that's why I invited her. I think she would've loved my Ma, but I'll show her the photos when we see her in September."

"Oh, still, it is a shame she couldn't be there in person." Tiffany winked at Emma.

Emma shot her a warning glance. Tiffany may be a talented dancer, but she was a horrible actress. Emma hadn't even wanted to let her in on the secret, but Simone was driving up to Todi on Friday after school. When she'd told him Signora

Renata wanted to come, he'd offered to pick her up from Termini Station and to deliver her to the hotel.

If Tiffany didn't ruin the surprise first.

"After the whirlwind courtship, it's amazing you were able to get everything organized so quickly," said Emma, changing topics.

"Thank God for small towns. It would never happen in Rome, where you need to book a church a year in advance. In Todi, everything was so easy. The priest is an old friend of Giuseppe's, and he was so happy to see him in love again. We booked right away. And, of course, Emma and Mark were so generous with the hotel. And Giuseppe's aunts and sisters have taken over all the cooking. His mother is supervising the menu—and I can guarantee my new *suocera* is a force to be reckoned with in the kitchen. I wouldn't even try." She chuckled.

"And you managed to get your whole family here so quickly?" asked Tiffany.

"They were afraid I'd never get married. Ma almost passed out when I told her the news. She booked the tickets the same day."

"I've spoken to Giuseppe's family. They're over the moon, too," said Emma. "In fact, almost the whole town is showing up—the mayor, the head of the police, everyone I see in the shops. We won't be able to have everyone for a sit-down dinner, but we will have drinks and appetizers outside the church before we walk back to the hotel. It will be beautiful."

"It *will* be beautiful." Annarita smiled. "But I'm going on and on about me—the stereotypical self-centered bride. I'm hardly the only one in love, and I'll be too busy with guests and wedding stuff to really talk these next days. What's new with you and Simone? Should we be expecting invitations soon for another event?"

Tiffany shook her head. "Eventually, but not quite yet. Things are great, and we're talking about maybe next summer—up in Perugia. We'll try to spend some weekends up there this summer. I want to spend more time with his parents and sisters, and he wants to see what I think about the town." She looked down at her emerald ring. "See if I might consider living there."

"You? Up in Umbria, too?" asked Annarita.

"I don't know. With more steady work and living with Simone, for the first time ever, I'm putting aside money. Simone's been saving up for a while. We couldn't hope to buy anything decent in Rome, but we'll start looking around at houses in Perugia. Simone knows he could teach at the high school there. He says I could work in a dance studio. Maybe eventually think about opening my own." She looked at them shyly. "It would probably be a good place to raise kids ... not that we're planning on that right now."

"But it's exciting news!" said Annarita.

"It is. It's nice to have a plan," said Emma. "I admit I had you pegged as the one of us who would stay in Rome."

"And we still might. There's no rush. But I know Simone wants to return home eventually, and I want to see if it's something I could do. It was always a sticking point between him and Ramona. He always assumed it might be with me, too, that I'd never want to leave Rome." She sat back in her chair and tilted her head up to the sun. "But I think I've changed a lot in the months we've been together. The things I used to think were so important aren't any longer. Television shows, and glamorous parties where people flaunt their money— those aren't things I chase after anymore." She took a deep breath. "Maybe I've finally decided to grow up."

"You're not the only one." Emma shook her head. "At least you have the excuse of youth. It took these months for me to grow up, too. I was always in a war with my ex, jealous of his new life and upset that I was stuck in a rut. And a few months later, I have a new man, a new job," she sighed, "what I hope will be a new life in Todi, if the kids can adjust." She reached out and took their hands. "And wonderful new friends."

"That's beautiful, Emma," said Annarita. "I know it sounds dorky to want to watch *Three Coins* before our wedding, but I really feel it was a turning point. It brought us together as friends. And, in its own way, it got us all rethinking our lives." She handed euros to the waitress.

"So we all got men, just like our 1950s sisters," said Tiffany.

Annarita shook her head. "It's more than that. We have what we dreamed of. Yes, okay, the men are part of it. But you're a dance teacher now. You say you might consider moving to Perugia and opening your own studio. You have your students dancing onstage at the National Theatre. Do you have any idea what an experience like that means to a teenage girl? And you, Emma. It's not just meeting Mark—although he's one of the most amazing men I've ever met. Giuseppe agrees. But you were complaining you never thought you'd work again. And look at what you've done!" She turned to Tiffany. "You should see Emma at work. She's always one step ahead of the guests. We're inundated with bookings. We've only been open a few months, but people really feel at home when they're with us. And that's all thanks to Emma."

Emma felt her cheeks burning.

"You're good at it. You could do this anywhere, but I'm glad you and Mark fell in love and want to make a go of the hotel. Because it's changed my life, too. I hated teaching English to spoiled students. I've always loved cooking, but I never thought I could make it my profession. But I've been so happy at the hotel. Not just because of Giuseppe, but teaching those classes, meeting the guests, knowing that they'll take our recipes home to Amsterdam or London or Tokyo, and cook dinner for people they invite to their homes. And when they do, they'll remember their week in Umbria with us. And as they're cooking their meat, or stirring their sauces, they'll forget all about their problems at work, or the car insurance that has to be paid, or an upcoming medical exam—and they'll remember when they were happy and relaxed." She smiled. "I love being a part of that."

"It shows," said Emma. "It's one of the reasons our guests are clamoring to come back. The cooking classes are such a hit. I was so scared Giuseppe wouldn't take to it. But I was wrong."

Annarita winked. "He may have had a little female encouragement to push him in the right direction. Who says you can't teach an old dog new tricks? So you see, after a rough patch, we all have our Hollywood ending." She looked at her watch. "Uh-oh, we'll have to pick up my family, and there's one thing I still want to do before we go."

"No more plaques, I hope."

"Nope. Hurry." She led them down the steps to the square, where Antonio was waiting for them. "Where we said, Antonio." They headed off to Piazza Venezia and continued on to Via del Corso. Traffic had picked up and the trip was fairly slow. Antonio dropped them off on Via del Tritone, finding a small spot in front of a hotel. "Wait for us here. We won't be long."

Annarita jumped out of the van, taking her friends by the hands and weaving through the crowds. They heard the sound of rushing water before they emerged at the side of the Trevi Fountain.

"Oh, you're kidding, Annarita," said Tiffany.

"Humor me. I promise not to make any more demands." She led them both to the front of the fountain. Despite the hour, tour groups were jostling for space. Crowds of Russians and Chinese threw coins in the fountains, bored tour guides stood nearby and texted as they waited for their flocks to return, sellers hawked cheap trinkets. Water rushed over the bright, white statues as Oceanus kept stern watch over the throngs paying court to him.

Emma walked by the fountain millions of times, but it had been years since she stood in front of it as a tourist.

Annarita plucked three shiny coins from her purse and distributed them. "Just like in the film. You knew I'd make you come here eventually. What better time than now?"

All three stood with their backs to the fountain. At Annarita's signal, they tossed their golden coins in the fountain, turning to see where they splashed.

"Thank you. Thank you for being my friends, and for being here for me on my special day." Annarita reached out and hugged the two women into her. "And now we better hurry before my family kills me." She bounded up the stairs. Tiffany and Annarita followed.

A few meters before reaching Antonio's van, a Bangladeshi hawker jumped in front of Emma, holding up a cheap, plastic replica of the Trevi Fountain. "You throw coin in fountain, you bring Trevi Fountain home, and you return to Rome."

"Thanks, but I don't need it. Rome is already my home." Emma smiled and stepped into the waiting van.

Acknowledgements

Although a debut novelist is bound to bore many in this section, there are simply too many people to thank for their time and talents in helping to finalize a first novel. Every reader brings different observations to the table, and I have benefitted from so many suggestions and ideas in revising this novel.

To my brilliant and always insightful friend, Maria Casa, who has always been my first reader, and whom I can trust to call me out if my Italian observations don't ring true.

To the members of "The Best" Roman writing group. Before everyone moved away and deserted me, I benefitted from help on early chapters from Terianne Falcone, Amber Paulsen and Kaushik Barua – and for all the encouragement, laughs and wine along the way. To Ashlinn Craven, who has read and critiqued earlier works and reviewed these chapters as well - thanks for all the wonderful thoughts and suggestions.

Special thanks to all the writers over at Critique Circle who joined individual chapters and provided invaluable advice, but especially to Grace Tierney, Linda G. and Chantel Rhondeau who reviewed the overall work and helped improve these chapters.

I am deeply grateful for Valerie Valentine's excellent editorial support – and for making the process such a pleasure! As someone who adores graphic design, I've never been a believer in the saying "You can't judge a book by its cover", which is why I was thrilled to bring in the immensely talented Joanne Morgante and Roberto Magini of Maxtudio to create my beautiful cover. *Grazie!*

And finally, gratitude to my husband, Francesco, and my sons Alessandro and Nicolò, for your patience when I'm writing instead of spending time with you. And thank you, especially, for helping me to become a "real" Roman.

About the author

KIMBERLY SULLIVAN grew up in the suburbs of Boston and in Saratoga Springs, New York, although she now calls the Harlem neighborhood of New York City home when she's back in the US. She studied political science and history at Cornell University and earned her MBA, with a concentration in strategy and marketing, from Bocconi University in Milan.

Afflicted with a severe case of Wanderlust, she worked in journalism and government in the US, Czech Republic and Austria, before settling down in Rome, where she works in international development, and writes fiction any chance she gets.

She is a member of the Women's Fiction Writers Association and The Historical Novel Society and has published several short stories. *Three Coins* is her first novel.

After years spent living in Italy with her Italian husband and sons, she's fluent in speaking with her hands, and she loves setting her stories in her beautiful, adoptive country.

kimberlysullivanauthor.com
Twitter: @kimberlyinrome
Instagram: kimberlyinrome

Made in United States
North Haven, CT
18 June 2023

37925411R00173